DANGEROUS RUSH

Also By S. C. Stephens

Furious Rush

Untamed

Thoughtful

Reckless

Effortless

Thoughtless

It's All Relative

Collision Course

'Til Death

Bloodlines

Conversion

DANGEROUS RUSH

S.C. STEPHENS

This is a work of fiction. Names, characters, places, brands, media, and incidents are either the product of the author's imagination or are used fictitiously. The author acknowledges the trademarked status and trademark owners of various products referenced in this work of fiction, which have been used without permission. The publication/use of these trademarks is not authorized, associated with, or sponsored by the trademark owners.

Copyright © 2017 by S.C. Stephens
Cover photography by Claudio Marinesco
Cover design © Hang Le byhangle.com
Editing by Madison Seidler Editing Services
Formatting by JT Formatting

All rights reserved.
Without limiting the rights under copyright reserved above, no part of this publication may be reproduced, stored in or introduced into a retrieval system, or transmitted, in any form, or by any means (electronic, mechanical, photocopying, recording, or otherwise) without the prior written permission of the above copyright owner of this book.

First Edition: 2017
Library of Congress Cataloging-in-Publication Data
Dangerous Rush (Furious Rush Series) – 1st ed
ISBN-13: 978-1546666721 | ISBN-10: 1546666729

This one is for Addy. Keep fighting the good fight.

ACKNOWLEDGEMENTS

First off, I'd like to thank everyone who read the first book, *Furious Rush*, and messaged me, clamoring for more! I had so much fun writing this sequel, and I hope you had as much fun reading it! And now on to book three!

A huge thank you to my agent, Kristyn Keene of ICM Partners, who was a tremendous help in putting this book together. Hugs to everyone at Forever/Grand Central Publishing, who have done such a great job promoting the series. Much love to Holly and Katie, for beta reading this for me. Your input was greatly appreciated, and thank you so much for fitting me in at a moment's notice!

Thank you to my editor, Madison Seidler, my formatter, Julie Titus of JT Formatting, my cover designer, Hang Le, and my web designer Lysa Lessieur of Pegasus Designs. I would be lost without your help! And to all the numerous blogs, readers, and authors who have supported me over the years—from the bottom of my heart, thank you so much! I wouldn't be able to continue in this business without your kind words and (sometimes daily) encouragement.

DANGEROUS RUSH

CHAPTER 1

~Hayden~
4 years ago

"Here you go, Hayden...the best shit your money can buy." Hookup handed me a manila envelope, and my fingers twitched as I took it. There was supposed to be an engagement ring inside, and not just any ring, but a ring fit for a queen. Fit for *my* queen.

Once I had the envelope in my hands, I was hesitant to look inside. Hookup wasn't that great with matters of the heart—his interests tended to revolve around making money—so I wasn't sure what to expect. He could have messed this up in so many ways, and I really couldn't afford to buy a ring like this twice. But when I'd told Hookup my plan to propose to my girlfriend, Felicia, he'd assured me that he knew a guy who knew a guy who could get me something I'd never be able to afford on my own. I was fairly certain I was holding stolen property.

Inhaling a deep breath, I pulled back the envelope flap to peek at the ring nestled in the crevice at the bottom. My eyes widened in surprise at the size of the rock Hookup had nabbed. It was so big it was almost gaudy. Pulling the shiny adornment out of its hiding place, I studied it for any obvious flaws that would proclaim it a knockoff; I couldn't find any. "Damn, Hookup. I don't want to know where you got this, but it's perfect. Thanks, man."

I clasped his shoulder in a quick hug; my cheeks were beginning to hurt, I was grinning so hard. "No problem, dude. Just remember, when you finally knock up Felicia, you're having a boy and you're naming him Tony, after me. Izzy already took care of naming a girl after me with Antonia. Speaking of which, we should get going. You know Iz will kill us if we're late."

Nodding, I stuffed the ring into my jacket pocket. "Yeah, let's go."

As we walked to our vehicles—a black, souped-up Acura for Hookup, a super-fast Suzuki for me—Hookup pointed to my pocket. "So, you gonna give that to Felicia today?"

Just his question made me feel lightheaded and dizzy. I'd been thinking about doing it today, and, of course, every time I thought about it, I felt like throwing up. But today was the perfect day to ask Felicia to marry me. In addition to being Antonia's third birthday, it was also my nineteenth birthday. Everyone I cared about was going to be at our joint birthday party. And to make things even better, timing-wise, Felicia was turning eighteen in another month. We'd both finally be free.

As I felt the hard ring in my pocket, I told Hookup, "Yeah, yeah, I think so." My gut twisted again, but I ignored it. The diamond resting in my jacket was the perfect embodiment of my relationship with Felicia, and it belonged on her finger. We'd known each other forever, but we'd begun dating when I was fourteen years old, and sure, maybe nineteen was a little young to settle down with just one girl for the rest of my life, but she was no ordinary girl, and the two of us had never had an ordinary life.

Both of us had been taken from our biological parents when we'd been about Antonia's age. We'd bounced around the system, floundering for someone or something to replace everything we'd lost. Instead of being handed what we'd needed to survive, the two of us had fought tooth and nail for every scrap. We were a team; we had each other's backs, and there was no one else I wanted by my side. Why wait another ten years to get married, when I already knew I wanted to be with her for the rest of my life? Always had, always would. She was my destiny.

A few minutes later, Hookup and I pulled into the parking lot of Izzy's apartment building. Being a single mom was hard on Izzy, but then again, having a baby at fifteen had been hard on her. The douchebag who'd knocked her up had bailed on her the minute he'd realized she wasn't just gaining weight, but was actually going to have a child. Having him split had been a walk in the park in comparison to having a kid when she was still a kid, but we—Hookup, Felicia, and I—felt like Antonia was ours, too, so we did everything we could for Izzy. And man... that kid... Antonia was something special. There wasn't anything I wouldn't do for her, and hell if I was going to let her have a childhood like mine. If it was the last thing I did on this Earth, she would know what having a father felt like. And, in a way, thanks to her, I knew what having a daughter felt like. I was there the day she was born. I'd changed mountains of diapers, fed her gallons of formula. I was the one who'd taught her how to walk, and my name was the first thing she'd said. Well, technically, it was

"Hay," but I was claiming it. That kid meant the world to me…which was why I was starting to get really concerned about her. She'd been sick a lot lately—run-down, tired, nauseous—like she'd caught something she just couldn't shake. Izzy was freaked out about it, so we all took turns reassuring her that Antonia was going to be fine. And she had to be; she was just a toddler after all. How bad could it be?

I had a huge bag full of toys for Antonia strapped to my back, the focal point of which was one of those American Girl dolls. I swear the thing cost as much as Felicia's ring. Thank God I was making decent money street-racing for Hookup. He'd turned Felicia and me onto it before we'd even been old enough to drive. That fact had never concerned me though. Since all of it was illegal, being underage had hardly seemed worth worrying about.

God, I loved racing, and I was good at it—damn good at it; I hardly ever lost. Beating someone to the line…it ignited something in me, something thorny and dangerous. Hope. Hope and dreams. And the more I competed, the more I began to believe that maybe one day I could race motorcycles for a living—legitimately. I couldn't think of a better life for me, and there was certainly nothing I wanted to do more. Felicia could probably race professionally, too, since she was top-notch. Yeah, the two of us racing for a team together…it sounded perfect.

Hookup caught up to me at Izzy's door. Banging on the hard wood once, I turned the knob and walked right in. Warmth and laughter greeted us as we stepped inside, and the first thing that drew my eye was seeing my girl, standing by a window, drenched in sunshine, smiling at me. Fuck, she was gorgeous. Long, dark brown curls cascaded down her back; huge, deep brown eyes glinted with playful mischief; full, pouty lips that I could suck on for days. God, just thinking about kissing her was exciting me. How long did we have to stay here before we could quietly slip away for the night? Because I'd really love to end this birthday with those arms and legs wrapped around me.

"Hey, babe," I said, sliding up to her side.

"Hi Hayden," she purred in return. "Happy Birthday." There was a gleam in her eyes that told me she wanted to end the night the same way I did, and from the heat I saw boiling in the dark depths, she was going to do things to me that were going to leave me walking funny in the morning. Sweet Jesus. We were leaving after cake.

Just as I thanked her for the acknowledgement, a tiny pair of arms wrapped around my waist. "Unckey Haydey!"

Felicia laughed in amusement. "Haydey…I like it. I'm using it."

I gave her a frown before bending down to scoop up Antonia; she was limp in my arms, almost weightless. Antonia looked just like her mom and Hookup, her biological uncle. She had their tan, Hispanic skin, tiny frame, and their dark eyes and dark hair, but right now, Antonia was pale, with deep circles under her eyes. She looked like she was about to drop from exhaustion at any minute. Squeezing her tight, I kissed her head of thick hair. "Hey, kiddo. Happy Birthday."

She sighed contentedly, snuggled into my arms, then didn't move. It took me a minute to realize she'd fallen asleep. Icy fear tightened my chest, but I shoved it aside. Izzy had taken her to the park this morning, and she was just tired from the long day. I'm sure it was close to her naptime anyway. It was nothing to worry about.

Looking around for Izzy, I spotted her standing next to the cake table with Hookup. She looked irritated, and I wondered if Hookup had told her about the ring. I knew she was excited about the idea of Felicia and me getting married, so that wasn't the problem, but Izzy hated Hookup's...extracurricular activities, and was probably ticked that the ring was hot property. She'd get over it, though. Izzy forgave Hookup a lot.

"Hey, Iz," I said, walking over. "Someone's done for the day."

Izzy swung her head my way, and, for the millionth time, I was taken aback by how young she looked. No matter how hard I tried to see her any other way, she always looked twelve to me. Probably always would. It made the instinct to protect her that much stronger. Blood or not, Izzy was my sister.

She frowned as she stared at her passed-out daughter. "I don't get it. She shouldn't be that tired. She didn't even go on the playground, she just wanted to cuddle..."

Her eyes watered with worry, and I tossed her an untroubled smile that I hoped looked believable. "She's fine, Iz. Just sleepy."

Looking a little comforted, Izzy held out her hands. "Guess I'll put her to bed."

Hookup frowned as I transferred Antonia to her mom. "No, wake her up, Iz. I want her to see what I got her." He rubbed his hands together and grinned like he was about to win an award for best gift-giving.

With a subtle glare, Izzy shook her head. "She'll open it later, Tony. Right now, she needs rest."

Hookup grunted, clearly annoyed, but he didn't say anything else. Felicia twined her fingers with mine as we watched Izzy disappear with her daughter. "I hope she's okay," Felicia whispered, leaning into my side. She smelled like her favorite Jasmine perfume, something that normally would have ignited my senses, but her words cooled my jets.

"Yeah, I hope so too."

Hookup waved an irritated hand at both of us. "She's fine. Kids get sick, it's what they do."

Without saying anything, Felicia and I looked at each other at the exact same time. She raised a brow, and I rolled my eyes, then we both let out a laugh. It drove our friends nuts, the way we communicated without words.

Hookup glanced at us, then returned his attention to the cake table. He stared at the two cakes for a solid ten seconds before finally saying, "Oh shit! It's your birthday, Hayden! I always forget you and Antonia are twins. So, where we goin' tonight to celebrate?"

I waved a hand at the room overflowing with balloons, streamers, and large, toddler-friendly confetti. "We *are* celebrating."

Hookup gave me an unamused, blank stare. "I meant after this, jackass. Go to a strip club, go down to Mexico, what do you want to do?"

"I want to be with Felicia, and since she can't do either of those things—"

"Or *wants* to do either of those things," she smoothly interjected.

Smiling at Felicia, I finished with, "So we're staying here. And besides, I've got that *thing* I was gonna do later." I stressed the word "thing" as hard as I could, but I really didn't know if Hookup got the hint. How he'd forgotten my plans to propose to Felicia in such a short amount of time was beyond me.

"Yeah, okay, fine. I was thinkin' of meeting up with Grunts later anyway. He's got a tip on an underground fight club that we're gonna check out. You guys want to place a bet if we find something?"

Felicia and I both said no at the exact same time. Placing bets with Hookup usually wasn't a good idea. If he did happen to win the bet, he usually took a pretty generous cut of the winnings. He called it a commission.

Hookup pursed his lips and shook his head, like he thought we were idiots for missing out. "Whatever. I'm gonna call Grunts, find out what time that shit's going down." He pulled out his phone with one hand, trailing his other finger along the edge of the cake. Smiling, he stuck the glob of frosting in his mouth as he walked away.

Finding myself alone with Felicia with an engagement ring in my pocket made my heart start to pound. Was now a good time? With Antonia sleeping and Hookup making plans? Should I wait until everyone came back together? Or maybe I should do it tonight, when it was just the two of us. Fuck, I didn't know, and I hated not knowing what to do.

Possibly sensing my turmoil, Felicia laced her arms around my neck. "You look nervous. That have anything to do with this 'thing' you're doing tonight?" Her lips twitched, like she was trying to contain a smile. Did she know what I'd been planning for the last two weeks? Probably…she knew me better than anyone.

With a casual smile plastered on my face, I told her, "I don't know what you're talking about."

Leaning in, she placed a light kiss on my lips; she tasted like chocolate, and I wondered if she'd swiped some frosting too. Great, now I wanted to smother her in chocolate and lick her clean. "You sure about that?" she murmured, her lips returning to mine. She sucked my bottom lip into her mouth this time, and a small groan escaped me. God...maybe we wouldn't stay for cake after all.

"Uh...pretty sure...no special plans...just hanging with you..."

With a small, seductive laugh, she brought her mouth to my earlobe. After trailing her tongue up the edge of my ear, she said in a low voice, "Really? So you weren't reminding Hookup about something...important?"

The sensual movement made a pulsing rush of desire go through me. God...what was she asking about? "Um... well..." I was just about to spill every single secret I had, when the shrill ring of a telephone cut through the air. Regaining my senses, I took a step back. *Nice try, Tucker.*

Felicia looked both amused and annoyed as she saw my defenses quickly reforming. Izzy rushed into the room as I unlaced Felicia's arms from around me. It would be easier to not spill my plans if we weren't touching. That girl could undo me so easily, it was embarrassing.

Izzy hurried from Antonia's room to pick up the phone handset. "Hello? Yes, this is Isabel. Do you have Antonia's test results back? Do you know what's wrong with her?"

Flicking a glance at Felicia, I heard Hookup hanging up with Grunts. Izzy had mentioned that the doctor had run some tests the last time she'd taken Antonia to see him. If they had some information for Izzy, maybe it would put her mind at ease.

All three of us turned to watch Izzy as she nervously chewed on her lip while she listened. After a second, her brows creased. "What do you mean you can't tell me over the phone?" She was silent a moment, then said, "No, I don't want to come in tomorrow and talk to the doctor, I want to know what the hell is wrong with my daughter right now!" In a quieter voice, she added, "If you know anything, please, *tell me*. I don't want to wait. I *can't* wait."

Eyes wide, Izzy scanned the room. Feeling like she needed me, I left Felicia's side and put a hand on Izzy's shoulder. She reached up to grab it with an iron grip that only got tighter with every passing second. "No…she can't have… She's only three years old…and today's her birthday…and she just can't…" She swallowed, then nodded. When she spoke again, her voice was flat, dead. "Of course, we'll come in tomorrow. What time?"

She listened to something, then hung up the phone without even saying goodbye. My heart was thundering now as I looked at her; her expression was void, numb, but I knew it wouldn't stay that way. "Izzy? What is it? What's wrong with her?"

Izzy looked up to meet my eyes, and, as she stared at me, the orbs filled to the brim with tears. "They still need to do more tests, but they're fairly certain…they think she's got leukemia…" Her voice trailed off, but the word she'd just spoken thundered inside my head with the ferocity of a raging storm. The tears spilled from Izzy's eyes as her face crumpled in desolation. "Hayden…my baby's got cancer…"

She completely fell apart then, dropping into my arms so heavily, I struggled to keep her upright. Racking sobs that were too big for her small body left her, and I felt my eyes sting with tears, felt the hot trails rolling down my cheeks. From behind me, I heard Felicia begin to cry, as her arms wrapped around Izzy and me. Hookup was cursing, then sniffling, then falling to his knees with his head buried in his hands.

No…it couldn't be true. It had to be something else—*anything* else. She was only three years old…

* * *

Weeks passed, taking the hope I'd been cultivating, and morphing it into complete and utter crap. Antonia was sick. Really, truly, devastatingly sick. Izzy was scared out of her mind that she was going to lose her. Fuck. *I* was scared out of my mind that I was going to lose her. She'd only been a part of our lives for three years, but she'd changed me, touched me; I couldn't imagine my life without her now. I didn't want to.

Oddly, out of all of us, Antonia was the one handling it best. Of course, she was too young to completely understand the situation. All she knew was that the nurses at the children's hospital in San Diego were nice, and that they lavished her with love, toys, games…whatever made her visits more bearable. Whenever she did get scared—usually when needles were involved—they were right there for her, soothing her with humor and kind words. They were great. I wished they could have soothed and comforted me with silly stories, because I sure could have used it.

Izzy didn't see Hookup much after the diagnosis. He disappeared, immersing himself in gambling, women, alcohol—whatever he needed to dull the pain. I dulled my own with Felicia. I held off asking her to marry me—now was definitely not the right time—but every free minute I had, I spent with her, usually in bed. Sex was as good a distraction as any, and besides the occasional street race with Hookup, it was all I had to keep me busy.

Panting, spent, I rolled off Felicia and stared up at the cracked ceiling of our apartment. My body was still flooded with endorphins, and for one moment in time, everything in the world was perfect.

Beside me, Felicia let out a satisfied groan. "God, Hayden, that was just… God…"

I knew exactly what she meant. I wasn't sure if it was the ramped-up emotions swirling all over the place, but the sex between us lately had been hot, passionate, all-consuming—two lit torches burning down the bed. I knew things would probably settle down again, but for now, I'd gladly take the heat.

But even as I thought that, a heaviness started weighing down the room. I felt it, and I knew Felicia felt it too. As the passion faded away, as our breaths returned to normal, a sense of unease clamped around my heart. Things weren't perfect. They were far from perfect.

"So…did you still want to go with me? Antonia is finally home from the hospital. I want to see how she's doing, give Iz a hug. I'm sure she needs one."

I thought she'd say yes right away, but she hesitated. When I looked over at her, she was chewing on her lip. She stopped as soon as she saw me watching. "Yeah, when did you want to go?"

Tossing the covers aside, I told her, "Now is good."

She shivered as the colder air hit her, her skin pebbling, her nipples hardening. For a moment, I reconsidered leaving. What harm would it do if we indulged in another go-around? If we delayed the inevitable just a little longer…

Knowing procrastination wouldn't help the situation any, I shook the vague erotic idea out of my head and got up. I hurried to get dressed, but Felicia stayed there on the bed, naked and exposed, staring up at the ceiling like she was lost in thought. That knot in my stomach tightened as I studied her face. "Hey, you okay?"

She instantly tossed on a smile as she snapped her eyes to mine. "Of course. Just feeling lazy." She ran her hand down her body in a suggestive way, and I knew it wasn't just laziness she was feeling. Like me, she was wanting to avoid reality for a little longer. It would be so easy to cave, to stay…but Izzy and Antonia, they needed me. It was time to grow up, time for both of us to grow up.

Not giving in to the small, sensual smile on her face, I reached out for her hand and started pulling her up. "Come on, sleepy, we've got places to be."

She sighed, but stood up.

There was a thickness in the air as we walked to our bikes, and I couldn't shake the feeling that something was wrong…something bigger than Antonia. As we were putting on our helmets, I asked her again, "You sure you're okay?"

Again, she smiled and nodded. "Yep, I'm fine."

I wanted to believe her, I really did, but there was a haunted look in her eyes. Felicia didn't like being pressed—me either—so I left it at that and hopped on my bike. She would tell me when she was ready. I just hoped she didn't freak out first. Felicia had a habit of running when things got hard. Without a word to anyone, she'd up and disappear. Vanish, like smoke. Her foster parents would freak out when they realized she was gone. They'd call the police, and because I was her boyfriend, I'd be brought in for questioning. Izzy and Hookup would be questioned, too—any "known associate" of Felicia who they could find…but it would never lead to anything. Felicia was a pro at becoming a ghost. But then, a couple days later, she would come back, acting perfectly fine, like nothing in the world had happened. Like she hadn't just freaked out everyone around her. That usually led to a nasty fight between the two of us. And some pretty spectacular makeup sex.

It was a gorgeous early evening in San Diego, the perfect night for a drive, but I wasn't enjoying a moment of it as Felicia and I rode north out of the heart of the city, toward Izzy's place. Things had been so intense lately, and in a really bad way. Felicia's eighteenth birthday had been a week ago today, and normally we all would have celebrated the hell out the momentous occasion of her freedom from the reins of foster care…but we hadn't even gone out. Izzy had wanted to stay with Antonia, and Hookup had left town with Grunts to bet on a boxing match.

I hadn't felt like doing anything, but I would have if Felicia had wanted to. All she'd wanted was a copious amount of sex, and while I'd been more than happy to give it to her, I felt like we'd missed an opportunity. A small way for all of us to temporarily put aside what was going on, and celebrate a life event. It would have lifted all our spirits, recharged us, given us a much needed second wind, but instead, we'd dwelled, avoided, and ignored the problem plaguing us. And now it was beginning to feel inescapable.

When I opened the door to Izzy's apartment, the mood inside felt just as somber as it had back at my place. Maybe it was me. Maybe I was carrying melancholy around with me, changing the tension wherever I went. As I gave Izzy a hug, I would have given anything to be able to lighten the feeling in the air. But jokes wouldn't work, good-natured ribbing wouldn't work; nothing would work. It was what it was, and it fucking sucked.

Felicia seemed to shrink inside herself as she absorbed the underlying feeling of hopelessness. She gave Izzy a hug after I did, but there was clearly a wall being erected; her full heart wasn't in the embrace. It worried me to see Felicia retreating, but if I asked her what was wrong again, she'd only tell me nothing. Felicia was always great, even when she wasn't great.

"Where's Antonia?" I asked, as Izzy and Felicia separated. Izzy had always been small, but she seemed downright frail now. I should come by more often, make sure she was eating enough. I was being selfish with my sexual indulgence.

Izzy half-smiled at me. "She's lying down. Her counts were good, so they let us check out, but now she's feeling sick. Doctor said that might happen off and on…a side effect of the chemo. I just have to watch for fevers. She could have stayed there a few more days though… maybe she should have… I don't know, she's been there for so long, I thought she'd want to be home, but maybe I was wrong. Fuck, I don't know what I'm doing, Hayden. What the hell do I do? How the hell do I pay for all this? I can't work, I can't leave her... I don't know what to do. I just don't know what to do..."

I could see her struggling, see her emotional walls crumbling. I knew she couldn't do this on her own, and I also knew she didn't need to do it on her own. She had me. Pulling her into my arms, I soothed her fears as best I could. "Hey, hey, hey, you're doing great, Izzy. No one knows how to deal with this shit. And don't worry about money. I've got you covered. I'll call Hookup, have him enter me in every single race he can find, and all my winnings will go to you. I've got your back, Iz, and I'm not going anywhere."

She started sobbing against my shoulder, simultaneously thanking me and wishing there was another way. The street racing made her nervous. It was a no-brainer for me, though. She needed money, a lot of it, and racing was an easy way to get it. As I held Izzy, I looked over at Felicia. If she raced with me, we could earn twice as much money for Antonia. Felicia had a strange expression on her face—one I couldn't read. It was a mixture of shock, fear, pride, and...something else I couldn't name.

Once Izzy had composed herself, the three of us went to check on Antonia. She looked tiny in her bed, like a doll instead of a human. The chemo had already ravaged her, and most of her thick, dark hair was gone. She was lightly snoring as she slept, but the rest was doing nothing to restore her pallor. She seemed drained, like she was only half-alive. Clutching her throw-up bowl in one hand, she had her American Girl doll clenched tightly in the other. Izzy said she never let it leave her sight. God, if I thought it would help her, I'd buy a thousand of those damn dolls. A million, if that was what it took.

As I stood beside the bed, one arm around Izzy, watching Antonia sleep, I heard Felicia breathing heavier. When I looked over at her, I saw that her dark eyes locked on Antonia were filled with unshed tears. Bringing shaking fingers to her mouth, she murmured, "She's so…she looks so…"

Releasing Izzy, I walked over to Felicia. "Hey, it's okay. It's gonna be okay, babe."

Swiping under her eyes, she glanced at Izzy before shifting her attention to me. Forced smile on her face, she told me, "I know."

I wanted to know what was on her mind, but I knew the answer wouldn't be something Izzy needed to hear, so I didn't even ask. I just pulled her in for a silent hug. Izzy watched us with a small smile on her face, then we heard Antonia stir. She groaned in her sleep, just before green vomit started spewing from her lips. Izzy rushed to her side and helped turn her head into the bowl. She heaved a few times, then stilled; she never even woke up.

Izzy took the bowl into the bathroom to wash it out. When she returned, she looked anxious and tired. "Hayden, I hate to ask this…but could you stay tonight? I'd really…I'd really like some help with this."

My answer was instant. "Of course." Then I turned to Felicia. "Is that…okay?"

She nodded, her face composed, but her eyes still bright. "Yeah, of course. I'll just…I'll see you in the morning."

I nodded, then leaned over and gave her a kiss. To my surprise, she grabbed my face and deepened the moment. There was almost a desperate frenzy to the contact, and instead of turning me on…it kind of freaked me out. Pulling back, I grabbed her arms. "Everything's gonna be okay. We'll get through this. Together." She nodded, but her face fell a little. I gave her a kiss on the cheek, hoping some sweetness would bring her around. She smiled, but I wasn't sure if it really worked.

Felicia stayed with us for another half hour, then she gave me a kiss goodnight and headed home. I made a meal for Izzy, then made her eat it. After that, I shuffled her off to bed. "I'll watch over Antonia tonight. You need rest."

Izzy protested for a long time, but finally I—and exhaustion—won, and she headed to bed. I did exactly what I promised I'd do, and kept watch over Antonia all night long. I sat in a chair beside her bed, watching her sleep, occasionally emptying her vomit bowl, and praying that everything really would be okay.

Antonia was still sleeping when Izzy woke up in the morning. She came into her daughter's room to find me trying not to nod off in the stiff-backed chair that had been my ass's home for the last several hours. "You didn't sleep at all, did you?" she asked.

Shaking my head, I told her, "I told you'd I watch her all night, and I keep my word." And I would always keep my word when it came to Antonia. If I couldn't fix what was wrong with her, then I'd fix everything else.

A genuine smile warmed Izzy's face. "Yeah, you do. You should go home, though...get some sleep."

Frowning, I looked over at Antonia's sleeping body. She hadn't thrown up in a long time, and I was taking that as a good sign, but I'd still feel better if I saw her eyes open, saw her smile at me. "I'd like to stay until she wakes up."

Putting a hand on my shoulder, Izzy looked down at me with the concerned eyes of a mother. "I'm fine now, Hayden. I can handle this. For today. But Felicia... something is off with her. I feel like...I feel like she's gonna run again. Go to your girlfriend, get her to talk to you. Then get some sleep."

I knew she was right, but even still, a part of me didn't want to leave. Sometimes I needed reassurance too, and seeing Antonia awake and happy would be very cathartic. Izzy was right though; something *was* going on with Felicia. She needed me too, and I needed to be there for her. "Yeah, all right. I'll get out of here for a little bit, get some sleep. If you need me to come back—if you *ever* need me to come back—just text me, Iz. Like I said, I'm not going anywhere."

"I know," she said with a smile, then kissed my cheek.

On my way home, I worried. Worried about Izzy, worried about Antonia, and worried about Felicia. How did everything fall apart so fast? But no...it hadn't fallen apart, it had just cracked. And I could fix cracks.

I struggled to keep my eyes open the entire ride home, and when I pulled into the driveway, I debated if I could go to bed first, and talk to Felicia when I woke up. No, even *I* knew that wasn't a good idea. She was my priority, and I should treat her as such. I'd talk to her first...then go to bed. As I twisted the knob, another thought occurred to me, a much happier one. I'd been waiting for a good time to ask Felicia to marry me, but there hadn't been the perfect moment; I was beginning to think there never would be one. So, what if I chose the wrong moment instead? What if doing it now—when we were at our lowest—was the best for everyone? It would give Felicia something positive to think about, brighten Izzy's spirits, and possibly Antonia's too. What little girl didn't love weddings?

My mind made up, I decided the first thing I'd do when I saw Felicia was drop down on one knee. I should give her the ring, too, though. I'd sneak into the bedroom, grab it from my underwear drawer, then drop down on one knee. It would be perfectly imperfect.

Plan in mind, I was quiet when I entered the house. She might be in the bedroom, of course, which would make things harder, but I was sure I could do it. I had quick hands.

Stealthily closing the door, I started heading for the bedroom. Something felt different in the apartment, but I couldn't put my finger on it…like the air felt stale. When I got to the bedroom, I poked my head in to see if Felicia was there. She wasn't, so I began tiptoeing to the dresser. I stopped when I noticed something…odd. The top two drawers on Felicia's side of the dresser were cracked open, the bottom one was completely open, and empty.

Straightening my stance, I instantly forgot about being sneaky. Walking over to the dresser, I started yanking open drawers. Felicia's were all empty. What the fuck? I switched to my side of the dresser…but everything of mine was still there, including Felicia's engagement ring.

I checked the closet beside the dresser, and found the same thing—Felicia's stuff was gone, but all my crap hadn't been touched. An icy feeling started clenching my chest, making it hard to breathe. Did she fucking run again? She hadn't done it in a while…I thought for sure she'd outgrown the compulsion. I hurried to the bathroom, but it was the same as everything else—void of her. Goddamn it. How could she bail on us now?

Maybe she hadn't left yet. Maybe I could fix this. "Felicia? Babe? You here?"

There was a panicked edge to my voice. I hated hearing it, but I couldn't help it. Felicia had never taken *all* of her stuff before. She'd always just fled with whatever she had on her at the time. Everything about this felt wrong. It felt pre-meditated. Felt...permanent. Fuck, this wasn't just Felicia running away for a few days to get her head on straight. This was Felicia running away...for good.

No. She wouldn't do that to me. We'd been best friends since I was ten years old. Something else was going on here. It had to be something else...

The bed was pristine, untouched. No clues there. Ducking out of the bedroom, I started searching everywhere for her. It was a small apartment, though, not a whole lot of space to check. When I got to the kitchen, I stopped searching. A piece of paper was lying on the table. For some reason, just looking at it made my heart beat faster. Felicia had never left notes when she ran. Ever.

I had to force my legs to move toward the table, had to force my eyes to focus on the paper, force them to concentrate on the words written there in an all-too familiar script. My heart was thundering when I was close enough to read what it said, but even then, my stubborn eyes refused to make sense of the letters. I had to close them and inhale a deep breath.

When I reopened my eyes, I wished to God I hadn't. In bold letters, smudged with dried teardrops, were two sentences that completely tore everything to pieces.

I'm sorry. I can't do this.

CHAPTER 2

~Hayden~
Present day

Shit. Why couldn't anything good in my life be simple, easy, strife-free? Why was I cursed with complications? Felicia. I hadn't seen her in four years, not since she'd walked out on me, walked out on everyone. And now that things in my life were just about as great as they could be, she was back to complicate them again. I wasn't just cursed, I was fucked. Royally, cosmically fucked. Someone up there seriously hated me.

I hadn't even thought about Felicia in years, not until Kenzie had steamrolled into my life. When I'd first laid eyes on Kenzie, for a full half-second, I'd thought she *was* Felicia. I'd quickly realized she wasn't, but those first few encounters with her had been difficult for me—confusing and disorienting. I'd wanted to get closer to her, had wanted to shove her away. Kenzie's snippy attitude toward me back then had actually made things a little easier. I'd been able to separate the two women into two distinct and individual personalities. And they were most definitely two different people—two *very* different people. For one, Kenzie hadn't bailed on me when things got difficult. She'd fought for me, she'd fought for *us*, and I respected her so damn much for that.

But Felicia...seeing her again yesterday had brought back some baggage I thought I'd firmly stuffed into a small compartment in the very back corner of my mind. When I'd spotted her, standing at *my* practice track in Benneti gear that matched *mine*, it was like I'd taken a bullet to the brain. Instant, blinding, painful. I'd felt like I was back at the New Jersey race, and was again smacking into a pile of motorcycles and men at 100 miles per hour. I couldn't breathe, couldn't see, and every organ hurt. I'd felt like that lost 19-year-old kid again, hesitant to approach a fucking piece of paper on a table.

The dam holding back my memories had cracked open, and a flood of unrelenting misery had threatened to drown me in grief. But Kenzie had been watching, and I hadn't wanted her to see the torture inflicted upon me, so I'd shoved the emotions back into their cage, securely locked the door on them, and then ran away with my girl. And I'd keep running away with her if I had to, because Kenzie was all that mattered now. Keeping her, satisfying her, making sure she was happy.

Because if she left me too... I couldn't survive another piece of my soul being torn away. I just couldn't. Fuck. Why the hell had Felicia returned? Why now, after all this time, when everything was finally going great with Kenzie? The two of us had gotten over every hurdle keeping us apart, and now this shit. I was such an idiot, thinking things in my life would be easier from here on out. Nothing came easy. Not for me.

I pulled up to the gate at the Benneti Motorsports Practice Track, wondering what today had in store for me.

Maybe it wouldn't hurt as much to see Felicia, now that I knew she was here. It was the shock that had unraveled me before. That was all.

Entering my key card into the slot, I punched in the code and waited for the gate to open before squeezing my motorcycle through the gap. It felt strange to be coming here without Kenzie today, like somehow, I was doing something wrong. We'd bailed early on Keith's "welcome" party for Felicia yesterday, and had gone for a drive up the coast. Riding along the winding roads with Kenzie had been euphoric and energizing, but it was nowhere near as amazing as it was to race against her. I missed that. A lot. But Kenzie didn't have a team anymore, and neither one of us was street racing anymore, so the odds of Kenzie and I being able to go full-out against each other anytime soon were slim-to-none. We'd have to be content with casual drives instead. Well, almost casual. We *had* gone ten to twenty miles above the speed limit at times. Our racing spirit could only be curbed so much.

I'd spent the night at Kenzie's house and left from her place this morning. I'd asked her if she wanted to come with me today, but she'd wanted to make some more phone calls. She was still trying to get on a racing team. Her father had sort of blacklisted her after his team fell apart at the end of last season. He'd given her an ultimatum—to break up with me or never race again—and she had miraculously chosen me. It still blew my mind. And made me feel really guilty. As much as I loved racing, I think Kenzie loved it even more. It was in her blood; Jordan Cox had been a champion before forming his own team. Kenzie had grown up in the world, and had wanted to be a part of it probably before she could even walk. And

I was the reason it had been taken from her. I had no idea how I was going to make up for that fact, or if I even could.

Hopefully, she would be able to contact a team today who hadn't been convinced by Jordan to reject her. Kenzie was an amazing rider, and she deserved to be on a team. Someone just had to see past Jordan's bullshit and hire her. All the local teams had said no, though, so Kenzie's only chance of keeping her dream alive would be taking a job far away from me. Something I didn't want to think about yet.

I made my way through the inner gate, to the heart of the complex. Stopping there, I looked around. The focal point of my view was the massive practice track itself. Movable concrete barriers defined the course, creating sweeping turns and exhilarating straightaways. The path was changed routinely, to keep us all on our toes; pushing myself through that gauntlet was one of my favorite things to do.

To the right of the track was the abandoned buildings of Cox Racing. All the team logos were gone, all the windows were dark, and all the doors were locked. A *For Sale* sign was the most prominent feature, a fact that had my boss, Keith Benneti, in an uproar. He wanted the track, but Jordan refused to sell it to him. To say there was bad blood between them was an understatement. I hated seeing the lack of life on that side of the track, but I was the only Benneti who felt that way. The "bad blood" between the owners had infected the rest of the team as well.

In contrast to the emptiness, the Benneti side, on the left of the track, was bustling with life. I could hear the whining of power tools and engines, could see people walking around inside the open garage bay doors. It was just another day at work, but somehow, it all felt different.

With a reluctant sigh, I turned my bike toward the Benneti garages and prepared myself for…well, for anything. There was a nauseous feeling in my gut as I approached the place that used to be my sanctuary. Okay, maybe sanctuary was a stretch. The other guys on the team had been reluctant to embrace me as a full-fledged member, and even now, it seemed they still had some lingering resentments.

Keith had found me on the streets a little over a year ago. I had no idea how he'd heard about the street racing, and I'd never seen him at an event after that night, but he'd been impressed, and had offered me a spot on his team afterward. With one stipulation, of course—I had to give up street racing. For good. Not because he cared if I was doing something illegal like that, but because he hadn't wanted to invest a bunch of time and money in me, just to see me banned from the sport. If Keith only knew that I hadn't entirely given it up last season, he would have gone ballistic.

But he hadn't found out, and he'd given me everything I could have ever asked for—a roof over my head, a motorcycle to ride around town, another motorcycle to race with on the track, and even spending money. It was difficult for me to feel so indebted to one person—my childhood had taught me that was an all-around bad idea. It helped to keep reminding myself that Keith was ultimately only interested in helping Keith. He wanted a champion, and he believed that could be me.

All the lavish attention Keith placed on me had severely pissed off my teammates, and whenever they'd gotten a chance, they'd done everything they could to take me down a notch. I could almost feel some of the bruises they'd given me. It hadn't helped matters any that they'd also suspected I was tampering with bikes to win, thanks to Hookup, who actually *had* been tampering with bikes. Asshole. He'd gone way too far this time. Cutting him out of my life completely was one of the best decisions I'd ever made. Besides dating Kenzie, of course. The crash I was in last season had smoothed things over with my teammates, though—since I obviously wouldn't let myself get hurt if I was the saboteur—and they were sort of civil now.

Rodney and Maxwell waved hello when they saw me pull up outside of the garage. "Hey, Hayes," Rodney said. "You see the new girl yet? Hot damn, that is one fine piece of ass. I'm not sure how I'm supposed to keep my mind on the race with *that* behind me."

Two very opposite emotions hit me at the same time. A knot of anxiety tightened my stomach so hard I was sure I'd be sore in the morning, and a surprisingly hot flash of anger swept through me. Since neither of those would help me deal with this asshole, I forced myself to respond with a joke. "What makes you think she'll be behind you?"

Maxwell snorted and held out his fist to me. I grudgingly bumped him, when all I really wanted to do was sock Rodney in the face. Why was I feeling protective of her? Felicia had never needed me to be her bodyguard; she could take of herself. And besides, I didn't owe her anything—she'd *left* me.

Turning my back on the guys and my dark thoughts, I headed for the garage. While I kept a calm smile on my face, an internal chant was repeating through my brain:

Don't let her be here, don't let her be here. I just wasn't ready to see her. Now, or ever.

A quick peek around the space told me the coast was clear. Nikki wasn't here yet, but that wasn't too surprising, since she was often late. She was one of the best mechanics I'd ever seen, though. She used to be Kenzie's, and I felt a little bad for swiping her, but Nikki had needed a job, and she hadn't wanted to leave the track. Keith had been all too eager to snatch her up. My guess was he'd expected her knowledge of the Cox side of things to give him some miraculous insight, something our side didn't already know. So far, there had been no new discoveries, but Nikki was a genius with a bike, and I was glad she was helping me.

I trudged upstairs to go hit the gym while I waited for her; I preferred Nikki to fully examine my bike before I took it out. When I got to the second floor, I passed by Keith's office on the way to the gym. His door was open, and I heard my name being called as I walked by. "Hayden!"

Stopping, I twisted to the doorframe. "Yeah?"

My heart sunk when I looked inside. Keith was sitting behind a massive oak desk that probably weighed close to a thousand pounds. He had on his signature aviator sunglasses, even though he was indoors, and was rockin' a pretty impressive pair of muttonchops. He was flipping a pen in his hands and giving me a smile that reeked of amusement. The source of his amusement, and my discontent, was lounging on a couch perpendicular to the desk. Felicia. My lungs compressed to nothing as I stared at her. She looked exactly like the eighteen-year-old girl I remembered—the eighteen-year-old girl who had run from me, leaving four insufficient words behind as the only explanation. *I can't do this.* Her thick hair covered her shoulders in dark curls, and her cool, dark eyes watched me like a raptor. I wasn't sure what she expected from me, but I knew what she'd get from me: nothing.

"I'm glad you're here," Keith said, bringing my attention back to him. I still hadn't taken a breath yet, so I couldn't respond. In my silence, he said, "You left the party so early yesterday, I didn't get a chance to personally introduce you to our newest rider, Felicia Tucker."

Hearing her name out loud was like having a hot poker jabbed in my eye. What the hell was she doing here? She rose from the couch and walked over to me with a roll to her hips that I knew very well. "We know each other," she said over her shoulder to Keith. To me, she added, "It's good to see you again, Hayden. It's been too long." A flash of pain crossed her face, and a visible ache was in her eyes. Was that regret? I didn't want to stay to find out.

I inhaled a much-needed breath and focused on Keith. "If you need me, I'll be in the gym." Turning, I immediately left the room. Fury made my feet fast, but not fast enough. The sound of jogging footsteps told me someone was following me...*she* was following me.

"Hayden! Wait!" I didn't. If anything, I started walking faster. *There's nothing I want to hear from you.*

Her hand reached out and grabbed my arm, stopping me. "Wait!" Enraged, I spun to face her. Being so close to those deep eyes and pouty lips flooded me with mixed emotions. *Why did you leave?* Fuck it. I didn't care.

Yanking my arm away, I bit out, "Don't touch me. You don't get to touch me anymore."

Her hand was shaking as she dropped it to her side. "You're right, I'm sorry."

Her voice was just like I remembered, smooth and sweet like honey. It pissed me off even more. "I don't know why you're here, but let's get one thing straight right now...I don't want anything to do with you."

"Hayden..." She took a step toward me, and I instinctively took a step back.

"I'm serious, Felicia. When you left, you closed a door." Closed it, doused it in gasoline, then struck a match and set it ablaze. "It's not reopening," I stated.

Her dark eyes grew misty. "I know, and I know I messed up. I just want a chance to explain, that's all."

Raising my hand, I shook my head. "There's no reason for you to explain. There's no reason for you to say anything. So don't. Don't talk to me, don't come near me, don't even look at me. We're done."

I started to move away, and she stubbornly refused to listen to my simple instructions. She grabbed my hand, and damn if the memory of holding her didn't instantly resurface at feeling her tender touch. "I know you're mad, but just hear me out. There was a reason I—"

Ripping her hand away, I tossed it aside...just like she'd tossed me. With a cold smile on my face, I quietly told her, "I'm not mad, Felicia. *I just can't do this.*"

Contempt dripped from my voice as I repeated her goodbye back to her, and her face fell at hearing it. The tears in her eyes finally dripped to her cheeks, and, not wanting to see her pain, I angrily pushed passed her.

I'd thought it would make me feel better to toss those words in her face, but it hadn't. I just felt empty. Maybe I wouldn't ride today after all. Maybe I'd just go home. But if I did that, Nikki would tell Kenzie I hadn't come in, and then she would wonder and worry. I didn't want to stress Kenzie out about this; she had enough on her plate with her family ignoring her and her current lack of employment. And there was nothing here for her to worry about anyway. Like I'd told Felicia...we were done.

I went to the gym like I'd told Keith I was going to, and worked out my aggression on the punching bag in the corner. An hour later, when I went back downstairs, I threw on a casual, no-care-in-the-world smile for Nikki. If Kenzie asked her about today, Nikki would tell her I was fine. And I was. Absolutely, completely, and totally fine.

For the rest of the day, I managed to live in a delusional bubble where Felicia didn't exist. When she was nearby, I purposely avoided looking at her. When she was speaking, I purposely avoided listening to her. It was like a black void of nothingness spawned to life whenever she was near, drawing in everyone around her until she left. Maybe it wasn't the best way to cope with things, but it worked for me. Avoiding her even helped me race—running from her was easy when I was flying down the road—and I scored the best times I had since my accident...something I probably shouldn't mention to Kenzie. I didn't think hearing that I was racing well without her would make her feel good.

When I left the track for the day, I was exhausted. Exhausted but hopeful. I'd found a way to deal with my newfound reality. I had a plan. Now I just needed Kenzie to believe in my plan, believe in *me*, then maybe Felicia coming back wouldn't change a damn thing.

The minute I got back to my apartment above Keith's garage, I texted my girl. *'Hey babe, I'm done for the day. Want to come over?'*

I knew what her answer would be before she even gave it. *'Not really. Want to come over here?'* Now that I was no longer in a cast, Kenzie avoided Keith's house like the plague. I didn't blame her. After some of the things she'd told me about Keith and her mom having an affair behind Jordan's back, I probably would have avoided Keith too.

Telling her I'd see her soon, I stripped off my clothes and headed to the shower. Once I was refreshed and dressed, I hopped on my bike again. Keith was in the driveway when I left. He watched me leave with a frown, but he didn't say anything. He didn't approve of me dating his worst enemy's daughter, and was only tolerating it because he was hoping Kenzie would convince Jordan to sell the track to him. That might work, if Kenzie and her father were on speaking terms. Regardless, I didn't care what Keith thought about Kenzie. He was my boss, not my father, and if he wasn't going to fire me for dating a Cox—a fire-able offense when I'd first started racing for him—then he could keep his opinions to himself.

Kenzie lived in the heart of Oceanside, in a modest one-bedroom home. When I'd first found out she was the daughter of a racing champion, I'd expected something a lot…grander. But Kenzie was a simple girl at heart, and I loved that about her. Her passion revolved around racing; it was all she'd ever wanted to do. God, I hoped she'd had some luck today.

Pulling my bike into the driveway, I turned it off and nearly ran to her door. It hadn't been the best day, and I really needed to see my girlfriend. I rang the doorbell to the tune of "Silent Night." It annoyed Kenzie to no end when I rang Christmas carols, but I think she liked it too. The door was pulled open long before I finished the song, and Kenzie was standing there in loose cotton pants and a tight Cox Racing T-shirt. God, she looked amazing, and now that I knew her so well, I could easily spot the uniqueness that made her completely different from Felicia. Seeing her was like walking outside into the fresh air after being cooped up in a stagnant room all day long—I could finally breathe again. Her long, dark brown hair was a mess of wavy curls, wild and untamable, just like her spirit. Her creamy skin was perfect, flawless, and her deep brown eyes danced with delight at seeing me. And irritation.

"I really wish you'd stop doing that," she murmured, a half-smile on her lips.

I knew she meant the rhythmic ringing, but I couldn't resist playing with her. "Staring at you like you're a meal I want to devour? Sorry, can't do that. You're just too damn appealing."

Stepping into her house, I wrapped my arms around her waist and pulled her into me. She gasped at the sudden movement, then smiled and laced her arms around my neck. As she gazed at me, I saw a flurry of emotions dance across her face: humor at my comment, desire at my words, interest, love, happiness, and a trace of...concern, fear. She would probably never say it, but she'd been worried about me going to the track today. Worried about me being around my ex all day. I needed to find a balanced way to convince her that she had absolutely nothing to worry about without sounding like I was overcompensating for something.

With a peaceful smile on my face, I lowered my lips to hers. "I missed you," I whispered, right before our lips connected. It was fire, passion, heat, and need when her soft skin met mine. I wanted more, wanted a deeper connection, wanted to scoop her into my arms, toss her down on her bed, and explore every inch of her. And before the night was through, that was exactly what I was going to do. But not yet. It might seem fueled by something else if I took her now. I needed to wait until she was assured that today had meant nothing to me.

"I missed you too," she told me when our mouths finally separated. With a sigh, she gave me a final kiss, and retreated from my arms. I watched the joy in her expression fade as she closed the front door.

"How did today go? Any leads?" I asked, crossing my fingers for a bit of good luck. Kenzie needed to ride, just as surely as I did.

She sucked a plump lip into her mouth as she shook her head. "I called half a dozen teams, and they all said the same thing: 'We'll let you know.'"

Smiling, I walked over and grabbed her hands. "On the bright side, that's not a no."

Lifting an eyebrow, she deadpanned, "That's not a yes either. I also tried calling my father and my sisters. Dad wouldn't even pick up. Theresa was as frosty as ever. She told me I was a horrible person for hurting Dad, then she hung up on me. Daphne bitched me out for twenty minutes straight. She wouldn't let me get a word in edgewise." A fiery look ran through her eyes. "I know I hurt Dad when I chose you over racing…over him…but they're all taking it to the extreme. They're acting like I'm intentionally trying to be cruel or something, but I'm not...I just want to be with the person I love."

I knew she meant that, and I knew she honestly believed she'd made the right choice by choosing me, but sometimes I wondered, and worried. Her father had pulled a lot of strings to get her rejected by nearly every racing team. He'd probably called in every favor he had, all so he could get Kenzie to end things with me. Why he hated me so much I wasn't sure, but I was also beginning to believe it wasn't really about me anymore. He was proving a point—no one crossed Jordan Cox and got away with it. Not even his own daughter. I should have a word with him. Several. But not until Kenzie had finally gone over there and spoken to him face-to-face. It was time for her to confront her father.

I opened my mouth to tell her something positive, although I had no idea what I could say to turn *that* problem around. Like she knew what I was trying to do, Kenzie swished her hands at me. "But I don't want to talk about my family right now. I want to hear about your day. How was... How were your times?"

By the slight pause and wary tone, I knew she really wanted to know about Felicia. God, that had to have eaten her up all day. It would gnaw at me, if our positions were reversed. In my head, I would have played out multiple intimate fantasies of the two exes reconnecting. I'd be a basketcase waiting for an answer—waiting for my world to fall apart. I didn't want Kenzie to feel that way, didn't want her to not know where she stood with me. And because I also didn't want her to know that I'd raced better today than I had in a while, I answered a question she hadn't asked. "Felicia approached me this morning, wanting to talk...and I told her that I had nothing to say to her, ever, and politely requested that she never talk to me again. And if she tries to anyway, I'll tell her the exact same thing again. I have no desire to hear anything she has to say. Ever."

My voice came out a little impassioned on that last part, and I cringed as I watched a light flush spread over Kenzie's cheeks. Her breath increased, just a little, and her eyes were wide as she stared at me. I hoped she was just trying to process everything I'd openly, unprompted, confessed to her, and I hoped she wasn't wondering about the heat in my voice. *I'm not hiding anything from you, Kenzie. You're the one I love. I promise.*

"She wants to talk to you?" she finally said, her voice quiet. "But you don't want to hear her out? You're not curious?"

She was trying to feel me out, figure out my exact feelings toward my ex. But there was nothing to suss out; I didn't have feelings for Felicia, just regrets. "Nothing she has to say is going to change what she did. She abandoned Izzy and Antonia when they needed her the most."

"And you," she softly added. "She abandoned you too."

A strange sensation started growing in my chest; it was like a maddening irritant lodged under my skin, unreachable, unfixable. Yes, she'd abandoned me, just like every shit foster parent I'd ever had. Just like my parents, when they hadn't done a damn thing to get me back. In the end, Felicia hadn't been the person I'd thought she was. And that had hurt. It had taken me months, *years*, to get over the betrayal, and even now...sure, it still stung. But I didn't want Kenzie to see that, didn't want her to know that. Kenzie was my world now.

"What Felicia did to me doesn't matter anymore, so why would I want to hear about it? You're all that matters, because you're the one I want. The *only* one I want. Okay?"

"Yeah...okay, Hayden." Her expression changed, and, for once, I couldn't read her mood. Was that relief I saw in her eyes, or compounded fear? Had I made things worse by bringing Felicia up before she did? Damn it, maybe she'd needed to ease into the conversation, but stupid me, I'd just dove right in and gone for broke. So much for trying to sound like I wasn't overcompensating. *So how do I fix this now?*

"Are you really okay?" I asked, seeking her guidance. I didn't want to steer the conversation wrong again.

The air thickened with tension as she studied me, and I suddenly had the feeling that we were standing on opposite sides of a giant plate, balanced on the sharp point of a slim spear, and we were each trying to find the tipping point. Any wrong move right now would disrupt the harmony and send our relationship tumbling into darkness and chaos. My heart started to beat harder as I waited for some type of response from her. She was either going to open up to me, let me see her fears and doubts, or she was going to start building a wall.

Just when I couldn't take it anymore, and I was about to ask my question again, Kenzie gave me a forced smile. "Yeah, I'm fine. It's fine. We're good."

I knew right then and there that we weren't. "Kenzie…"

Ignoring me, she indicated the kitchen. "Are you hungry? I tried making Pad Thai. I'm not sure if it turned out, but I know you love it so I figured you'd eat it anyway. I thought we could eat it in bed. Naked."

There was a look on her face, a silent plea to accept the distraction she was offering, to accept the Thai food and sex, and let the lingering doubt between us remain untouched, unexamined, undisturbed. And I knew if I did that, if I let her steer us down this road of avoidance, this uneasy feeling between us would only get bigger. But I had to admit, the idea of avoiding this—just for right now—sounded damn appealing. I'd had a long, emotional day, and all I really wanted was to see Kenzie smile, to enjoy the meal she'd made for me, and to kiss every single inch of her body. I didn't want a heartfelt, painful conversation that would probably lead me down a rocky road of torturous memories and years-long, built-up suffering. I just wanted to be with her. Happy, content, oblivious. We could deal with reality tomorrow.

And that was why I responded to her suggestion by pulling her into my body and growling, "Okay, but can we skip right to the naked in bed part?"

She giggled in response, but there was a hollowness to the sound that haunted me. Had I already fucked this up?

CHAPTER 3

~Hayden~

Like I'd been doing a lot lately, I spent the night at Kenzie's house. Sleep was elusive though. I kept tossing and turning; no position was comfortable. My mind refused to settle down, and my day replayed over and over in my head. I kept analyzing my conversation with Kenzie, trying to figure out how she'd taken my words. Then my thoughts turned to Felicia. Not to her personally, but to the brief encounter we'd had. Could I have handled that differently? Been more assertive? Why the hell was she back?

Thinking of Felicia got me thinking about the rest of my original pack. Did Izzy know Felicia was back? I should probably tell her. Then she could tell Hookup, if he didn't already know. Although…maybe I should talk to him. Maybe I'd handled that situation wrong, too, and I should try to make some sort of peace with him. I wasn't sure, but it was weird not having him in my life. God, what to do. I'd felt lost several times in my life before, but nothing quite like this.

My pillow felt like a rock, the sheets felt like sandpaper, but eventually I found a somewhat comfortable position, and started relaxing as the pull of sleep began to take me under. The thoughts tumbling through my brain slowed into languid visions—some of my past, some of my present. A memory of running through the rain with Felicia morphed into running along the beach with Kenzie. Racing through the streets alternated between Felicia and Kenzie beside me, and then oddly, both women were there. Exploring Felicia's body, nervous and fumbling as I tried to figure it all out, shifted into masterfully bringing Kenzie to the brink, then keeping her there for hours.

As my body began to shut off for the night, my thoughts turned weirder and weirder—flying cats, Keith telling me he was my father, my bike having a conversation with me. Then, deep in dreamland, I found myself walking into the Cox Racing garage. It wasn't empty, like it was in real life, but bustling with activity and energy... like it used to be.

Mechanics, riders, and crew members milled about the room, endlessly going from space to space. Nikki was in the center of the garage, laughing over something with her friend, Myles, as she worked on Kenzie's bike. I looked around for my girlfriend, but she wasn't anywhere to be seen. Starting to worry about her, I took a step toward Nikki. A hand on my shoulder stopped me. I expected to see Kenzie standing behind me when I spun around. It wasn't her though.

"Felicia? What are you doing here?" Confusion rang through my brain as I tried to make sense of all the out of place images: a full garage, Kenzie gone...Felicia here.

She stared at me with a calm smile that was edged with sadness. "I'm here for you. It's time to go, Hayden."

Ice tightened my spine, and I glanced around the room again for Kenzie. The entire garage was empty now, though—not a trace of the people or the machines remained. Thinking I should tell Felicia I wasn't going *anywhere* with her, I said, "Time to go where?"

Holding both my hands in hers, she whispered, "Time to go home."

I woke up with a start. My heartbeat was fast, and I was breathing heavier. Thing was, I wasn't sure how I felt about the dream, other than relief that it *was* a dream. A part of me had been crushed, while another part of me had been hopeful. I didn't want to think about it, and I definitely didn't want to analyze it. Sometimes a dream was just a dream, and there were no hidden meanings.

A soft, comforting hand touched my chest. "You okay?" Kenzie mumbled, voice thick with sleep.

Not wanting her to feel my racing heart, I grabbed her fingers and brought them to my lips. "Yeah, just a weird dream. Go back to sleep."

She popped up on her elbow to look at me, and even in the bleak grayness of her room, I could see the concern in her eyes. "Dream? About what?"

God, why did she have to ask that? There was no way on Earth I could tell her. There was just no way to explain it without making myself look bad. Or making my subconscious look bad, at any rate, since that was a completely unauthorized dream. If I could, I'd fire somebody.

"I don't really…I don't remember much. It's fuzzy." I felt horrible lying to her, but in this case, it was the absolute right call. Sometimes the truth opened a door that couldn't be shut again.

Kenzie frowned, like she could sense the deceit, and I silently begged her not to pry. *Don't make me confess what you don't want to know.* Like she'd heard my plea, she smiled and leaned down to kiss me. "Well, you don't need to worry about the boogey man, I'm here to protect you."

My ears picked up a slight emphasis on the words, "I'm here." It was subtle, but she was definitely stressing the fact that *she* was the one in bed with me, in a relationship with me. That she was the one who hadn't abandoned me. *I know. And I love you so much for that.*

I couldn't say that to her without confessing my small sin, so instead, I cupped her cheek and drew her mouth back to me. "I love you so much," I said between tender kisses.

"I love you too…so much." Her kiss grew more frantic after her words, more passionate, like she was trying to show me how much she cared, then she slipped her leg over mine and repositioned herself so she was straddling my hips. I already knew she loved me, and she didn't need to do this to prove it, but I had something to show her too, so I pulled her hips into mine and let her deepen the kiss.

With her rubbing against me, I was hard in an instant, straining against my underwear. Kenzie moaned as she rocked against me. Sitting up, she pushed her chest out to me and dropped her head back. I took the opportunity to reach out and feel her firm breast through the fabric of her light tank top. Her rigid nipple called to me like a beacon, and I desperately wanted it in my mouth. Sliding my fingers up her ribs, taking the top with it, I slowly exposed the tender flesh. Kenzie's gaze returned to me, and with a small smile on her face, she lowered her breast to my lips.

A groan escaped me when I felt that hard peak in my mouth. I rolled my tongue around it, savoring it, cherishing it. Kenzie sucked in a quick breath, then dug her hips into mine, hard.

As the pleasure ripped through me, my mouth parted and her breast escaped me. Kenzie quickly ripped off her shirt, then circled her hips in a pattern that was going to make me lose control if I didn't pull my shit together. I could *not* come before I'd even entered her. Wanting to drive her wild before she sent me over the edge, I slid my hand between our bodies, searching for that warm wetness I loved so much.

I slowly slid my finger between her legs. Kenzie cried out, gripping my shoulders so hard I thought I might be bruised tomorrow. "Fuck, you're so wet…you feel so good." I wasn't sure if this was the right moment for dirty talk, but I couldn't stop myself from saying it, and it felt great to tell her the truth.

Kenzie made some incoherent noise as I traced a slow circle around her core. Then I heard her mumble, "I need you." There was so much sincerity in the sentence, that I pulled my hand away and rolled her onto her back.

Looking down into her eyes, I lovingly told her, "I need you too." I prayed she understood that I didn't mean sex. Very few people understood me like she did—our interests, our competitiveness, our tragic pasts, our fiery passion—it was like she was designed specifically for me. Thank God fate had put us on a path toward each other.

A warm look softened Kenzie's eyes as she stared up at me. Doing my best to not break eye contact, I pulled off her underwear, then my own. Once we were bare, I slid inside her. Then I had to close my eyes—the sensation was so great, I had no choice. "Oh God," I heard her say beneath me. I internally echoed the sentiment. Nothing felt as good as being buried inside her; in this, too, it was like we were built for one another.

To make this connection last, I kept the pace slow and steady, almost tortuous. Kenzie was writhing before too long, panting with need. Her desire fed my own, and I reluctantly picked up the pace; I never wanted this to end. As we drove into each other, the building pressure inside me told me I wasn't going to last for long. *Just let her come first, please.* Adjusting our hips, I tried a different angle. Kenzie's mouth popped open, and she whispered my name followed by three yeses. Then her head dropped back and her body stiffened. A long, erotic cry left her, and I hungrily devoured the sounds and sight of the wondrous woman beneath me. God, she was amazing.

I forced myself to wait until her orgasm was almost through before plunging deep into her, working on my own release. It didn't take long to find the exact right trigger point, and I groaned in relief and ecstasy when the buildup finally exploded into a euphoric climax.

Kenzie wrapped her arms around me as I came, and a feeling of belonging swept over me. My dream was wrong...*this* was home.

Once the shockwaves of pleasure were gone, I slowly pulled out of her. Shifting to her side, I gently kissed her shoulder. "I love you," I murmured, my breath still quick.

"I love you too," she said, an unstoppable grin on her face. The smile quickly shifted into a frown, though, and she studied me for a moment before asking, "Are you sure you're okay?"

Scoffing, I indicated my bare body with my hand. There had to be visible waves of bliss rising off my skin with how good I felt. "Don't I look okay?"

Her eyes slowly scanned my body, and the surveillance started reigniting me. God, I just couldn't get enough of her. "Always," she murmured. Then her expression grew serious. "But the dream...and even before that, you weren't sleeping well. I could tell."

I hated the fact that I'd disrupted her rest. This was her house, so she should be able to sleep soundly inside it. "I'm sorry about that. I really am fine, though, Kenzie. I promise." Hoping I truly meant that, I kissed her soft skin again. "Hey," I said, propping myself up on an elbow. "Since we're up early, do you want to go for a run or something?"

For a moment, the look on Kenzie's face was really strange. It was almost like she was looking for deceit or a cover-up in my eyes. I kept my face as unchanging as possible. She wouldn't trust me with my feelings for Felicia overnight. I just had to keep trying to show her that she had my heart in her hands; one day she might believe it. "Sure," she finally answered.

We took our time getting out of bed, and there was plenty of touching, kissing, and fondling before we finally threw off the covers. It was still pretty chilly, so we both dressed in long layers—luckily, I had clothes and a pair of athletic shoes tucked in her closet from a previous run.

The sun was just rising when we stepped outside—red and orange painted the sky in a colorful mosaic. Kenzie extended her arms over her head, slightly exposing her belly; immediately, I thought we should still be in bed. Lifting her foot, she grabbed her ankle and pulled it in for a quick stretch, then she bounced on her heels to warm up. I was frozen in place, staring at her, and she laughed when she noticed my rapt attention. Giving me a devilish grin, she murmured, "Race me or chase me, Hayes," then she took off like a bolt of lightning.

Still dazed by her beauty, it took me a second to stop staring and chase after her. It didn't take long for my competitive spirit to kick in, though, and, before I knew it, I was drowning in endorphins almost as powerful as the ones I felt during sex. God, I loved racing this woman. Even on foot.

The two of us ran until the sun crested the horizon, neither one giving up first place for long. The farther we ran, though, the more I felt the pull of exhaustion; with every mile, my feet felt more like concrete, weighing down my steps. Endurance training just wasn't my strong suit. On the final stretch back to Kenzie's house, my body refused to go any faster, and she pulled ahead. When she reached her driveway before me, she jumped up and down with her hands in the air. Even though it was technically poor sportsmanship to celebrate winning like Kenzie did, I loved every second of it. It made me want to find a way for her to compete again, hopefully at Daytona in a few months. Somehow, it just had to be possible.

"Good job, 22," I panted. "You got me."

She gave me a breathless grin, but it slowly fell off her face as my words sunk in. I'd called her my old pet name for her—the number she'd raced under. In one sentence, I'd reminded her of everything she'd lost. Goddamn it.

"Kenzie, I'm—"

She stopped my apology with a quick question. "Hungry? I can make a couple of protein shakes for breakfast."

I nodded. "Sounds great." Wanting to lighten the mood, I asked, "Can we have bacon too?" She raised an eyebrow, then shook her head and laughed. Mission accomplished. Although, I hadn't really been joking about the bacon.

The entire time Kenzie made the shakes, I felt like I should apologize. I was beginning to feel like that a lot lately, and it was exhausting. But it couldn't be helped. Everything seemed to be conspiring against us recently. Story of my fucking life.

"Here you go," Kenzie said, a smile in her voice as she handed me my bacon-free protein shake.

I took it, but my expression wasn't nearly as happy as hers. "A little grease never hurt anyone, you know," I told her.

"A little *less* grease and you might have beat me," she retaliated. I scowled at her, but hearing the humor in her voice made a warmth bloom inside me. Humor meant we were okay.

There was a challenge in her deep brown eyes that was captivating, like a moth to a flame, I couldn't look away. I was just about to tell her exactly what I could do with a little grease when my cell phone on the island chimed with a new message. Smirk on my face, I causally walked over to peek at the notification. What I saw was confusing, so I picked up my phone to check it out. I didn't recognize the number ending in double fives and double sixes, but the message was clear enough.

'Hey, it's Felicia. Keith wanted me to remind you about the team meeting this morning. I guess it's important, and he doesn't want you to be late. See you soon.'

Anger boiled through my veins as I stared at my phone. What the hell? I hadn't had this number when we were together, so Keith must have given it to her. Shit.

"What is it?" I heard Kenzie ask.

Tearing my eyes from the screen, I cursed myself for staring at it for so long, and with such a hard expression on my face. I should have played it cool, no matter what it was. Trying in vain to fix my face, I debated what I could tell her—the truth was obviously out. "I…um…Keith…there's a team meeting this morning, so I have to go soon." That was kind of true, so I didn't feel too guilty saying it. The fib still stung my conscience though. I was trying to convince her I was being faithful by being dishonest. How fucked up was that?

Kenzie's brow scrunched, and her eyes darted to the screen. Crap, could she read it from her angle? As discreetly as I could, I deleted the message. Kenzie wouldn't handle it too well if she knew my ex was texting me. Damn it, this was quickly turning into a nightmare. Maybe I should just tell her. But then she'd worry…and there was nothing to worry about. I was over Felicia. One hundred percent over her.

"Oh, okay…" Kenzie mumbled, looking confused.

Not wanting her to dwell on my answer, I quickly tossed out, "Want to go to the track with me today? Say hi to Nikki? Or…do you have more phone calls to make?"

Kenzie sighed, and I could tell she'd let the text go. "I don't have it in me right now to make more phone calls. Maybe this afternoon I'll try again…"

She let out another weary exhale, and I wrapped my arms around her waist and pulled her in for a hug. She needed it. Damn Jordan and his damn vendetta. I was sure she was tired of hearing me say I was sorry, so I remained quiet as I held her, but the words reverberated around my soul anyway.

Like she could see the words on my face, Kenzie avoided direct eye contact with me. "We should shower before we go," she murmured.

Normally those words would have riled me up, but that wasn't the feeling in the air right now. "Okay, sweetheart, let's go shower."

Kenzie laughed and looked up at me. That word had incensed her when we'd first met. I supposed always having to prove herself in such a male-dominated profession had placed some pretty heavy chips on her shoulders. Coming from the world of street racing, a sport that did *not* go over well with my new peers, I understood the feeling. My feminizing her like that had instantly raised her hackles, turning her from somewhat cordial to a raging bitch. It amused her now, though, especially since she could repeat the sentiment back to me. "We better get going, *sweetheart*. Wouldn't want you to be late."

She looked at me over her shoulder as she left the room, and I mentally photographed her flirty grin so I could forever store it in my memory. *That one's a keeper.*

After a joint shower that was way too quick for my tastes, we got dressed for the day and rolled our street bikes out of Kenzie's impressively-sized garage. After the door was closed and locked, Kenzie pulled on her helmet and started her engine. I took a long moment to appreciate the beauty of her on a motorcycle before putting on my own helmet. There was just something about Kenzie on a bike that got all my juices flowing—I wanted to hold her, kiss her, race her, and undress her, all at the same time.

Kenzie revved her engine, teasing me, and I quickly straddled my bike and started it. We might not be able to race like we used to, but we could still compete in some small ways. In one smooth move, I turned my bike around and pulled onto the street. Kenzie was a breath behind me. My grin was uncontrollable as I surged forward.

We took it easy as we drove through the town of Oceanside, California, but the second we merged onto the highway, we both leaned over our bikes, lowering our wind resistance, and letting down our guards. Freedom and excitement rushed through me as the thrill of riding with her took me over.

Knowing we needed to be careful, I glanced down at the speedometer and cringed; we were already fifteen miles over the limit. Not having the ability to push me and my bike against Kenzie and hers was annoying. To Kenzie, it must be stifling, like a leash tethered to her neck. I wanted to go faster, not slower, but I didn't really have a choice—Keith would have my ass if I got a speeding ticket.

Reluctantly, I reduced my speed. That was when I noticed Kenzie starting to inch past me. Doing everything to keep her from winning was too ingrained in me to keep slowing down, and I gently laid on the throttle, increasing my speed. Just a little, just enough to keep her at bay.

I cast quick glances her way, surprised she was open to racing with me…and even more surprising, I was open to it too. I knew I shouldn't even entertain the idea…but it had been ages, and I was jonesing. After finally accepting that this was happening, I leaned forward and pressed on the speed. I could easily envision Kenzie smiling under her helmet; I certainly was. *Game on.*

As I quickly moved around her, my heart accelerated to match my pace. There were so many reasons we shouldn't be doing this, but I just couldn't stop myself. Forcing my gaze to stay on the road and not my speedometer, I curved low through dips and corners with Kenzie right on my tail. Memories flooded through me as I raced —the bank of lights holding me back, then releasing me, the various flags used to warn or encourage, the multitude of other riders, giving their all for a win, the concrete barriers creating the manufactured roads, the thrill of competition, the strain, the stress...the satisfaction. I couldn't wait for the racing season to start, but God...if only Kenzie could start it with me. Things wouldn't be the same without her.

I ended up beating Kenzie to the turnoff that led to the practice track by mere seconds. Raising my fist into the air, I glanced over my shoulder to where she was close behind me, then I lifted my ass in the air and smacked it. Kenzie shook her head, but I knew she was amused. Joy lightened my heart, giving me a euphoria that was difficult to duplicate. I loved beating Kenzie. I loved competing with Kenzie. I missed racing with her. So much.

Kenzie moved up beside me as we approached the outer gate. Raising my visor, I gave her a triumphant smile. *Got you.* Lifting her own shield, she rolled her eyes at me. Laughing at me helped distract Kenzie from the sign looming over our heads: *Benneti Motorsports Practice Track*. It was twice as big as the old sign had been, even though it only had one name on it now. And to make the fact that he owned it even clearer, Keith had enhanced the sign with a tacky tagline that Kenzie truly hated: *Where Champions Reside*. Even though he hadn't outright said it, I was pretty sure the slogan was a dig on Kenzie's dad, since he no longer "resided" there. Kenzie scowled whenever she noticed the sign.

Wanting to hurry past it, I used my key card and code to open the gate, and Kenzie and I rode through together. It had to be odd for Kenzie to no longer have a key card to this place, but she'd told me John had collected hers when she'd picked up her bikes. Jordan Cox had been conspicuously absent that day. And every day since from what I knew.

As we rode through the parking lot, the euphoria from the ride began to dissipate, and something darker replaced it. Glancing over at Kenzie, I saw the same frustrated expression on her face that I was feeling. Or maybe it was trepidation. The last time she'd gone to the track with me, it hadn't exactly turned out well for her. Or for me really. Damn Keith. Why the hell had he hired Felicia? And was there really a meeting this morning? He hadn't mentioned anything to me yesterday.

We drove through the open inner gate that led to the training complex, and the first thing that I always noticed when I came here filled my view—the mammoth practice course. Flanked on either side by large buildings that held offices and garage bays, the track was the focal point upon entering the inner sanctum. Kenzie's helmet shifted to the right side of the course, where dark empty buildings held the ghosts of Cox Racing. Never properly repaired or maintained, the garages were run-down, dilapidated. It had been sad before the business closed, but now it was kind of heartbreaking.

I veered my bike toward the Benneti side of the track, but Kenzie turned her bike toward the Cox side. Coming here was so difficult for so many reasons; I honestly wasn't sure how she got the strength to ride through the gate. It had to be like returning to the scene of a tragic crime and being reminded of the trauma over and over. It must kill her to come with me. I shouldn't even ask her to step on the property. Man, I was so selfish.

Feeling horrible, I hesitated just a moment before following her. She stopped fifty feet from the Cox buildings, like she was reluctant to go any farther. The *For Sale* sign was huge this close to the building, and the cracked windows seemed somehow supernatural, like they were sucking life out of the air, making everything around them dark and dreary. Knowing the building was cold and vacant reminded me of my dream—Kenzie gone, Felicia pulling me away. A shiver went up my spine as I stopped my bike beside hers.

She looked my way, and I sighed. "I'm so sorry, Kenzie. It must suck for you to be here. I shouldn't ask you to come with me."

She gave me a wry look that told me I'd just said something she thought was utterly ridiculous. "I wouldn't come here if I didn't want to be here, Hayden. And...I don't know, for some reason, I like coming here. I like seeing this."

Her gaze returned to the abandoned buildings, and my eyes widened in shock. "How could you possibly like seeing this?" That made no sense to me.

Still scanning her old stomping grounds, she shrugged. "I'm not sure exactly. It's just…seeing it empty like this…it gives me hope. If it's empty, then it's not gone. Not really." She looked back at me, and there was a fervent passion in her eyes. "I feel like, so long as the buildings stay empty, there's somehow this microscopic chance that Cox Racing could return. I know it's probably not going to happen…but if no one takes ownership, then I can pretend we'll rebuild. I have to carry that hope with me, Hayden. It's all I have left…" she whispered.

It didn't help my guilt one tiny little bit to hear her say that. It was like having a carving knife shoved through my chest. Repeatedly.

Her expression was suddenly so void of emotion, I knew a chaotic storm of feelings was swirling within her. Her career, her team, her dad…Felicia. One more thing would break her right now, I was sure, and I desperately didn't want to be that one more thing. "Maybe I can talk to Keith. Convince him to let me train with you, since that's how I got my best times last year."

The look on her face told me she thought I'd have a better chance telling a whale to stop swimming in the ocean. She gave me a smile that almost reached her eyes. "Yeah…sure. Couldn't hurt anything at this point."

We turned our bikes around and headed back to the Benneti side. I'd spotted a brief glimmer of hope on Kenzie's face when she'd lowered her visor, and I prayed Keith went along with my idea; Kenzie desperately wanted to race again, and I'd given her a possible way to do it. If I couldn't come through… Fuck, I hated disappointing people I cared about.

Pulling up to the garages, we stopped our bikes before one of the open rolling doors. I removed my helmet and set it on the handlebar, then watched Kenzie do the same. She always fluffed out her ponytail whenever she took off her helmet, and I loved watching the wavy strands slide through her fingers. It was such a simple movement, but somehow, she made it erotic.

Kenzie smiled at me when she was finished, then we walked inside hand in hand. I felt her fingers clench mine, and saw her scan the room out of the corner of my eye. My chest tightened in a painful way when I realized she was looking for Felicia. God, what if Felicia said something to her about the text message this morning. I should have just told Kenzie the truth; this could backfire.

I discretely looked around for her, too, but she was, thankfully, nowhere to be found. And even more thankfully, Nikki wasn't late for once, and was at her work station, fiddling with my bike.

The cheery Latin American girl gave us a wide smile when she noticed me approaching with her best friend. "Hey Hayden, Kenzie. How's it going?" she asked, wiping her dirty hands on a towel.

I'd worried in the beginning how the guys here would treat Nikki, but it wasn't a problem. Nikki was charming and personable, always going above and beyond to get to know the crew and the riders. Plus, she was a mechanic, not a racer, and from all I'd seen, anyone who worked hard to make a Benneti bike better was practically lifted to godhood around here. She was doing just fine at her new job, and she seemed to really enjoy working on my Honda CBR600RR.

Kenzie smiled as she answered her ex-mechanic's question. "It's good. How's it going here?"

Nikki's dark eyes sparkled with delight. "Excellent." She shifted her gaze to me. "Just finished sprucing up your bike. She should really fly now."

I gave her a wide grin. "Awesome! I can't wait to take her out." My gaze drifted to Kenzie, and I instantly felt sorry that she couldn't come out with me. But maybe she could... I'd talk to Keith about it at the meeting. He had to see reason. I needed her.

Just as I was about to tell her my plan, someone nearby called my name. All of us twisted around to see Keith hobbling toward us. Kenzie let out a small sigh, and she kind of looked like she wanted to hide. Or run. She hated being around Keith, hated speaking to him even more.

I straightened my stance as Keith approached, and Nikki instantly busied herself with my bike; she obviously didn't want her boss to think she was slacking off. Keith shot Kenzie deadly daggers the entire time he strode our way. I found that really irritating. It was no secret that Keith didn't like Kenzie. Not only was she the child of a man he hated, she was the spitting image of her dead mother, a woman Keith had supposedly loved. He'd lost her to Jordan at the end, and the animosity between the two men had instantly become fixed in stone. Keith didn't need to take that bitter rivalry out on Kenzie though; none of that had been her fault, and as I'd told Kenzie once, their problems weren't our problems.

Stopping in front of me, Keith gruffly said, "You get my message about the rider meeting? It's in ten minutes. My office. Don't be late. And don't bring your little galpal." His dark eyes shifted back to Kenzie, and the sneer on his face deepened. My momentary relief that he hadn't mentioned the fact that he'd used Felicia as his delivery person faded. He shouldn't look at Kenzie that way, and he shouldn't call her my "gal-pal." It reeked of contempt.

Before I could call him on it, he started speaking to Kenzie. "You still haven't convinced your dad to sell his side to me, Mini-Cox. Every day he holds out is another slap in the face." He pointed a pudgy finger at her. "You better fix this fast, or I'll completely ban you from the track."

Shock and anger competed for space inside me. He didn't have the right to do that to her. The brief flicker of hope in Kenzie's eyes—hope that *I'd* kindled—began to die at Keith's statement. Stepping in front of her to refocus his attention on me, I firmly said, "No you won't, Keith. If you want me to come in, then you'll let her come in too. We're a packaged deal."

My plan worked, and Keith shifted his attention to me; his anger too. "Don't threaten me, Hayes, and don't underestimate what I will and won't do to help my team win." With a sleazy smile on his face, he lifted his free hand. "Now, I'm not saying I'd stoop to bike tampering like Jordan, but—"

His comment instantly enraged Kenzie, and she didn't let him continue. "My father was *not* a part of that!"

Keith's cool eyes looked back at her, and while he shrugged, it was clear he wasn't swayed by her passionate words. "If you say so…"

"It wasn't him!" she snapped. "It was—"

I could tell she was about to leak a secret that might bite all of us in the ass, so I snapped my gaze to her, and silently begged her to not say Hookup's name.

Meeting my gaze and instantly understanding, Kenzie fumbled for different words to say. "It was someone else."

"Whatever," Keith blandly stated. "Just get your daddy to sell. Until you do, consider yourself trespassing the moment you pass through the gate."

"Keith…" My voice came out both insistent and pleading at the same time. He couldn't do this to us.

Keith's eyes rolled my way, then he sighed. "Fine. She can go to the Cox side, and watch from there. You can briefly visit her when you're not training." I was so stunned, I could only stare at him in response. He shook his head. "Don't look at me like that, Hayes. You can't keep allowing non-employees into the garage. It's not that kind of job." He shuffled off to go tell others about the meeting, and once he was gone, I was surprised to find I was breathing heavier.

"Asshole," Nikki murmured from her hiding place behind my bike; she cautiously looked around after she said it, to make sure only Kenzie and I had heard her. Goddamn Keith. After that conversation, I knew, without a doubt, that Keith would never agree to Kenzie and me training together. He'd rather see me fail than do anything that might help Kenzie.

Kenzie was pale but composed when I looked back at her. "I'll talk to him, Kenzie, get him to come around." How, I had no idea.

She shook her head as she studied me. "Don't bother, Hayden. He's right. I *don't* belong here." Looking around, she rubbed her arms, like she was feeling chilly eyes watching her every move. Keith wasn't the only one who would love to see her gone, even I knew that. Things had been tricky for me at first, but the guys had come around eventually. They hadn't with Kenzie. She was an ex-Cox racer *and* Jordan Cox's daughter. If all they did was ignore her, I considered that a good day.

Hating the facts being ruthlessly shoved in my face, I softly whispered, "You do belong here, though. You belong wherever *I* am."

She gave me a small one-sided grin that made me want to kiss her. "You should get to that meeting before Keith gets really mad."

I sighed in defeat, then gave in to my desires, and lowered my lips to hers. The tender exchange was much too short for my taste, but she was right. I did have somewhere to be. After telling Kenzie I'd see her tonight, I trudged upstairs for that damn rider meeting.

The conference room that Keith used for meetings was on the far end of the building. It was empty when I got there, so I took a seat and waited. And waited. And waited. Just when I was about to call it quits, someone finally walked into the room, and, of course…it was Felicia. Nothing about my day was going to go right, apparently.

She closed the door behind her, and I immediately stood up. If there was going to be a meeting today, I'd come back when everyone else was here. I'd rather be late than stuck in a room with my ex.

Felicia's dark hair was pulled back into a ponytail. She tilted her head, exposing her long neck. "You got my message?"

"I got *Keith's* message," I said in rebuttal. Looking around, I snapped, "Where is everyone?"

Felicia shrugged, then started walking around the long table toward me. "I don't know. Did you keep it?"

I wanted to back up, but like my feet were glued to the carpet, I couldn't. "Keep what?"

"My number," she answered, her dark eyes warm and welcoming.

I felt like the room was heating as she approached, fire flared up my neck, roasting my face. Where the hell was Keith, Rodney, Maxwell…anyone would be great.

There was no way in hell I was going to confess that Felicia's simple number was burned into my brain, so I said the only thing I could. "No, I didn't."

Determined to go around her, I turned and made my way to the other side of the table. Felicia changed her trajectory to block my exit. Great. So we were playing keep away now? "Move," I told her, my voice hard.

"Listen," she countered, her voice equally rough.

I sensed a fight coming, an epic fight four years in the making. Those fights had always ended in makeup sex before, but not this time. This time, there wouldn't even be a fight. I would say my piece, then leave. Stopping where I was, I stared her down. "Once upon a time, I thought you were my destiny."

Her face immediately brightened. "I am."

My scowl deepened. "No…you ran." She flinched, like I'd struck her. Ignoring the hurt I was inflicting, I continued spelling out my own pain. "You were always running, but you'd never run from me before. You're not my destiny, because I don't want to chase someone for the rest of my life. Not like that."

"Hayden, I—"

Holding up my hand, I cut her off. "Did you know, I held out hope that you'd come back? That it was just another one of your disappearing acts? I kept telling myself you'd show up one day, acting like everything was fine, and things would go back to normal...so I put my life on hold and waited. Izzy was worried about me, Hookup thought I should be committed, but I didn't care what they thought. I knew you'd come back to me. It took a year for me to realize you weren't returning. A *year*, Felicia. It took me a solid year to give up on you. And what...it took you *one* evening alone to give up on me?"

With tears in her eyes, she shook her head. "Antonia was sick, I couldn't deal, I just—"

"You couldn't deal?" I asked, incredulous. "So you abandoned her? Like our parents abandoned us? She deserved better than that." Contempt written all over my face, I snipped, "We've been friends since I was ten, lovers since I was fourteen. I thought I knew you...up until that day. We needed you, and you abandoned us. *All* of us."

"Hayden," she pleaded. "I just needed time."

"Four years? No one needs four years. You ended us. You were done. And now, for some reason, you're having second thoughts about that. Well, tough shit. You're gonna have to deal with whatever it is you're going through, because I'm done waiting for you. I've moved on, and I'm happier than ever."

I stormed past her, on a mission to get to the door. She didn't try to stop me, but she turned her head as I passed, and I heard soft words escape her mouth. "Are you?"

Opening the door, I left the room without a response. Her question burned through my mind though. *Yes, of course I'm happy.* Then why had I already lied to Kenzie about who'd texted me? Why had I already broken my promise? I'd told Kenzie I wouldn't engage in conversation with Felicia. But I had. And it had felt damn good getting all that off my chest. And the fact that doing anything with Felicia made me feel good, also made me feel incredibly guilty. Kenzie would be crushed if she knew I'd deceived her. So, I'd just make sure she never found out. It wasn't like it was going to happen again anyway.

CHAPTER 4

~Kenzie~
Three months later

The phone shook in my hand as I carefully listened for the voice on the other end of the line to say something. They were either going to give me a chance to race for them, or they were going to completely destroy my dream. Even though I wanted to stay cool and detached, wanted to pretend this phone call wasn't the most important phone call of my life, my heart was pounding a furious rhythm against my ribcage; each pulse struck harder than the beat before, and I was positive I was going to be bruised inside.

Ever since I was five years old, I'd known what I'd wanted to do for a living—follow in my father's footsteps and race motorcycles. There was never another option, never a Plan B. I never doubted my decision or waffled on my career choice. I'd done what I'd had to do to make my goal a reality. And, for one glorious season, I'd lived that dream to the fullest. Then I'd let it go. I couldn't deny that it had killed me to release it…but in the back of my mind, I'd never truly believed it was gone. Until now. Today was my last chance to get on a team before the new season started.

The air in my kitchen seemed to solidify, and every breath was a struggle. *Jesus, just say something already.* Then a weary exhale met my ear, and I knew my fate before he even said it; I'd heard that sigh before. "We *do* appreciate you reaching out to us, Ms. Cox, and we truly wish there was something we could do for you, but unfortunately, we can't take on any more riders at this time. I know you understand how expensive this business can be, and we're a small team to begin with. There's just no room."

Not wanting my last chance to slip away from me so easily, I quickly spat out, "I know, but I'm willing to work with you. I have my own bikes, I can buy my own—"

He cut me off with a curt, "I'm very sorry…but the answer is no." From his tone, I knew debating with him would get me nowhere.

There was a tearing sensation in my chest as his rejection settled into my brain. It was like the pocket of my soul where hope was fervently held tight had just been tapped and drained; I felt lightheaded, faint. Then anger and grief rushed in to fill the void. The mixture was thick and heavy, weighing me down instead of lifting me up.

My mouth felt too dry to speak, but somehow, I managed to form words. "If you'll only reconsider, I'm sure we could work out something—"

The other line disconnected before I could finish my futile attempt at persuasion. Feeling numb inside and out, I slowly lowered the phone to the counter. That was it. The very last racing team in the ARRC…and they'd turned me down. Full to the brim of stunned disbelief, I couldn't even completely comprehend that it was over. My dream was done. What was I going to do now?

Pricks of pain swept over me as I contemplated a lifetime of being blocked from the sport I loved. How would I go on? Should I just let it go? Be content with the fact that at least I'd gotten the chance to live my dream for a short time? Many people never got that far in life, after all. But I'd done it. I'd tasted glory, felt the blood-pumping thrill of competition, reveled in the euphoric high of success. I'd touched the sun. And now all I was left with were memories, stories...and scars.

Dad was the reason no one would hire me. He was furious over the decision I'd made at the end of the racing season last year—to give up competing so I could stay near Hayden. In an effort to keep us apart, Dad had tried manipulating my life by making plans to ship me off to a racing team back east. When I'd refused, he'd given me an ultimatum—quit the boy or quit racing. I couldn't say goodbye to Hayden, so I'd left racing behind, rejecting and hurting my father in the process. Quickly after that, Dad had contacted every team, and, using his remaining respect and influence, he'd blacklisted me. When Dad wanted to make a point, he made sure it stuck.

The entire ordeal was gut-wrenching for me. Despite our differences, my father and I had always had a good relationship before this; his approval, guidance and support had been the cornerstone of my career. The Hayden-sized wedge between us was a razor-sharp slice across my heart that wouldn't properly heal. Knowing Dad was hurt, angry, disappointed...it *killed* me, but I loved Hayden—with everything inside me—and giving him up just wasn't an option. But I truly believed that if Hayden and I stayed tight and true, one day Dad would accept him and forgive me. He had to...we were family.

But, in the meantime, none of my family members were making things easy. Dad was still completely ignoring me. I called, left messages, and texted all the time, but I never received any response. He probably thought I'd break down and cave if he froze me out of his life. Theresa and Daphne were still angry; every conversation I tried to start with them ended in a fight. It sucked. I wanted my family *and* my career *and* my boyfriend. I shouldn't have to choose. And I wasn't going to. The cost was high though. Bonds were breaking that could never truly be repaired. I hoped Dad realized just what he was risking by freezing me out, because the more time that went on, the more I could feel our family fraying.

Between the loss of my family and the loss of my career, my soul was bleeding out. There was one good thing that hadn't been taken away though. No, one amazing thing: Hayden. And I took a great deal of comfort in the fact that he and I were still going strong, despite everything that seemed to be trying to come between us.

Since I still wasn't welcome at the Benneti garages, Hayden and I spent as much time together as we could outside of his practice schedule. He stayed at my place most nights, and while I loved having him there, it could be challenging at times. Hayden was many things—sexy as hell, brave, fearless—but he was also kind of a slob. At least, compared to me.

I liked things to be a certain way—a place for everything and everything in its place. I preferred order, tidiness, simple lines, clean curves and absolutely *no* clutter. Hayden just dropped whatever he had on him wherever he happened to be, and he only picked his crap up again when he needed it. It drove me insane, but I really liked having him around…so I was trying to not let the little things bother me. I had enough on my plate.

Like right now, when my world felt like it was imploding. I could feel defeat bubbling inside me, feel pockets of despair bursting open, coating me. *My dream is over.* Trying to hold in the tears stinging my eyelids, I stared at the island counter. It used to be completely bare, but Hayden frequently used it as his dumping area. Currently, it was overrun with papers, receipts, pens, small tools, and handfuls of candy; the boy had a soft spot for sweets.

We'd made love on this counter once, but now there was no room for that to even be a consideration. The urge to clean up *something* in my life had me itching to grab a large garbage bag and sweep all his crud into it. I could toss the bag in the garage and it wouldn't really make it *any* harder for him to find things. *A* system had to be better than no system at all, and less junk would certainly help my sanity. For a little while.

Having convinced myself that project One Bag was a great idea, I headed to the sink to retrieve the lucky garbage sack that was about to store all of Hayden's treasures. That was when Hayden strolled into the kitchen, wearing frayed jeans, a plain white T-shirt, and his black leather Benneti Racing jacket.

Running a hand through his shaggy blond hair, he gave me a warm smile. Then, like he knew exactly what I was thinking, he pointed a finger at me and stated, "Don't you dare touch that. I'll clean it later." I raised an eyebrow at that, since I'd heard it before, and Hayden did a quick X over his heart. "Promise."

My thwarted plan to clean something made me want to sigh in frustration, but at the sight of Hayden's crooked smile, the sound came out wistful and airy; just seeing him could lift my mood sometimes. He was so damn good looking, like a mad scientist had artfully combined the DNA of David Beckham, Scott Eastwood, and Chris Hemsworth to create the perfect male specimen; the result was just as amazing as it sounded. Sometimes it was hard to believe that Hayden wasn't a model selling underwear for a living, or some famous movie star's son. He was just another professional road racer, like me. Or like I used to be, at any rate.

His green eyes sparkled, reminding me just how in love he was, but then his expression fell. Glancing at my cell phone on the end of the cluttered counter, he quietly said, "You heard from the last team, didn't you?"

His question reignited my grief and disbelief. *I can't believe they all said no.* Over the last several weeks, I'd been systematically calling every single ARRC racing team, trying to find one who would take me. Local, distant...I didn't care anymore. I needed to race. My dream might have died, but it was still a part of me, and I still yearned for it.

Blinking away the moisture that instantly clouded my vision, I nodded. "Yeah. It's official, nobody wants me..." Saying it felt like plunging a dagger through my throat. *It's really over.*

Hayden's supportive arms were instantly around me, and I inhaled his strength, his salt and surf scent, and his sun-like warmth. Being near him brought to mind all of my most happy places—my solaces—tearing it up on my motorcycle, gliding through the ocean on my surfboard, and being surrounded by unconditional love. Hayden merged all my favorite things into one firm body that I constantly craved to touch.

"I'm so sorry," he whispered in my ear. Pulling back, he gave me a tender smile. "If it's any consolation, *I* want you."

That was actually a huge consolation; it was what made all my sacrifices worth it. "Thank you," I murmured in response.

The haze in my vision cleared as I pulled back to stare at the amazing man before me. Knowing that I was free to kiss him at any moment of my choosing was a heady feeling, one I really wanted to indulge in right now. Taking advantage of our newfound freedom, I lifted my mouth to his. The minty hint of gum tickled my nose, making me want to maintain the intimate contact for as long as possible.

I could feel Hayden smiling as I slipped my tongue into his mouth; he craved this too. But after a long moment that was entirely too short for me, he pulled back. There was clear concern on his face as he searched my eyes, and echoes of the conversation I'd just had with my last hope of racing this year ghosted through my brain: *We truly wish there was something we could do… We can't take on any more riders…* I'd heard similar rejections from everyone else I'd talked to—no room, no need, no way.

Cupping my cheek, Hayden again said, "I'm so sorry, Kenzie. I wish I could fix this…" His eyes were dark with helplessness. It was a feeling I understood, since I felt it daily.

"It's not your fault, Hayden. This was my choice." I told him this so often, I probably said it in my sleep. It never seemed to ease his guilt though.

He gave me a smile that wasn't really a smile. "Have you reconsidered confronting your father? I really think that if you talk to him face-to-face, he'll change his mind. If nothing else, at least you'll finally get him to speak to you. I mean, he can't ignore you if you're standing right in front of him."

A humorless laugh escaped me as I thought about that. "Don't underestimate Jordan Cox." Shaking my head, I looked around the cluttered kitchen. "I've thought about stopping by his house a thousand times, but whenever I start going through the motions, I freeze up and talk myself out of it. I'm not sure if it's fear or anger holding me back, but I really can't talk to him." My hands inadvertently clenched into fists, and I had to force myself to relax them. "He sabotaged my career, blacklisted me from *every* team that might have hired me. He screwed me over, and then he shut me out." Just saying it killed me a little; a phone endlessly ringing haunted my dreams sometimes.

With a sigh, Hayden gently kissed my forehead. "I know, and I know how much family can suck. *I'm* here for you though, Kenzie. You and me…we'll get through this on our own. We don't need anyone else."

There was an edge to his voice that caught my attention. Pulling back, I studied his face. Family was a tricky topic for Hayden. He'd been bounced around from foster home to foster home as a kid. With no parental consistency to speak of, he'd found consistency and security in his friends—Hookup, Izzy, and…Felicia. They'd been the four musketeers, always together. But inevitably, things had changed. Izzy's daughter, Antonia, had been diagnosed with leukemia, Felicia had cut all ties and vanished, and Hookup had let his pride and gambling demons take over. The group—his family—wasn't what it used to be.

"You okay?" I asked, looping my arms around his neck.

Hayden's fake smile didn't change. "Of course." I gave him a flat stare until he finally sighed. "I've just been thinking about things a lot."

That made a knot of anxiety tighten my stomach. Proving that he truly was a vindictive son of a bitch, Keith had somehow found and hired Felicia, and now Hayden had to be around her every day at the track, a fact that made me feel like someone was continuously wringing out my stomach.

Hayden didn't talk much about her, and I knew he was doing that to protect me, but there were holes in his stories where I knew she fit. The only thing he would easily confess to me was that he was ignoring her existence and refusing her requests to talk. God, I hated every moment that I knew he might be with her, but I had to suck it up and deal with it. I *had* to trust him, or we would never make it. But it was really fucking hard.

I'd lost everything I had but Hayden. Professionally, Felicia had just been given everything I'd lost. She had everything *but* Hayden. Neither of us was content with our situations—Felicia wanted Hayden back, and I wanted racing back. Thinking about Felicia made breathing almost impossible, but I wasn't about to let her chase me away. I wasn't going to let anything else be stolen from me.

"What…kind of things?" I hesitantly asked.

Hayden's expression grew guarded as he studied my face. I could almost see him trying to figure out what I was thinking. Then he sighed and shook his head. "This is going to sound strange, but I've been thinking about Hookup. I keep thinking maybe I should try talking some sense into him again or something."

His words surprised me. Things between them were tense, at best. Hayden's last words to Hookup had been a threat to permanently stay away from him, from both of us. "Did he approach you? Or Izzy? Have you heard from him?"

Shaking his head, Hayden quickly said, "No, I haven't heard from him since the hospital. Which is what I've been thinking about..." I bunched my brows, not understanding, and Hayden let out a heavy exhale. "He fucked up, that's for sure...but maybe...maybe I handled that all wrong. I don't know. It's just weird for me not having him around. He's been a part of my life for so long. When no one else gave a shit, he was there. It's hard to let that go. Maybe I gave up on him too quickly..."

For some odd reason, I felt like he wasn't just talking about Hookup anymore. Everything he'd said could also be said about Felicia too. "Yeah...but he's trouble, Hayden. He's gone off the deep end, and he'll just drag you down if you try to save him. You don't need him anymore." *You don't need her anymore either.*

Hayden's eyes lowered to the floor. "Yeah, I know. I was just thinking about it, doesn't mean I'm going to do it."

"Good...I guess." It was a sad situation all around, but it was for the best. Hookup was bad news for Hayden.

For Izzy and Antonia too; eventually, his greed would bring them down.

Inhaling a deep, cleansing breath, I tried changing the subject. "How were your times today?"

Hayden smiled, but I saw the tightness around his eyes. He didn't like talking about work with me, and he was generally very vague whenever he did talk about it. It really bothered me that the thing that had originally brought us together was now a taboo topic, but I understood why. It was difficult for me to watch him ride, difficult for me to hear about the world I longed for. I wanted to be supportive though, so I tried to not let my discomfort stop me.

His answer was brief. "Fine."

Knowing he was being elusive to protect my feelings, I didn't let him off the hook. "Close to where you were last season?" Asking him that made a wave of pain slice through my gut. He'd been going to ask Keith if we could practice together, since racing against me had dramatically improved his times last year. But after Keith had banned me from the Benneti garages...he hadn't asked. There was no point. Keith would never give me something I wanted, even if it helped Hayden too. Not until my father sold him the track.

Hayden's lips pressed together so tight, they turned white. There was turmoil and uncertainty in his eyes, and I knew he didn't want to answer my question...and, in doing so, he silently answered my question. "They're better than last season, aren't they?" I said.

He swallowed before nodding. "Just a little better... not by much..."

My gut inadvertently clenched like I'd taken a physical blow. *His times were better. He didn't need me.* Forcing an encouraging smile, I said, "Good. Daytona is only a little over a week away, so…that's really good. You're going to have a great year…" My voice trailed off as a mixture of anger and sadness clashed inside me. The new season was nearly upon us. Hayden was about to go off and live his dream—live *my* dream—while I stayed here, staring at the walls, straightening his messes, and worrying about his ex.

Hayden put his finger under my jaw and made me look up at him. When our gazes met, I saw compassion in the depths of his jade eyes. "It's because of you that I'm doing well. You know that, right? You gave me the foundation, helped me build on it. Everything I am, is because of you, Kenzie."

His words touched my heart, and as I lost myself in his eyes, my emotions began swirling within me, faster and faster, like a tornado inside my chest threatening to rip my insides apart. Love, fear, anger, joy, uncertainty, desire…it all swirled together, combining to form one super-intense emotion that I couldn't even begin to describe. Dad had always gotten after me about controlling my feelings. It had been easy for him, but it was something I'd always struggled with. But then again, letting go had served me much better last season than reining myself in all the time had ever done. Maybe in this, Dad and I were just different—he needed rigidness, I needed freedom. And Hayden was my freedom.

Grabbing his face, I pulled his mouth to mine and released the wall holding all my emotions in check. I instantly felt my eyes burn with unshed tears, and instead of pushing away the feeling, I embraced it. As our mouths moved together with almost frantic need, hot tears started coursing down my cheeks.

Hayden pulled back. "Kenzie…"

Eyes clamped shut, I shook my head. "Don't. I'm fine, I need this. I need to let go. Help me let go…" My voice was shaking, and I let it. I needed to fall apart, and I needed him to be there to put me back together.

Returning his lips to mine, Hayden swooped me into his arms and carried me away. When he set me back down on my feet, we were in my bedroom. His thumbs gently brushed the tears off my cheeks, but more silently replaced them. I could tell by the look on his face that he didn't want to do this, not while I was upset. But I didn't need conversation; I needed his arms and legs wrapped around me, supporting me, engulfing me, reminding me that everything was going to be okay.

Needing to distract him from my pain, I pulled off my shirt and unhooked my bra. His gaze traveled down my chest once my breasts were free, but I could still see hesitation. Kicking off my shoes, I shrugged out of the rest of my clothes. "Take me," I whispered. "I'm yours."

His eyes lifted to mine. They were heavy with lust, but he was still holding back. Grabbing his hand, I brought it to my chest, to my heart. The ring with three looping infinity symbols was the only item left on me; it seemed to shine in the darkness. "Take me…please," I repeated.

Any lingering uncertainty dissolved from his eyes as he stepped in to my embrace. Pulling my body against his, he crashed his lips down to mine. He hurried to strip himself of his clothes, then when he was bare, he slowed down, so he could gently lie me on the bed. My tears had finally dried up, but I still felt an emptiness in my heart... one he could help me fill. "Make love to me," I murmured in the darkness.

Hayden exhaled a shaky breath as he settled onto the bed beside me. His hand slid over my hip as his lips traveled up my throat. Closing my eyes, I let the sensation of him overwhelm me, silence my brain. When his mouth got to my ear, he softly said, "Kenzie...talk to me."

I could feel him retreating, feel seriousness begin to blanket the room. Shaking my head, I told him, "I don't want to talk, I just want to feel." Grabbing his hand, I led his fingers to the focal point of my need. Exhaling a heady breath in my ear, he gently lowered one finger, then slowly slid it between my legs. An explosion of euphoria swept over me when he touched me, and crying out, I gripped his shoulder tight. *Yes, this is what I need.*

Hayden groaned at hearing me, feeling me. I heard him mutter, "Okay," then his mouth started traveling down my body. He teased me as he went, licking and sucking every sensitive spot I had. Then his tongue slid over my core, and every thought in my head vanished. My emotions calmed as pure pleasure took me over, and I held nothing back as I completely let go.

The sensation of his mouth moving over me was so swift and strong, starbursts exploded behind my eyes. A loud moan left me, and I squirmed beneath him. I wanted him to move harder, faster. More...I needed more. Hayden stubbornly refused to let me dictate the pace though. He kept up his slow, erotic torture, until I felt like I was tumbling, weightless. When I was just on the edge of releasing, he moved back up my body, kissing every inch of me as he went, igniting me even as he retreated. When our chests were flush again, I felt him slip between my thighs, rubbing against me. It was a glorious promise of something I desperately needed—something deeper, more intense. I adjusted my hips, giving him a better angle, and almost accidentally, he slipped inside me.

Hissing in a quick breath, Hayden paused his movements. Needing more, I reached up to grab his hips and pull them toward me. "God, Kenzie...yes," he groaned, pushing into me, filling me, sending me toward the brink of something intensely profound.

Clutching the edge of the bed, my heart racing, my breath a pant, I started rocking into him. He eagerly met me, and with every thrust, the blissful energy at my core started cresting, rising, leading to something too incredible for words. All I could do was moan, "Yes," while I screamed inside my mind for more.

Moments later, I reached the point of no return. Stiffening, a long cry escaped me as the shockwaves radiated through every cell, every nerve ending. Hayden slowed his pace and groaned as he came, and we clutched each other tight as we rode out the bliss together.

And for a second, while we drifted off to sleep, I was hopelessly, endlessly, and completely untroubled.

CHAPTER 5

~Kenzie~

When I woke up the next morning, I didn't feel quite as blissful, but I felt better than I had before Hayden had made love to me, less of an emotional rollercoaster. As the gray light of early morning softened the room, Hayden stirred beside me. He let out a long, satisfied sound as he stretched, then his warm, naked body wrapped around every single inch of my warm, naked body.

"Good morning," he whispered in my ear before kissing my cheek.

"Good morning," I murmured in return.

Gazing down at me with adoration in his eyes, he studied me a moment before saying, "Last night, you were… Are you…?" With a sigh, he looked away. I was just about to tell him I was fine, and yesterday was just a much-needed outlet of emotion, when he peeked up at me and asked, "What are you going to do today?"

I smiled as brightly as I could. "Same thing I do every afternoon." Nothing. Now that there was no point even going to the track, I generally floundered for something to do. I'd been spending a lot of time with Izzy and Antonia lately.

Understanding that I had difficulty filling my day with productive activities, Hayden gave me a small, sympathetic smile. I wished he would ravage me again, just to change the look on his face. I was fine, we were fine, last night was fine. I would find something to do with my life. Eventually.

Sitting up, I grabbed the sheet and wrapped it around my body. "Maybe I'll go surfing today. It's been a while, and it will feel good to be back on the water." It would clear my head, if nothing else.

Hayden nodded, but his expression didn't change. I could practically feel his worry hovering in the air between us. "Okay," he finally said. I started to stand, but he grabbed my hand. Pulling me into him for a quick kiss, he murmured, "You mean everything to me, Kenzie."

I gave him a heart-stopping kiss in answer, and there was fire in his eyes when I pulled away. Smiling, I hopped off the bed before he could drag me back into it. It was so nice to be with him whenever I wanted, and so incredible to be with him all night long with no worry, no fear. At least *that* stress was gone from our lives.

Hayden got out of bed a moment after me, and started collecting his clothes. His phone chimed with a text message as he was putting on his jeans. Glancing down to where the phone had fallen from his pocket onto the floor, I saw an unsaved number flash on his screen, unreadable tiny text beneath it. I didn't know the number, but it seemed oddly familiar, like I'd seen it before somewhere. Double fives and double sixes…

Hayden snatched his phone from the floor like the hardwood was suddenly lava, and dread filled my stomach. He unlocked the screen, glanced it for a second, deleted the message, then shoved his phone into his back pocket. I waited for an explanation, but he only smiled at me and picked up his shirt.

"Who was that?" I asked, my guts twisting into knots.

Shaking his head, he put on his shirt, then said, "Keith. Just reminding me of a...work thing."

It didn't make sense to me that Keith's number wasn't programmed into his phone, but Hayden's expressionless face wasn't giving anything away; I couldn't tell if he was being honest or not. Remnants of his previous lies back before we were dating flashed through my mind, peppering my skin with anxiety-filled goosebumps, mixing with all the doubts I'd had recently. Was he still hiding things from me?

Deciding that I couldn't live my life suspicious of everything he said, I forced the feeling of unease to the back of my mind. "Oh...okay." Maybe it was my imagination, but I could have sworn I heard him sigh in relief when I excused myself to use the bathroom.

After a quick bathroom break, I changed into my swimsuit. Hayden groaned when he saw me. He'd gotten completely dressed in my absence, and the front of his jeans was quickly thickening as he drank me in. Rubbing himself, he shook his head. "You couldn't have waited to put that on until I was gone?"

"You'd prefer it if I'd stayed wrapped in a sheet?" I asked.

With a pained expression, he nodded. "Yes, seeing you hiding behind a sheet would have been much easier than seeing all of my favorite things highlighted in tight black spandex. God, that ass..." He mimed squeezing my backside.

I laughed at his movement, then raised a finger at him. "Just be glad I'm in my one-piece, not my bikini." This particular suit even had long sleeves for warmth, not that you'd know that by Hayden's reaction.

"Jesus," he groaned.

Still laughing, I gathered up the rest of my stuff and headed to the garage. I paused in the doorway when I saw my two racing motorcycles. They were collecting dust in the corner, sad mementoes of a golden age that I hadn't even realized was perfect. I'd probably never get to use them again. Briefly closing my eyes, I let the grief pool in my chest, then pushed it away. The past was the past, and I'd done my grieving yesterday. It was time to move forward. Somehow.

I headed for my surfboard and began attaching it to my truck. Hayden popped in to say goodbye with a sweet, lingering kiss. Raising the garage door, he walked outside to his bike waiting in the driveway. He put on his helmet, then popped open the visor and lifted his hand in goodbye. His eyes held a deep look of empathy; it was a familiar sight on him.

Faking my best happy grin, I waved goodbye. Hayden didn't appear to buy my forced cheer, but he had places to be, so he slammed down his visor and twisted his bike around to leave. My smile fell the second he was gone. I was so tired of having nothing productive to do. I was so tired of hating almost everything about my life.

Putting away my pity party, I climbed into my truck and headed for the beach. Several minutes later, I was pulling into my favorite surfing spot. After unstrapping my board from my truck, I headed down an almost indecipherable trail. It led over a small hill, and then through a patch of bare trees until it finally reached the ocean. The beach was thankfully empty this morning, and I was grateful for that; I wanted to be alone.

The chill instantly pressed upon my skin when I stepped into the ocean, constricting and contracting until my feet felt a little numb. Ignoring the sensation, I laid the board on the rolling surface and paddled my way past the waves. I was breathing heavier by the time I made it over the breakers, but it was mainly from excitement. My ride was about to start, and in the back of my mind, I clearly saw the bank of red lights that preluded the start of every motorcycle event.

Sitting on the board, I lined up with the waves, and waited for the perfect one to show itself. When it did, the mental lights in my head shifted to green, and I dug my hands into the brisk water to pull myself closer. *Go, go, go!*

Much like motorcycle racing, timing and balance were everything in surfing. My form was absolutely perfect as I popped up to stand on the board, and as the speed of the wild surf rocketed me toward the shore, joy pounded through my veins. This was what I'd been missing. Almost.

The rush of the free-flowing movement made me want to giggle, and while I knew this substitute for racing wouldn't satisfy me forever, it at least made today a little more bearable.

After a couple of hours on the waves, my body was spent, and I knew it was time to pack it in. Trudging back up to my truck, I reattached my surfboard, hopped inside, and made my way back home. I'd just pulled into the driveway when my phone chimed with a text message.

Even though I knew the odds were slim, my heart raced at the thought that maybe it was my dad…maybe he was caving on his tough-love discipline.

Hope in my heart, I mentally crossed my fingers as I grabbed my phone and glanced at the screen. My mood deflated like an untied balloon when I saw the screen. It wasn't my family. Not my actual family, anyway. It was Izzy, the woman who was like a little sister to Hayden; she was quickly becoming a little sister to me too. *'Hey, girlie. Want to come over for lunch?'*

Smiling at her text, I responded, *'Yeah, I need to change, then I'll be right over.'*

After a quick rinse-off in the shower, I threw on some clothes then headed out the door again, but on my bike this time. Izzy lived in an apartment building south of Oceanside, just a little outside of San Diego, so she could be close to the children's hospital—it was one of the top ten in the country. Unfortunately, Antonia was there all too often.

Hayden had been nervous to take me to Izzy's in the beginning. Meeting her had sort of been like meeting his parents; it had been a big step for our relationship. I'd instantly bonded with Izzy and her daughter, and we'd been fast friends ever since. There were days I literally didn't know what I would do without her. Wondering if Antonia would be joining us for lunch or if she'd be in school, I gingerly knocked on Izzy's door. When she opened it a few seconds later, her smile was wide and welcoming, but there was fatigue on her face and exhaustion in her eyes; it never seemed to completely leave her.

"Hey, Izzy," I said, wrapping her in a warm hug.

"Hey, Kenzie," she responded, holding me tight.

The embrace was a little too firm, though, and I instantly knew something was up. "Everything okay?" I asked.

She sighed as she pulled away, confirming what I'd already suspected—everything wasn't okay. "Yes, no…I don't know."

"What's going on?" I asked, stepping all the way inside. I could smell something amazing coming from her kitchen. It made my mouth water, but I pushed the hunger aside so I could focus on my friend.

Closing the door, she told me, "Antonia. She's been struggling with eating lately. The doctors have been telling her she can't afford to lose any more weight, but she hasn't been getting much down. Her doctors finally admitted her yesterday, so they could put in a feeding tube and get some nutrition in her. She's so upset…she didn't want to miss school. She's getting so sick of this, and frankly, so am I. She's just a little girl…"

Her tiny body was shivering with restraint as she tried to keep her torment inside. Seeing her on the verge of a breakdown made me desperately wish that I instinctively knew what to do in these situations. Heavy emotions made me so uncomfortable; I just wanted to bury my head in the sand and pretend everything was fine. Not knowing what else to do, I pulled her in for another hug; she immediately started crying.

"I should be at the hospital with her right now, but I just…I needed a break. I felt like I was going to shatter into a thousand pieces if I didn't get out of there." Pulling back, she looked up at my face. "Am I a horrible mother?" she asked, fat tears dripping down her cheeks.

White-hot grief ripped through me at seeing her pain, and my own eyes filled with tears as I rushed to reassure her. "God, no, of course not. You're the best mom I know," I said. "A person can only take so much...and when you go back, you'll be refreshed, ready to take on more. Knowing your limits is a good thing." And something my dad often reminded me of.

Izzy smiled, and I saw the relief in her eyes. "Thank you, I really needed to hear that. I've been feeling awful." Drying her cheeks, she nodded her head toward the incredible smells. "Come on, let's have lunch. I made tamales."

Oh God. I didn't know whether I should hug her again, or smack her for leading me into temptation. I wasn't exactly keeping up with my old exercise routine right now, and I was getting a little doughy. But Izzy needed me, and she needed me to partake in this with her, so I was going to gladly eat a mountain of delicious calories. Because that was what friends did for each other.

As we sat down with plates of heaping food, I took a quick look around Izzy's modest home. Most of her life was dedicated to her little girl and that was evident everywhere I looked. "Aside from what's going on now...how are you holding up?" I asked. "Financially, I mean. Do you have everything you need?"

Izzy smiled as she pulled the husk off a tamale. "Hayden has been exceedingly generous with his winnings, and I'm very careful with what I spend money on...so yeah, we're fine for now. It's sweet of you to ask, though."

I shrugged as I pulled apart my own tamale. "You and Antonia are the closest thing I have to family, now that mine are pretty much out of the picture. I want to make sure you're okay."

Izzy frowned as she absorbed that. "They really cut you out? Because of Hayden?"

"Because of many things, but yeah…it basically all boils down to Hayden. They just don't see what I see." That he was amazing, that he loved me unconditionally, that he'd do just about anything to protect me. Dad just couldn't get over our beginning to see that.

"Hayden is the type of person you have to get used to," she laughed. "They'll come around." As I watched her take a bite of her tamale, I truly hoped so.

Izzy watched me take a nibble of the amazing meal she'd prepared. The corn flour and meat hit my taste buds and my eyes rolled back into my head. So good. Izzy smiled at my reaction, then asked, "So, how have things been going for you and Hayden…lately."

I knew by the odd pause in her question that she was asking about Felicia. I didn't really want to talk about Hayden's ex, but she *was* on my mind. Or rather, Hayden's loyalty to his past was on my mind. "I don't want to burden you with that. You've got enough to deal with without having to listen to me whine."

Izzy gave me a wide grin before taking another bite. "Please…burden me." Her expression more somber, she shook her head. "This might sound strange, but it's nice to focus on problems besides my own. It makes things seem less…overwhelming."

I gave her a rueful smile. I definitely understood avoidance. "I get that. Okay…well…Hayden mentioned something odd last night, and it's kind of got me thinking." Izzy lifted a dark eyebrow in expectation, and I sighed. "He's been debating contacting Hookup. After everything Hookup did…I just don't understand why Hayden would want to mend that fence."

Izzy didn't seem as confused as me. With a slow shake of her head, she murmured, "Hayden and his damn loyalty. It's difficult for him to cut people out of his life. Once you're in with Hayden…you're in for life. Even if you don't deserve to be."

God, I was afraid of that. "And…does that go for Felicia too? Is she…in for life with him?" I could barely get the words out, and once they were, a part of me wasn't sure I wanted to know the answer. If I could have sucked them back in, I would have.

With another tamale halfway to her lips, Izzy hesitated before saying anything. "You don't know how badly I want to say no, Kenzie. I like you. I *really* like you, and I think you're amazing for Hayden. I've never seen him happier…but…"

"But once you're in, you're in," I sighed.

"Yeah…" Setting her food down, she added, "My brother and Hayden, this isn't their first fight, although, it's certainly been their most serious one. But they always make up. Hayden *always* forgives him. He *always* lets Tony back in…"

From the way she stressed the word *always*, I knew exactly what she wasn't saying. "And her too, right?"

Izzy's lips firmed into a hard line. "In the past…yes. Felicia too." Her face relaxed after she said it, and she gave me a small, encouraging smile. "But who knows, maybe this time it will be different. He has you now, after all."

I gave her a quick smile before shoving the tamale into my mouth. *Right, he has me now.*

The last few months of my life circled through my head as I said goodbye to Izzy. I didn't want to go back to hiding in my house, futilely waiting as the world revolved around me. No, I needed to act. I needed to swallow my fear and finally face my father. It was time for the cold war to end. Besides, dealing with my father sounded easy in comparison to dealing with Izzy's statement. *He always forgives her, he always lets her back in.* No, this time it would be different.

Shoving that worry from my head, I gathered my courage and headed to my father's house. Even though I'd made this drive fifteen million times before, it felt foreign. It used to always give me a feeling of homecoming when I came back to the place where I grew up, but today, all I was filled with was trepidation. I hadn't talked to Dad in so long, I wasn't sure what I would say. Or if he would even let me say it. There was a very real possibility that he would keep pretending I didn't exist, even if I was right in front of him. He was *that* stubborn.

A curve in the driveway showed me the modest two-story farmhouse that had been my childhood home. Mom had loved animals, and Dad had given her every sort of creature he could find—horses, cows, ducks, goats, chickens, rabbits...you name it, and Mom had raised it. Of course, Dad hadn't kept up on the livestock after Mom had died. Or the house, really. Everywhere I looked, the home was spotted with age. Just like the track, it was slowly being abandoned, neglected, and it broke my heart to see it crumbling to pieces.

Dad's truck was in parked in front of the faded red barn when I got there. At least he was home. One of the barn doors had fallen off its top hinge, and was resting haphazardly against the other door. It had been like that for years, and I knew Dad had no plans to fix it; there was nothing inside the barn anyway. Nothing but ghosts.

Parking my bike next to Dad's truck, I shut off the engine and looked around to see if he was watching me. It didn't appear that he was. Removing my helmet, I inhaled the fresh air of my youth, trying to calm the butterflies inside my belly. Feeling nostalgic, I hopped off the bike and walked past the barn, to an oval ring of asphalt in the backyard. Dad's makeshift motorcycle course was the only thing he'd ever truly kept in tiptop shape around here, but I could see signs of disuse growing in the weeds inching closer and closer to the concrete. A pang of remembered joy went through me at seeing the simple racetrack. I'd first started practicing my corners on it, going one direction, and then turning around and going the other. Every day I'd come out here, rain or shine, filled with dreams of how amazing my life would be when I was old enough to compete. I never imagined it would end so soon.

"Mackenzie? What are you doing here?"

Shaking off that melancholy thought, I spun around to see my father standing there with a stern, disapproving look on his face, like he'd caught a trespasser. And I supposed I was trespassing at the moment. I was so happy to see him, though, that I could feel the tears pricking my eyes. God, I missed my family. "Hey, Dad. I was hoping…we could talk."

Crossing his arms over his chest, Dad examined me with curious eyes. The blonde hair he'd genetically gifted to my sisters was mostly gray now. The aged color had seeped into his eyes too, darkening the bright blue to a steely gray. He looked worn to the bone, with dark circles under his eyes, like none of the stresses he'd faced recently had eased with closing the business. Was that because of me? "You've broken it off with that Benneti boy then? Good, I'm glad to hear you've come to your senses," he said, his voice gruff.

I wanted to roll my eyes and tell him to knock it off and just let his stupid feud with Keith go. It had already cost him way too much; he might have been able to salvage Cox Racing if he hadn't lost control and punched Keith at an event. "No, I haven't. But I'm not here to talk about him. I'm here to talk about us. You can't shut me out forever."

Like I'd just told him everything he believed in was inconsequential, Dad's expression crumpled; his stern mask of disapproval was back mere seconds later though. Face firm, he started turning away from me. "If you're not here to tell me you're done with that foolishness, then we have nothing to discuss," he said over his shoulder.

Fury expanded from my chest to warm every inch of me, and even though there was a refreshing breeze in the air, I felt like I was standing in the Sahara Desert, parched with thirst. "Don't you dare walk away from me!" I yelled.

Startled at my outburst, Dad stopped and turned my way again. He seemed angry now, too, but he was keeping his emotions in check much better than me. "You still have issues with control, I see."

My fingernails dug into my palms. "This has to stop, Dad. You can't keep ignoring me. I'm your *daughter*."

Sadness swept over Dad, crushing my heart and diminishing my fury. "You're the one who placed this barrier between us, Mackenzie. I can't fix this, only *you* can. You know what to do, you just refuse to do it." Heat finally entered his voice, and I saw the hurt and anguish he was going through in the brief crack in his facade; this was killing him.

Inhaling a deep breath, I slowly and calmly approached him. "It doesn't have to be him or you. There's room for both of you in my heart."

"There's not room for him in mine," he snapped.

I tossed my arms out to the side. "So hate him! That's fine! Just don't shut me out because you don't like my boyfriend! Don't end my career because of him!"

Dad's eyebrow lifted at my words. "Your career? That's why you're really here, isn't it? This has nothing to do with repairing your family, you just want to ride again."

Guilt tore through me—in a way, he was right—but he was oversimplifying the problem. "Of course not. My family means more than racing; my family means everything. I miss you all...so much." My eyes started watering as the truth of those words hit me. Crazy, obsessive compulsive Daphne, easy going Theresa...my stern, emotionally-reluctant father...my life would never be entirely complete if they weren't a part of it.

Dad's eyes softened as he studied the pain in my watery gaze. He opened his mouth, then shut it. As I watched, helpless, I saw his features harden with stubborn determination. "If we mean everything, then you'll have no problem doing the right thing. And...I think you should do it before you come back here again."

Anxiety coiled my stomach into a knot. "Are you saying I'm not welcome here?"

With a gaze void of emotion, my father only hesitated a second before calmly placing another wedge between us. "If you're still with him, then yes…you're not welcome here. I'm sorry, but until you're single, Mackenzie…I need you to leave."

Ice-water filled me as I stared at him in shock. *That's it?* Him or me, no exceptions, no compromise, no …nothing. I couldn't believe he was actually going to take it this far. Because he didn't approve of the guy I was seeing? Because he didn't like that I'd stood up to him and made a shocking, and rather hasty, decision about my career? Because he thought he was helping me, and thought I'd eventually come around if he stuck to his guns. Bullshit.

"Fine," I bit out. "Give Daphne and Theresa my best." Turning around, I headed back to my bike. Might as well go, since there was nothing here for me.

I left a deep rut in Dad's gravel driveway, I squealed out of there so fast. I knew he'd be pissed about that, but at this point I didn't care. He'd blacklisted me, and now he was disowning me. So much for the unbreakable bond of family.

Tears coursed down my cheeks as the grief took me over, and the road blurred in my vision. I'd known choosing Hayden over Dad would damage our relationship, but I'd had no idea just how deep the cut would go. And I hadn't realized that I'd lose Daphne and Theresa too. I thought they would be able to see that Dad was overreacting, but they were being just as silent as Dad.

Well, screw them. Like Hayden had said: we didn't need anybody.

Not wanting to go home, I headed to the practice track instead. Since I didn't have a key, I snuck in through Hayden's secret entrance in the chain-link fence; I never in a million years thought I'd be using it without him. I knew I wasn't supposed to be at the track, not on Keith's side at least, but I was fuming. I needed a release or I was going to explode. Dad had screwed me over, yet again, and rage and anguish were battling for dominance inside me. I needed Hayden to calm me down, to see me through the turmoil.

Nikki approached me the minute she saw me step into the Benneti garage. "Kenzie, you're not supposed to be here." She paused a second, then asked, "What's wrong? You look like you just got canned, but since you're not working right now, I know that's not it…"

Her voice trailed off as her expression grew apologetic.

Stepping away from her, I lifted my hands into the air. "I'm fine, just thought I could talk some sense into my father, but apparently, I can't, and I don't know why I even…" My throat tightened with emotion, choking off all speech; I wished I could claw it back open. Swallowing a few times, I quickly asked Nikki, "Do you know where Hayden is? I really need to talk to him." He was my center—he would realign me.

A strange look passed over Nikki's face. "He's upstairs with Felicia."

Anxiety chilled my skin, down to the bones. "As in, they both happen to be upstairs at the same time, or they purposely left together to go upstairs?"

She held her palms up to me. "As in, Keith asked them both into his office. I don't know why."

Great. I tried to move around Nikki to get to the stairs, but she blocked me. "Where are you going?"

I pointed to the staircase behind her. "I'm going up there. And Keith can bitch and moan all he wants, I really don't give a shit anymore." Slipping around her, I dashed toward the stairs.

"Kenzie, wait!" she cried out, but I didn't wait. I stormed up the stairs; Nikki followed right on my tail. "Kenzie," she hissed. "You shouldn't be here. I can get Hayden for you…just wait outside." She was looking around the entire time she spoke, like she expected a ghost to come out and startle her. Or Keith to walk out and fire her.

As I tromped down the hallway, I found the door to the locker room, the gym, and the storage closet, but I couldn't seem to find the door I really wanted—the one to Keith's office. "It will be fine, Nikki. Keith isn't going to—"

Just then, Keith stepped out of a doorway to stand right in front of us. "Keith isn't going to what?" he asked, his dark eyes flicking between Nikki and me.

My heart leapt into my throat, and I instantly cursed my stupid luck. I wasn't sure what Keith could do to me, other than keep me from seeing the Cox side of the track, too, but I didn't want to see him, didn't want to talk to him. Just being in his building was bad enough; everything here smelled like him.

Nikki started sputtering an excuse as she pulled on my arm. "Oh, hey, Mr. Benneti. Kenzie and I were just heading outside..."

Keith's eyes narrowed as he locked onto her. "You. Go downstairs and get back to work. Now."

Nikki gave me a sorry smile before immediately turning and dashing back to her station. When Keith and I were alone in the hallway, I straightened my shoulders and faced him as proudly as I could. "Keith...I know you don't like me being here, but I need to speak to Hayden, and Nikki said you asked him—"

Shifting his weight on his crutch, Keith eyed me up and down before coldly interrupting me. "Has anyone ever told you...how much you look like your mother?"

His question completely caught me off guard, and everything I'd been about to say fled from my mind. "Yes," I murmured, feeling chilled all over. "I hear that a lot."

A smug smile spread over Keith's face. "Yeah, I bet you hear a lot of things...and I bet all of them are one-sided. Do you want to know the real reason why your mother came to me?"

I kept my mouth firmly closed. No, I really didn't want to hear his version of the "real" reason. I didn't want to hear about anything that had happened between them.

Keith continued liked I'd said I'd love to hear all about it. "Your father can be a real piece of work sometimes...cold, vindictive, manipulative. Whether it's an argument or a race, he needs to win, at any cost, and he's not afraid to burn bridges to get what he wants. Surely you've noticed his tenacity?"

Yes. Unfortunately, I had. I couldn't keep looking at Keith, and had to avert my eyes.

Keith made a sound that was both approval and disgust. "Yeah, thought you might have. I heard he blacklisted you from *everyone*...made deals so no one would let you race. All to keep you from my boy, I'm guessing. Interesting. And you probably still think that between the two of us, I'm the asshole."

My eyes returned to his then, and even *I* could feel the affirmation in my glare. Keith smirked. "Daddy's little girl," he murmured.

Having had enough of this sort-of conversation with him, I started backing away. "I should probably get back to—"

"Why haven't you asked me about a job?" Keith asked, his face completely serious.

I froze in my tracks, and my heart started thudding in my chest. Honestly, I didn't think he'd ever hire me—he hated me, had banned me from his building—so I'd never truly considered asking him. That, and I despised him too. "I...I didn't think... Would you hire me?" my voice was a squeaky whisper, and I hated how desperate I sounded.

A smug smile spread over Keith's lips, and he stroked one of his muttonchops while he mulled over my question. My heart was pounding so hard, I thought I might pass out while I waited for him to say something. God, I hated even the idea of the name Benneti on my back, but if it meant I could ride again...

"No." The singular word burst my bubble so hard, I actually flinched. As defeat poured over me, Keith shrugged. "Not as a racer anyway. Since I hired Felicia, I'm full for the year. And I'm not about to fire her for you. She's absolutely incredible." A creepy smile spread over his face as he closed his eyes and reveled in the wonder that was Hayden's ex-girlfriend. I didn't even want to know what he was thinking about.

When he reopened his eyes, he lifted an eyebrow. "But I might have a job opening for you...if you're interested."

I stepped forward in my enthusiasm. "Yes, I'm interested. What would I be doing?"

He shrugged. "Book a flight to Daytona. I'll fill you in there."

Feeling like I was having some bizarre dream, I nodded. "Yeah...okay."

"Good." Turning around, he shuffled down the hallway toward the stairs.

God, I'd never imagined in a million years that an encounter with Keith would end up with me having a job. And even though it lifted my spirits to have something in this racing world to look forward to again, I couldn't help but feel like I was covered in a layer of grime now. I wanted to stand under a shower for an hour, and scrub every inch of me. Was this what selling out felt like?

I was still standing there in a daze, when Hayden finally appeared from around the corner. He was storming down the hallway toward me, coming from somewhere farther back in the building; he looked upset, but he stopped in his tracks when he saw me standing there. "Kenzie? What are you doing here?"

Still dazed, I feebly pointed where Keith had gone. "I was just..."

Words failed me as Felicia appeared from around the same corner that Hayden had just come from. Nikki's comment, that they were in a meeting with Keith—who I had just been speaking to—flashed through my brain. White hot sparks of suspicion nearly blinded me. "Where were you?" I asked, looking back at him.

Hayden flicked his eyes Felicia's way before answering my question. "Conference room."

That was all he had time to say before Felicia was upon us. She never slowed her sauntering catwalk pace, and her bedroom eyes never left Hayden; I could almost see the smoky vapors rising off her seductive skin. Twisting her body so her breasts were facing Hayden, she edged her way between us. "Always a pleasure talking to you," she murmured as she passed through the slim opening, brushing against Hayden in the process.

Right.

The heat in the hallway seemed to leave with Felicia. The air was so frigid, I was surprised I couldn't see my breath. Hayden lifted his hands like he was facing a wild animal that might charge him at any moment. "That wasn't what you're thinking it was."

Multiple scenarios flashed through my brain, none of them good. "I'm not thinking anything," I murmured.

He gave me a disbelieving face. "Bull. You're thinking I was alone with her because I wanted to be, and that's not it at all." His expression turned hard as he lowered his hands. "Fucking Keith. He called us in for a meeting, then left and never came back. He's been doing that lately...it's really starting to piss me off."

Now that I knew about it, it was starting to piss me off too. "Oh," I responded, my anger toward *him* diminishing, and my confusion toward Keith increasing. What was he playing at?

"What are you doing here?" he softly asked, clasping my hand in his.

My mind felt like Jell-O as I answered his question. "I was looking for you, and then…I ran into Keith…and he offered me a job."

Hayden's face looked just as shocked as I was sure mine had been. "What? A racing job? Really?"

Shaking my head, I frowned. "No, he said he couldn't take on another rider, but he has something else for me. He said he would tell me at Daytona."

A look passed over Hayden's face that mirrored my own feelings—distrust. Even though Hayden held Keith in high regard, he understood that when it came to me and my father, all bets were off. That was what made all of this so odd. What the hell did Keith have in mind for me? Did I really want to go to Daytona to find out? Yes, I did. Because whatever he had in store, it had to be better than sitting at home, wishing I was still a part of the racing community. This would most likely bite me in the ass, but I had to see it through.

With a small, worried smile, Hayden agreed with my summation. "Well…at least you'll be a part of the world again."

Yes. But at what price?

CHAPTER 6

~Hayden~

I was still reeling from the news that Keith had given Kenzie a job, something he'd seemed adamantly against earlier, when Kenzie hit me with another bombshell—Antonia was in the hospital. We left as soon as she told me, and traveled straight to see her. Making that kid happy was far more important than racing against time on a clock.

Kenzie was in a state of shock. I could tell, because she didn't try to beat me as we rode down the freeway. In some places, she even fell behind, and I had to slow down for her—something I'd never had to do before. I was worried, but I wasn't sure what I should be worried about. The melancholy she could slip into so easily, the fact that Keith had caved and given her a job, and who knew what that job might be, or the fact that I was lying to her, more and more frequently it seemed.

Felicia was texting me all the fucking time now, and for some reason…I read every fucking message. The first few were just messages passed along from Keith—Felicia testing the water. The last few had nothing to do with our job. *Please talk to me. I have so much to say. I'm so sorry. I miss you so much.* That last one had come in while I'd been with Kenzie. Reading it had double-socked me with guilt and pain. *She misses me?* Well, she should have thought about that before she deserted me. I had someone else now, someone great, and I didn't need her.

So why couldn't I stop reading the messages? Curiosity? Was I looking for meaning in her texts? A reason she left, a reason she was back? Yes, I supposed it was closure I was seeking. I wanted to know why she'd bailed. But I knew enough about Felicia to know she'd never explain in a message. If I really wanted to know why she'd ran, I was going to have to have a sit-down conversation with her; she'd make sure of that. Because getting closure might lead to a reconciliation. That was how she saw it at least. And I was too worried she was right to test the theory. There was a *lot* of history there, and sometimes being around Felicia felt too…familiar. I didn't want to put myself in that situation. I *wanted* to be with Kenzie.

Fuck. Kenzie. If she ever learned about the texts, if she ever figured out what was going on in my head, I'd have some serious explaining to do. Hopefully she'd be calm enough to listen. Hopefully I'd be able to come up with an excuse. Hopefully it never happened. Jesus. I was digging a hole around my feet so fast, it was only a matter of time before I fell inside it.

I forced myself to shove that worry aside when we got to the hospital. Antonia needed me to be strong, undistracted, the rock she relied on to come through for her. Izzy needed that too. And Kenzie, in a way. Kenzie and I held hands as we walked through the hallway. She looked lost in thought, and I couldn't help stealing glances at her. She was going through so much, same as me, but different. She wasn't being tormented by an ex-flame, but instead, she was being completely barred from what she loved. That last rejection had killed her, and when she'd fallen apart in my arms, instead of making her talk about it, I'd let her distract me with sex. I was screwing up so much lately, I couldn't tell up from down anymore.

When we stepped inside Antonia's hospital room, I had to stop and collect myself at the sight of her. Her hair was coming back, about an inch long now, but she looked so tiny and frail against the bed sheets, especially with the slim tube up her nose keeping her constantly fueled. I wanted to rip it out the second I saw it, but I knew it was serving a purpose, a very important one; I just hoped she wouldn't have to have it for long.

Izzy spotted us standing there, and stood up to greet us with a hug. Antonia noticed us a second later, and gave me a huge, tired grin. "Uncle Hayden."

Releasing Izzy, I walked over to Antonia's bed. "Hey, Bookworm. Didn't I say you weren't allowed to come back here?" I said, mock sternness in my voice.

Antonia's smile turned shy and amused. "Sorry, I didn't mean to."

"It's okay," I said, kissing her head. "Just don't let it happen again."

She laughed, then sighed and closed her eyes. She looked exhausted, a sight I was all-too familiar with. While Kenzie sat on the bed on the other side of her, I looked back at Izzy. "How is she doing?"

Izzy's smile was almost as tired as her daughter's. "Better. Both of us are better." Her warm smile shifted to Kenzie. Kenzie had been there when Izzy needed her. Kenzie hadn't abandoned her, and never would. That wasn't her style.

Antonia dozed off and on for the next hour. I knew they'd kick us out sooner or later, but I really didn't want to leave. Maybe I'd say I was her dad, pull up a chair, and sleep all night here. That really wouldn't be fair to Kenzie though. She was making the best of the situation, reading a book to Antonia while she listened with drooping eyelids. She'd be out again in no time.

Izzy approached where I was standing by the sink, listening to Kenzie's story. Gently, she tugged on my elbow. "Care to get some coffee with me?" she asked.

Kenzie paused, turned to smile at me, then resumed reading to Antonia. Kenzie probably didn't realize it, but Izzy wasn't a big coffee drinker. She wanted to talk to me alone, to spare Kenzie's feelings, and that meant she wanted to talk about Felicia. Great.

"Sure, Iz," I replied, a tight smile on my face.

Slight fingers wrapped around my elbow as Izzy walked us out the door and toward a coffee vending machine on the other end of the hallway. I sighed when we were well away from Antonia's door, out of earshot. "What is it?"

Izzy was silent for a few more steps, then she said, "Kenzie told me you want to contact Tony."

We arrived at the machine, and I separated us so I could look at her. "I said I was *thinking* about it. Big difference."

Izzy smiled, but it looked sad to me. "I knew you'd change your mind. You always let your past back in...no matter how hard it hurts you."

Studying her face, I slowly asked, "Are we still talking about Hookup?"

Her face scrunched in concern. "It took you three weeks to tell me Felicia was here. That she was *working* beside you every day. Why?"

"Because she...she bailed on you. She hurt you. I didn't want to..." A heavy sigh escaped me. That wasn't why, and Izzy knew it. "I don't know. I just...didn't want to have this conversation, I guess. I wanted to ignore it. Ignore her..."

Grabbing my arm, Izzy squeezed it tight. "You've got a good thing with Kenzie, Hayden. A really good thing. Don't fuck it up. Especially not for *her*. She doesn't deserve your forgiveness...yours or mine. And she definitely doesn't deserve you. But Kenzie does."

"I'm trying not to fuck it up, Izzy. You've got to believe me...I'm trying..." There was a sharp, cracking pain in my chest, and confusion burned like acid inside it. I didn't want to hurt Kenzie, but Felicia... I had so many questions, so many memories, so many...loose ends.

Izzy wrapped her arms around me, holding me close. She patted my back like I was a child, whispering that everything was going to be okay. Normally her mothering would have annoyed the hell out of me, but right now...I kind of needed it.

* * *

We visited Antonia every evening for the next few nights. She was slowly getting better, slowly gaining weight, but the doctors didn't want her to go home yet. It was hard to leave her every night, but Saturday night was the hardest of all. Keith was having a pre-season celebration, and every Benneti rider and crew member was required to attend. Unless we were on our deathbeds, we had to be there, maybe even then too. Kenzie was less than thrilled about going. I think she'd only truly agreed to go because Nikki was going and bringing Myles as her date.

I wished we could have stayed at the hospital all night, but eventually we had to leave to go get ready for the party. Antonia was upset to see us go. "Please stay, Uncle Hayden."

"I wish I could, but this party is required for work. Not going isn't an option. But when you get better and you get to go home, I'll bring you something great to celebrate."

Antonia's eyes lit up at the promise of a gift. "Like what?"

"I don't know...how about a puppy?" I said with a shrug. Izzy was going to kill me, but Antonia had always wanted a pet.

Her mouth dropped wide open in shock and surprise. "Seriously?" she asked, trembling with excitement.

A second later, Izzy chimed in. "Hayden," she said in warning. Izzy hated dogs.

I gave her a one-sided grin. "Every kid needs a puppy, Iz." This one more than most.

Antonia squealed in delight as Izzy sighed in consent. I knew she'd give me this. When it came to spoiling her daughter, there wasn't much Izzy wouldn't let me do. Except buy her a motorcycle. She was still adamantly against that.

As soon as we got back to Kenzie's place, I hopped on the computer to start researching pets. Kenzie left me to it, and grudgingly got ready for the party. Having a positive way to help Antonia made me smile in a way nothing had lately, and by the time I joined Kenzie in her bedroom,

I had the prefect breed all picked out for her. Maybe tonight wouldn't be so bad.

A few hours later, Kenzie was snuggled on the back of my bike as we made our way to Los Angeles. She was wearing a short skirt that exposed nearly all her trim thighs as she sat behind me, and she was showcasing what she was showing with a pair of sexy knee-high boots; she looked like a million bucks. I was going semi-casual tonight, with black boots, black jeans, a crisp white button-up shirt. I was wearing the team leather jacket that Keith had handed out to everyone. It was an article of clothing Kenzie hated, since Benneti was sprawled across the back. I wouldn't be surprised if I woke up one day and the thing was ripped to shreds. I wouldn't blame her either.

The closer we got to L.A., the tighter Kenzie held me. She had to be a little nervous about this party. She'd be surrounded by my teammates—men she'd been conditioned to dislike. And then there was Felicia. She was going to be there, and, for the first time, the two women were going to be occupying the same space for an extended period of time. Come to think of it, I was a little nervous about the party too.

Letting go of that worry, I focused solely on the feeling of Kenzie's arms and legs embracing me. There was something erotic about having her on my bike. Dipping low through the curves, I could feel her thigh muscles flex and firm, and her fingers had drifted down my stomach. They were sitting so low on my waistband that if she reached down just a tiny bit, she could stroke me through my jeans. God, just the thought was making me hard, and if going to this party wasn't required, I'd turn the bike around and take her home. And if the drive home was just as stimulating, I might take her the second we reached her driveway.

I let myself imagine every single indulgence I would have with her later, and by the time we pulled into a parking garage beside the hotel hosting the party, I was hard as a rock. Damn. Maybe she'd be up for a quickie in the parking lot.

After finding an empty spot on the fifth floor, I shut off the bike and lowered the kickstand into place. Kenzie hopped off, removed her helmet, then fixed her hair and her dress. God, I loved when she did that. Her tight outfit and her bright red lipstick were doing nothing to stop the surging desire coursing through my veins. I needed her. Right now.

Seeing that I hadn't moved yet, Kenzie gave me an inquisitive look. "Did you change your mind about going to this?" she asked.

Removing my helmet, I placed it on my lap. "No, I just need a moment to calm down. You're the sexiest thing I've ever seen," I added, my voice low, near a growl.

A warm flush highlighted Kenzie's cheeks as she stared at me, then a slow smile curved her lips. "I'm not sure if I should let you calm down…or hop on that bike and have my way with you."

A throb went through me, painfully pushing sensitive parts against rough denim. "Jesus, Kenzie," I said with a groan.

As she let out a husky laugh, someone on the other side of the garage yelled, "Move your ass, Hayes! Keith's fining anyone who's late."

Kenzie and I both looked over to see Rodney and his date strolling to the elevator, and just like that, my hard-on was gone. Asshole just ruined what could have been a beautiful moment. I hopped off the bike and set my helmet beside Kenzie's. She glanced at my jeans and sighed, then looked up at me with a small, sad smile on her face.

"Ready?" I asked her.

"No…but let's get this over with."

I nodded at her, and we walked through the garage, hand-in-hand. When we stepped into the hotel, I moved us toward the conference room Keith had rented for the evening. I knew exactly which room it was once we got close enough—a pair of scantily dressed girls were flanking the doorway. They each had wild, overdone hair, expertly manicured nails, and heavy makeup that you could probably see from space. Keith had dressed them in standard model-wear: knee-high boots, tight leather shorts, and bikini tops covered with the Benneti Motorsports logo. Each girl was holding a tray of wine as they welcomed the riders and guests, and, with a forced smile, I took two glasses and handed one to Kenzie.

She was slightly frowning at the models, but didn't say anything about it. Keith thought the best way to advertise the team was to show off skin, and Kenzie knew that. It annoyed her though. She'd struggled so hard to be an equal to her rivals; having female sexuality shoved in her face at events like this was demeaning. But a job was a job, and Keith paid his models well; I didn't blame them for wanting to strut their stuff. They had nothing on Kenzie, though.

"Even wearing three of layers of snowsuits, a Hazmat suit and a mumu, you'd still look better than both of them combined."

Stopping, she twisted to look up at me. Her face was a mixture of adoration and awe, like she'd never expected me to feel that way about her. But I did; she was the most beautiful thing in the world to me. Considering how I'd grown up—bounced around from here to there, never fitting in, never belonging to anyone or anything—it blew my mind that I'd found love—healthy, reliable, reciprocal love. Kenzie wasn't going anywhere, wasn't taking off at a moment's notice. She was with me, hell or high-water, come what may, and I'd do just about anything to keep her. Once someone had my loyalty, I fought tooth and nail for them. But Izzy was wrong…once a bridge was burned, it stayed burned. I wasn't letting Felicia back in. There was no room for her now.

Kenzie leaned up and lightly placed her lips on mine. The softness of her kiss was pure heaven—I didn't think I'd ever get enough. Unfortunately, it didn't last long. We were tackled out of the moment by a pair of enthusiastic arms wrapping around Kenzie's shoulders. "Kenzie, you're here!" Nikki squealed.

Once Kenzie regained her balance, she squeezed her friend back. "Hey, Nikki." After they separated, a forlorn sigh escaped Kenzie. "I can't believe the season is about to start again." Grief passed over her face; whatever she'd be doing for Keith, it wouldn't be racing. Shaking her head, I could see her struggling to push aside the sadness. "Speaking of the new season…where is Myles?"

Nikki said a quick hello to me before returning her eyes to Kenzie; her smile was a mile wide when she answered her question. "He's totally pissed that I made him come with me tonight, but he's here somewhere." Turning around, she scanned the room for their friend. The back of her form-fitted dress was completely open, nearly to her tailbone. More than one Benneti rider was checking her out, and I was sure, if she wanted to, Nikki could go home with one of them. And if she did and they were asses to her, they'd have me to deal with. Nikki was important to Kenzie, and that made her important to me.

Waving her hand in the air, Nikki got the attention of Myles on the other side of the room. He was at the snack table, adding onto a plate that was already piled ridiculously high with food. I doubted he planned on eating it all; he was probably just sticking it to Keith in the only small way he could by wasting the expensive food. The old feud with Benneti still ran strong in Myles. It applied to me too. Myles might have grudgingly accepted that Kenzie and I were together, but he still didn't like me, and he definitely didn't trust me.

Nikki headed his way, and Kenzie followed her. I started to go with them, but something in my peripheral distracted me. Keith was talking to a small group of Bennetis. One of them was a girl in sky-high heels, a shapely dress, with long dark hair cascading down her back. Felicia. She was sipping on a glass of wine, smiling at something Keith was saying. Then, like she could sense me watching her, her eyes flicked my way. Our gaze met and held, and my chest constricted in a weird, disorienting way. She gave me a brief smile, but there was pain and longing in her eyes. Seeing it made the compression in my chest feel like my heart was being pressed flat, and one word echoed throughout my brain: *why*?

Swallowing, I tore my eyes away from her, and searched for my girlfriend. She had stopped on her way to Myles when she'd noticed I wasn't with her, and she was looking back at me with a confused expression on her face. My heart sank as I watched her slowly shift her gaze to where I'd been looking—to Felicia. Her lips parted when she spotted my ex, and I mentally kicked myself. Why the hell hadn't I looked away immediately? How could I explain that to Kenzie?

Kenzie turned on her heel, and I hurried to catch up to her. I tried holding her hand, but she subtly resisted. I settled on grabbing her wrist instead. "I'm sorry," I muttered, "I just..." I just what? Couldn't help myself from staring? From wondering? From ruminating on why she'd thrown us away like garbage?

Kenzie suddenly grabbed my hand. She squeezed my fingers so tight, they went numb. "It's fine." Her tone was cool, and her eyes were liquid fire. It wasn't fine, but she was trying to let it go. God, she was amazing. With a tight smile, she added, "We should hurry if we want any bacon-wrapped scallops. Looks like Myles is going for a world record."

Fuck. Five minutes in, and I had already screwed up. Well, the least I could do was let Kenzie pretend she was fine. We could talk about it later. If we had to. Fuck, this crap made me miss when our biggest problem was the Benneti Ban. That was easy compared to this confusing, emotional crap.

Agitation and regret coursed through me. Myles's deep brown eyes narrowed as they took me in, then he shifted his gaze to Kenzie. Holding a soaring plate of food her way, he said, "Here, take this so I can fill up another one."

"No thanks, Myles," she responded with a smile.

Shrugging, he handed the plate to Nikki instead, then grabbed another one and started piling it with food too. It wouldn't surprise me if he spent the evening filling plates then leaving them untouched on all the various tables spaced throughout the room.

Kenzie dropped my hand so she could give Myles a hug. For some reason, I was reluctant to let her go. Maybe it was because I could still feel Felicia's eyes boring into me, trying to draw me away again. But I wouldn't get sucked into that trap twice. Kenzie had all my focus now.

When Myles and Kenzie pulled apart, Kenzie sighed. "It's so good to see you, Myles. It's been too long. And with the season starting, we're going to see you even less than we do now." I knew the truth of that. Myles had made it down from his new racing team in San Francisco a couple times a week earlier, but now that training was in full swing, Kenzie hadn't seen him in a while. And she might not see him outside of events for months after tonight.

Myles frowned at her and Nikki, his two best friends who he'd had to leave behind when Cox Racing fell apart. "Yeah, I know. That's the part of all this that really sucks the most."

Looking sad, Kenzie nodded. In the silence, I asked Myles a question that I hoped would shift the mood in the air. "You ready for the new year? How are you feeling?" My gaze flicked down to his neck. Myles had been in a bad crash last year, a wreck that had ended his season early. Everything else had healed on him, but from what Kenzie had told me, his collarbone still ached on occasion.

Myles didn't seem entirely thrilled to be talking directly to me, and he ran a hand through his scruffy brown hair before he answered. "I'm feeling good…feeling ready." He unconsciously brought his fingers to the sore spot, and rubbed it a little. For a time, Myles had believed that I was the one responsible for his unfortunate accident. And in a way, he was kind of right. Hookup had hurt him, and I was the one who had brought Hookup into the world. Indirectly, I was one hundred percent responsible for his wreck. Thank God he was okay now.

The lights in the room suddenly darkened, then swirling spotlights started circulating, making me dizzy. A voice coming through the speaker system welcomed everyone to the greatest party of the year. That made Kenzie roll her eyes. When the announcer started highlighting Benneti Motorsports achievements, she almost turned and left. Squeezing her hand tight was the only thing that kept her in place.

When the accolades stopped, the spotlights focused on one person—Keith. Larger than life in a powder blue tux, a jewel encrusted arm crutch, and his signature aviator sunglasses, Keith gave the applauding masses a grandiose bow. Microphone in hand, he proudly exclaimed, "Welcome honored friends and guests, to our annual Benneti Bash! I hope you enjoy the food and drinks, and hope you partake in...whatever your heart desires this evening." His face stopped directly on mine when he said that, and annoyance churned in my stomach. What was he playing at?

While I cast a quick glance at Kenzie, Keith pointed off to his right. "I'm sure you've all met the absolutely stunning Felicia Tucker by now, but what you might not know is how talented this devastating beauty is. Felicia...come up here and show yourself off."

As I looked around the room, I noticed something I should have earlier—cameras and reporters—Keith had invited the media, so he could show off his newest acquisition. I had a feeling he wasn't going to stop there though. Now I wanted to leave too. Keith had only required that we show up on time; he hadn't said anything about staying.

While the crowd whistled their approval of Felicia, I opened my mouth to ask Kenzie if she was ready to go. I never got the chance though. Keith's voice interrupted me. "Between Felicia and Hayden, Benneti Motorsports just might have the best-looking riders in the championship. Hayden, where are you? The reporters want to see how great you and Felicia look together."

Before either of us could disappear, a spotlight burst into life around us; it was angled in such a way that I was nearly blinded, and Kenzie was drenched in darkness. As all eyes turned to me, I debated what I could do. Snub Keith and run? His assholeness toward Kenzie, and his constant little manipulations with Felicia were really starting to piss me off, but...he *had* given Kenzie a job, and he *had* given me my shot. I owed him for that. So much more than I could ever repay.

Keith's voice boomed over the speakers while I closed my eyes in frustration. "Hayden, get your ass up here."

Praying Kenzie understood why I had to do this, I reopened my eyes with a resigned sigh. Giving her an apologetic smile, I turned and headed to where Keith and Felicia were waiting. Felicia was practically glowing as I approached her; the hope in her eyes was evident for everyone to see. She was wearing a slinky cocktail dress that was cut down the front to her waist. A long Y-necklace was resting between her breasts, and she played with the end of it while she waited for me to join her. The second I did, she immediately looped her arm around mine.

I instantly yanked my arm free and stepped away from her, and she grabbed my hand instead. I tried shaking her off, but she had a death-like grip on me. She was all smiles for the camera now, and by the way she was leaning on my arm, it probably looked like we were a lot more than teammates. Goddamn it.

My face tightened in anger and my body tensed. And that was when some clever asshole shouted, "Bend her over, Hayes! Give her a real Benneti Bash!"

Felicia laughed like the crude suggestion was funny. Kenzie's face went bright red, and she said something to Nikki. I watched as Nikki said something calming to her in return, hopefully defending me. But then Myles said something to both of them. I couldn't hear what he said, but it seemed to piss Nikki off, and Kenzie's face was ghostly pale when she looked back at me. Shit. He'd gotten to her. We were definitely going to have a talk after this.

I wanted to pull away from Felicia, but Keith snapped, "Stop fidgeting and smile. Half this job is showmanship, Hayes, and I've just guaranteed that people will be talking about you. Both of you. Even people who don't watch the sport will want to know all about the golden couple of racing." Over my shoulder, he winked at Felicia. "Give him a friendly little kiss, dear, something to fan the flames."

My face was flaming red as rage surged through me. This was absolutely ridiculous. I turned to Felicia to tell her not to touch me, but she took the moment to make her move. Lightning fast, her fingers cupped my cheek, holding me still, and her lips firmly landed on mine. My world spun as two very different realities pummeled me. Was I still in the present? Because the past was crashing all around me as her familiar taste and smell filled my senses.

I came back to myself almost instantly, but it was still too late. Pushing Felicia away, I searched the room for Kenzie. I didn't see her—just the spot where she had been. Myles was glaring at me, Nikki was fighting her way through the crowd, chasing after Kenzie. Fucking Keith. Twisting back to him, I growled, "Make a spectacle of me like that again, and I'm through." He raised his hands in the air, like he was completely innocent, but he flashed a victorious glance at Felicia. Asshole.

When I found Kenzie, she was in the hotel lobby with Nikki, who had her hands on her shoulders, calming her down, but Kenzie still looked like she was having trouble breathing. Fuck. She was going to kill me. Inhaling a deep breath, I headed their way. Might as well get to the hard part. "Kenzie…"

Nikki stepped back, and Kenzie lifted a finger at me. "Don't. Nikki is going to give me a ride home. I'm leaving."

Sighing, I looked over at Nikki. "Can you give us a minute?"

She nodded, then patted Kenzie on the shoulder. I waited a second after we were alone. Kenzie wouldn't look at me, and I could feel the rising tension between us, sliding across my skin like a wet snake. "I know you're mad," I finally said.

Kenzie snapped her eyes to mine. "Mad? No, why would I be mad? Your ex-girlfriend is only trying to seduce you back into her bed, and your boss is trying to help her. Why the hell would that make me mad!"

"That's not what's going on…" I let my weak defense die. Yes, in a way, that was exactly what was going on. Felicia wanted to reconnect with me, Keith wanted the buzz that came from two sort-of celebrities getting it on. It was a win-win for them. "I would stop them if I could," I whispered.

Kenzie crossed her arms over her chest, not at all relieved by my words. Wishing I could do more to ease her fears, I asked her, "What did Myles say to you?" Her cheeks heated and she averted her eyes. It was bad then. "Tell me."

Peeking up at me, she said, "Nikki told me you were being good at the track. You and Felicia, she said I had nothing to worry about. But Myles…" Pausing, she swallowed an emotional lump in her throat. "Myles told me that wouldn't last. That no man could resist temptation forever. He said you'd eventually cheat, you'd eventually leave me…"

She started crying, and I instantly pulled her in for an all-consuming hug. Pulling back, I began kissing every inch of her face. "No, I won't. She's not what I want. You're what I want, you're all I want." Cupping her cheeks, I made her look at me. "You're my life, you're my everything. Don't throw us away, Kenzie. Please." *Don't be like her. Don't run.*

Her tears had stopped spilling, and her watery eyes stared at me so unflinchingly that fear began to crawl up my spine. Why wasn't she saying anything? Was she going to end us…over this? I hadn't made it happen, hadn't wanted it to happen. I would give anything to be able to go back in time and stop it from happening. But I couldn't…it *had* happened.

Kenzie finally closed her eyes and inhaled a deep breath. When she opened them again, she quietly said, "I want to leave. Please take me home."

Wrapping my arms around her, I nodded in her shoulder. "Okay, sweetheart." She couldn't run if I was with her. And she wouldn't. Kenzie didn't bail; she faced things head on.

Hours later, we were lying in her bed, both fully dressed. I couldn't sleep. Keith wanted Felicia and me together, to hurt Kenzie and her father and to generate buzz for the team…so why had he given Kenzie a job? And what was she going to be doing? What was Daytona going to be like for us? Damn it. How did things go from being so good, to so convoluted, so fast? Fucking Felicia. How could *one* woman fuck up my life twice? And why were her lips still on my mind?

Just as I was dwelling on that, my cell phone chirped on the nightstand. I glanced over at Kenzie, but she was sound asleep. Mentally cringing, I grabbed my phone and unlocked the screen. The text was from the unsaved number that I knew was Felicia's. In two simple sentences, she had my stomach twisted into knots. *'I enjoyed kissing you again. Did you enjoy kissing me?'*

I typed a response without thinking, and immediately hit send. *'No, I didn't.'*

She replied with a smiley face, and I knew it wasn't because of my answer. It was because after weeks of ignoring her, I'd finally responded to her text. I'd cracked open the door. Shit.

CHAPTER 7

~Kenzie~

A handful of days after that disastrous Benneti Bash, we touched down in Daytona. I still wasn't over everything that had happened at that party—and I frequently had nightmares of Felicia's mouth on Hayden's—but being here at the track helped. And hurt. The sights and smells assaulted me with memories when I stepped inside the speedway. Everywhere I turned I was faced with ghosts from my past—some from my first and only race last year, some from visiting the track with my father before I turned pro. The bright team colors merging to create a chaotic yet beautiful mosaic. The sound of revving engines underscored by whining power tools, shouts, and laughter. The younger riders showing off wherever they could get away with it, the older crew members shaking their heads at the ridiculousness of youth. The rows of bikes awaiting inspection. The smell of engine oil, grease, popcorn, and beer. The heat, the excitement, the fans, the anticipation. Every recollection was a slash across my heart. God, I missed this.

But at least I was here and a part of the world, although I still had no idea what I was going to be doing—a fact that had my stomach dancing with anxiety.

Hayden held my hand tight as we walked to the area assigned to Benneti Motorsports. Even though I knew there wasn't a spot reserved for them, I still looked around for Cox Racing; it was so strange to think they weren't here. That hadn't happened in...ages. It truly was the end of an era. A fact that Keith was exuberant about. I'd never seen him so giddy as we entered the garage area here at the track; he beamed at everyone who approached him.

Staring at the portly man adorned in an oversized Benneti jacket made me sigh. Hearing the trepidation in my exhale, Hayden looked down at me. "Do you know what you're doing yet?" he asked.

Shaking my head, I tore my eyes from Keith and looked up at him. "No. You haven't heard anything either?"

Hayden frowned as he looked Keith's way; he looked a little worried, which didn't make me feel any better. "No. He changes the subject whenever I ask." Shifting his gaze back to me, he smiled. "I'm sure it will be something great, something worthy of your skill."

I raised my eyebrows at that. Keith wouldn't waste this opportunity to humiliate me. No, I was going to be doing something menial—Keith's personal fetching girl or something. But whatever it was, I'd do it with a smile on my face. Being here was all that mattered.

From over my shoulder, I heard a familiar voice say, "Hey guys! Isn't this exciting! We're back at Daytona!" I twisted around to see Nikki standing there, dressed in her red and black Benneti jumpsuit. She frowned when she met my eyes. "I mean, we're kind of back at Daytona. It's not the same of course, but it's still kind of fun…right?"

She looked so guilty over the fact that she was enjoying herself that I had to laugh. "It's okay to love your job, Nikki," I told her. I'd sure loved mine. And hopefully I'd like whatever Keith had in store for me too.

Nikki looked relieved. Then she brightened. "You guys are coming out with Myles and me tonight, right? He found a speakeasy he wants to check out. Apparently, the front of the place looks like a candy store. You don't even know you're going into a bar until they open a secret door behind the counter."

I had to roll my eyes at Myles's never-ending ability to find the oddest places. I looked up at Hayden to see if he wanted to go. He shrugged, then nodded, and I told Nikki we'd be there. As Nikki gave us both a thumbs up, I happened to notice Felicia stroll into the room. She was in Benneti racing leathers that matched what Hayden was wearing, and her long brown hair was pulled back into a slick ponytail. The sight of her prepped for a race stung worse than I thought it would. *That should be me.*

Inadvertently, I found myself squeezing Hayden's hand harder and harder. He glanced down at me, then looked over to see what had my attention. I heard him sigh when he spotted Felicia. She was walking over to Keith now. Cool and confident, she looked like she'd always been a part of this world. It made me wonder, if she hadn't left town a few years ago, would Keith have brought both her and Hayden onto the team? Probably. They would have come on as the king and queen of Benneti Racing, and Hayden and I never would have happened. But she *had* fled town, and now that she was back, things weren't the way she'd left them.

Keith and Felicia suddenly both turned my way. Straightening my stance, I raised my chin. *You don't worry me.* Keith smiled like he knew what I was thinking, then he turned back around and reached into a box in front of him. Curiosity killing me, I watched as he grabbed a few things and handed them to Felicia. When she took the items, she tossed me a small smile. I had no idea what that meant.

Keith jerked his thumb my way, and Felicia started sauntering over. Great.

With Hayden on one side of me and Nikki on the other, I felt like I had bodyguards. I didn't need them, though; I could handle Felicia. Since it was obvious she wanted to talk to me, I squeezed my way through Hayden and Nikki, so I was standing slightly in front of them. Felicia's eyes swung Hayden's way and she gave him a charming smile. "Ready for the race tomorrow, Hayden?"

Hayden frowned, like just her talking to him irritated him. "I don't think you've been properly introduced to my girlfriend yet. This is Mackenzie," he said, ignoring her question. I loved the fact that he'd used my full name.

I could almost see Felicia inwardly sighing as she slowly turned her head my way; her smile now was clearly forced. "Right...your girlfriend. It's nice to meet you... I've heard a lot about you."

Disliking that she'd heard *anything* about me, I murmured, "Likewise."

Felicia flashed a glance at Hayden. "All good, I hope?"

I could feel my jaw tightening. "Not really," I answered truthfully. *Kiss my boyfriend again, bitch, and I just might rip that smile off your face.* Was that smugness I was seeing? Or longing?

She brought her eyes back to me, and they grew heated with an emotion I finally understood. Anger. She opened her mouth to say something, but before she could, Hayden cut her off with a gruff voice. "Keith gave you something for Mackenzie?"

Felicia glanced at him before returning her eyes to me. "Yes…your new uniform."

She handed me a small bundle of black and red material. Confused, I unfolded the pieces—one was a bikini top, the other a very short pair of spandex shorts. "What the hell is this?" I asked, my eyes snapping to hers.

Felicia shrugged. "Keith said you were the new spokesmodel for Benneti Motorsports. Congratulations, I hear it's a very competitive market." From her voice, I couldn't tell if she was being serious, or insulting me.

My jaw dropped to my chest as my heart fell to the floor. I could not wear this *here*, around people who used to be my peers and rivals. It was a blow within a blow, and that was exactly why Keith had done it. I should have known the humiliation would have come in this form. Keith knew how hard I'd worked to be seen as an equal in this sport. Of course he'd want to lower me in the eyes of my ex-competitors. I should have known.

Crumpling the material, I debated throwing it on the ground and walking away. I couldn't possibly do this. But I refused to let Keith win, and I refused to let Hayden's ex see me defeated. If this was the task I'd been given, then I would do it to the best of my ability. Even if it meant strutting around the track with Benneti Motorsports plastered on my ass.

"Great, thank you," I muttered. My cheeks felt hot, and I prayed she didn't see how flustered I was.

With a quick flick at Hayden, Felicia softly said, "No problem." Hayden's eyes were daggers, but Felicia only smiled in response, then walked away.

The second she was gone, Hayden turned to me. "You don't have to do this. Give the outfit back to Keith, and tell him to go to hell. I know you want to tell him that anyway," he added with a smirk.

While that was true, I was already in too deep to back out now. "The sad truth is…this is the only way I can be a part of racing now, Hayden. And I want that so much."

Hayden's eyes grew soft. "You nearly ripped my head off when I assumed you were a model…and now you're willing to pimp Keith's team with your body?" God, was I really going to give him what he wanted?

"It's a means to an end, until I can find something else. But look on the bright side," I said, holding the "uniform" up to his face. "I'll be strutting around in basically a bikini all weekend long."

Nikki snorted, then walked away. Fire danced in Hayden's eyes. "Well, that certainly is a bright side… although, I don't think I'm okay with every other guy around here seeing you like this." His gaze shifted to where Keith was standing, laughing with Maxwell… probably about me. "I'm going to go talk to Keith. This is going too far."

I put a hand on his chest. "This is the job he has for me, Hayden. If you tell him this isn't okay, then he'll just fire me and send me on my way."

Hayden put his hand over mine. "That's fine with me. If he fires you, then you'll be here as my guest, and not as his...trophy."

Smiling, I stroked my thumb over the coolness of his leathers. "I need to be a part of this world, Hayden. Not as a fan, not as a guest, not as a third party who is just in the way. I need to be an *active* part, with purpose. And as meager a role as this is...it *is* advertising, so at least there is a small amount of purpose to it." Hayden opened his mouth to interject, but I interrupted him. "Yes, maybe this isn't a role I ever thought I'd play, but it's better than nothing, so I'm going to do it." Not much better than nothing, but I didn't want to tell him that.

He again looked like he was going to object, so I leaned up and kissed the rough stubble along his cheek. "I'm going to go change. There's a fan walk soon, and I'm sure Keith wants me there to entertain the crowd." Hayden's jaw tightened with my words, but he didn't say anything, and I knew his mind was spinning with reasons why I shouldn't do this.

My smile was joyful as I clutched my outfit tight and left Hayden to find a bathroom, but joyful wasn't how I felt. I was fuming, burning with an anger hotter than the sun's core. Fucking Keith. I made a vow as I watched him while I walked. He would never see my pain. All he would see was happiness—happiness that I was here, happiness that I was with Hayden. And in that way, I would come out of this the winner. Keith's team might claim the championship this year, but I was the one who would be victorious.

Felicia caught my eye as I walked through the door, and a surge of acid-filled jealousy hit me. She was an equal to the men around me—a competitor, a rival. And I was about to be strutting around in my underwear. Fuck my life.

After finding a bathroom to change, I took a hard look at myself in the mirror. I wasn't the most buxom person, but I was practically spilling out of the tight top. And the shorts…Jesus, there were going to be kids at the event, and they should *not* be subjected to this much skin. But it was what Keith wanted, so it was what Keith was going to get. Jerk off.

Gathering up my belongings, I trudged back to the Benneti camp. I felt more and more eyes on me with every step. It was hard to not hunch over and hide, difficult to stand as tall and straight as if I had on a shimmering ball gown, but that was what I made myself do. Keith wouldn't destroy my spirit. Not now, not ever.

When I stepped back inside the garage, Maxwell and Rodney spotted me first. They let out loud cat calls that echoed throughout the room. I flipped them off. Since I was technically an employee, could I sue them for sexual harassment?

The noise got Hayden's attention, and I spotted him stepping away from the bikes to see what was going on. When he saw me, his reaction was a mixture of approval and disgust—like he wanted to hide me away…by shoving me into his bedroom. Keeping my head held high, I ignored the stares and whistles around me and strutted his way. Holding my things out to him, I calmly said, "Is there somewhere I can put these?"

He hesitated before taking them, and I could tell he wanted to wrap me back up in the material. "Yeah, I'll just…stash this with my… Are you sure about this, Kenzie?"

I nodded as firmly as my courage allowed. "Yes. Now, I need to find some boots. My Converse aren't going to cut it with this outfit." Hayden's eyes slowly drifted down my overly exposed thighs to my comfortable shoes. His gaze washing over me made a rush of excitement dull the embarrassment. Maybe if he mentally undressed me the entire time, I might actually make it through this.

It took every ounce of determination I had to survive the autograph session, and when it was over, I had a newfound respect for what models had to put up with. I was openly leered at, crudely hit on by men who had their children in tow, and once or twice I felt a palm on my ass. I couldn't even tell the creepers to get bent. I had to smile, wave, and offer them 8x10s of the Benneti racers.

But none of that compared to how it felt to watch the racers greet their fans. Seeing Maxwell and Rodney giving guys high-fives, seeing Hayden tousle the hair of young kids, and seeing the fans' faces as they approached their idols—it was an excruciating reminder of what I'd lost. Watching Felicia's table was the worst. Hearing the fans tell her how excited they were to see her race, the young girls looking at her with dreams in their eyes…it was utter torture being forced to take a back seat while she lived the life I wanted.

My heart was cracked to pieces by the time we got back to Hayden's hotel room, and I fell onto his bed, absolutely drained. As I stared up at the ceiling, I felt Hayden compress the mattress beside me as he sat down. "You all right?" he asked, concern in his voice.

With a great amount of effort, I shifted my gaze to him. "No. Take this off me. Now." When I'd gone back to the Benneti garage to change into my street clothes, I'd discovered that some jackass had "moved" them. Everyone claimed they didn't know anything, but, by the way Rodney and Maxwell had been chuckling, I was sure they'd had something to do with it. Just as easily could have been Keith though, or Felicia. Regardless, my clothes were AWOL, and I'd had to return to the hotel in my eye candy outfit. The cherry on top of the suck-fest that was my day.

Hayden's jade eyes brightened at hearing my command. "Gladly," he murmured.

While I laid on my back, comatose, he slowly peeled off the black, knee-high, motorcycle-style boots that Keith had decided completed the outfit. Once my feet were bare, he started on the atrocious spandex shorts. He didn't just rip them off like I'd hoped though. No, he folded them down, inch by inch, pausing to kiss the new skin as it was exposed. The exhaustion started shifting into something a lot more stimulating, and my body tingled with alertness. A satisfied murmur escaped me as I wriggled my hips in anticipation. This was as good a way as any to forget my horrendous afternoon.

A soft laugh escaped Hayden as he pulled the shorts all the way off. Leaving my underwear on, he moved up to my ridiculous top. Kissing each breast through the fabric, he lowly said, "I know you hate this outfit, but damn, baby, you look good in it. I was hard during the entire autograph session."

A smile broke over my face as he unhooked the back. "Well, good thing you were sitting. That probably would have surprised your fans otherwise."

Hayden began pulling the hated fabric off my skin. As he did, he quietly said, "You had fans there...did you see?"

His words froze me, and I looked down to see him peeking up at me. "I had fans there?"

Sitting up a bit, Hayden nodded. "Yeah, they had your shirt on, and were holding photos of you. Keith, he …"

He looked away, and a knot of anger stirred in my belly. Whatever Keith had done, by the look on Hayden's face, I was positive I wasn't going to like it. "Keith what?"

Looking back at me, Hayden sighed. "He told them all you weren't available for autographs. Said it would interfere with your new job...then he directed them all to Felicia."

I sat up on my elbows, incensed. "Those were *my* fans. He had no right! And he sent them to Felicia? That son of a bitch!" I sat up so suddenly, Hayden had to scoot away to avoid getting injured. Storming away from the bed, I tossed out, "I need a shower." I suddenly felt like I was covered in filth.

"Do you want me to join you?" Hayden asked. Without answering him, I briskly shut the bathroom door. No, I really didn't want him around me right now. I needed to decompress in peace.

The steaming water helped me cool down, but it didn't change the bitterness in the back of my throat. Everything I'd once loved was slowly being stripped away from me, and I hated it. But I also didn't know how to change it. My life was tumbling out of control in a direction I'd never expected it to go, and just when I thought I was on my way to stabilizing my trajectory, something else came along to knock me off course. Where I was going to end up now was anyone's guess.

I dressed in a Cox Racing T-shirt when I emerged from the shower—maybe I was feeling nostalgic. Hayden had a concerned expression on his face the entire time he watched me cover up. "You okay?" he asked. I was getting really tired of him asking me that.

"I'm great," I said, my voice tight. "But I could really use a drink." Grabbing my phone, I texted Nikki and asked her where this speakeasy bar was. The sooner I had alcohol in me, the better.

Hayden came up behind me and started playing with my damp strands; the waves were a lot curlier when I let them air dry. Wrapping a dark section around his finger, he leaned down to kiss the crook of my neck. "Let's go get you a drink then."

Forcing myself to relax, I turned and gave him a soft kiss. This wasn't his fault, so I shouldn't take it out on him.

Hayden changed into some going out clothes while I waited for Nikki to text me back with an address. When she gave it to me, we made our way down to Hayden's sporty rental car. "You want to drive?" he asked, opening the driver's side door. It warmed me that he was being so sweet, and normally I would have leaped at the chance to drive this racy-looking thing, but I just wasn't in the mood.

"No, I'm good," I said, opening the other side.

A small sigh escaped Hayden as he slid behind the wheel. I knew he wanted me to perk up, to be sunny and bright like I usually was, and while I was trying to fake happiness, I just couldn't fake it to that degree right now. Maybe after a few margaritas.

While Hayden drove us to this place called The Shoppe, I put my hand on his thigh and tried to focus only on the fact that we were together, and about to spend a fun evening with our friends. Well, with my friends who had grudgingly accepted the fact that Hayden was my boyfriend.

When we got to the address Nikki had given me, Hayden frowned. "You sure this is the right place?" The brightly lit building was clearly a candy store, with rows of shelves full of yummy treats visible from the outside.

"Yeah…she *did* say it looked real," I said, stepping out of the car. Hayden stepped out with me, and we both stared in silence at the unlikely bar before us.

As we were staring, a couple cars pulled into the parking lot. Seconds later, I was surrounded by people I knew and loved—Nikki, Myles, and a bunch of ex-Cox Racing team members. I was struck with painful memories as I hugged Ralph, Eli, and Myles's mechanic, Kevin. God, it was good to see them.

Kevin, always the practical one, gave Myles a confused glance once we separated. "Are you sure about this, Myles? It seems like a candy store to me."

Myles raised a playful eyebrow. "Would a candy store have a bouncer?"

We all took another look, and, sure enough, there was a burly guy standing by the front door, arms crossed in a classic posture of intimidation. Myles gleefully clapped his hands before grabbing Nikki's hand and pulling her toward the store; she giggled the entire way. Ralph, Eli, and

Kevin gave Hayden a once-over before following them. While the ban between our old team and Keith's was no longer an actual thing, it had to be strange for them to be hanging out with a Benneti. Maybe it would be a little easier for them since Nikki was one now too. And me, I supposed.

Hayden and I brought up the rear of the group. The bouncer by the door eyed our group, then said in a monotone voice, "Password."

Everyone looked around at everyone else. We needed a password? Seriously? Myles scratched his head, then slowly said, "Let us in so we can get fucked up?"

The bouncer eyed him for a second, then turned and opened the door. Nikki gave Myles a high-five as we all stepped inside. A girl wearing a crisp uniform that looked like it was straight from the 1800s greeted us on the inside. "Welcome to The Shoppe," she said. "Right this way." She led us behind the counter and into a back room. Just as I was beginning to think we'd all been duped and we were about to be murdered, she pushed something on the wall, and it swung open to reveal a spiral staircase. "Have fun!" she said, her voice bright.

Myles and Nikki headed toward the sound of thumping music. Hayden and I glanced at each other, and he held my hand extra tight before we followed them. The actual bar of the speakeasy was like some gothic fantasy come to life. Thick black curtains separated areas into private rooms, every source of light was fashioned to mimic candle flames, and all the chairs in sight were plush, throne-like pieces straight out of a Dracula movie. Considering where we'd just come from, it was a pretty spectacular sight.

The waitresses were all in black corsets and shorty-shorts that made my Benneti spandex briefs look like sweatpants. Myles flagged one down and ordered a round of shots for everyone, then found us a table in a back room that looked like it belonged in some medieval nobleman's dining room.

Hayden and I sat down across from Myles and Nikki. Eli and Kevin sat next to Myles, while Ralph sat down next to Hayden, although he left a chair between them. I rolled my eyes at my ex-teammates, but I didn't say anything; they'd get used to Hayden eventually.

While we waited for our shots to arrive, I asked Myles, "So how do you like Stellar Racing? Is it as bad as you thought?"

Myles groaned. "It's worse. Luke Stellar is a dick, and Jimmy's a stuck-up asshole. The only decent people there are Kevin and Eli." He tilted his dark head in their direction and they both grinned at me. "But I'm surviving, and it's good to be racing again." Myles's brown eyes locked onto Hayden, and I could see the gears turning as he studied my boyfriend. "So...should we expect any mishaps this year, Hayden? Or is everything back to status quo?"

Silence blanketed the table. It was broken only by the shots arriving. Hayden kept his eyes locked on Myles while the waitress doled them out. I wanted to kick Myles under the table, but I resisted the temptation. Instead, I lifted my shot glass. "Cheers!" I exclaimed, once everyone had theirs.

Hayden and Myles took their drinks with their gazes still focused on each other, and I knew this conversation wasn't over. When Hayden set down his glass, Myles shrugged. "So? What do you think, Hayden?"

Hayden looked around the table before meeting Myles's eyes again. "I'm certainly no expert on the subject, but yeah…I think it will be a normal year."

Myles narrowed his eyes. "As opposed to last year?" Myles knew Hayden had somehow been involved with the tampering last year, and he wanted answers, but here and now was not the place to get them.

Interrupting, I said, "Next round is on me. What would everyone like?"

Ralph, Eli, and Kevin seemed grateful that I was breaking the tension in the room, and eagerly gave me their orders. Nikki piped up with her request, and eventually Hayden and Myles let go of their conversation and gave me theirs too. Just as I was scooting my chair back to head to the bar, a voice to my left said, "I'll take a whiskey Coke, Mackenzie. Diet please."

I looked over to see who had spoken, and my heart almost stopped beating. Felicia? What the fuck was she doing here? While I gaped at her, dumbstruck, she calmly settled herself in the empty seat beside Hayden. Even though every person was staring at her, Felicia looked perfectly at ease, like she wasn't crashing a party she hadn't been invited to.

Minutely moving his chair away from her, Hayden asked the question that was blazing through my brain. "What are you doing here, Felicia?"

She smiled, like his tone had been warm and friendly. "It's the night before a big race. I'm unwinding, same as you guys." Looking around the table, she asked, "Is everyone ready for the big day?"

Ralph, Eli, and Kevin looked unsure if they were supposed to answer that. Myles looked annoyed, while Nikki kept flicking heated glances between Felicia and me; she looked like she was ready for a throw down...I just had to say the word. While I scooted my chair back to the table—hell if I was going anywhere now—Hayden said, "You should go, Felicia. This is a private function."

Looking over at me and then Nikki, she answered with, "Looks like a Benneti function. I'm a Benneti now." Lifting her hand in the air, she flagged down the waitress. "Another round of shots, please," she said, indicating the empty glasses on the table.

Eli, Kevin, and Ralph relaxed since she was buying them alcohol. They even smiled and thanked her. Myles and Nikki were staring at me, waiting to see what I wanted. Hayden narrowed his eyes at Felicia, then turned his gaze my way. Leaning over, he said, "Want to leave?"

Yes. And no. It was clear Felicia wasn't going to go anywhere voluntarily, but I didn't want her to chase me away either. If she wanted to be stubborn, well, two could play that game. Locking eyes with Felicia on the other side of Hayden, I told him, "No, everything's fine here." *Unless she tries to kiss you again. Then we'll have an issue.* Hayden let out another long exhale, then shook his head in disbelief.

Felicia and I stared at each other until the drinks arrived; I didn't even let myself blink until she did. As the waitress passed out the shots, Felicia coolly said, "So, Mackenzie, how did the autograph session go? I was too busy with my line to see much of you. Did you enjoy yourself?"

Did I enjoy looking like a play toy in my old workplace? Fuck no, I didn't enjoy that. I wanted to sling back my shot as soon as it was in front of me, but I refused to take mine before Felicia took hers. Tension built around the table again as people waited for my answer; Myles and the guys looked confused…they didn't know what my job today had been. "I think I made a real impact with the fans," I finally said. God, was that the right thing to say? I wished I could have just said, "Go to hell." That felt more appropriate.

"What do you want, Felicia?" Hayden suddenly asked.

Felicia's gaze swung from me to him, and the awkwardness at the table tripled; everyone but the three of us started downing their drinks one by one.

"I want to have an actual conversation with you, Hayden, where you say things, and then I get to say things in return. I want to explain what happened four years ago."

Shaking his head, Hayden looked away from her. "You're barking up the wrong tree. No need to explain anything…doesn't matter anymore."

Somehow, the tone of his voice sounded all wrong, and I knew he was lying. Felicia knew it too. "I'm sorry I left, Hayden. And I hope that one day you can forgive me…like Izzy has forgiven me."

Hayden's eyes snapped back to her face. "Izzy forgave you? I don't believe it. She's pissed that you took off when Antonia needed you most. She said she'd *never* forgive you for that."

Felicia's eyes sank to the table, and she started slowly turning the glass in her fingers. "Yeah, well…I talked to her before we left to come here. She forgave me, and she said she thought you would too," she added, her voice almost too quiet for me to hear.

"Why would she possibly think that?" Hayden snapped, a hard edge to his voice.

Myles suddenly slapped his hands on the table. "Who wants to play darts?" The others shot to their feet, and, within seconds, they were all gone. I didn't blame them; the concrete-like tension in the air would have had me bailing too.

To my surprise, Hayden slowly stood up after them. "Darts sound great." He held his hand out for me. "Kenzie, want to play?" From the look in his eye, I knew what he was really asking was, *Want to sneak out the back and leave now?*

Felicia was still staring at her glass, and the curiosity was killing me. Why had Izzy so readily forgiven her? And why the hell did Izzy think Hayden ever would? Felicia had abandoned him, made him afraid to let people in again. She'd scarred him. That sort of pain wouldn't easily go away.

Taking Hayden's hand, I let him pull me to my feet. "Sure," I whispered, wondering if we should actually leave.

Felicia looked up when we started to move. "Hayden." He stopped, exhaled a deep breath, then looked back at her. Heart in her eyes, she told him, "You're right, it was wrong of me to leave. I have so much to atone for…to everyone. I'm trying to make things right. That's all."

Even as she said it, I knew that wasn't entirely accurate. She was trying to make things the *same*…big difference. But Hayden looked genuinely affected by her statement, and there was clear turmoil in his eyes; the depth of the pain I saw there worried me.

"It's too late for that, Felicia," he said, his voice unsteady. Grabbing my hand tighter, he yanked me away from the table. As I glanced back at Felicia, I saw my own internal question reflected in her shimmering eyes.

Was it really?

CHAPTER 8

~Kenzie~

I didn't sleep well that night. I kept tossing and turning while my mind spun. While Hayden never acted like he was awake as well, I got the feeling sleep had evaded him too…there was something in the haggardness of his eyes the next morning that confirmed long hours of restlessness.

Not wanting yet another outfit of mine to go missing, I dressed in my sleazy Benneti gear at the hotel. Hayden let me wear his jacket over the top, which helped a lot, but I still felt skanky and underdressed as I walked through the hotel lobby. I'd only just begun, and I was ready for the day to end.

When we got to the track, Hayden still looked speculative. I wanted to ask him what he was thinking about, but I already knew what—or *who*—he was thinking about, and I didn't really want details on his thoughts. Especially if they were along the lines of: *maybe I should talk to her, maybe I should forgive her, maybe I should get back to together with her.* Just the thought of him thinking that, even only for the briefest moment, made me feel sick to my stomach. We were so great together, everything the two of them hadn't ended up being, and he knew that. *He had to know that.*

The second Keith saw me, huddled up in Hayden's jacket, he snapped his fingers and said, "That comes off the second you're at the event. I want everyone to see the goods." For a horrible instant, I wasn't sure if he meant the logo plastered all over me, or my body. Both amplified the queasiness in my gut.

Hayden frowned at Keith's pronouncement. "Keith, she just got here. Ease up."

Keith frowned at his star racer, then a smarmy smile spread over his lips. "Hayden…the man, they myth, the legend…tell me you're ready for this race."

Hayden glanced at me once it was obvious Keith was going to ignore his statement, but then he nodded. "Yeah, my times are good. I'm ready." The knowledge that he'd moved on and was now comfortable enough racing to procure amazing times without my help still stung. And the sad part was, I didn't even know if the same held true for me. God, it had been forever since I'd pushed myself on a bike.

Keith wrapped an arm around Hayden's shoulders, and started leading him away to a meeting for racers and the crew…basically everyone but me. Hayden looked back at me as Keith swept him from my side, but he didn't get out much more than, "I'll see you later."

On the far side of the room, Keith and Hayden were joined by more team members, including Felicia. Keith dropped his hold on Hayden and stepped back, just as Felicia stepped into his side. Hayden looked uncomfortable to be walking side by side with her, but, uncomfortable or not, he left the room that way.

Keith's crew chief, a beefy man very appropriately named Butch, was busy watching the bikes until they were inspected. That was where the problems had started last year—some time right after the pre-race inspection. While I knew there wouldn't be any problems like that this year, the rest of the teams weren't as sure. In a lot of people's opinion, the ARRC had never adequately explained what had happened.

Since I'd never been a model before in my life, I wasn't entirely sure what I was supposed to be doing. Keith usually hired a handful of girls for these events, but, for some reason, there was only me. I supposed that was to make me feel as isolated and uncomfortable as possible. Having females to bond with and complain to would have been an outlet. Maybe I should find other models to hang with. I had a feeling Keith would have an issue with me being around other team's or non-affiliated sponsors' models though. No, I was on my own.

I ended up grabbing some promotional material and wandering aimlessly around the property. Then I found myself in the stands, staring at the finish line. Sitting with a handful of strangers, I watched some practice laps and then some qualifying laps. Hayden had an amazing run, qualifying in the 3rd position. Myles qualified in 2nd. Felicia was going to start in 8th, a fact that both impressed and incensed me; I'd qualified 10th my rookie year. Every single part of watching them killed me, and yet, I couldn't turn away. Each time a rider crossed that magic line, a small piece of me died. I felt numb inside.

"Hey, there you are. Keith's looking for you."

I glanced over to see Hayden walking down the bleacher, heading my way. Shit. I'd been so engrossed in watching the bikes, I'd forgotten all about the job I was supposed to be doing. "Is he pissed?" I asked with a cringe.

He scrunched his face in an adorable expression that made me want to kiss him. "Define pissed…"

Great. Groaning, I shook my head. "I just wanted to sit out here for a couple minutes, to remember why I was demeaning myself." Smiling, I inhaled a deep, exhaust-laden breath. "Despite it all, it's good to be back here."

"I know," he said, his voice low as he sat beside me. "I just wish *you* were out there with me."

From his tone, it was clear he was saying he wished I was out there with him instead of Felicia. A pang hit me as I wished the same thing. "You're starting in 3rd…that's amazing."

His grin was wide and pleased. "Thanks. I'm still a little shocked about that. I was just a hair below Myles too. Next time I'll get him."

I wanted to make a comment about Felicia besting my time, but I also didn't want to bring her up. She seemed to hover in the air around us anyway, and I knew she'd linger there until one of us took the elephant in the room by the throat, so I decided to be the one to throttle the beast. "What Felicia said last night…do you really think Izzy forgave her?"

Hayden's expression fell as he stared at his hands. "Yeah…I've been stewing on that. I don't know. I really don't see why she would after one conversation." He looked over at me. "Felicia's just messing with my head. She does that. If she wants something bad enough, she'll do just about anything to get it."

His words filled me with icy dread. "Well, it will be easy enough to solve this mystery. We'll just talk to Izzy when we get back."

Hayden nodded, then reached out for my hand. When I placed my fingers in his, he squeezed them tight. "I love you, Kenzie. That hasn't changed, and it isn't going to change...even if Felicia was telling the truth."

My eyes stung as painful hope filled me. "I love you too." *And Felicia isn't the only one who will do anything to get what she wants.*

Knowing I couldn't put Keith off any more than I had, I followed Hayden back to the Benneti area. Keith berated me for a solid fifteen minutes on what he expected from me during events, then he handed me an umbrella and told me to keep the racers cool while they waited in their grid boxes. I couldn't believe it. I used to be the one lined up in the grid box, waiting for my shot at glory, and now I was a freaking umbrella girl. It was an additional blow that I wasn't sure my ego could take right now.

To make it as bearable as possible, I made sure I was the one holding the umbrella for Hayden. His face was a mixture of pity and pleasure as he cast not-so-discrete glances at my body. I knew he wanted me to have more than this, but he was clearly glad I was the one on display for him.

Eventually it was time for the race, and the officials made everyone leave who wasn't riding. Having to get off the track was like having a long piece of duct tape wrapped around me then slowly pulled off. I felt the burn all the way to the innermost part of my core being. I couldn't even really watch the race either. Keith was hoping to land a new sponsor after today's event, so I was sent to the VIP section to "entertain" them on his behalf. I spent the entire race getting the pair of men drinks and slapping their hands away from my ass. Keith probably would scold me for not letting them touch, but there was a limit to just what I'd do for this job. And for him.

When the race was over, I was as exhausted as if I'd participated. But I was brimming with anxious energy when I finally got away from the sponsors long enough to check out the standings. A part of me wanted Hayden to finish behind where he'd finished last year, but I knew that was born from insecurity, so I hurriedly pushed it from my mind. I loved him, and I wanted him to do well, even without me. When I saw the final times, my jaw nearly dropped to my chest. Myles won the whole damn thing! And Hayden was second. And Felicia…was fourth.

Seeing her name beside the placement I'd fought tooth and nail for last year—and lost—was like having a javelin punched straight through my chest. All the breath left me, and I couldn't inhale again. She'd beaten me. She'd also beaten the record for a female racer on this track. Handedly. She was in the record books on her very first race. *She did everything I couldn't do.* My mind swam, and everything in my vision suddenly tinted red. She was doing everything I wished I could be doing…and she was doing it better than I ever had. I thought I might throw up, but I couldn't tear my eyes away from the board.

My vision hazed, and I felt darkness swallowing me. I fell into a crouch, with my hands on my knees, and finally drew in the breath my body desperately needed. Jesus. Why did she have to be good? If she had been lousy, I could have handled her living *my* dream more easily. But her excelling at what I wanted…it was too much, too painful. *I shouldn't be here.* But sadly, there was nowhere else for me to go.

Not even caring if Keith fired me, I decided to go back to the hotel instead of back to the garage area. Fate wasn't with me though. Maxwell spotted me plodding through the crowds, and stormed his way over to me. "Hey, Cox! Keith wants you with the winners. He wants you standing beside Hayden while he's being interviewed."

Well, of course he did. He could advertise Benneti with my chest while simultaneously embarrassing me and my family name on national TV. Maybe seeing how far I'd fallen would actually get my father's attention, and he'd call a cease-fire to the cold war. Then at least one good thing would come out of all this.

Clearly not trusting me to go there on my own, Maxwell grabbed my arm and started pulling me. Feeling even worse than before—something I hadn't even realized was possible—I let him lead me. Last year, I'd had so much anticipation and expectation placed on my shoulders, I'd felt a crushing amount of pressure. I'd doubted myself, but had wanted to rise above and prove my worth. Now there was nothing to prove to anyone, but I still felt laced with doubt. Had I ever been good enough to compete at this level? As much as I hated to admit it, without Hookup's interference last season, I might not have done nearly as well as I had. Maybe it was all a fluke, and maybe I couldn't get a job simply because I wasn't good enough and the other teams knew that. Maybe Felicia was the one who truly belonged here, and I was the outsider.

When I got to the celebration area, I instantly spotted Hayden. His helmet was off and his sweaty blond hair was sticking up every which way. A broad smile was on his face and his jade eyes were gleaming with joy. He was mesmerizingly attractive, and I no longer needed Maxwell's help to get closer to him; in his arms was the only place I wanted to be.

On my way to my boyfriend, I caught a glimpse of Myles. He was practically glowing as he shook up a celebratory bottle of champagne. The exploding liquid spewed out of the bottle, covering Myles in suds while he laughed; I'd never seen him happier. My heart felt lighter watching his joy—he deserved it, after his nightmare year last year. I couldn't have been prouder of him.

Hayden was looking right at me when I shifted my eyes back to him. The expression on his face faltered, and I saw some of the light in his eyes die. He felt sorry for me. I was ruining his moment just by being here. Not wanting him to feel anything but elated right now, I threw on a smile. *This is okay. You did amazing, enjoy it.*

Holding my head high, feigning confidence I didn't truly feel, I strutted up to him and tossed my arms around his neck. His arms wrapped around my waist, and I heard him laugh in my ear as he picked me up. "Second place! I did it, Kenzie!" Pulling back, his grin grew. "*We* did it."

His lips lowered to mine, and bliss overwhelmed me; it was almost as sweet as competing. From all around us, I heard chaos, noise, and celebration. It was intoxicating, but not nearly as euphoric as Hayden's embrace. There were reporters nearby asking Hayden to answer some questions, and he reluctantly pulled away from me. "Stay close?" he asked.

Indicating my outfit, I said, "Have to. Keith wants me as your window dressing." Hayden's smile started shifting into a frown, and I raised my finger to stop him. "Don't. This is your moment, and for once, I'm glad I have this job, because otherwise I might have missed it."

One side of his lip curled up into a crooked smile, making my heart beat faster and harder, then he turned that charming grin toward the camera; the red record light instantly turned on, capturing it. Hayden was going to ignite the racing world with a smile like that, and I knew that any female fan who had somehow missed him his rookie year, was not going to be able to miss him this year.

As Hayden began talking about his epic finish, I moved around to stand beside him. Throwing on a smile, I hoped no one recognized me. If all people saw was a random Benneti model, I might get through this relatively unscathed.

It was nerve-racking standing there, but after a few minutes with no outburst of recognition from the crowd, I started to relax. Then I saw someone who hadn't placed in the top three, and who didn't need to be a part of the post-race interviews: Felicia. Helmet off, long hair wild and free, she was swaying her way through the reporters, apparently on a path to Hayden. The smile on her face was enormous, and the feeling in my gut intensified, turning to concrete. I could easily imagine the after-race euphoria that was coursing through her veins right now—I'd been there myself before. Seeing the joy on her face and knowing I would never again feel that way…it killed me.

Hayden's smile tightened when he noticed her, but it didn't completely fade. While I watched in horror, Felicia wrapped her arms around his neck, then leaned over and kissed his cheek. "Congratulations, Haydey!"

The cameras caught the entire nauseating event, and the rock in my stomach started to boil, churn, and liquefy into white-hot molten lava. She had no right to put her lips on him—again—congratulations or not. And Haydey? What the hell was that about?

Hayden jerked away from her touch, but the reporters instantly latched onto the effervescent woman. "Felicia, please stay. We'd love to ask you a few questions."

In a nonchalant way that made it look like Hayden wasn't rejecting her, Felicia deftly removed her arms and beamed at the reporters. "I would be honored," she purred.

"Well, first off, we must congratulate you on your record-breaking finish. We haven't seen a ride like that in...well, we've never seen a ride quite like that," the reporter said with a smirk.

Really? Never? My eyes narrowed with hatred at the reporter who'd spoken, and that was when I recognized him. It was the same asshole who'd aired that fateful interview I'd given last year, when I'd inadvertently slammed my ex-teammate, Jimmy Holden.

Felicia flashed a glance over her shoulder at me, and the heat in my eyes grew even hotter. I would have given anything to have superpowers at that moment. She would have been nothing but a pile of goo beside Hayden. "Thank you," she answered the reporter, her voice both light and luxurious. "It's a remarkable beginning to what I hope is a remarkable year...for both of us."

She grabbed Hayden's arm and squeezed, and hell if they didn't look like some picture-perfect couple from some goddamn romantic comedy. If she didn't back off right now, I was going to give the cameras a show they'd never forget.

The reporters beamed at Hayden and Felicia together, and I could already see them spinning a story about the two of them, and that was probably exactly what Keith wanted; a born-on-the-track romance was gossip gold. "You two were both brought into the ARRC by Keith Benneti. How has it been racing together?"

That made me want to scoff. They'd competed together *once*. Were they supposed to have developed a career-worthy bond in that short amount of time? Felicia gazed at Hayden like he was the beginning and end of her day. Hayden pointedly removed her arm from around his. He opened his mouth to say something, but Felicia beat him to it. "It's been amazing. We're teammates first, competitors second. We're here to help and encourage each other. I couldn't imagine a better partner than Hayden."

Hayden's eyes blazed as he looked at her, and I saw something in the gaze that iced my stomach. It wasn't that he was upset, that was understandable—I was furious too. No, it was the level of anger that I saw in his eyes that concerned me. There was passion in the glimmering jade depths. A negative passion, true, but passion nonetheless.

"I wouldn't be where I am today without my *team*," Hayden said, his jaw tight. That one simple sentence was oozing with multiple meanings. Hayden was being as politically correct as he could be for the cameras, but by his tone, I knew he wasn't including Felicia when he said *team*. Regardless of her allegiances, she was on the outside looking in with him.

His double words were lost on the reporter though. With a knowing smile, he said, "I'm sure that's true. Congratulations again on your second place finish, Hayden, and Felicia…it was wonderful talking to you. We wish you both the best of luck at Road America next month."

The light on the camera died and the group left in search of new targets to talk to. A twinge of bitterness hit me as I watched them walk away. They hadn't even noticed I was there; I'd wanted to go unnoticed, but what I'd become was invisible.

Hayden stepped away from Felicia. "What are you doing here?" he asked, the vein in his neck pulsing.

Untroubled by Hayden's mood, Felicia calmly crossed her arms over her chest. "I'm doing exactly what I told them I was doing…supporting my teammate." The way she said teammate was almost intimate.

Extending his hand, Hayden reached out for me. After I grabbed his fingers, Hayden pulled me into his side. "I have all the support I need right here," he said, squeezing me tight.

He turned me to start walking away, and Felicia called out his name. I wanted to keep going but Hayden stopped. Inhaling a deep breath, he turned his head in her direction. A look crossed over Felicia's face that was equal parts relief, equal parts pain. "I know what Hookup did around here last year, and I know you feel responsible…but it wasn't your fault."

Surprise washed over Hayden's face, then he quickly looked around to see if anyone had heard her. When it was clear no one had, Hayden returned his eyes to hers. He opened his mouth, then shut it and clenched his jaw. He was silent a few more seconds, then muttered, "Thanks," and started walking away. A small smile graced Felicia's lips as she watched us leave.

"Fucking Izzy," Hayden growled as he stomped off. The farther away we walked, the tighter his hand clenched mine.

"Hey," I said, placing my other hand over the pair of ours. "Calm down."

Stopping in his tracks, he rounded on me. "Izzy had no right to tell her everything that's been going on with me! She shouldn't have said two fucking words to her!"

Alarmed at his anger, I gently placed my palm on his cheek. "He's her brother. Izzy was sharing her own story."

Hayden sighed, "I know...but Felicia didn't need to know. She *walked away*. She lost the right to care..." His voice grew heated again, and his eyes darkened to match. There was age-old hurt in his expression that I had no idea how to fix, if it even could be fixed.

"I'm sorry," I told him. There wasn't anything else to say.

His face softened as an exhale left him. "I'm the one who's sorry. I didn't mean to dump this on you."

Hearing him call his feelings about Felicia "this" made a sharp pain go through my chest, like a burst of static electricity touching my soul. Ignoring the sensation, I wrapped my arms around his neck. Even though it upset me to see the hurt, seeing something real from him concerning Felicia was heartening. "You don't have to be sorry. I'm your girlfriend...that's what I'm here for."

Smiling, he shook his head. "I guess I'm still not used to that. It's been a while since I've...yeah..." He ran a hand through his hair, discomfort suddenly on his face. Right. His last serious girlfriend was Felicia. Again, I felt her presence hovering between us. Even when she wasn't here, she was here.

* * *

We went out to celebrate that night, once again meeting up with Myles, Nikki, Eli, Ralph, and Kevin. Thankfully, Felicia didn't crash the party this time, and the mood in the room was a lot less tense. Even Eli, Ralph, and Kevin seemed less stressed being around Hayden. Myles's win had everyone riding high.

When Hayden and I stumbled back to his hotel room afterward, I wasn't thinking about what I was missing, or how estranged I was from my family, or why Izzy had forgiven Felicia, or if she and Hayden would ever get over their past and find their way back to each other. No, all I was thinking about was how amazing my boyfriend's hands felt on my body. The simplicity was refreshing.

But when I opened my eyes the next morning, the uncomplicated freedom vanished and the weight of the world settled in on me again. Would there ever be a time when everything in my life was going the way I wanted? Or was asking for perfect peace just too much? Yeah. Probably.

The flight back home to Oceanside was uneventful, although quiet. Hayden seemed lost in thought as he stared out the window at the blanket of clouds beneath us. Again, I didn't want to ask him what he was thinking, and I again, I hated that I was too scared to ask.

After the plane touched down, Hayden's phone chimed three times in a row with new messages. I peeked at the screen when he unlocked it, and was a little surprised to see that it was the same unsaved phone number—double fives and double sixes. Keith. I couldn't read the messages from my angle, but I thought I saw the words "miss you" before he deleted them. What the hell?

Frown on his face, Hayden shoved the phone into his pocket and didn't say a word. He clearly didn't feel like he needed to tell me who was contacting him, and I wasn't sure if I had the right to keep asking. This was one of those touchy, privacy gray areas that I was clueless about. Did I keep prying, or did I let it go and hope for the best? I tried to put myself in his shoes, to think about what I would be okay with, but the only thought screaming through my brain was—*Was that really from Keith? Why the hell would he miss you? And why do you make a point of deleting all the messages?*

Hayden could see me staring at his jacket pocket, where his phone was tucked out of sight, but he still didn't feel the need to enlighten me. My skin felt tight as I slowly looked up at his face. *Can't you just make this easy on me? I shouldn't have to ask.*

Hayden's expression was blank, and I didn't know if that was because he was silently daring me to ask him, or if he was just genuinely clueless that I was beginning to drive myself crazy imagining who that text had been from. But he would tell me if Felicia was texting him. He wouldn't keep that to himself. It must be Keith. He was giving him a ride home, after all; maybe he was just making sure Hayden didn't miss his ride. The man had zero patience.

"Something going on?" I asked, hoping that was vague enough to be respectful. And hoping that he answered me with a hell of a lot more than a one-syllable answer.

I indicated his phone, just in case my question wasn't clear, and watched as Hayden patted his pocket. "Huh? Oh …yeah…just…Keith. Everything's fine," he added in a hurry.

A flood of suspicion washed through me at his less than comforting answer. Feeling like my skin was a size too small, I snipped, "Why don't you have his number programmed into your phone? After all this time…that's kind of weird."

Hayden's eyes widened as he stared at me, and he chewed on his lip before he answered. "Yeah, I just… haven't gotten around to… I was going to call Izzy when I got home, set up dinner with her tomorrow night. I think I should talk to her about…about what went down with her and Felicia."

His abrupt change of subject hit my stomach like a wrecking ball. I couldn't tell if he just felt stupid for not having programmed his boss's number yet, or if he was hiding something. But then what he said sunk in, and a web of anxiety crawled up my shoulders, making a knot that no amount of massaging would loosen. "Yeah…that's a…good idea." Shit.

Maybe seeing that I wasn't thrilled about the suggestion, Hayden slowly said, "I can go alone. I know you aren't thrilled to be a part of a conversation about my ex."

Inhaling a deep breath, I considered taking his offer as an easy way out. Then I groaned and cursed myself. Avoiding this wouldn't solve anything. "No…I want to be there. She wasn't just an ex-girlfriend, she was family…a part of yours, and a part of Izzy's. I want to know why your family hurt you just as much as you…don't want to know."

Hayden shook his head, then turned his gaze to the window. "Yeah…" I was just about to ask him what he was thinking about, when he turned back to me and said, "I love you so much. I think you might just be the best thing that's ever happened to me." His words, and the sincerity I heard in them, soothed my fears. For a time.

We went our separate ways after the airport; Hayden went back to his place for clothes, and to catch up on his life, trivial things that often slipped by the wayside, like mail and bills, while I went back to my place. Hayden left baggage claim with Keith. Watching them be all buddy-buddy was still extremely difficult. It probably always would be. Keith was just so…vile…but Hayden had a different experience with him, and while he disliked how Keith treated me, he looked up to him. Kind of.

Casting aside all thoughts of the man I despised, I grabbed my bags, found my truck, and headed home. My mind still wouldn't quiet down, so I turned up the radio and rolled down the windows. Noise was good. It drowned out the voices in my head, soothed my worried soul, and made me forget there was a uniform fit for a strip club in my bag.

As I pulled up to the driveway of my house, the radio blaring country music all but vanished to my ears. I was suffering from shock. I knew it, but I still couldn't comprehend it. Parked in my driveway was my father's enormous heavy-duty pickup truck, and the figure in the driver's seat told me Dad was waiting for me. My heart began to race as I wondered if my outlandish job had somehow succeeded in breaking the ice between us. Would he forgive me now? Would I forgive him? He'd ruined my career, written me off and cast me aside, all because he didn't like who I was dating. But he was my father, and I knew I'd forgive him of everything to have him in my life again. I was loyal too.

Pulling my truck up beside his, I turned off the engine, disbelieving he was really here. Had I fallen asleep on the plane, and all of this was just a bizarre dream? But no, as Dad stepped out of his truck, I knew this was reality. Even my own head couldn't perfect the scowl on my father's lips. If this wasn't a thaw between us, then it must be something more sinister. But what more could he possibly do to me? That realization made me feel more at peace as I exited my vehicle. The worst was over.

"Dad...what are you doing here?" I asked, shutting my door and walking over to him.

Dad's face hardened as he tried to stare me down. Raising my chin, I held my ground. "I saw you on TV," he said. My gut clenched, but I did my best to not let it show on my face. Dad's eyes glinted with distaste. "You looked like a two-bit whore, Mackenzie."

And there it was. Dad truly wasn't holding back any punches; he must be desperate to make me crack. Well, he wasn't going to today. "It was the only job I could get, Dad." Tilting my head, I asked, "Are you really upset about the outfit, or is it the name on the outfit that bothered you so much, you felt the need to wait on my doorstep to tell me how awful I looked?"

Dad averted his eyes, and his face grew stormy. He usually kept a tight rein on his emotions, but like water trickling from a leaky faucet, they were slipping through the facade. "You working for him isn't right. You don't belong there," he said, his eyes snapping back to mine.

There was pain in his features and in his voice. This was killing him. It was killing me too.

Taking a step toward him, I snapped back, "I know! I belong on a bike, racing for a team who understands and supports me. But *you* took that from me!" Before I could stop myself, I poked him in the shoulder.

Dad glanced down at where I'd touched him, and when his eyes returned to mine, the stern stoicism was back. "I did what I had to do to show you what a huge mistake you were making. As a parent, that is sometimes necessary. But not once was anything ever meant to intentionally harm you." His arm lifted, and he extended a finger in the direction of the practice track. "But taking a job with *him* was a definite and deliberate attempt to harm *me*. Your mother would be horrified," he said, lowering his arm. "If the sickness hadn't already put her in an early grave, your betrayal would have."

His words cut so deep, I felt like I was bleeding out; my legs even started shaking. "That's not fair. I only took the job because you...you left me no..." My voice warbled until eventually the emotion swallowed it.

I couldn't believe what he'd just said to me. It wasn't just mean, it was cruel. Anger reignited my voice. "I'm sorry you lost Cox Racing, Dad. I'm sorry you're eventually going to lose the building to Keith. And I'm really sorry you don't like Hayden...but none of that should affect *our* relationship, it shouldn't divide our family! My job aside, the man in my life aside...I'm blood, *we're* blood! And blood should mean more than all that crap!"

Dad only raised an eyebrow at my outburst, but that one gesture spoke volumes to me. "Exactly, Mackenzie. Blood should mean more." Heat flared in my chest as we stared at each other. He was calm and cool, while I was breathing so hard, I looked like I'd just run a marathon.

With those final words, Dad turned around and got into his truck. I stared in shocked silence as I watched him back out of the driveway. By his expression, you'd never know he'd just verbally slapped me in the face. Keith had called him manipulative, vindictive, cold, and I'd never once in a million years thought I would agree with anything that man said, but in this case…goddamn it…Keith was right. My father was taking this too far.

CHAPTER 9

~Hayden~

It was a weird weekend, full of high highs and low lows. And Keith seemed to be behind a lot of it. I knew he wanted the world to see Felicia and me as a couple, but did it really matter? Our racing would speak for itself. And that fucking uniform he was making Kenzie wear... God, it really pissed me off that he had taken someone of her caliber and talent and made her a fucking umbrella girl. She could have worked on the pit crew, she could have been a liaison to the press, she could have been freaking security. There were a hundred jobs he could have given her, but he'd chosen the one that was the most beneath her skill level. He'd done it on purpose to kill her spirit, and hell if I was going to let him get away with it.

Keith's driver was waiting for us in the loading area of the airport when we got there. As we stepped up to the sleek, oversized SUV, I turned to Keith. "We need to talk about Kenzie. That job you gave her is completely—"

Keith interrupted me by holding up his hand. "Hold that thought." Handing his bag to the driver, he told him, "We've got one more joining us, Tom."

Scrunching my brows, I stupidly asked, "Who?" I hadn't even finished my one-word question before I saw Felicia strolling out of the airport, rolling bag in tow. Fuck. I really should have seen that one coming.

Turning to Keith, who was smugly watching his new protégé approach, I murmured, "I'll catch a cab."

Keith snapped his gaze up to mine; he was a good half-foot shorter than me. "You'll do no such thing. If you want to keep racing for me, then you'll get in the car. We have things to discuss."

Anger boiled through my veins as I stared at him. He could blacklist me exactly like Jordan had Kenzie. It would be even easier for him to do it to me too. All he had to do was tell people where he'd found me—confirm the rumor, so to speak—then tell people that I'd hadn't given up that life. No one would take a chance on a rider who was potentially participating in an illegal activity that could get them banned from the sport. I was a high-risk rider, and, because of that, Keith was my only option. Fuck.

Turning my back on him and Felicia approaching, I tossed my bag into the rear of the SUV then hopped inside. I might have to ride home with them, but I didn't have to be friendly. Keith glared at me as he hobbled over to the passenger's side, but I didn't care. If he was going to act like my father, then I would act like his petulant son.

When Felicia caught up to us, she handed her bag to the driver, then got into the back seat with me. An oddly shy smile was on her face as she scooted over as far as the seat would allow. She was wearing the Jasmine-scented perfume that she had frequently worn when we were together. It rewound me back to that time, made it hard to remember that everything had changed between us; sometimes being near her was far too familiar. I scooted closer to the window to get away.

"Hey, Hayden. Great race this weekend," she murmured, her voice smooth and sweet, like velvet over bare skin. Swallowing, I ignored her. She was repeating something she'd already told me anyway.

The driver started the car and pulled it away from the curb, and Keith turned in his seat to look at us. "My two stars...hot damn you two look good together."

That snapped me out of my mood. "We're not together, Keith. Not anymore."

Keith dismissively waved his hand, like that fact was inconsequential. I desperately wanted to mention Kenzie, wanted to talk to Keith about the demeaning job he'd given her...but I was *not* going to bring that up around Felicia. She didn't need to know Kenzie was struggling.

Keith turned his attention to Felicia. "Cutting in on that interview like that was great. They're replaying it almost nonstop. You're getting more exposure than that crybaby who actually won the damn thing. Keep it up." He turned back around, clearly finished with the conversation. That was it? He could have said all that on the sidewalk. And I really didn't think Myles was a crybaby. I wasn't about to defend him to Keith though. That was a fast-track to his bad side.

Shaking my head, I returned my gaze to the window. Unbelievable. Keith just wanted Felicia and me together in the backseat. Like we were going to reconnect with him chaperoning us. Not that we were ever going to reconnect. But even as I thought it, I felt Felicia's fingers brush against my thigh. I pulled away, but I was already squished against the door…there was nowhere for me to go.

"So…sorry about all the texts earlier. Plane rides make me nervous."

Unwillingly, I peeked over at her. Bullshit. The girl I'd known hadn't been afraid of anything. She'd been fearless then, almost recklessly so. I found it hard to believe that she could have changed that much, that something like an airplane ride freaked her out now. Like Keith, she was playing me.

I turned back to the window, ignoring her, but like her incessant texting, that didn't stop her from engaging me. "Does Kenzie know that we speak like that? Does she know we text each other almost every day?"

Keith's eyes were on us in the rearview, and I knew he was listening to everything she was saying. Snapping my gaze back to her, I spit out, "We don't speak. You text me, but I don't respond because I don't want to talk to you."

Reaching up, she put her hand on my thigh. Comfort and disgust washed through me at the same time. "You responded once," she purred. She didn't say it, but I clearly heard the words, *And you'll respond again.*

Flicking her hand off my leg, I turned back to the window. "That was an accident, one that won't happen again."

Felicia was silent as she minutely pulled away from me, but I could feel her smiling. She didn't believe me. And the sad thing was, I didn't entirely believe me either.

Like Keith wanted me to know where Felicia lived, we dropped her off first. I tried not to take in where she was staying, but I couldn't help but look. It was a small house, oddly similar to Kenzie's place. Jesus. Was fate trying to kill me by making them so similar?

Uncrossing her legs in a slow, tantalizing way, Felicia waited for the driver to open her door. Once it was propped open, she looked over at me. "I hope you talk to Izzy soon. Then I hope you text me back. We're good together, Hayden."

Staring straight ahead, I swallowed the sudden lump in my throat. No, we *were* great together. But that all ended the day she walked away.

Felicia sighed at my silence, then exited the car and shut the door. Moments later, we were on the move again. I knew I should take the opportunity to talk to Keith about Kenzie, but I couldn't. That damn boulder in my throat wouldn't let me speak.

Once we were back home, I darted out the door, grabbed my bag and fled to my apartment above Keith's garage. I just wanted to be alone. But being alone didn't help my spinning thoughts. I took a long shower to try and relax my mind, but the only thing I got out of it was clean skin.

Kenzie and I hadn't talked about me coming over later that night, and I kind of felt like I should have my head on straight before I saw her, so I laid down on my bed and stared at the ceiling. All I could think about as I laid there, attempting to quiet my thoughts, was whether I should tell Kenzie that Felicia had gotten a ride home with me and Keith. And she was texting me. And she wanted what we had back. I was sure Kenzie already knew that last part, thanks to that damn party and that damn interview, but she didn't know the other things, and I didn't see how anything good could come out of her knowing.

Giving up on relaxation, I turned on the TV and flipped to ESPN. Just like Keith had said, they were showing the interview that Felicia had crashed. They were also splicing in the kiss from the party. They cleverly weren't showing the part where I'd pushed her away from me. To anyone not in the know, it looked like Felicia and I were teammates *and* lovers…ratings gold. God, I really hoped Kenzie hadn't seen this. It would freak her out even more than she probably already was.

When I finally shut off the TV, it was dark outside. The sun had set hours ago, and I hadn't even noticed. It was a little weird to me that I hadn't heard one peep from Kenzie. Did she make it home okay? Grabbing my phone, I looked to see if I'd missed a text from her, but I hadn't. A little worried, I called her.

A sleepy voice met my ear. "Hello?"

"Hey…you okay? You sound weird."

She sighed, and the sound electrified me. I missed her already. "Yeah, I'm fine…just a rough night."

I sat up on the bed, concerned. "Why? What happened?"

"My dad was here when I got home. He told me… He was just being his typical asshole self." Her voice warbled with emotion, and rage surged through me. Why were both of our "father figures" being such dicks lately?

"God, Kenzie…I'm sorry. Why didn't you call me?"

She didn't answer right away, and nerves started attacking me like rabid animals. Was she hiding something too? "I don't… Nikki's my best friend…I just…I called her without thinking. She came over, and we spent the entire night talking, laughing, bitching. I'm sorry, after she left I felt better, and I...I just didn't think about calling you."

I felt like she'd just socked me in the gut and pulled out my insides. She didn't think of calling me? I was her boyfriend, her rock...shouldn't I be her first phone call? But then, we'd left things kind of strange at the airport. Felicia had texted me on the plane and I'd lied about it to Kenzie. Again. But this time she'd called me on it, and I'd had no good explanation. I was a dick, and I deserved to not be forefront on her mind.

"It's okay...Nikki's your best friend, I get it. Can I come over now though? I'd really love to see you." I had a lot to make up for.

I could hear the smile in Kenzie's voice when she answered. "Yeah, of course."

Thank God. As long as she still let me come over, things were fixable.

I made the drive to Kenzie's house in record time, and, on the way, I came up with something I knew would make her feel better. I was so giddy when I rang her doorbell that I forgot to tease her with a Christmas song.

She looked worn when she opened the door, but happy too. Pulling her to me, I inhaled her fresh lavender scent as I hugged her tight. As we separated, I told her, "Grab your bike, your *good* bike, and follow me."

She raised an eyebrow at my strange request. "Why? Where are we going?"

Smiling, I told her, "We're going to do something we should have done a while ago."

Kenzie looked confused and curious as she stepped inside to get her jacket, but she was smiling too. Part one of making her feel better was complete. Now for part two.

Opening the garage door, Kenzie walked over to her pair of Ducatis. They were both covered in a thin layer of dust, a truly sad sign, and something I was kicking myself over—I should never have stopped taking her where I was about to take her.

Hanging on the wall next to Kenzie's bikes was her old Cox Racing leathers. Pointing to them, I told her, "Take those too. You're going to need them."

Kenzie gave me an incredulous look, but she yanked them off the wall and stuffed them into a backpack. "What are you up to, Hayes," she murmured.

"You'll see," I answered.

A few minutes later, we were on the road, heading to a place we both knew all too well—the place where our love affair had begun. Kenzie popped open her visor when we stopped in front of the gate to the practice track. With wide eyes, she simply stared at me in disbelief.

Laughing, I told her, "Even if you don't have a team to race for, there's no reason we can't still train together. In secret. Just like we used to..."

Her eyes were misty with emotion as she nodded at me. It felt so good to make her truly happy for once; I was flying high as I entered my key card and punched in the code. I picked the lock to the inner gate to get us inside the complex, then picked the door to the Benneti garage, so we could change and prep.

Kenzie changed into her leathers right there in the middle of the dark garage, and I was so captivated, I couldn't move until she was completely dressed. She laughed as she looked me over. "You racing in your jeans?"

I almost told her I'd race naked if she wanted. God… Kenzie naked on a bike. That image would haunt me for days if I ever saw it.

After I finally changed and grabbed my racing bike, we turned on the lights and headed to the entrance of the track. Inhaling a big breath, I absorbed the midnight memories as well as the oxygen. So much had happened here late at night between Kenzie and me that it almost felt like an entirely different track in the moonlight. This was our special place, and ours alone.

Revving my engine, I looked her way. "Race me or chase me, Cox."

I slammed down my visor and immediately accelerated, but Kenzie beat me to the draw, and was a breath in front of me as we entered the track. *That's my girl.*

We breezed through the course for countless laps. We weren't keeping score, weren't watching the time, weren't racing for pride or for our team…we were just having fun. I could tell Kenzie was surging with adrenaline when we finally rolled to a stop. Tearing off her helmet, she callously tossed it to the ground. I took mine off as well, setting it down on the concrete, so I could take in her magnificence with no obstructions.

Her face was beaming as she smiled at me. "That was amazing, Hayden. It was everything I needed, everything I've been missing for so…"

Her words trailed off as she stared at me, then she hopped off her bike and stormed over to mine. I wasn't sure what she was going to do, and I tensed for a second. But then her hands were around my neck and her mouth was on mine, and I groaned in delight. Her kiss was wild, passionate, unrestricted; it ignited everything inside me. *Fuck…yes.*

While she kissed me frantically, I felt her tugging at something. Flashing a quick peek, I saw her unzipping her leathers. God, what was she doing? She had her jacket off and was working on her pants before I could stop kissing her long enough to ask her.

"Kenzie," I panted, "What are you…?"

Pulling back, she stared at me with fire in her eyes. "I want you. Right here."

I looked around at where we were, out in the open, sitting in the entrance to the track, bright lamps engulfing us in light. Fuck, having her right here would almost be like having her in public. I was instantly hard, throbbing with need.

Lifting a leg, I started to get off my bike, but she shook her head. "No…stay there."

God, I'd always wanted to have sex on a bike. I wasn't sure if it could even be done, but I was more than willing to try. Seductive half-smile on her face, Kenzie started slowly undressing. When she was down to just her bra and her underwear, I started working on my pants. Free…I needed to be free.

She reached down to help me, and I hissed in a breath when her fingers grazed me. Fuck, I wanted her so bad. It took some work to remove me from my leathers—I was pretty sure we ripped them—but finally I was free and clear for all the world to see. Kenzie smiled, then leaned over and wrapped her lips around the tip of me. Goddamn, she felt so good, just that little caress made me feel like I was going to come.

She groaned around my cock as she took more of me in, and I gripped the handlebar to steady myself. "Now, Kenzie," I muttered. "I need you now." I needed to be inside her.

Slipping off her bra and underwear, she straddled my bike, facing me. It took some finagling to get into the right position, but once her legs were comfortably over mine, her chest delightfully in my face, she carefully eased herself onto me. Being so deep inside her stole my breath for a second, and I could only grunt as I strained to keep us steady. *Oh, God...*

Straddling my thighs, her feet just barely reaching the pedals, she gently lifted her body, moving her hips away from me. She was in complete control of this; I couldn't do anything but hold us in place, and I loved it. I loved her owning me like this. As she lowered her body and reconnected with me, her face was a mixture of euphoria and concentration. Her moving against me felt so fucking good, sensation was exploding within me, begging for more.

She pressed her chest against me as she rocked our hips together, and I gratefully took a nipple in my mouth; I needed to distract myself, or this was going to be the shortest sex ever. Kenzie's head fell back with a loud cry that echoed around the empty space as I teased her sensitive skin. The sound reminded me where we were. I would never look at the track the same way again, and that made the moment even more electric.

As she bucked against my hips more and more frantically, I had to hold onto the handle bars harder and harder. The bike squeaked beneath us, in harmony with the grunts and groans we were releasing. My feet lost footing on the suddenly unstable concrete more than once, and I almost lost my hold on the precious balance keeping us upright, but as the tension started building, I stopped caring. We could completely fall over and I wouldn't mind—I was so close, and so was she. Panting, her legs shaking, she verbally expressed her need for me with escalating moans and cries. I pressed my head against her chest, my own breaths fast and ragged. *Fuck, I'm almost there…*

Just as my strength was about to give out, I felt it approaching—the rising tide that was going to leave me quivering with bliss. Moving harder against me, Kenzie moaned my name, and I knew she felt it too. The explosion hit her a second later, and she clung to me as she fell off the edge. Groaning, I released a moment after her. The bike beneath us jostled and wobbled, but I somehow managed to keep it steady as we both came.

Spent and exhausted, Kenzie slumped against me. The bike lurched to the side as I lost control, but I immediately adjusted my numb feet and righted the motorcycle. Looking up at her, breath still fast, I panted, "Jesus, Kenzie…that was…Jesus…"

Laughing, she giggled, "I know. I love you, Hayden. Thank you for this."

I knew she meant the midnight racing, but I honestly felt like I should be thanking her for fulfilling a fantasy. Instead, I wrapped my arms around her and whispered, "It was my pleasure, Kenzie. I'd do anything for you."

* * *

Once we were back in Kenzie's bed, spent and satisfied for the day, I dwelled on my promise to her at the track. I *would* do anything for her, and it was time I started. She needed a champion, someone to fight for her in the places where she was failing, and that champion had to be me. It was time for me to use my voice. I was time for me to talk to her father.

The next morning, instead of going to the track, I headed to Jordan Cox's house. I'd never been there, but luckily for me, Kenzie was a little old school; she kept an address book under her telephone in the kitchen, and I'd found Jordan's address inside it.

When I reached the driveway that I knew led to Jordan's place, I began to wonder what I'd say to him. Maybe I should have thought up a concrete argument before coming here. I wanted to command him to stop being an asshole, to get his daughter a decent job, and convince the family to talk to her again, but I knew that a head-on confrontation like that wasn't going to get me anywhere. I'd have to be…nice.

Jordan's truck was parked in front of the farmhouse when I got there. I parked my bike beside it, inhaled a deep breath, then shut off the engine and prepared myself for what was about to happen. Climbing off the bike, I pulled off my helmet and set it on the handlebar. Staring at the hard material, I wondered if I should keep it on. Head protection might come in handy if Jordan got violent again. No…it wasn't going to come to that. I hoped.

Imagining Kenzie, I summoned as much confidence as I could and strutted up to Jordan's door. I knocked, then rang the doorbell twice. I wanted to do it again, but I made myself resist. Pissing him off before he even knew it was me wasn't a good plan.

The sound of shuffling feet met my ear, then the door cracked open. I instinctively puffed up my chest when Jordan's face appeared in the slim space. A tense feeling buzzed through my skin, reminding me of confronting a sore loser after a hard race; I was already in fight or flight mode, with a heavy emphasis on fight. I tried to tone it down, but the instant anger on Jordan's face made that impossible.

"What the hell are you doing here?"

Hoping my voice came out steady, I met his steely gaze without flinching. "I'm here because of Kenzie. What you're doing to her isn't right. She deserves better, Jordan."

That was probably the wrong thing to say. The front door flew open and Jordan stepped onto the porch with me. "And that's you? You're better?"

"I didn't say that," I said, my hands slightly lifting in defense. Inhaling a soothing breath, I knew I needed to fix this before it was too late. "You know what Kenzie's doing for work right now…she told me you came by. I'm hoping, I'm asking…if you could just call in a favor and get her a racing job, she could give up that shit. She has plenty of time to train before Road America, she could be back on the path she's supposed to be on. And she's supposed to be racing, Jordan. It's in her blood."

There was a pleading tone to my voice that I didn't care for, but I hoped it moved him. Kenzie needed this. But his gaze only grew harder, his blue-gray eyes sharper. "Mackenzie made her bed, and now she needs to live with her choices. I'm not going to make it comfortable for her just because she's unhappy with her decisions."

The lid on my anger snapped right off. "She's unhappy with *your* decisions. You're the one who blacklisted her. Without your interference, she'd be racing right now."

"I could say the same thing about you and your interference," he stated, his voice icy.

I tossed my hands into the air. "How can you be such an asshole? She's your daughter!"

He took a step toward me, so we were almost toe to toe, and the desire to battle tinted my vision red. "You don't think I know that?" he snarled. "It kills me to see her throwing it all away…for you. You're not worthy of her."

I know that. Rage fired every cylinder inside me, prodding me toward violence. I wasn't going to start this fight though; Kenzie would never forgive me. But I would definitely end it, if Jordan wanted to take it that far. "You gonna pop me again, old man?"

Jordan took a step back with my words. He shook his head, and the anger on his face diminished. "No," he said quietly. "You're not worthy of me either."

Without another word, he turned and walked back into the house. The door softly closed behind him, and that pissed me off even more. He was dismissing me, like I was nothing. Less than nothing. A lifetime of being treated like dirt beneath people's shoes flooded my brain. I was so sick of being looked down upon. I really thought racing professionally would turn that around, give me just a tiny bit of respect, but apparently not. In some things, I'd never be good enough.

I needed to hit something, needed to do some sort of damage to something. There was nothing around but my helmet resting on my bike though. Picking it up, I chucked it down the gravel. It skidded and tumbled for fifteen feet, long scratches marking up the black paint, making it look worn and trashy. Great. Goddamn it.

Hands clenched into fists, I tried to calm down. I'd known this probably wouldn't go well, I don't know why I was surprised. I wanted to call Kenzie and vent to her, but I couldn't. She couldn't know I'd gone behind her back to confront her dad. She'd be pissed. She didn't want help when it came to her family, she wanted to handle it on her own. And she didn't want me to feel guilty about everything she'd given up for me. But I did, and no matter how often she said she was fine, I knew she wasn't. And I knew it was because of me.

My phone buzzed in my pocket. Pulling it out, I unlocked the screen to see a new message from Felicia on the screen. *'Missing you at the track. Hope everything is okay.'*

I knew I should ignore it. I knew I should automatically delete it and then block her number…but I was fuming, and I needed some sort of release, and Felicia knew exactly what it felt like to be looked down upon. We'd grown up in the same gutter. *'Not really. People are assholes.'*

As soon as I hit send I felt sick. Fuck. I shouldn't have done that. Her response was instant. *'I know. Want to talk about it?'*

Shoving the phone back into my jacket pocket, I kicked a large rock in the gravel. Goddamn it. Now she thought I wanted a conversation. I didn't. I was just venting, that was all. Shit.

Walking over to my helmet, I picked it up to examine the damage. It looked like crap now, all scratched to hell. Putting it on, I stormed back to my bike, started it, and got out of there as fast as I could. I shouldn't have even bothered trying to talk to Jordan. He'd never see me as anything other than garbage someone left on the street.

My rage had somewhat cooled by the time I got to the practice track. Knowing Felicia was probably on the lookout for me, invigorated by my stupid ass text, I did my best to sneak upstairs unseen. When I ran into Keith in the hallway, a new idea started forming in my mind. If I couldn't talk some sense into Jordan, maybe I'd have better luck with Keith.

"Hey, Keith…I'm glad to see you. Can we talk in your office?"

Keith sighed, like he knew what I was about to ask, then he indicated down the hall with his hand. I closed the door once we were inside the room; we definitely needed privacy for this conversation. Keith shuffled to his desk, then sat down beside it. "What's on your mind, Hayes?"

I paced in front of his desk for a moment, collecting my thoughts this time. Maybe if I'd done that with Jordan, things wouldn't have hit the fan quite so fast. When I felt I had a win-win path in front of me, I turned to face him. "The job you gave Kenzie is beneath her. You're wasting her talent. Give her a job. A *real* job. Racing."

Keith sighed as he removed his signature aviator sunglasses. Setting them on his desk, he scrubbed his face before answering me. "I don't have a racing job for her, Hayes. I gave her what I had available, and it might be beneath her, but it's all there is." His eyes turned dark as they narrowed at me. "And I don't like being told what to do. Don't forget that *you* work for *me*."

I shook my head. "I haven't. You gave me everything, and I appreciate it more than you know. In fact, I appreciate it so much…I'm going to get you everything you want."

Keith tilted his head, interested. Good. "What do you mean?"

Holding my breath, I prayed Kenzie forgave me for this. "Cox Racing. You give Kenzie a job as a rider…and I'll get you Jordan's side of the track." *I'm sorry, Kenzie. It's the only way.*

Keith's eyes widened in surprise a second before narrowing again. "How?"

I gave him my most charming grin. "I have my ways."

Keith tapped his fingers against the desk. It was the longest ten seconds of my life. Finally, he said, "All right. I'll make her a racer on my team…*after* you get me the track. You have my word."

My gut felt like he'd punched a hole straight through it. He'd give her a racing job *after* I got him the track? I hadn't actually thought out that part of the plan yet. But…if that was what it took to give Kenzie her life back, then I would find a way to do it. I would need a guarantee though. I owed Keith everything, but that didn't mean I entirely trusted him. Not when it came to Kenzie. "Before I agree to anything, I want assurances."

Keith gave me a calculating look. "What assurances?"

I knew Keith wasn't going to like this, but it seemed like the only way I could win here. "If I get Jordan to sell the track to me…then you make me a partner in Benneti Motorsports." Keith started laughing, then stopped when he realized I was serious. He couldn't back out on giving Kenzie a job if the business was partly mine; I'd just go around him. Raising my hands, I told him, "I'm not saying you have to give me fifty percent, but I want a say in what happens around here. A *substantial* say."

Keith's gaze turned ice cold. "The only way that is going to happen, kid, is if you put your money where your mouth is. No one gets something for nothing. You want in, then you bring me Jordan's side of the track…on your own dime."

My jaw nearly dropped to the floor. "And where exactly am I supposed to get that kind of cash?"

A delighted smirk lightened Keith's expression. "You have your ways, remember?"

CHAPTER 10

~Hayden~

My mind was spinning when I left Keith's office. How the hell was I going to buy the track from Jordan? I'd made good money street racing, but most of it had gone to Izzy and I wasn't a part of that world anymore, so I didn't have a way to get more. I had next to nothing in savings, and what I did have, I was holding onto for Izzy, just in case. And then on top of that, there was the additional problem of Jordan willingly selling his half of the track to me. I'd say he detested me almost as much as he hated Keith. He'd never sell his dream to me. Fuck. One problem at a time.

Nikki was her normal cheery self when I stepped downstairs. Spotting me, she looked around the garage, like I'd appeared from thin air. She waved and was just about to ask me a question, when an unexpected and unwelcome voice interrupted her. "Hayden…do you want to talk now? By your text, it seemed like you were upset."

I was just a couple of feet away from Nikki, staring into her deep brown eyes. They were wide with surprise; there was no way she hadn't heard Felicia say that. Great. My day was getting better and better.

Over my shoulder, I told Felicia, "I said no and I meant no. I'm fine, and I don't need to discuss anything with you."

Felicia's voice was calm and quiet. "All right, Hayden. But if you change your mind, you know how to get ahold of me."

I could hear her boots walking in the opposite direction, but I couldn't pull my eyes from Nikki's to look. Nikki's gaze had alternated between Felicia and me that entire exchange, but once Felicia was gone, her eyes focused solely on me. They were so heated with anger that I thought I better defend myself before she crucified me.

"Keith gave her my number. She's texts me, I ignore her. But this morning...this morning just sucked, and I inadvertently answered her, and I'm begging you to not tell Kenzie about any of that."

Her eyes grew cold, and I knew I'd lost ground with her by asking her to keep something from her best friend. "And why would I do that?" she asked.

Closing my eyes, I inhaled a deep breath. "Because it will fuck us up if you tell her. It has to come from me, it's the only way she'll believe the truth—that I didn't start this, and I don't want it to continue."

She crossed her arms over her chest, clearly not believing me. Great. If *she* didn't, how the hell would Kenzie? Locking eyes with her, I said, "I swear, with everything I have and everything I am, that I don't want Felicia. I want Kenzie."

Nikki scrutinized my face for a few more seconds, then nodded. "I'll give you time to tell her first, but you better tell her."

I nodded, temporarily relieved. "I will. I promise." *When it's right, when it won't hurt her and make her feel like I betrayed her, I'll tell her.*

* * *

After practice, I picked up Kenzie and we made our way to Izzy's for dinner. To talk about Felicia. God, I just couldn't get away from her today.

I felt distant from Kenzie as we rode our motorcycles south. The guilt of what I was doing was weighing me down. There were so many little secrets Kenzie wouldn't approve of, and some she'd downright hate. I knew I shouldn't let the guilt push me away from her, but I couldn't help it; just looking in her direction filled me with shame. She'd given up her entire life for me, and I was lying to her, talking to my ex—however briefly—and contemplating stealing her father's legacy right out from under him. Jordan was right...I wasn't worthy of her. One day she'd realize that, and then *I* would be the one who lost everything.

A brief part of me wondered if I should just get out now, spare myself some pain. But the more logical part of me knew that wouldn't stop the agony. I was fucked either way. And that was exactly why I hadn't wanted to fall in love again, why I'd resisted this. Loss was inevitable, and never easy. Desperately wanting to hold onto something you had, only made the inevitable loss of it all the more excruciating. Staying free and clear of everything was really the only way to avoid pain. After all, you couldn't have the rug pulled out from under you if you never purchased a rug in the first place.

But God...being alone fucking sucked. There had to be a balance somewhere, some way to win in this fucked-up life, some way to have it all. But if there was a way, I had no clue what it was.

When we got to Izzy's, my mood sank for an entirely different reason. Izzy had been just as dead set against letting Felicia back in as me. *She doesn't deserve us.* Those had been her words, not mine. But then, in just *one* conversation, she'd forgiven Felicia from bailing on her—on *us*—when we'd needed her most. And then she'd told her intimate things about our lives that Felicia didn't need to know. It made no sense.

I was so lost in thought, I didn't feel Kenzie trying to hold my hand until she grabbed my wrist to stop me. I gave her a sheepish smile, then clutched her fingers tight. The feel of her soft skin in mine was surprisingly comforting, and I drew strength from her as I knocked on Izzy's door.

Izzy's smile faded when she cracked the door open and saw my face. Letting out a weary sigh, she swung the door wide. "Come on in," she said.

Antonia stepped from her room into view, and I could feel my mood brightening as she skipped to the door. "Hey, Bookworm, you broke out of prison. Good for you." Releasing Kenzie, I reached down and wrapped my arms around Antonia. She beamed up at me. Her feeding tube was still connected, but she looked much better. She was still too thin though; her tiny body was so frail in my arms, it seemed like a heavy breeze could snap her in two.

"Uncle Hayden! Did you bring me a puppy?" she asked, her dark eyes scanning the room for her new pet.

An ache ripped through my chest. With so much going on in my life lately, I hadn't had time to take care of that yet. I needed to move that up my list of priorities. With a heavy exhale, I shook my head. "Sorry, kiddo, I'm still working on that one."

Still not sold on the puppy plan, Izzy gave me an annoyed look, but it quickly fell off her. "How was the race?" she asked. Her hands played with a ring on her finger, twisting it over and over—a nervous habit.

Flicking a glance at her hands, I snipped, "I think you already know the answer to that, Iz."

She sighed, then threw her hands up. "I can explain, Hayden."

Anger began boiling within me as I stared at Izzy. "You talked to Felicia. You told her things she didn't need to know, Iz. And you *forgave* her? After everything she did to…to us?" *After everything she did to* me.

Kenzie cringed, and by the look on her face, it was clear she knew what I'd really been thinking. A hole in my chest cracked open a little bit as I pondered if bringing Kenzie here was a bad idea. I wasn't going to be able to keep my anger in check, and she might take that the wrong way. But this wasn't about Felicia and me, it was more about Izzy and me. Maybe if I thought that enough times, I'd actually believe it.

"Why the hell would you forgive her?" I asked. *Why the hell would you betray me? We were supposed to be a team about this.*

Izzy shifted her attention to her daughter. "It's time for your bath, Antonia. Go hop in the tub, please." Not wanting to leave me, Antonia let out a long, annoyed whine at her mother. Snapping her fingers, Izzy pointed to the bathroom and Antonia finally shuffled off.

"Come on in and sit down, Hayden," Izzy softly said, indicating the couch.

Annoyance surged through me as I trudged inside and took a seat on the couch. Kenzie sat beside me while Izzy closed the front door. Once Izzy joined us, I snapped, "How could you do that, Iz? What could she have possibly said to you that would take back four years of...nothing?"

Kenzie looked uncomfortable, like she felt out of place. I was torn between making her feel better and pressing Izzy for answers. Izzy hesitated, then put a gentle hand on my knee. "I can't tell you why I forgave her, but I did."

Surprise ripped through me like a wildfire. "You can't tell me? Why the fuck not?"

Her expression tightened in irritation before relaxing into a sigh. "It's not my story to tell, that's why. It's Felicia's story, and I promised her that I would let her tell you...when she was ready."

Looking away from her, I felt my face hardening. I knew she had a good point, but Felicia didn't deserve Izzy's loyalty. Not anymore. "There's nothing Felicia can say that will change the fact that she left me. The two of us were..." Flicking a glance at Kenzie, I stopped myself from saying that Felicia and I were on the fast-track to marriage. Kenzie didn't need to hear about that, didn't need to know that I still had Felicia's ring in the very back of my closet. Looking back at Izzy, I said, "She vanished, and it's just too late, Iz."

Izzy gave me a small, sad smile; it made my chest compress like someone was sitting on it. "Yeah, I thought the same thing, Hayden, and sure, it might be too late for some things…but it's never too late to hear someone's side of the story. It's never too late to listen. You should give her a chance."

A chance? Never. Not in this lifetime, and possibly not in the next. Izzy lifted her hands like she was warding off an angry spirit. "Okay, wrong choice of words…but you should at least hear her out."

I'd really been hoping Felicia had been lying about Izzy forgiving her. Now that I knew she wasn't, I didn't know what to think. I felt like the world had been flipped over, and north was now south; I had no idea what direction to take.

Kenzie fidgeted beside me, and a small sigh escaped her. I avoided looking her way while I thought over my options. I didn't owe Felicia anything, but Izzy was right about being open to listening to someone. If I'd hurt someone as badly as Felicia had hurt me, I'd hope that person would at least listen if I was trying to make amends. But fuck, that was so much easier said than done. And would hearing Felicia out hurt Kenzie? Izzy was contradicting herself by telling me to not fuck things up with Kenzie, then turning around and telling me to give Felicia "a chance." I couldn't do both.

I felt the heat of Kenzie's stare all over me; it was like I was inside an oven. When I opened my mouth to give Izzy some sort of response, a firm knock on the door interrupted the silence. Izzy frowned at the front door, then got up to answer it. Still not sure what I was going to do, I avoided looking at Kenzie. We weren't touching anymore either. We were sitting close together on the couch, but I felt like an ocean was between us—an ocean filled with my past, and her sacrifices.

Izzy's soft voice from the door broke the cold front forming in the room. "Hey, now isn't a good time. How about you come back tomorrow night?"

My eyes snapped to the door at hearing her words. *Please tell me* she's *not here.* But it wasn't Felicia at the door. It was worse. Hookup was standing there, trying to come inside, but Izzy had her hands on his chest, physically keeping him out, like her small frame really could. At hearing Izzy's words, Hookup refocused his gaze into the room and instantly spotted Kenzie and me on the couch. "Well, if it isn't my two favorite ex-racers. How's it hangin', guys?"

Confusing feelings of happiness and trepidation swirled through me like a chaotic cyclone. It had been forever since I'd seen Hookup, and a part of me missed him, crazy as that was. I didn't trust him, though, not for a second. I instantly hopped off the couch and stepped in front of Kenzie, shielding her from whatever Hookup might do. "Izzy's right, man, you shouldn't be here."

"Bullshit," Hookup said, pushing his way past Izzy like she wasn't even there. "Iz and Antonia are my family. My *actual* family. I'm not some stray they picked up and decided to keep."

For a second I was so stunned at his comment that I couldn't respond. *Did he really just say that to me?* Son of a bitch.

Izzy seemed to feel the same way. "Tony," she barked, grabbing his arm. "Go, and come back tomorrow."

Hookup shrugged her off and stepped up to me. "I have every right to be here. Unlike some."

Like dogs guarding our marked territory, Hookup and I stared each other down, hackles raised, teeth bared. I was taller than Hookup, and had a bigger build, but even so, I wasn't sure which one of us would come out ahead if the rising tension turned to blows; Hookup was small and scrappy, and I knew from experience, he didn't fight fair.

Clearly worried about me, Kenzie moved out from behind my protective stance. Stepping forward, she put a hand on his arm. "Hookup, don't."

Hookup gave her a look laced with poison. "I don't remember asking your opinion, bitch."

Oh...I don't fucking think so. Lunging forward, I grabbed Hookup's throat and started squeezing. Kenzie's admonishment immediately switched to me. "Hayden, don't!"

I glanced over to see her brown eyes wide with fear. Knowing her concern was for me, I shoved Hookup back. "Don't ever call my girlfriend a bitch again," I seethed.

Hookup rubbed his throat, then predictably, made a move for me. Izzy tackled him from behind, stopping him. Arms around his shoulders, she screeched, "Knock it off, Tony!"

Hookup tried to shake her off, but she wasn't about to let go. "Just leave, Hookup!" I yelled.

And that was when a tiny voice from the hallway brought everyone back to the realm of sanity. "Uncle Tony? Uncle Hayden? What's going on?" We all twisted to look down the hallway. Antonia was standing there, her tiny body engulfed in a massive pink robe. Her dark eyes were wide and watery, and her face was even paler than before.

Izzy instantly let go of Hookup and rushed to her daughter. "Nothing, baby. The boys are just talking. Let's get your pajamas on." She swept Antonia into her bedroom, but not before shooting Hookup and me a warning look.

Hookup coughed into his hand while I obsessively ran my fingers through my hair. Antonia shouldn't have to see crap like that. I should have held it together. The tension in the room melted away, and Kenzie let out a relived sigh. "I'm sorry for sort of choking you," I quietly told him.

"I'm actually glad you're here, man," Hookup said, the look on his face thoughtful. "I've been thinking about stuff…"

A strange surge of hope went through me. Had Hookup finally hit rock bottom? Finally realized that he couldn't keep going on the way he had been? God, for his sake, for Izzy's sake…and for my sake…I hoped he had. "Yeah…what stuff?"

Hookup shuffled his feet and cracked his fingers. "Ah…yeah…well…Izzy said Felicia is back. Crazy, huh? You talked to her yet?"

Irritation cut through the hope in my chest; why was he bringing her up? "I'm pretty sure Felicia isn't what you wanted to discuss."

Hookup gave me a derisive sniff. "No, man…she's not." His small brown eyes shifted between Kenzie and me, and when he spoke, he indicated both of us. "Look, things haven't been the same since you two stopped racing. I haven't been able to find anyone worth half a shit to replace you. I'm not making fucking anything anymore!"

With a sigh, I started turning away from him. He hadn't realized anything, hadn't changed one single bit. Grabbing my arm, he stopped me. "Come on, man, race for me again! I'll be good this time…I promise." I was mildly surprised that he'd actually hinted at doing something wrong in the first place, although he'd certainly skated around outright admitting it.

Shaking him off, I said, "No, I'm done. I told you that already."

Hookup held up his hands as he took a step back. "I know, I know, but there's this big race coming up…50K to enter, man. It's like a mini-Mondo! And since that race went to shit, we've *got* to do this!" His eyes were shining with the promise of a big score, and even I could see the euphoria of addiction swimming in his eyes. "Come on, H," he pleaded. "One last big race, then you walk away and I never bother you again, and everything between us is cool." His hope-filled face twisted to take in Kenzie. "Between all of us," he added.

Kenzie raised her eyebrows at that. "One last race is supposed to make up for the fact that you tried to kill me?" Maybe Hookup sabotaging her bike wasn't attempted murder, but what he'd been doing wasn't exactly a precise science. If I hadn't removed that mini-bomb thing from Kenzie's bike, who knows what could have happened to her.

Hookup rolled his eyes like she was being a drama queen or something. "Please, nobody died. Both of you overacted to that whole situation…which I had nothing to do with," he quickly added, his eyes scanning the room like he was searching for a camera. Wow, paranoid much?

Crossing my arms over my chest, I shook my head. "There's not going to be one last race, Hookup. That ended the day I got hurt in that…unfortunate pileup." My eyes turned to stony fire. It could have been Kenzie in that wreck instead of me. "Thank God nobody *died* in that mess…"

Hookup suddenly looked very uncomfortable, but then he shrugged it off, like it didn't matter—or he didn't want to think about it. He was very good at avoiding what he didn't want to deal with. "Look, I'll give you fifty percent, sixty, whatever it takes. I just...I need to be in that race, Hayden."

Closing my eyes, I let out a soft sigh. "My answer is still no, Hookup. I left that life behind for a reason." Opening my eyes, my expression turned hard. "And you should leave it behind too. That world...it will eat you alive. Things will only end badly for you if you don't get out. For you, and for Izzy and Antonia." Taking a step forward, I pleaded, "If you care about them at all, Tony, then you'll—"

"Screw you, Hayden," Hookup snapped, taking a step back from me. "You don't know what the hell you're talking about. I'm fine, Antonia and Izzy are fine. The only problem we have is the fact that you're being a selfish asshole. *You're* the one who doesn't want to help the family—"

My eyes brightened with fire. Was he fucking kidding me? *I* was being selfish? "Well, as you pointed out, Tony, *I'm not family*! And I really don't see a reason to be here anymore." I held my hand out for Kenzie, and she eagerly took it. She'd probably been ready to leave ages ago.

Izzy came back into the room right as we were approaching the door. "Hayden?" she asked, her voice tinged with sadness.

Pausing, I looked back at her. "I'll think about what you said, Iz. Give Antonia a kiss goodnight for me, okay?" As Izzy nodded, I pulled Kenzie out the door.

My mind was once again spinning as we rode home. We shouldn't have gone over there. In this case, ignorance would have been better. When we got back to Kenzie's place, she was quiet, contemplative. I felt like the distance between us had grown even wider, and I desperately wanted to pull her tight again, but I didn't know how to scoop out the baggage that was wedged between us, expanding every day.

A forlorn sigh escaped Kenzie as she trudged to the kitchen to get some water. Feeling guilty, torn, confused, and a million other things, I followed her. "Are you okay?" I quietly asked as she filled a glass with water from the sink.

She only nodded in answer before taking a long gulp, and I saw right through it. She wasn't okay. At all. "I'm so sorry about all that. I never expected Hookup to show up…he's been MIA lately, and I kind of thought he'd stay that way. I certainly never expected him to ask us to race again." I shook my head in disbelief. After what had gone down last year, did he really think we'd say yes?

Kenzie gave me such an odd expression, that I instantly knew she hadn't been thinking about Hookup. Her tongue loosening, she said, "You told Izzy you'd think about hearing Felicia out. Are you really going to talk to her?"

Even more guilt flooded through me. Why had I told Izzy that right in front of Kenzie? Why was I even thinking about it? "I don't know, Kenzie. Maybe, maybe not. I feel like…" *I feel like Felicia is taking over my life and I'll never get it back until I talk to her.* But I couldn't say that to Kenzie; she wouldn't understand. I wasn't sure if *I* did. Walking through that door wouldn't help anyone. Except maybe Felicia. She wanted my forgiveness, but sometimes I felt like holding it back from her was the only way I could put some distance between us. Why did she leave? Why was she back?

My gaze shifted to the ground before looking back up at Kenzie. "I feel like I shouldn't be talking to you about this." *And I definitely shouldn't have let you come with me tonight.*

Sadness washed over Kenzie's face, like she knew that wasn't what I'd almost said. With lies, secrets, and missed opportunities to communicate blasting us left and right, I felt like our relationship was beginning to slide backward, and while I hated that it was, I didn't know how to stop the momentum.

Kenzie didn't say anything, but she looked pained. Needing to ease her stress, I stepped so close to her that our chests were touching. Cupping her cheek, I softly said, "I'm not going to talk to her. You mean more to me than anything she has to say, and that makes my choice pretty damn clear. Felicia can go to hell. I don't need her anymore, or her explanations."

A true smile finally brightened her expression. "Really?"

Feeling like I was finally doing something right, I nodded before lowering my mouth to hers. "Absolutely."

Kenzie tossed her arms around my neck, and I felt the space between us slowly begin to dissolve. As I kissed her as deeply as I could, I reveled in the bliss of our commitment. It was still just Kenzie and me in this relationship—the two of us against the world—and we were going to be just fine.

I hoped.

But even still, hours later, when we were lying on Kenzie's bed and dawn was inching closer and closer, I worried, and I doubted. Things would never be truly right between us until Kenzie was racing again. That was the only way we were going to work. She shouldn't have given it up for me. I was immensely grateful she had, because I couldn't imagine life without her, but it had changed things too much. Changed *her* too much. She needed it back, and the only way to get it back was by giving Keith Jordan's side of the track.

Bits and pieces of what happened at Izzy's place floated through my mind as the darkness lightened to a deep gray. I forcefully blocked out Izzy telling me she'd forgiven Felicia—why the hell would she do that?—and made myself only think of later, when Hookup had shown up. *There's this big race coming up. 50K to enter. I'll give you fifty percent, sixty, whatever it takes.*

If I was making that kind of cash again, I could have enough money to buy back the track in no time. That didn't solve all my problems—like Jordan refusing to sell it to me, and it definitely added additional problems—like hiding from Kenzie that I was street racing again—but it did solve *one* problem. Finances. I could even help Izzy again too; Kenzie was giving her money from her winnings last year, but Kenzie was living off that money, and it would only last for so long. If I could stock up cash to purchase the track for Keith *and* supplement Izzy's income at the same time, it was a win-win. Or it could be a major bust.

But I'd never know until I tried.

Carefully slipping out of Kenzie's bed, I grabbed my phone off the nightstand and quietly made my way to the kitchen. Wondering if he'd be up at this hour, I texted Hookup. *'Okay, I'm in.'*

His response was immediate. *'Fuck yes! You won't regret this, man.'*

Too late, I kind of already did. *'I have a few stipulations though.'*

'Like what?'

'One, I get seventy percent.'

I could almost see Hookup groaning at my request, but the response he typed back was, *'All right. Anything else?'*

Inhaling a deep breath, I typed, *'Yeah...I do this straight-up on my own skill. You don't touch the bikes—any of them. And nobody can know about this. Nobody.'*

I wasn't sure how Hookup would take that either. Saying yes would sort of be admitting that he'd once tampered with bikes. It would also be shooting himself in the foot by taking away his "edge." He'd have to trust me to get the job done, and Hookup wasn't good with trust. He loved to gamble, but he wanted a sure thing.

His response took a solid two minutes to get to me. *'Fine.'*

Closing my eyes, I set my phone on the cluttered kitchen counter, a counter I still hadn't gotten around to cleaning. It was done. I was going to start racing for Hookup again. This time, my goal was to save Kenzie, but I was going to have to lie my ass off to do it. Great. How the hell was I supposed to do that?

CHAPTER 11

~Hayden~

For the rest of the week, I stewed about the upcoming street race with Hookup. I had no idea how I was going to keep what I was doing from Kenzie, but I knew I had to keep her in the dark. She wouldn't approve. Back when she'd been racing with me, she'd begged me to quit—and that had been before she'd known what Hookup had been doing to make sure we won the races. Her fear of us getting busted by the police and kicked out of the ARRC had finally made her decide the reward wasn't worth the risk. She'd never willingly let me delve into that world again. Not for her. And truly…I wasn't sure if she would be happy with me buying the track for Keith, just so she could race for him. It was a double-edged sword for Kenzie, but it was the only option left for her.

Before I was ready, it was Saturday, and the megarace was finally upon us. Somehow, I had to get away from Kenzie without looking like I was getting away from her. I had no idea how I was going to do it, and maybe, because of that, because of the massive guilt I felt crashing through my chest, I was overcompensating in other areas with Kenzie. Like cleaning her entire house, including the super-messy kitchen counter.

The look on her face when she got back from surfing was priceless. "What...happened?" she asked. By the way she looked around the kitchen, it seemed like she was trying to figure out if she was in the wrong house.

"I told you I'd take care of it," I said, a tired but satisfied smile on my face.

Kenzie grinned as she shook her head. "That was so long ago...I really didn't think you'd come through."

Hating that she thought I'd fail her in anything, I pulled her into my arms. "I will *always* come through for you." My voice had gotten intense on me, and the room suddenly felt thick with meaning. I tried lightening things with a brief laugh. "It just might take me a little time, is all..." *But I will get you your career back, Kenzie. I promise.*

Kenzie wrapped her arms around my neck and looked up at me with love-filled eyes. Pain tightened my chest. I was holding back too much from her; I should tell her one of the many secrets I was keeping. Definitely not racing. Maybe that Felicia was texting me like a mad woman, and I occasionally...responded. But how could I possibly tell her that? She'd be pissed, and that loving gaze would instantly shift into doubt. I hated that look, and I couldn't bare ruining the moment by seeing it. One day I'd have to confess, and soon, before Nikki broke down and told her. But today wasn't that day.

"Is this why you didn't want to go surfing with me?" she asked, her tone amused. "It wasn't because you were too tired?"

That was the excuse I'd given her this morning, and considering all I was doing behind her back, I suddenly felt horrible for telling her that; I was sick of lies. And surrounded by them. "Yeah...I just wanted to surprise you."

"Well, it worked. I am officially surprised." She leaned in to kiss me, and the smell of sand, surf, and sun nearly overwhelmed me. The ocean was one of my favorite places, and nothing beat the way it smelled. Not even engine exhaust, burnt rubber, and fresh gasoline could top it.

Letting the kiss sweep me away, I allowed myself to momentarily forget what was happening tonight, what I was about to keep from her. But in the end, wasn't it just another surprise? A large, dangerous, potentially disastrous surprise that was either going to fix everything...or destroy it. That did not relieve my guilt at all. No, this had to turn out just right if she was ever going to forgive me. And when had anything in my life ever turned out *just right*?

Pushing that negative thought from my mind, I focused instead on Kenzie. Her hair was still in a ponytail and still a bit damp; water droplets from the ends occasionally splashed onto the kitchen floor. Having her in front of me, seeing the life, energy and vitality in her eyes, seeing the love and happiness on her face, it made me want her, made me want her arms and legs wrapped around me, made me want to never let her go.

"You know...there's something we haven't done in a really long time...and now that the counter is clean, I think this would be a perfect opportunity..."

Her eyes sparkled with playful mischief as she looked up at me, and I knew she was onboard with my idea, even before she playfully said, "Yeah?"

As I stared at the heat in her eyes, I instantly regretted cleaning off the counter; sweeping everything to the floor would have been much more satisfying. Squatting down, I picked her up so I could sit her on the counter. She giggled as she laid down on the Formica. Memories assaulted me as I watched the way the spotlights over the island highlighted her body. The first time we'd done this, we'd been keeping secrets too, but from other people, not each other. Well, maybe I hadn't been forthcoming with what I'd suspected about Hookup, but I'd never outright lied about it. Not like now. *I should tell her. And break her heart? She'll leave. Everyone leaves eventually...*

Kenzie sat up on her elbows as she studied me. "You okay?"

That was when I realized I'd been so lost in an internal argument, that I hadn't done anything for a while. Goddamn it. Throwing on a devilish smile, I told her, "Just admiring. Some views need to be savored."

Sitting up all the way, she wrapped her arms and legs around me, devouring me with an all-consuming kiss. *Yes.* Her voracious lips on mine finally silenced all the voices in my head. *Thank you.* I slipped my fingers up her waist, under her shirt, then started pushing up the material. She shivered as my light touch tickled her skin, but I didn't increase my pace or my pressure. Teasing her was almost better than the actual sex. *Almost.*

Pulling her shirt all the way off revealed her slightly damp bikini top. Fuck. Just one more reason I loved the ocean. She reached around herself to undo the back, and I grabbed her wrists to stop her. "Nuh-uh, that's my job."

She grinned and rolled her eyes, then arched her back, sticking out her chest. Letting go of her wrists, I reached behind her back and unhooked her top. As I slid it off her shoulders, I marveled at the creamy skin that no other man got to see. It made a growl of possession want to escape from me. She was mine, and I had no intention of ever giving her up. Not without a fight.

I could only admire her perfection for so long before needing a taste. Leaning down, I sucked a nipple into my mouth. Kenzie moaned, then dropped her head back. She accidentally hit one of the swinging spotlights overhead, making a bright circle of light swirl around her body. Laughing again, she laid down so she was completely on display for me. Damn.

My body hardened as white-hot, urgent need coursed through me. I needed her. Putting my hands on either side of her hips, I grabbed the loose cotton shorts she was wearing and pulled. When I realized she'd removed her bikini bottoms before leaving the beach, I just about came. I had to unbutton my jeans to relieve the pressure.

"Jesus, Kenzie, you're so fucking sexy."

I wanted to tease her, taste her, draw this out for a solid half-hour, but her body bare beneath me was too much, and combined with the turmoil I'd been feeling for the last several days, I couldn't hold out. I needed to be pumping away my frustrations in the warm, loving safety of her body.

Completely undoing my jeans, I shoved them and my underwear down my hips. Then I grabbed Kenzie and slid her closer to me. When we were at the perfect angle, I plunged into her. Sensation overload hit me as her firm body took in all of me. Kenzie let out a loud cry that amplified the pleasure running through me. I could barely breathe it felt so good, and I had to pause, to get myself back under control.

Kenzie squirmed her hips, then wrapped her legs around my waist and pulled us tighter together. Fuck, yes. Hands still firmly on her hips, I inched my body away, then slammed back into her, over and over. The erotic noises leaving her let me know that she was loving every second. I wanted to slow down, wanted to savor it, but I needed more, needed harder, needed faster. When it came to Kenzie, I'd never be sated.

Suddenly, Kenzie's hips lifted and her back arched away from the counter. Even before she let out a long, shuddering cry, I knew she was coming. I slowed my hips so she could enjoy every second of her release, then, when I couldn't take the restraint any longer, I shoved into her again. The explosion hit me seconds later, and I stiffened as the tidal wave of euphoria nearly knocked me over. God, I loved making love to her.

I continued to rock slowly as we both came down. Kenzie slowly lowered her body back to the counter, then removed her legs from around my waist. She stayed there, breathing heavy, all sprawled out on her clutter-free island counter, and I vowed to never get it dirty again.

After carefully removing myself from Kenzie, I helped her get off the counter. While I fixed my clothes, she picked hers up off the floor. Holding her things in her arms, she beamed at me, then kissed me on the cheek. "I'm gonna hop in the shower."

I told her okay, then laughed when her bare butt skipped away from me. For a brief moment, everything in my life felt absolutely perfect. She was perfect, she loved me, we were perfect, and I actually felt like everything was going to be okay.

And that was when my phone chimed with a text message. Even though I'd watched Kenzie leave, I double-checked the hallway before I looked at it. I'd changed my phone so that all the messages sounded the same, so I didn't know if it was Felicia or Hookup texting me; neither one would be explainable if Kenzie saw it, reminding me just how far from perfect we really were.

Guilt nearly blocking my throat, I checked my phone. The text was the unsaved number that I knew was Felicia's. Reading what she had to say made me cringe. *'Izzy told me she talked to you. Are you ready to listen now?'*

No, I'm not.

I managed to have enough control not to type that. But Felicia texted me again like I had. *'Why are you still refusing to talk to me? Is it her? Is it Kenzie?'*

I couldn't stop myself that time. I instantly typed back, *'Yes.'*

She's who I want.

In my mind's eye, I could see Felicia's brows drawing together, could perfectly see the annoyance in her eyes, could easily picture the frustration on her face; I'd seen that look a time or two. *'You can't keep denying fate. And you can't protect her forever. One way or another, she's going to get hurt.'*

I wasn't sure why, but that sounded ominous to me. *'Is that a threat?'* I asked her. I could practically feel my hackles rising. If she thought she could physically start something with Kenzie to get her out the way, then she was in for a brutal surprise; I hadn't entirely left the streets behind me.

Felicia's response sounded condescending, even in text form. *'I don't threaten people, Hayden. It's just the truth.'*

Knowing I should just ignore her, I typed back, *'Not necessarily.'*

Her answering message took a little bit to get back to me. *'Some things are certain. You and I are one of those things.'*

I turned off my phone after that. Felicia wasn't all-seeing or all-knowing. She was guessing I'd go back to her because of all the history we shared, but I wasn't trading in my present for the past. History wasn't enough.

When Kenzie came back into the room a few minutes later, I was still staring at my turned-off phone, contemplating. "Something wrong?" she asked, a clear note of suspicion in her voice.

I felt sick over what she'd just missed witnessing—and over the fact that I'd carried on a conversation with Felicia; I was slipping faster and faster—but there was an opportunity here, and I had no choice but to take advantage of it. "Actually…I kind of have bad news. Keith…he just texted. There are these sponsors he wants me to schmooze. I have to go to this thing in L.A. tonight…and it might run late." My stomach roiled as I stared at her, and I was sure I was about to throw up. *It's all for a good reason.* I just had to keep reminding myself that.

Kenzie's face fell, and her expression grew just a touch more distrustful. "Oh…does he want me to go too? Show off my…goods?"

That instantly enflamed me; her "goods" weren't for anyone but me. Keith had no right to pimp them out. "No. If I see some guy pawing you, I'll punch his lights out…and that won't get us sponsors." I managed a sheepish grin on the end that wasn't entirely fake; that was a true concern, the only part of this conversation that *was* real.

Kenzie smiled at my answer, then frowned. "Is…is everyone going?" she quietly asked.

I knew by everyone she meant Felicia. Having another truth to tell her loosened the shame in my chest. "No…it's just me."

A large grin erupted on her face before she schooled her features, and it made me feel better that at least I'd made her smile.

* * *

To help sell the lie that I was going to a party with Keith, I left Kenzie's house a lot earlier than I needed to. I killed some time in my apartment above Keith's garage, then, when it was late enough, I quietly left Keith's place and headed north to Los Angeles.

Hookup had called me earlier with an address, and I made my way to an area of the city that was routinely plagued with criminal activity. Since what I was doing could not only get me arrested, but banned from my chosen career, I planned on keeping my helmet on and my license plate covered. Hookup had created this ingenious sticky, magnetic film that slipped right over the plate, making it completely unreadable. I'd look like just another random racer in a sea of random racers, and that was the way I needed it to be.

I immediately knew when I hit the right place; both sides of the street were littered with flashy cars and even flashier bikes. I spotted Grunts almost right away. Hookup's massive friend was easy to pick out, even in a crowd. Hookup was standing on the sidewalk just to the left of Grunts. He was on the scrawny side to begin with, but next to Grunts, he looked like a child. When I pulled into a small space next to them, I could see they were still getting organized. Good.

Hopping off my bike, I walked over to Hookup. He gave me a blank look until I lifted my visor and he saw it was me. "H-man! You're here!" He started rubbing his hands together like he was warming them up. "This is gonna be so fucking awesome! God, I can't wait until you cream these wannabes all over the pavement."

"Yeah…remember not to use my name."

The glee on his face instantly shifted to annoyance. "Why the hell not? Your name sells you. People remember golden-boy Hayden Hayes. Bets double when you ride, just because you're a household name."

Shaking my head, I told him, "I know, but I can't use it anymore. I should have dropped it the second I started racing for the ARRC…but it's fine, I'll start over, create a new name for myself."

"Hayden…" he whined.

I crossed my arms over my chest so he'd know I wasn't negotiating on this. "No, Hookup. No one can know I'm racing. And if you're not okay with that, then I'm walking, right now."

Disgust on his face, Hookup spat on the sidewalk. "Fine, we'll ditch the name we spent years building. Not a problem." His tone dripped with sarcasm. He briefly looked over at Grunts before returning his eyes to me. "We'll call you Speed Demon instead."

I cringed. "No."

"Speed Killer?" he countered.

"No."

"Lady Killer," he said with an amused grin.

A small explosion of irritation went off in my brain. "Definitely, no."

Hookup's grin widened as he looked over at Grunts again; his quiet friend smiled back at him. "What?" Hookup said. "It's appropriate. I hear you have Felicia number one *and* Felicia number two both choking your chicken."

His choice of words made me want to roll my eyes, but what he'd said enflamed me too much. Who the hell was spreading rumors about me? "Where did you hear that?"

He shrugged. "Nowhere...I'm just assuming."

Of course he was. Hookup assumed everyone of the opposite sex was doing it. The only person he hadn't ever accused me of sleeping with was his sister. Even though Izzy had a kid of her own, I don't think it occurred to Hookup that she was fully capable of having sex.

"Well, you're wrong," I told him. "Kenzie is the only one who's choking my..." I stopped myself from repeating his stupid phrase, and reworded my answer. "Felicia and I aren't anything anymore."

Hookup smirked, like I'd just said something outlandish that no one in their right mind would believe. "Right. You still have her ring?"

His question caught me off guard. "What?"

He pointed at my pocket, like I had it with me. "The engagement ring you had me get for you. You still have it tucked away? Ready to give it to her when the 'time is right'?"

Shit. I did still have it tucked away, but not to give to her. That was over and done with. As was this conversation. "I'm not here to chitchat, Hookup." I pointed at him, then me. "You and I, we're not on solid ground."

Hookup gave me a derisive sniff. "When the fuck did you get so touchy? That Kenzie chick...she's murdered the fun part of you. I should file a police report."

"You do that," I said, rolling my eyes. "I'll be over there, racing." Not wanting to talk to him anymore, I slammed down my visor and returned to my bike.

It wasn't too much longer before the eager swarms of onlookers started vying to place bets. I didn't look his way, but I heard Hookup loudly announcing me to the crowd. "Ladies and gents, so glad you could all make it. Tonight's race is gonna be epic, and my boy here is going to steal the show. I call him Fun Killer, but don't let his name fool you, he actually can ride...he just can't take a joke."

Looking his way after that comment, I flipped him off. Asshole. Some of the crowd laughed, and I heard bets being placed under my new name. Wonderful. Oh well...the fact that people were betting on me was all that mattered.

When it was my turn to go up, Grunts strapped the camera to my helmet. The guy I was going up against was riding an older Yamaha. My Honda shouldn't have a problem beating the bike, but for a moment, I wished I'd nabbed one of Kenzie's Ducatis from her garage. Her racing motorcycles were slightly faster than my street bike, and I wouldn't mind having the extra edge right now—I needed to win. Immediately after having the thought, I dismissed it. Stealing Kenzie's bike would be a major violation, one she wouldn't quickly forgive me for. Especially if something happened and I damaged it. In the back of her mind, Kenzie hadn't entirely given up on her dream yet—otherwise the Ducatis would be for sale. She was still hopeful for her future, and so was I. Kenzie was going to need those bikes again soon.

Grunts gave me the green light, and I eased my bike onto the street. The crowd around me was screaming, cheering on their preferred racer. The familiar noise and chaos filled me with intoxicating adrenaline. Racing in the ARRC had its own highs, but it didn't quite compare to the raw intensity of street racing. There was a real element of danger here, not the watered-down version on the track. More could go wrong than right on the streets—the crowd knew that, and so did the racers. It amplified *everything*.

When I got to the crosswalk start line, I froze in a ready position. Just like in the ARRC, a bank of lights started the race. My body tensed in preparation as I waited for the red to shift to green. My heartbeat sped up, my breaths quickened—everything inside me wanted to go fast. I could barely contain my need to release the pent-up energy.

Neither could the guy beside me. He kept revving his engine, showing off how eager he was. Rookie mistake. When the moment came, he was either going to stall his bike, or be late on the draw. Either one worked for me. I waited as patiently as my impatient body would allow. The light suddenly changed, and I punched it; I beat the showoff beside me by a solid three seconds.

The crowds dissipated as we sped further into the city. We started hitting traffic as we raced for the checkpoints. Hookup had been scouting the course all week, finding out the best routes to get to each pre-determined place. He'd noted obstacles, construction, higher-patrolled areas, anything that might "legally" give me an edge. Earlier tonight, when he'd called me with the address, he'd spent an hour on the phone with me, debriefing me on everything he'd found out, and while the call had been tedious, I was grateful for his attention to detail; I stretched my lead to five seconds at the first checkpoint, seven at the second.

After I passed the third checkpoint, the final required destination before I could head back to the starting point, I felt damn-near invincible. I had this in the bag! But being behind had given my competitor a much-needed boost, and before I could blink, he was right on my tail, almost riding my rear tire. Cursing my ego for calling the race early, I hunched over the handlebars and pressed on the speed. Faster. I needed to be faster.

I'd developed racing skills in the last year that the average rider didn't know, and I applied them all to give myself a slight advantage. I hung my body off the bike, I ducked low in the corners, rising at the last possible moment. Whatever it took to gain me fractions of a second.

We breezed through red lights, blew past traffic like the cars on the road weren't even moving. My brain catalogued the danger, but my heart didn't care; this was for Kenzie.

The starting line came into view. My heart thudded against my ribcage; he was still too close. One small mistake on my part and he could blow right past me. No. I did *not* go through all this, hide all this from Kenzie, just to lose. Losing wasn't an option. Knowing Hookup wasn't going to help me miraculously win this time, that it was my skill and my skill alone that would save me, I pressed my bike to the max. I just had to not screw up. If I held it, I would be fine.

Clearing all doubt from my mind, I focused on an image of Kenzie. Her warm brown eyes, her full pouty lips, the look on her face when she said she loved me, the way her entire body seemed to glow when she raced.

I was so absorbed in my mental play by play of Kenzie, that I didn't even notice when I crossed the finish line. I didn't notice the race was over until I spotted crowds of people rushing onto the street, forcing me to slow down; I still almost clipped a few. I slammed on the brakes as safely as I could, then turned back toward the finish line to see who had crossed it first. My competitor was slamming his hands on his handlebars, looking pissed, and the swarms of people were heading my way, engulfing me now that I was stopped. Holy shit. I'd won!

Momentarily forgetting that I was hiding, I popped open my visor and scanned the crowd for Hookup. He was striding toward me, hands in the air. "You're back, baby!" he yelled. I wanted to object, but I really couldn't. I *was* back. For now. Until I had enough money to buy the track and return Kenzie to where she belonged.

The boisterous crowd around me was a little overwhelming, but I managed to break free and direct my bike toward Hookup. I was dying to know how much I'd made tonight. I stopped dead in my tracks when I saw who was behind him. No...it wasn't possible. The bystanders were starting to clear out of the street now, as the next race was getting underway. I was still stopped in place, though, staring at a certain someone who shouldn't be there. Felicia.

When Hookup was a couple feet from me, I pulled my attention away from her, and directed my gaze his way. "What the fuck is she doing here?" I forcefully pointed at the intruder behind him.

Hookup looked over his shoulder and shrugged. "I don't know. She showed up, figured she was with you. Great race, man!"

Hopping off my bike, I ignored him and stormed over to her. "You shouldn't be here."

A small smile graced her lips. "I could say the same of you."

As I watched Hookup and Grunts rolling my bike off the street, out of the way, I inhaled a long, calming breath. Barking at her would get me nowhere. "What are you doing here?" I asked, my voice almost civil.

Felicia indicated the sidewalk, and we both started walking that way, following my bike. "I heard about the race, and figured Hookup would be here. I figured it was as good an opportunity as any to try to make amends with him. I had no idea you were still racing for him." When we reached the sidewalk, she turned my way. "Why *are* you still racing for him?"

My answer was instinctively defensive. "I'm not." She raised an eyebrow, and I sputtered an exhale. "It's complicated, and none of your business."

Her smile turned sad. "Seems like everything with you is none of my business these days."

Damn straight. I held in that thought. It was really hard to do.

Felicia sighed in response to my silence. "Hayden, I know I hurt you, I know you don't want to listen to Izzy, don't want to listen to me, don't want to hurt your...your girlfriend...but I need you to understand. It's killing me that you won't even give me a chance—"

"Like the chance you gave us?" I snapped.

With clear remorse on her face, she averted her eyes. Looking around at where we were, I suddenly realized that Felicia now had the upper hand. She could make my life utter hell if she wanted, and if I pissed her off enough, she might want to. But I really didn't want to hear what she had to say. Ever. I just couldn't let her know that. I needed time.

"I'm not ready," I whispered. It was a small enough kernel of hope that maybe she wouldn't rat me out. But still, it surprised me how much the words stung with the pain of truth. I *wasn't* ready. And even if Kenzie was completely out of the picture for some awful reason, I didn't think I'd ever be ready to hear what Felicia had to say. To hear her excuse for ending us. Didn't mean I wasn't dying to know though.

A beautiful smile graced Felicia's lips, throwing me back in time. I'd seen that smile on her so many times before, been the cause of it on so many occasions... The day we'd met, when I'd stopped a group of boys from picking on her. The day I'd made my move and had kissed her for the first time. The day I'd placed an anonymous tip with CPS and gotten her removed from a really bad situation. The day she'd sworn to me that she'd never run away again... So many times before she'd given me that smile, but it had never once hurt like this. *Why did you kill us?*

"Hey...you want to...get something to eat?" she asked. "I bet that diner that we used to go to is still around."

I immediately shook my head. "I don't want to talk about us. There is no *us* to talk about."

Her face softened in compassion. "I know you don't want to talk. That's why I asked you if you wanted to eat. Maybe we'll run into some people we used to know. Remember Kyle? Had high hopes of being a rock star. You ever hear from him?"

I knew what she was doing. Trying to get under my skin by reminding me of our shared history. And fuck if it wasn't working. I was swirling in the past, mesmerized by who we used to be, back before things got complicated. We'd been wild and free then, nothing holding us back or tying us down. We'd done what we'd wanted, when we'd wanted. Antonia had been healthy, and while Izzy had struggled to make ends meet, she'd been able to get by enough on her own. I'd raced for fun, not necessity. I hadn't felt guilty over ending someone's career, felt obligation to do everything I could to help a sick child, or stressed about how long I'd be able to balance it all. My entire life hadn't revolved around other people...just myself. And Felicia.

"Not recently," I answered. "Heard he moved up north."

Felicia grinned, then pointed at the scar going through my eyebrow. "Seeing that sure takes me back. I was absolutely positive we'd get expelled."

I laughed at the memory of her terror, back when I'd gotten the scar trying to pull off a high school prank. The sound fell short when I also remembered that she'd disappeared for an entire weekend soon after that night. That was Felicia. She ran when she got scared. And I'd known that almost my entire life. Could I really blame her for being who she was? Who she'd always been?

Yes. Yes, I could. She hadn't left me for a couple days…she'd left for *four years*. Clearing my throat, I told her, "I need to go. Kenzie's waiting for me."

Her face fell, either because I was leaving, or because I was going to my girlfriend. I wasn't—Kenzie would have questions if I went to her place this late at night—but telling Felicia that put some much needed space between us.

"Okay, Hayden. Another time, maybe."

No, there wouldn't be another time. Not for us.

CHAPTER 12

~Kenzie~

I thought going to events would get easier, but as I stood in the stands at Road America, watching the riders going for their qualifying laps, I felt more despondent than ever. Last year, that had been me down there, busting my ass to prove myself as an equal. And now look at me, strutting around in shorty-shorts and a bikini top. I tried to put on a brave face, but it was difficult. Dad's words kept flashing through my mind: *Your mother would be horrified.*

Having died when I was little, I really didn't know what my mother would think of me, but as much as I hated to admit it, Dad might be right. She probably would have been horrified. Not over what I was wearing, or who I was working for…but because I'd settled. Settled for something that was beneath my talent, beneath the legacy my father had forged for me, beneath my potential. I *belonged* on a bike.

Thinking of my parents didn't help my mood any. I was still the black sheep of the family. I hadn't talked to my dad since that day he'd made those hurtful comments, and I'd finally stopped calling my sisters; it was pretty clear by now that they didn't want to talk to me, they just wanted to argue *at* me. I was blocked from my family just as much as I was from the sport, and every day was just a little more tortuous than the last.

It didn't help things that I was finding myself alone more and more often. Hayden had been absent a lot the last month, doing "appearances" for Keith. I thought it was a little strange how often Keith was pimping out his Golden Boy, but then again, maybe not. Keith would do just about anything to promote his team, and to get Hayden a championship win. The only true surprise was the fact that Keith wasn't taking the opportunity to flash Felicia around too, especially when he could flaunt her next to Hayden, but Hayden assured me that Keith was only taking him to these…parties. That made it slightly more tolerable.

Hayden and Felicia were together now, doing a pre-race interview for ESPN. A part of me wanted to go down to the Benneti garage and watch the whole thing being filmed, but I couldn't do it. I couldn't stand seeing them together. It was like having splinters driven under my fingernails: it hurt like hell *and* it pissed me off. I knew it was nothing but clever marketing—for Hayden, at least—but it still left an ache that took forever to heal.

Eventually, I knew my absence from the garage would be noticed, and I pulled myself away from the glorious sounds of maxed-out engines. I felt like dragging my feet as I sulked back to my post. Keith had hired a couple of other girls this go-around, so at least I wasn't alone, but the pair he'd hired were hardcore, and they got after me for every misstep. Mainly, my job was to keep the riders happy and smile for fans. Their exact words had been, *Flirt with the fans so hard that they think they can take you out back and bend you over*, but hell if I was going to do that.

When I approached the garages, I felt my body tensing. *Please let their interview be done.* Luckily for me, the camera crew was gone when I stepped inside. Unluckily, Felicia was still glued to Hayden's side. He looked frustrated at having her so close, but he didn't seem to be encouraging her to go away.

Even as I noted how naturally good they looked together, angry hairs started rising on the back of my neck. *Back off, he's mine.* Like he somehow heard me, Hayden's gaze swung my way. His scowl softened as he locked eyes with me. Then he cast a nervous glance at Felicia. He said something to her, and she glanced my way too. When she looked back at Hayden, he said something else to her. She asked him a question, and he gave her a brief nod. She smiled in response, then started walking away. What the hell was that about?

I hated seeing them talking to each other, but I knew as teammates they were going to have to chat occasionally. At work. And about work. Anything else would be unnecessary, and Hayden had said repeatedly that he didn't want unnecessary conversations with her.

"Everything okay?" I asked, stepping up to him.

With a devilish smile on his lips, Hayden's gaze raked over my mostly exposed body. "Everything is great now."

There was an excitement in his eyes that made all the unwanted leering I'd experienced today worth it; I'd put up with a lot more to see that look on his face. "What was—?" I stopped myself from asking what he and Felicia had been talking about; it was work, and none of my business. Instead, I asked, "How did the interview go?"

Small frown on his face, Hayden looked over my shoulder. I didn't need to follow his gaze; I could feel Felicia boring holes into my back. "It was…fine."

By fine, I took it he meant misleading and sensationalized. Great. If she'd kissed him again, I just might superglue her lips shut.

I sighed and Hayden wrapped his arms around my waist. "Hey, it really was fine. I swear." I nodded, but I wasn't entirely convinced. With a crooked smile, Hayden asked, "Want to sneak into Keith's trailer? I could give you a backrub?"

By backrub I knew he meant sex. And while having sex here at the track somewhere sounded intriguing and arousing, I was not doing *anything* of that nature in a place where Keith did…Keith things. "I'm good, thanks."

Hayden started laughing, just as Nikki approached us. "Hey, you two…what's so funny?"

"Nothing," I said, an amused smirk on my face.

Nikki smiled like she was in on the joke, then she clapped her hands together. "You guys are going out with Myles and me, right?" Before we could answer, she added, "It's tradition, you have to."

I laughed at her, then looked over at Hayden. He was cringing like he had bad news, and my heart sank. "Sorry, I've got a thing tonight, I can't go." He turned to me. "But you should still go."

Not wanting to appear startled in front of Nikki, I tried keeping it together, but I wasn't sure if I succeeded. "A Keith thing? Way out here?"

His cringe deepened. "Yeah…sorry."

A frustrated sigh escaped me. "It's fine, you have to do what you…have to do."

"Thanks for understanding. I love you." He kissed my cheek, but for some reason, it felt cool instead of comforting. When he pulled away, he seemed…uncomfortable. "I'm gonna go…get ready for my laps."

I nodded as he gave me another kiss on the cheek. Nikki pouted when he left. "You're not going to go now, are you?"

"No, I'll go," I told her absentmindedly. Hanging out with her and Myles would be a good distraction anyway. "Hey, do you know what Keith has planned for Hayden tonight?"

Tilting her head, she thought for a moment before saying, "No. I do my best to avoid talking to Keith. He freaks me out."

I gave her a half-hearted smile. Damn. "Yeah, me too." But not today. No, today I was going to talk to him, and find out just what he was doing with my boyfriend.

It took me a while to get up the nerve to approach him. It wasn't that I was nervous, more like…repulsed. Seeing a chance to speak with him alone, I got over the roiling sensation in my stomach and stepped in front of him.

Lowering his overly large sunglasses, he looked down at me with contempt clear on his face. "What do you want, Cox? If you have a question about your job, ask one of the other girls." With a sigh, he shook his head. "I really wish you filled out that top better. I can barely read the logo."

My cheeks heated so fast I felt like someone had set a match to them. Digging my fingernails into my palms, I made myself ignore the insult. "You're taking Hayden to a party tonight?"

His bland expression didn't change one bit. "Yeah. What's it to you?"

A sense of relief filled me; Hayden had told the truth. It was quickly followed by irritation. "Do you need a model to accompany you?" Keith's gaze shifted over my shoulder, to where I could hear one of the other girls giggling. Before he could invite one of those women to spend all night with Hayden, I quickly amended my sentence. "Do you need *me* to accompany you?"

Keith's lips twisted into a look that was both a sneer and a sarcastic smile. "I think we'll do just fine without you. Now get back to work, and don't worry about what Hayden and I have going on. It's none of your business anyway."

With that, he limped past me, leaning heavily on his crutch like he was trying to emphasize the fact that a Cox was the reason he'd had to end his career, and he would never forget it or forgive it. Jerk.

* * *

Nikki and I met up that night around the same time that Hayden met up with Keith. I tried not to think about what my boyfriend was doing while we joined up with Myles, but it was hard not to think about him when Nikki decided we should all go dancing. Being stuck between hot, sweaty bodies made me want *my* hot, sweaty body. But he was busy. With Keith. Again.

It was really beginning to annoy me, especially when I stumbled back to our hotel room early in the morning and he still wasn't back yet. That was when annoyance turned to worry.

"You were out late last night," I said in the morning, when we were getting ready to go to the track. Since Hayden and I didn't live together, and he didn't come over on nights when he went out with Keith, I had no idea if what time he'd come home was typical. Was he always gone that long with Keith? What the hell did they do at these parties that kept them out until the crack of dawn? Fear and doubt mixed inside me, churning into anger. "I'd think he wouldn't want to do that to you, right before a race."

Hayden's eyes went wide as he stared at me. Was that concern? Guilt? The expression shifted into a smile before I could pinpoint it. "Yeah, I know. I keep telling him that, but you know Keith...stubborn."

That much was true. "I asked Keith if I could come along. He said no."

His hands froze from buttoning his jeans. "You talked to Keith?" he asked, his eyes on his motionless fingers.

A humorless laugh escaped me at the memory. "Yeah. He told me it was none of my business." Asshole.

Hayden seemed to slump. He stayed there a couple seconds before looking up at me, and when he eventually did, his smile was apologetic. "I'm sorry he said no. I would have loved to have you there." His eyes were so sincere when he said that, that some of the doubt began to burn away.

I looped my arms around his neck, and his gaze drifted down to my Benneti bikini top. "Well, I hope your late night paid off for you. I hope you scored someone great." I squeezed my arms together, giving him the best view of my cleavage that I possibly could.

His lips lifted into a seductive smile, and his heated eyes locked onto mine. "Oh...I did," he murmured.

I knew from his tone of voice that he wasn't talking about a sponsor. Pressing my lips against his, I reveled in the fact that, even if it was a painfully short amount of time, at least we were together right now.

Unfortunately, that brief moment ended all too soon, and we were on our way to the track before I could even think to ask Hayden to strip my slutty uniform off me. A wasted opportunity—a phenomenon that seemed to be happening more and more often with us.

When we got back to California, I didn't see Hayden for more than an hour at a time for almost a week straight. I was dying to have an entire evening alone with him—possibly another late-night rendezvous at the practice track—but he was just so busy with work and with Keith, that it never seemed to happen. By the time he did have the night off and he was able to make time for me, I almost didn't want him to.

'You sure you want to come over tonight? The place is a mess and I need to wash my hair.' I almost groaned after sending the message. Was I really using that excuse with him? It was as transparent as a window pane, and just as thin: *I feel neglected, come comfort me.*

'I don't care about messes, and I'd love to help you wash your hair.'

His message ignited a fire that had been dormant for far too long. My fingers typed out a response before I could stop them. *'Okay.'* Yes, please.

Ten minutes later, my doorbell was playing "Winter Wonderland." I tried to stop the smile on my face, but I couldn't. I'd missed him. Tossing open the door, I grabbed his jacket and pulled him inside. Then my arms were around his neck, and my mouth was all over his. He instantly responded, his fingers roving up and down my body.

"Kenzie," he murmured, breaking away from me. "You're naked…"

"I know. You should probably do something about that," I breathed, finding his mouth again.

I felt him shift his weight, heard him kick my front door shut, then he was picking me up and hurrying me to my bedroom. His clothes were half off by the time he laid me down on the mattress. And as he plunged deep inside me, I prayed for time to stop, so this moment with him would last forever. But after that night, he practically became a ghost for the next three weeks.

It was really hard to enjoy the time that we did have together, when I knew that once it was done he'd be gone for…for who knew how long. I was mad at the endless parties, mad at Keith for having them…and mad at Hayden for going to them. It felt like everything in my life was transpiring against me, and I just couldn't win. My job sucked, my family sucked, and my boyfriend…kind of sucked.

I wanted him to make me a priority, to place me above everything else. I had placed him above my career after all. Wasn't it his turn to do the same for me? But he didn't. Night after night he chose Keith, and night after night I grew more and more unhappy.

* * *

Mid-June, we were back at an ARRC event. One of my favorites—Barber. Again, it was torture and bliss to be there, and I began to believe that standing on the outside looking in would never get easier.

Closing my eyes during the qualifiers, I pretended the sound of straining engines was coming from me, from a bike underneath me. I got so carried away in the fantasy, that I could practically feel the movement of the bike, feel the vibration of the road beneath me. It was a glorious, painful daydream. Speed wasn't something I'd felt much of lately. Hayden and I hadn't been spending a lot of time together, and we hadn't snuck into the practice track in forever. I missed it so much. I missed a lot of things.

"Hey, Kenzie, how you doing?" Nikki asked.

My fantasy fizzled around me, and I cracked an eye open to look at her. "Fine."

Nikki grinned like I'd said something really amusing. "You're getting better at doing that. I almost believed you."

Once upon a time I'd been really good at hiding my fear, doubts, and insecurities. But with everything that I'd been bombarded with this year, I'd lost a lot of that deceptive skill. I supposed that was a good thing.

Nikki's smile shifted to a frown. "Hey, I know you don't want to hear this, but once the season is over, maybe you should look for something else. Maybe a job in a different field?"

I opened both eyes at hearing that, and tried my best not to scowl; she only wanted me to be happy, and even a blind man could see that I wasn't happy. But still, racing was my life. How could I leave it behind? Especially when I didn't have anything substantial to fill it with, since Hayden was AWOL most nights. "Thanks, Nik, but this is where I want to be. It will get better." It sure as hell couldn't get any worse.

Nikki sighed, then scanned the room. "Are you and Hayden going out with us tonight?"

Trying hard to completely mask my feelings, I threw on a bright smile. "Hayden's got a thing, but I'll be there." Hayden's "thing" was another party with Keith. God, if these parties didn't end soon, I might lose my ever-loving mind. And hopefully, that was all I lost. Because I really didn't think I could handle losing anything else.

Nikki seemed to believe me this time. She gave me a soft smile before getting back to work on Hayden's bike. Of course, I hadn't confided in her how often Hayden abandoned me, so she didn't have a reason to think that I was anything other than satisfied with my boyfriend. I just hadn't found the courage to talk about it. Doing that would somehow make it seem even more…real. And I wasn't ready for "real." Leaving Nikki to her job, I got to work on my job—shaking my ass.

* * *

When we returned to California, nothing much changed. Hayden still ran off all the time, my family was still on the outs with me, and my job was still incredibly demeaning. To say that life was wearing me down was an understatement. My soul was running on fumes, and I had no idea how much longer I could go before I completely puttered out.

A whimpering noise beside me distracted me from my dark thoughts, and I looked over to see a wet nose pressed against the cage door of the small kennel resting on Hayden's lap. Dark, sad eyes looked back at me from behind the bars, and a mass of black and white fur shivered nonstop.

"We're almost there, sweetie," I cooed at the puppy, trying to reassure her. Casting a quick glance at Hayden, I said with a frown, "I really think you should just hold her. She wouldn't be as scared in your arms." I knew that worked on me.

"She's safer in the carrier," he answered, his expression completely serious.

His comment made me smile; Hayden caring about safety was pretty humorous, considering all he'd done in his life. He'd come a long way from the first time we'd met. At least, I hoped he had.

A few minutes later we were pulling into the parking lot of Izzy and Antonia's apartment building. I parked my truck close to Izzy's door, and Hayden hopped out. His smile was a mile wide; he was so excited to finally fulfill his promise to Antonia. Izzy was less excited, but she had no intention of telling her daughter she couldn't have a companion.

Pet carrier safely tucked under his arm, Hayden strolled up to the door and rapped on it with his knuckles. Izzy answered immediately. Her grin was bright at seeing us, but then her gaze shifted to what Hayden was holding. She sighed as she opened the door wider for us. "Come on in, she's just finishing dinner."

Hayden's playful grin grew as he stepped through the door. He'd been wanting to do this for months, but Keith had been keeping him so busy, this was his first real chance. That, and it had taken him forever to find Antonia's "perfect" dog.

I gave Izzy a hug as I stepped through the door, and she sighed again; I patted her back in commiseration. Having something you didn't want thrust upon you was never easy.

"Hey, Bookworm," Hayden called, stepping into the living room. "I got something for you."

I instantly heard a chair scraping, a fork dropping, and feet pounding toward us. Antonia practically skipped out from around the corner leading to the kitchen. She was pale, but her cheeks were bright with spots of color. Her feeding tube had been gone for a while, and she was much healthier looking. Even her hair was coming in nicely; you wouldn't know what she was going through by looking at her.

Antonia's eyes instantly locked onto the pet carrier Hayden was setting on the floor. "Oh my gosh, is that my puppy?"

Instead of answering, Hayden sank to his knees, opened the kennel door, and pulled out the shivering bundle. Antonia squealed when she saw the Shih Tzu puppy in his arms. Izzy groaned. "Hayden...those dogs are little hairballs."

Hayden's grin was a mile wide as he handed the puppy to Antonia. "Then Bookworm will have to get really good at brushing her. Right, kiddo?"

Antonia was nodding enthusiastically as she hugged the puppy to her chest. "I'll take great care of her, Mom. I promise."

There was so much hope and joy in her eyes, that Izzy finally smiled. "I know you will, honey," she whispered.

She looked over at me, then over at Hayden, and a sudden seriousness blanketed the room. Hopefully she would have a really long time of taking care of her dog ahead of her.

Clearing her throat, Izzy said, "What do you tell Uncle Hayden?"

Antonia instantly wrapped one of her arms around his neck. "Thank you! This is even better than the American Girl doll that you get for me every year." Pulling back, her expression grew serious. "I'd still like to keep getting the dolls though. I love them."

Hayden laughed. "We'll see, kiddo. We'll see." From his expression though, it was obvious he'd be getting dolls for her until the end of time. It warmed my heart to see how much he loved that little girl, and for a moment, I forgot that things between us weren't exactly perfect.

I remembered later that night, when we got back to my house and Hayden excused himself for a "party" with Keith. Maybe it was stupid of me to assume that we'd get to spend the entire evening together, but I really thought I'd get to have him all night long; I was so sick of him leaving all the time. "Again? Just how many sponsors is Keith trying to take on?" I snapped.

Hayden paused in grabbing his jacket. Straightening, he walked over to me and wrapped his arms around my waist. "I know it sucks, but it's something I've got to do. I'm free tomorrow night though? All night, no interruptions. We could go to the track? Break in the break room," he said with a suggestive wriggle of his eyebrows.

God, all that sounded amazing, but I wanted it *now*. I didn't want to have to wait twenty-four hours to spend some quality time with him. I was tired of waiting. "Why do you have to go? You don't owe Keith *all* your personal time. He's got other riders to win sponsors for him."

Hayden's hands started running up and down my back in a soothing pattern, and while his face didn't show any sort of turmoil, I got the feeling he was stalling for time. "I know you don't like Keith," he finally said. "And I know you don't trust him, but...I'm trying to fix things by doing this."

His answer surprised me so much, I felt my eyes bulge. "Fix things? What things?"

Hayden sighed, then shifted his gaze to the floor. When he raised them to meet mine again, they were shining with sincerity. "I'm trying to get your job back. I'm trying to convince Keith to..." Closing his eyes, he shook his head. Reopening them, he whispered, "You belong on a bike, and I'll stop at nothing to get you there."

There was heat and determination in his tone that sent shivers up my arms. That was why he was going to all these parties? To woo Keith into letting me ride? While it was a sweet thought, I had to wonder...what would Keith have him do in exchange for helping me? What *wouldn't* Keith have him do? Fuck, I did *not* like this.

"I've never asked for you to do anything to get my job back," I told him. "I'll get it back on my own." Somehow. And I'd do it cleanly, without making a pact with the devil.

Hayden gave me a sad, lopsided smile. "You've tried everything you can, Kenzie. Your father's influence has blocked you at every turn. Your only chance to race...is leaving me. And I hope you can see why I'd do anything to avoid that."

I could, and I hated that I could, because it gave justification to his actions. Whatever he was doing, he was doing it for me…and that only made it worse. Goddamn it. Why couldn't there be a simple solution to this problem? Why couldn't my dad let me make my own decisions? Why couldn't he just be happy that I was happy? Or I *had* been happy, at any rate.

Shaking my head, I told him, "I hate this. I hate all of this." Felicia, Keith, my job, my family…it all sucked.

With a heavy exhale, Hayden rested his forehead against mine. "I know. I hate it too. But I *will* fix this, Kenzie. You have my word." Before I could ask him what his masterplan was, he kissed my forehead, grabbed his coat, and walked out the front door. As the heavy wood shut behind him, an ominous tremor rang through my body. It felt like something had been cut with him walking away without an explanation, I just wasn't sure what.

I couldn't get my heart to calm down after he left; it was like the stupid organ was trying to break free from my body. The walls around me were suddenly so confining, I knew I'd suffocate if I stayed here any longer. Grabbing my phone, I texted Nikki. *'You home? I'm coming over.'*

Her response didn't take long. *'Yeah, no prob. Everything okay?'*

No, yes…I don't know.

'Just going stir crazy,' I answered. Hopefully she didn't ask where Hayden was, and why he wasn't occupying my time; I didn't feel like explaining it in a text message.

In true Nikki fashion, she didn't ask, she just accepted. *'I'll open some wine.'*

Smiling, I grabbed my jacket and the key to my bike. I sped on my way over to Nikki's apartment. I couldn't help it. Hayden and I hadn't gone midnight racing in forever, and his tease of possibly doing it soon had me itching; I needed relief. I managed to keep it under 80mph though, and that took an extreme amount of willpower.

When I knocked on Nikki's door, she opened it with a bottle of wine in her hand. "You sounded like you needed this."

I smirked at her, but I took the bottle. As soon as I got into the house, I flopped onto Nikki's couch. Somehow being here, where the doubt and mystery surrounding Hayden hadn't seeped into every floorboard, made it easier to breathe. Nikki handed me a large wineglass and I filled it nearly to the brim. Her eyes were as big as saucers when she took the bottle and poured herself a glass about half the size. Sitting beside me, she took a dainty sip. Mine wasn't so dignified.

"So…" she slowly began. "What's up?"

Laying my head back on the couch cushion, I stared at her ceiling and debated what to tell her. "I don't know. I think everything is just starting to get to me." Rolling my head over to the side to look at her, I said, "I miss my life." And truly, that was the crux of my problems. I was in mourning. Still.

Nikki carefully wrapped her arm around me, drawing me in for a quick hug. "I know you do. But…it's temporary. You'll get it all back." Her words were hopeful, but her tone said she didn't entirely believe it. We both knew how stubborn Jordan Cox could be.

I gave her a smile anyway, and she brightened at seeing it. "And you have Hayden to get you through it in the meantime." There was something in her voice that made her sentence more of a question than a statement. She was probing.

With a sigh, I stared into my massive glass of wine. Might as well tell her. "Yeah...thing is...I'm not so sure I do have him anymore." I felt something crack inside me after I said it out loud. I'd been hiding behind denial for so long now, actually admitting that something was wrong was torturous.

Nikki's face was full of concern when I glanced up at her, but not surprise. "What do you mean? What happened?"

A small laugh escaped me as I shook my head. "That's just it...nothing has happened really. But..." I felt my face hardening as I thought of his many disappearing acts. "He leaves all the time, and I really have no idea where he goes. He's says he's doing stuff for Keith, and Keith confirmed that, but..." My chest tightened as anxiety trickled through every inch of me. What the hell was he really doing? "I know relationships are all about trust, but something's off...I know it."

My eyes watered, and I quickly blinked back the tears. Nikki's face morphed from concern to anger. "Maybe he's with her..." she murmured, almost too low for me to hear.

I *did* hear her though. "Her who?" I asked, fear raising the hairs on my arms. "Felicia? Why would you say that?"

"Nothing, no reason," she quickly answered.

Bull. She was lying, I knew it. "That wasn't a nothing comment, that was definitely something. Spill it, Ramirez." *Before my heart leaps out of my throat.*

Nikki shook her head, regret clear on her face. "No, I just... I don't know... It was...wine," she finished, lifting her glass and pointing at it.

Taking the glass from her, I set it on the table. "No, it wasn't wine that made you say that. You said it for a reason, and I want to know exactly what that reason is."

Looking around the room, like she was searching for an escape route, she groaned, "It's nothing, Kenzie. I just...I overheard him and Felicia one day, and...I guess she texts him." Locking gazes with me, she shook her head. "After what you said, I was just making a bitchy conclusion and assuming they were sleeping together. But they're not...I'm sure they're not. Shit."

"Jesus, Nikki. Why didn't you say anything?" And God...was he meeting up with her?

Nikki seemed nervous, which did *not* make me feel any better. Finally, she raised her hands and said, "I would have told you ages ago, but Hayden said he was going to tell you. He said it had to come from him or you'd freak out...and I thought he was right, so I didn't say anything. I like you and Hayden together. I didn't want it to be anything, so I didn't press him. I just sort of left it alone. And then it got to be so far after the fact that I just assumed you knew and didn't want to talk about it. And I couldn't bring it up, in case you didn't know, because then you'd wonder why I hadn't told you, and... God, I suck."

Heat flooded my cheeks as anger mixed with terror. "So, you think he's going off to be with her? You think he's sleeping with her?"

She shook her head. "No, I don't. Not really. It was just the first thing that popped into my head when you said he was disappearing all the time. Jesus, Kenzie. I'm so sorry. I shouldn't have said that. I shouldn't have said anything. They're not sleeping together. There's no way he would do that to you. He loves you. Like, deep-down, soulmate type love."

Setting my wine on the coffee table, I stood up. "He loved her too." And he still might. And even if he wasn't sleeping with her, he'd promised me he wouldn't talk to her, wouldn't rebuild that bridge. Either way, he'd lied to me. He *was* lying to me. And it only made sense that she was the one he was meeting with all the time, not Keith. He could be with her *right now*.

Nikki sighed as she looked up at me. "What are you going to do?" she asked.

Considering the rage that was beginning to burn away the fear and panic inside me, my voice was surprisingly calm when I answered. "I'm going to Hayden's to wait for him to come home." *Or I'm going to scour the streets, looking for him all night.*

Standing up, Nikki put her hand on my arm. "Please don't kill him. You're too young to spend your life in prison." I smiled at her joke, but there was no humor on my face. With how I was feeling right now, I couldn't promise her anything.

I blew past the 80mph mark on the way to Hayden's. I thought the speed might help me calm down, but it really didn't. How could he lie to me? And how long had he been lying to me? Nikki had implied that it had been going on for some time. Had he been talking to Felicia for months? Slowly building reconnections that he'd promised he'd let die? Had he taken it to the next level? Was he screwing her, at this very moment? That son of a bitch! I'd given up everything for him! He was doing this to help me, my ass! He was helping himself.

By the time I got to his place, I was steaming. No...I'd left steaming behind ages ago. I was Mount Vesuvius, about to erupt all over his ass. His lights were on when I got there, which pissed me off even more. *He's still home?* He'd left my house almost an hour ago. What time was this supposed *party*?

Not able to hold back the inferno inside me, I banged on his door with all my strength; the heel of my hand stung a little when I was finished. Hayden opened the door a few seconds later, confusion and irritation on his face. His eyes shifted to surprise when he saw me. "Kenzie? What are you doing here?"

"What are *you* doing here?" I countered. "I thought you had a party to go to?"

He ran a hand through his dirty-blond hair as he drew his lower lip into his mouth. "It got rescheduled. I was just debating if I should call you, or let you sleep."

Right.

Hayden smiled and reached out for me, but I stepped back. His grin fell with his hand. "What's wrong?"

In my anger, my response was blunt. And vague. "She texts you?"

Hayden's brows drew together, and he started to ask who, but then understanding filled his face and he let out a long sigh. "I think you should come in," he said, turning sideways so I could enter his apartment.

He knew what I was talking about. That meant he really was texting her. I hadn't doubted Nikki, but I'd been hoping... Fuck.

I brushed past him, knocking his shoulder in the process. I kind of wanted to tackle him, but I knew that was excessive; I loved him, so I needed to calm down and hear him out. Although, I couldn't possibly think of an excuse that would make his lying okay.

Hayden sighed again as he closed the door; it was heavy with guilt. He turned around to face me slowly, reluctantly. "Look, I—"

I didn't even let him begin his explanation. Storming forward, I shoved my finger into his chest. "She texts you and you text her! You swore up and down that you didn't want to hear a single word she said, then you go behind my back and have conversations with her like it's nothing? What the hell, Hayden?"

He grabbed my hand to stop me from poking him, then he tried interlacing our fingers; I pulled my hand back before he could. Frown on his face, he said, "She texts *me*. I can't stop her from doing that. And I don't have conversations with her. Sometimes she pushes my buttons and I…inadvertently respond. That's it."

"And I should believe that?" I asked, shifting my hands to my hips. "Why didn't you tell me?" I snapped. "You didn't think your ex texting you was worth mentioning?"

"So you could react like this?" he said, indicating my stance. "I was trying to avoid this."

"Maybe if *you* had told me instead of Nikki, I wouldn't be reacting like this. Did you ever think of that?" I asked, staring him down.

He closed his eyes and clamped his jaw shut; I could almost see him counting to ten in his mind. When he finally reopened his eyes, he said, "Yes. That's why I asked her not to tell you. I was trying to figure out how to talk to you…without pissing you off."

Folding my arms over my chest, I told him, "Well, you failed."

"I can see that," he said, lips pursed.

Annoyed by this entire conversation, I tossed my hands into the air. "How did she even get your number, Hayden? Did you give it to her?" If he did, that made his defense one gigantic lie.

His face hardened. "No, Keith did. He gave it to her so she could 'pass on messages' for him," he said, using air quotes. He rolled his eyes. "Like he can't talk to me directly or something. He's meddling in shit he shouldn't be meddling in."

That was the first thing he'd said that I truly believed, and my anger cooled. Slightly. "Do you still have them? Can I read them?"

Hayden hesitated before answering me. "No."

I cocked my eyebrow, confused. "No you don't have them, or no I can't read them?"

He let out a soft sigh. "No, I don't have them. I delete whatever she sends me."

His answer warmed me, but at the same time it made me wonder…was he trying to hide something by deleting them? I almost wished he'd kept them, just so I could see for myself what was going on behind my back. "What does she say to you?" I asked, then immediately wished I hadn't.

Hayden cringed, like he also wished I hadn't asked. "Don't go there, Kenzie. Please."

There was a sudden lump in my throat that I had to swallow three times to get rid of. "Why?" My heart began to pound with anxiety as I waited for him to answer me. *What do you say to her?*

Hayden's eyes drifted to the floor before returning to mine. "Because…I don't want you to get hurt. I don't want to tell you…about another woman wanting me. That can't be something you want to hear about."

It was a perfectly reasonable response, and a one hundred percent correct assumption. I didn't want to hear about Felicia's desires for my boyfriend. Just seeing it in her expression was bad enough. But was that *all* that was going on here? Was this truly as one-sided as he was making it seem? "Do you want her back?" I whispered.

He immediately stepped forward and gently placed his hands on my arms. "No, of course not, Kenzie. I want *you*. That's why I'm with *you*." Was that true? Or was he with me because he felt guilty about everything I'd sacrificed for him? Did he feel obligated to love me? Was his loyalty the only thing holding us together? And did that loyalty extend to our sex life? Or was being my boyfriend enough in his mind, and he felt free to…dabble…in that area? Jesus, I hoped not.

My voice tight, I asked him, "Then where do you go all the time? Where were you *really* going tonight?"

Looking away, he let out a heavy exhale. Was there still guilt in it? I couldn't tell. "Keith's parties, Kenzie." Returning his eyes to mine, he said, "It's work, you know that."

I felt like a rock had firmly settled in my belly. Was he being honest with me? "I know you tell me that," I quietly answered.

His face was a mixture of sadness and remorse. "You don't trust me now." It was a statement, not a question.

"That number that you always said was Keith's...the fives and sixes...that was Felicia, wasn't it?" Hayden nodded, and I felt something in my heart crack. "You've been lying to me about who was texting you. For months. That kind of destroys the whole trust thing."

His gaze drifted to the space between our bodies; even though we were only a foot apart, it felt miles wide. "I know...and I'm so sorry, Kenzie." Eyes pleading, he looked up at me. "I know you don't agree with what I did, what I kept from you, but I swear I did it to protect you. *Everything* I've done is to protect you. You're my world."

The naked sincerity in his eyes, in his voice, it softened the split in my heart, began melting the hurt, filling the chasm. "Then let me in, Hayden. Tell me the truth, always."

Worry morphed his face, and when he opened his mouth, I knew he was going to tell me something big, something I wouldn't like; my heart started beating faster in anticipation. But then his face relaxed into a warm smile. "I will...I promise."

I wanted to question him about that look he'd just given me, but his mouth lowered to mine, and the memory of his face evaporated under his tender touch. I was still angry, still hurt, but I loved him so much...I needed the sincerity I'd seen in his gaze to be the absolute truth, the real bond holding us together. I needed him to love me, needed him to mean every word he'd just said, because that was how I felt about him, and I couldn't handle this being one-sided. I couldn't handle losing him too.

The passion in our argument spilled over into our kiss. It was fiery heat, splashed with a drizzle of chilly ice; the combination instantly ignited me. I ran my fingers through his hair, pulling him into me. His hands explored my body, one running up my back, the other running over my ass. I wanted his fingers over every inch of my bare skin, wanted his mouth over every section of my body, wanted to drown in the ecstasy that would consume us.

Desire overcoming my senses, I moved my mouth to his ear, "Hayden..." I murmured.

His response was a nearly a pant. "Yes?"

"I need you to do something for me," nibbling on his earlobe.

Both of his hands squeezed me tight as an erotic noise left his lips. "God...anything, Kenzie."

Pulling back, I looked him in the eye. His were sizzling with lust; it nearly changed what I was about to say...but there was something I desperately needed from him. "Take me to the track. Race me. Let me feel the rush with you. Then make love to me on the track...and make me feel truly alive."

He groaned, but didn't say anything. He just scooped me up and carried me out the door.

CHAPTER 13

~Hayden~

I was fucking up. I knew it, but I couldn't stop it. Not when I was so close to victory. I had enough money stockpiled from street racing, that I finally felt like I could approach Jordan. What I was going to say to convince him to sell the track to me, I had no fucking clue, but the money was nearly there. Step one was almost complete.

But at what cost? Kenzie was suspicious, even a blind man could see that. If I told her what I was really doing though, she'd ask me to stop. She'd say it was too dangerous, say she didn't need my help bailing her out, tell me that making a deal with Keith would never work and everything I was doing was pointless. Yeah, if I did the right thing and told Kenzie the truth, she'd never get her old life back. And if I kept lying to her...I'd probably lose her. Rock. Me. Hard place.

It didn't help matters any that I'd been juggling so much lately, I'd let something fall through the cracks. Nikki and those damn texts. Goddamn, I wish I'd seen that one coming. I wish I'd told Kenzie about Felicia getting on my case from the beginning. But for some reason, the words just wouldn't form around Kenzie. How could I tell her something that I knew without a doubt would hurt her?

Kenzie was still sleeping beside me. She looked peaceful for once, a small smile on her full lips. It had been far too long since I'd taken her to the track. I was failing as a boyfriend, on multiple levels. All for a good reason, but that would hardly hold up in court.

Carefully getting out of bed, I made my way to the living room to grab my cell phone. Kenzie and I had taken off so quickly last night, I'd left it behind. Good thing too. After I plucked the contraption out of my coat pocket, I saw about a million missed calls and texts from Hookup. I didn't need to read or listen to them to know he was pissed at me. I'd bailed on the race, and he'd had to forfeit the entrance fee. Hookup hated losing money, which was why he'd done what he'd done last year. But being a no-show had been unavoidable. There was just no way I could have gotten away from Kenzie last night, not with her that riled up. So, I'd made a split-second decision, and now I was going to get my ass chewed out for it.

Kenzie finding me at home when I was supposed to be out with Keith had only doubled her suspicions. Problems compounding problems. I'd have to hang out with Hookup from now on before races, to prevent that from ever happening again. That, or come up with a different lie to tell Kenzie. God, I really hated that those were my options. The lie was still working, though, so my best bet was to keep going with it. And besides, Keith was backing me up.

When I'd ask him about talking to Kenzie about it, he'd simply said, "I don't want to know what the hell you're doing, so long as you're doing it to get me Jordan's side of the track."

I'd assured him that was exactly what I was doing, and he hadn't said another word about it. He had to know I was street racing again—he wasn't stupid—but I guess the potential benefit for him outweighed the risk of him losing me if I got caught. And didn't that make me feel special.

Irritated with the complexities of my life, I decided I'd deal with Hookup when I saw him again for the next race in a couple days. Right now, my priority was making sure Kenzie was happy, and figuring out what to say to Jordan to convince him that I was somehow a better option than Keith. No problem.

"Hey, why didn't you wake me?"

I turned around to see Kenzie in the doorframe, wearing one of my T-shirts, and nothing else from what I could tell. Her wavy hair was wild, crazy, unrestrained, just like she'd been last night when we'd shucked all our clothes and had sex on the track. Fuck. That memory was going to stay with me for the rest of my life.

"I thought you needed your rest. We were up pretty late, after all." Slipping my phone back into my jacket pocket, I walked over to her. Kenzie's eyes tracked the movement of my cell, but she didn't ask me anything. The question was burning in her eyes though.

"No messages from Felicia," I assured her, and it felt so good to finally tell her the truth about something. I should have fessed up to that one a long time ago.

Kenzie smiled, but it was a sad one. I wished there was more I could do to let her know she had my heart—my full heart. Felicia was just…a loose end, dangling from my past. One I had every intention of snipping.

"Good," she murmured, but I could tell by the way she was fidgeting that talking about my ex wasn't the way she wanted to start her day. I didn't blame her; I'd rather not talk about her either.

Smiling, I leaned down to give Kenzie a soft kiss. "What are you going to do today?" I asked when our lips parted.

The look of reluctance didn't change as she shrugged. "Don't know. Hang out with Izzy, I guess."

I wasn't too surprised by her answer; Kenzie often spent her free time with Izzy. Keith had relaxed his stance on Kenzie coming to the track, since she was technically an employee now, but he still wouldn't allow Kenzie to use the track—not even on her own bike—so she hadn't come by. I gave her another kiss, since it was all I could do. For now.

We went our separate ways after breakfast, and while Kenzie looked better than she had last night when she'd wanted to rip my head off, I could tell she wasn't happy. I didn't know how long I had until that unhappiness turned to resentment, but I knew the clock was ticking. I needed to fix this, fast.

While Kenzie took off in her truck, I took off on my bike. Not for the track though. I had a pit stop to make first. One that I hoped went well, even though I knew it was a long shot.

Nerves started tugging at my stomach as I rode up Jordan Cox's driveway. The last time I'd attempted this, it hadn't gone so well. And considering what I was about to ask him, I didn't think this time was going to be any better.

When the two-story farmhouse came into view, I let out a long, slow exhale. Compared to all the things that I'd done in my life, this was easy. It was also the most difficult; I'd never cared so much before, never wanted something so much before. I didn't see Jordan anywhere when I pulled up, but his truck was in front of the house, so I figured he was home. Everywhere I looked, I saw something that was broken or breaking. Jordan was doing everything he could to hold onto the track, even let this place fall by the wayside. This wasn't going to be an easy sell.

Pulling my bike up next to his truck, I turned off the engine, removed my helmet, and hopped off. The minute my feet touched the gravel, they felt like they were incased in concrete—every step was a challenge. I couldn't give up and turn back though. I needed Jordan to cave on this, needed him to come through and help me make Kenzie's dreams a reality. I needed a win.

Stepping up to his front door, I paused a moment, then banged on it. I could hear shuffling and grumbling inside, so I waited as patiently as I could for Jordan to appear. In my head, I began running through what I might say to him, but by the time the door cracked open, I still had nothing good.

Jordan's steely blue-gray eyes focused on me, then narrowed into lasers meant to slice me in half. "You're back. Didn't you get the message the first time?"

I couldn't help but frown at that. "Yeah…loud and clear."

"Then what the hell are you doing here?" he asked, his voice gruff.

Trust me, old man. I wouldn't be here if I didn't have to be. "I have an offer for you."

He immediately interjected, "And in return you'll leave my daughter alone? Sold."

My mouth shifted from a frown to a scowl. "Not on the table. If you'll hear me out, I think you'll find that my offer is to your benefit."

Jordan folded his arms across his chest. Lips pursed in amusement, he said, "My benefit. Really."

Glad that he at least hadn't kicked me out, I nodded. "Yes." I inhaled a big breath, then crossed my fingers and blurted out, "Sell me the track." Jordan's eyes widened to almost twice their size. He opened his mouth to speak, and I held my hands up to stop him. "I know the track is sucking you dry, and I know you don't want to sell it to Keith. Sell it to me instead. You'll get that burden off your back, you'll be able to breathe easier, and you'll be able to say that you didn't cave to Keith." God, I hoped that last part wasn't taking it too far, although, it seemed a valid reason to me.

From the stony look on Jordan's face, I wasn't sure he agreed with me. "I'm not selling you the track just so you can give it to Keith, kid. Don't think I don't see the leash around your neck."

I hated that analogy—I was no one's pet—but I understood his fear. "You wouldn't be giving it to him directly. He's making me a partner in the business, so you'll be giving it to me." He still didn't look convinced, so I hastily added, "Please…if you do this for me, I can give Kenzie her life back. I can get her back on a bike. She's drowning without it…"

As my voice trailed away, his smile grew. It was like he was pleased that she was unhappy. "I can get Mackenzie back on a bike with *one* phone call."

Irritation broke through my calm. "Then do it!"

He stubbornly shook his head. "Not until I know she's thinking clearly. And she's not yet." Scowl on his face, he spat out, "Prancing around in Benneti underwear, ignoring the fact that she's hurting her family. You've changed her."

I couldn't believe what he was trying to blame on me. Did he really think I was the cause of all that? "Are you serious? *You're* the one who changed her. Everything she's been doing—you forced her into it!"

"Did I?" he asked, calmness returning to his expression. "Or did her pride send her on this journey?"

Her pride? How delusional was he? "Your pride, her pride...what difference does it make if you're both miserable?"

Jordan's eyes fell to his feet at hearing that. Good. Maybe I was finally getting to him. "Please, Jordan...let me help her."

He didn't do or say anything right away, and a surge of hope flared through me. If he'd just say yes, if he'd just help me do this, then I could get to work on fixing everything.

Finally, Jordan let out a soft sigh and slowly raised his head. I'd been hoping to see resignation in his eyes, but what I saw was about as far from that as you could get. "Selling you the track is essentially giving the track to Keith—partnership or not. And letting Mackenzie race for Keith isn't helping her. My answer is the same as it's always been for Keith. No."

"But, Jordan, I'm not—"

Lifting his hand, he pointed to the driveway. "I've heard your offer, and rejected it. Since there's nothing else to say, you can get off my property now." Lowering his hand, he said in a quiet, lethal voice, "If you come back again with some inane offer from Keith, I'll have you arrested for trespassing." A small smile graced his lips. "Of course, that might be a blessing in disguise. You being locked up might finally help spur Mackenzie to the correct choice of action."

With a shake of my head, I bit out, "Go to hell, Jordan," and turned and walked away. If I didn't leave, I might slug him. His preferred "choice of action" was for her to leave everything in Keith's world behind, including me, and hell if I was going to sit back and let that happen.

I was fuming as I peeled out of Jordan's driveway; I always seemed to leave his house that way. He just excelled at getting under my skin, and no matter how much I thought I was prepared for him, I never was. Kenzie would never fully accept Keith, but I didn't think I'd ever fully accept her dad.

Slightly speeding, I headed straight to the practice track after Jordan's. I needed to work out my aggression in a productive way. When I got to the parking lot inside the compound, I skidded to a stop in shock. Hookup and Grunts were standing there, arms crossed over their chests, looking pissed at everyone and everything. What the hell were they doing here, and how the hell had they gotten inside? You needed a key card and a code to get through the outer gate, and as far as I knew, they didn't have those.

After looking around to make sure no one else was in the parking lot, I pointed my bike in their direction. Stopping beside them, I ripped off my helmet. "You guys shouldn't be here," I hissed. "And how'd you even get in?"

Hookup rolled his eyes like I'd asked him how he'd tied his shoes. "Please. You're not the only one who knows about your secret back door into this place." That surprised me. Years ago, I'd cut a hole into the chain-link fence that surrounded the property, but I'd never told Hookup about it; he knew more about me than I realized. Shit. Was he spying on me?

Shaking my head, I repeated, "You shouldn't be here. Why are you here?"

Hookup's gaze grew icy. It matched Grunts's expression; he always looked annoyed. "To collect you, asswipe. Apparently, we've got to make sure you go to races now, since you feel like they're optional. Where the fuck were you last night?"

Guilt made me want to cringe, but his tone of voice annoyed the hell out of me. "I'm sorry about that, but Kenzie stopped by my place last night. I couldn't exactly kick her out."

Hookup didn't look moved by my argument. "Sure you could have. You just chose not to. And because of that, I lost eight grand."

"I'll reimburse you," I flippantly tossed out.

He nodded, like he was the one who'd suggested it. "Damn straight you will. You'll also race again for me tonight." Grunt made an agreeing sort of noise as he stared me down.

I looked between the two of them, annoyed. "I thought I had tonight off."

Hookup crooked a smile. "You did, but now I have some cash to make up, so you don't. And, word of advice…if you don't want your girlfriend to know what you're doing, come up with a better lie. See you tonight, asshole. We'll be by later to get you."

Great. Now I had a chaperone. "You don't need to do that, Hookup. I'll be there."

"Sure you will," he said, his voice dripping with sarcasm.

I was about to tell him where he could shove his sarcasm, when another person on a bike joined us. My heart started racing as I snapped my gaze over to see which one of my teammates had just busted me. A startling wave of relief hit me when I saw it was Felicia. Her dark eyes quickly scanned the scene, before focusing on me. "Something wrong here, boys?"

Oddly, her presence felt like backup. Maybe that was because she'd frequently been my shield against Hookup and his mood swings. "No. Hookup and Grunts were just leaving."

Eyes locked on mine, Hookup gave me a disdainful sniff. "Yeah…leaving." Shifting his gaze to Felicia, he said, "See you tonight, Felicia."

My brows drew together in confusion when she responded, "Yep, I'll be there."

Not wanting to question her in front of Hookup, I waited for him and Grunts to walk out of earshot. They were heading for the back of the property, where their car must be waiting near the gap in the fence. Great. I hoped nobody had spotted and reported it.

When I was sure they could no longer hear me, I turned to Felicia. "You're watching the race again tonight? Why?" Was that because of me? Did I want it to be because of me?

Her answer surprised me more than finding Hookup at my place of employment. "No, not watching. Entering."

"Why the hell would you do that?" I snipped. My eyes drifted to the open gate leading into the interior of the track. I knew why I was risking it all, but why the hell would she?

Felicia's quiet exhale drew my attention back to her. The expression on her face was sad, full of remorse. "You're not the only one I need to make amends with, Hayden." Her lips broke into a small, mischievous smile that brought back a lifetime of memories. "And Hookup is just about as stubborn as you. The only way he'd hear me out was if I raced for him. For free, of course." She laughed after that, like it didn't matter. To me, it seemed like the only thing that did...why else risk it?

"You're not taking a cut?" I asked, dumbfounded.

Shaking her head, she said, "I'm not in it for the money."

Didn't she understand that what I was doing was dangerous for multiple reasons? "If you get caught...you're done," I stated, wanting her to get it.

"So are you," she countered, her lips in an amused smile.

"It's worth it to me." *Kenzie* was worth it to me.

Felicia's smile faded and seriousness blanketed her expression. "It's worth it to me too."

There was nothing I could say to that, and an odd but comfortable silence fell around us. I wanted to look away from her, head into the racetrack, but I found that I couldn't move, couldn't leave. The resemblance to Kenzie in her features was downright uncanny, but still, there was something about Felicia's face that was uniquely hers.

Memories of holding that face, of kissing every inch of it, of watching it morph into ecstasy, filled my mind. We'd experienced so much together, from such a young age. Sometimes it was so easy to forget the "now" around her, and fall into the past.

Felicia chewed on her lip while we stared at each other, then she said in a rush, "Hayden, I know you needed time, but maybe—"

I snapped back into the present so fast my head hurt. Holding up my hands, I backed my bike away from her. "I can't, Felicia. It's been a really fucked up day, and I just…I can't…"

Remorse was in her eyes again, but she nodded like she understood. "Okay…I can keep waiting. That's worth it to me too."

Like I was fleeing, I turned my bike away from her and hurried to the inner gate. Encounters with Felicia lately were feeling too familiar. The barrier of anger I'd had in place for so long was beginning to fade the more she was around me. And even though I was a dick to her more often than not, I didn't actually want to hurt her. I didn't want to get close to her either. I just wanted to forget she was back and never see her again. But, of course, life wasn't about to let that happen, and now we were teammates off the track as well as on the track. Fuck my life.

After practice, I headed over to Kenzie's, to spend some quality time with her before I had to leave for the race. I really hated that I had to lie to her again about a sponsor party—and right after I'd promised to tell her the truth—but that was all I could think to tell her, and I knew it was something Keith would back me up on. I didn't have a choice but to spout the lie, and it really fucking sucked. I felt shitty all the time, and feeling that way kind of made me want to avoid Kenzie.

Trying to keep things normal, I rang her doorbell with a peppy Christmas song. She opened the door with a smile, and relief poured through me like a flash flood. Thank God, she wasn't angry, which meant she hadn't found out something else in my absence; I really hated this tightrope I was walking.

"Hey, babe, you look amazing." Wrapping my arms around her, I inhaled her sweet, salty scent. Her hair still faintly smelled of the ocean; she must have gone surfing today.

She laced her arms around my neck, and momentary peace filled me; the world was right when she was in my arms. Then she said something that broke the calm. "We going back to the track tonight? I'd really love to…do that again." She let out a seductive giggle at the end of her sentence that made me want to ditch Hookup again. If Jordan wasn't going to sell, then why the hell was I raising money? But I couldn't bail on Hookup. He really would track me down if I didn't show, and then I'd have things to explain to Kenzie that I just couldn't explain.

"Uh…actually…you know that party that was rescheduled? Well, it's tonight." *Fuck, let her believe me.*

Kenzie's arms around my neck stiffened, then she slowly pulled away to look me in the eye. Doubt was all over her face. She didn't believe me, but she didn't want to not believe me either. She was torn. We were both drowning in our own personal miseries. *I'm trying to save us. I swear.*

"Really?" she asked, and by the way her dark eyes were studying me, I could tell what she was really asking was—*are you telling the truth?*

No, I'm lying like a dog. Forgive me.

Swallowing a knot in my throat, I nodded. "Yeah...I'm sorry. I'll talk to Keith, get him to ease up on the parties. You're right, it's getting ridiculous." And pointless, since Jordan would rather see me behind bars than see me get his daughter racing again.

That seemed to satisfy her, and I prayed I could deliver. Hookup was obsessed with gambling, and unfortunately, he had me by the balls. He knew I didn't want anyone to know about my nighttime activities; he knew his blackmail against me far outweighed what I had on him—which was basically nothing since he could easily tie me to the meager evidence I had on him for the bike tampering last year. I was clearly Hookup's bitch now. All he had to do was threaten to tell Kenzie everything and I'd cave and do whatever he wanted. Fuck. Why couldn't Jordan just pull his head out of his ass and sell the track to me? Then all this deceit could be over with.

"Oh...good. I hope he lets up on your schedule. I'd love to actually see you again." Kenzie laughed as she said it, but I saw the hurt in her eyes, saw the tightness in her smile. She'd given up her dream for me, and I was failing her.

I had to bite my tongue to stop myself from confessing everything. Maybe I should confess my sins. It was over with Jordan, so what was the point now? But no...I couldn't give up on Kenzie's dream too. One of us had to stay strong. Jordan couldn't hold out forever. And maybe there was still a way...

"What are you thinking about?" Kenzie asked, jolting me from my thoughts.

Knowing I couldn't tell her anything real yet, I said something relatively close to the truth. "How amazing you look, sprawled out on your bed, wearing nothing but the ring I bought you."

She twisted the silver ring with three looping, intersecting infinity symbols. Then she gave me a devious smile and started walking backward toward the hallway. "What time do you have to leave?" she asked, her voice low and sensuous.

God, I wished I could say never. "Not for a while," I answered, my body already stiffening in response to her.

"Good." She gave me a playful smile, then turned and dashed into the bedroom. It took me exactly three seconds to catch up with her, but when I did, half her clothes were already on the floor. I helped her get the other half off, then laid her down, wearing only her ring.

The silver shone in the bright lights of her bedroom. As beautiful as the infinity ring was, I knew I would be replacing it one day with a proper engagement ring. Something even better than what I'd had Hookup get for Felicia. Assuming Kenzie would still have me after all this was over with. And God I hoped she did, because she was who I wanted. *She* was the girl of my dreams.

I kissed her ring finger, sealing that unknown promise, and Kenzie's gaze turned adoring. "I'm still mad at you," she whispered.

"I know," I murmured. She had every right to be, for more reasons than she realized. Her anger was something I would never hold against her.

Wanting to distract myself from my troubles, I kissed all the way down her bare body. When I worked my way up her smooth legs, Kenzie started squirming in anticipation. I was rock hard, ready to be inside her, but I owed her a little euphoria first. I slid my tongue between her legs. Kenzie cried out, one hand clutching the bed, the other clutching my hair. Desire shot through me so hard, I thought I might come just by listening to her.

Needing to make up for my sins, I slowly stroked and teased her, giving her as much pleasure as I possibly could. Within seconds, both of her hands were clenched in my hair, and her back was arching as a series of breathless pants shifted into one long moan.

I pulled away from her, letting her enjoy the orgasm, and she pulled on me, leading me back to her mouth. Her kisses were fast, hungry, like coming once hadn't been enough for her. She was more aggressive than she usually was, nibbling on my lip, raking her nails down my back. It brought to mind other times…with someone else. Someone I shouldn't be thinking about right now.

As my body throbbed with need, on the edge of exploding, Kenzie groaned in my ear, "God…that mouth… I'll never get enough."

Maybe it was guilt, maybe it was the passion I felt simmering off her, maybe it was desire-induced delirium, but Kenzie's words made it impossible to forget the past, and Felicia suddenly filled every corner of my mind. Her husky voice saying those exact same words flooded my ears, while memories of her body bounced around my head, throwing me into confusion. I couldn't keep thinking about my ex with Kenzie writhing beneath me, it was so wrong. But fuck, I'd never been this turned on before. If I could let it continue, just a moment longer…

Fingers wrapped around me, urging me inside. *God, yes…* Felicia's dark eyes filled my vision—that hungry, needy look she'd get when she was climbing the walls she was so ready for me. And fuck, I was ready for her too.

I pushed my way inside, and even through the overwhelming bliss, a part of me wanted to stop, wanted to take a minute to pull my shit together and focus on who I was really with. But as our hips rocked together, all self-control left me. This felt too good…it was too much to resist, and I couldn't redirect my thoughts. The fantasy pulled me under, swept me away…and I let it. Kenzie's wavy hair tossed over the pillows became Felicia's. Kenzie's breasts under my fingertips became Felicia's. And Kenzie's erotic gasps quickly sending me to the edge were Felicia's. God, I'd nearly forgotten how good she felt.

With the pleasure building higher and higher, I sped up my hips. I needed to come in her, needed to claim her, needed to make sure she never left me again. Felicia met me thrust for thrust, calling out my name. Then she stiffened beneath me, letting out a long, loud cry as she came a second time. Her body internally squeezing mine was too much, and the explosion hit me a split-second later. *Fuck…Felicia…yes.*

As the high wore off, realization hit me like sucker punch to the gut. What the fuck had I just done? My stomach churned with disgust as the memory of my fantasy roiled through me. I'd turned Kenzie into Felicia…and I'd loved it. Holy fuck. How could I have done that to her? And was that cheating? I had no fucking clue, but I knew I felt sick, so…it must be…in some strange way. Goddamn it, I was gonna throw up, but I had to act like nothing was wrong. Like it had just been great sex. With my girlfriend. And no one else. Shit.

I wanted to jump out of bed and bail on Kenzie I felt so wretched. But I couldn't. I had to stay there and cuddle with her while my stomach churned and acid burned my throat. Jesus, I was a horrible person. And the fact that I had to leave Kenzie to go meet up with Felicia didn't make my gut feel any better. I deserved to get caught.

Eventually it was late enough that I could leave Kenzie without suspicion. My heart wasn't in it when I gave her a kiss on the cheek. She shouldn't let me kiss her. "I gotta go, babe. I'll see you tomorrow night?" *Say no. Say you never want to see me again.*

Twisting to her back, Kenzie gave me a warm, satisfied, untroubled smile. "Yeah."

Flashing her a quick smile, I kissed her cheek again, then got out of bed. As I hurriedly dressed, I hoped I'd start feeling better once I was away from Kenzie. I didn't. At all. That sick feeling stayed with me the entire time I waited out the evening at Hookup's place, and as we drove to the event that night, it intensified so much I thought I might have to cancel. Hookup would kill me if I missed two nights in a row though. I had to do this.

It wasn't long after arriving at the bike-lined street that I saw the object of my confliction. Helmet under her arm, Felicia was walking my way with a smirk on her lips and a sway to her hips. The memory of coming inside Kenzie with Felicia on my mind struck me so hard, I had to look away from her. Shit. This was not good.

"Hey Hookup, Grunts…Hayden. How are you boys doing?"

The low tone of her voice sent a shiver through me, and I flashed her a quick glance. Did she know? No…there was no way she knew. It wasn't possible for her to be in my head. Thank God.

Hookup clapped her on the back, like everything between them was back to normal, like she'd never abandoned us. "Ready for this, girl?"

I could feel her smile on me as she answered. "Born ready. This is just like old times, right, Hayden?"

Fuck. Why did she have to bring up old times? I was trying to forget, not remember. Still not looking at her, I mumbled, "Right…old times." Twisting away from them, I turned to my bike. I overheard Hookup explaining the road to Felicia, but I barely paid attention. I needed to dig the thought of her body beneath mine out of my head. That was a long time ago, and some things were better left in the past.

After a moment, I felt her presence directly behind me. With a slow exhale, I turned my head to look at her. A curious expression was on her face as she studied me, and I suddenly wished I could discretely shut the visor on my helmet so she couldn't see my eyes. Erotic moans filled my ears, and I had to turn away again. "What is it?" she asked.

"Nothing," I murmured, squatting to examine my tires.

"Bullshit," she said. "That wasn't a nothing look. You feel guilty about something."

Closing my eyes, I cursed internally. She could still read me like a book, and I really hated that she could. Standing, I made myself face her. She might have been the vision in my head, but I'd still been making love to Kenzie. Not her. "Being here isn't exactly good for my relationship, so yeah, I feel a little guilty." About several things.

She tilted her head to the side in a familiar look of curiosity. "Then why are you doing this?"

Maybe it was the fantasy's fault, but I couldn't help answering her this time. "To get Kenzie's life back. She gave up everything to be with me, and it's not...it's not right." Pain squeezed my chest at admitting that.

Understanding lit Felicia's eyes. "Ah, I see. The two of you make so much more sense now. You feel obligated to her."

Heat boiled my veins, obliterating the guilt. "No, I don't. I love her."

She nodded, like she didn't doubt that. "Sure...but overriding that is this...debt...you feel toward her. How long do you think you have before that feeling drives you absolutely crazy?"

She lifted an eyebrow in expectation, and I clenched my fists. "It's not obligation, Felicia, it's loyalty... something you wouldn't know anything about."

The heat in her eyes grew to match the anger I felt blazing under my skin. "You don't know anything about my loyalty, Hayden. Because you're too scared to find out."

"Scared? You think I'm scared of you?" I seethed. "Hardly. Fine, Felicia. Tell me this huge secret that you think will instantly make me forgive you." Even as anger coursed through my veins, my heart started thumping in anticipation. No...I didn't want to know. I didn't want to forgive her. Especially after that fantasy...

Felicia opened her mouth while I willed her to stop. Thankfully, Hookup grabbed her arm before she could say anything. "All right, girl, you're up!" His head swiveled from her to me, and his grin grew mischievous. "Did I interrupt something? You two need a moment before the race?"

He wriggled his eyebrows suggestively, like I was going to take her around the corner and screw her or something. "No. You didn't interrupt a thing." I turned my back on her then, and stayed turned. If she wanted to speak to me, she'd have to speak to my ass.

I heard her grunt in irritation, then heard her leave with Hookup. Good. Moments later, she was at the starting line, waiting for the light to change. Hookup dragged me to the van to watch her helmet cam. I didn't want to, but it was hard to look away once the race started; the adrenaline of the crowd swept me up.

Felicia made it to the first two checkpoints before her rival, and the crowd was seething with energy, expecting a win from her. Hookup was bouncing up and down, his glee nearly uncontrollable. And that was when the unthinkable happened. Felicia was racing down a main street, when a car suddenly turned in front of her. She managed to swerve and miss most of it, but her rear tire clipped the tail end of the car, and then she was rolling and spinning, her helmet cam showing a dizzying display of alternating dark sky, bright lights, and black concrete. I was on my bike, speeding her way, before I consciously realized it.

When I got to where her bike and body were sprawled on the sidewalk, I skidded my motorcycle to a stop. Leaping off, I dropped to my knees beside her. "Felicia?" I asked, gently raising her visor. Her eyes were closed, and I couldn't tell if she was breathing. Studying her face for signs of life, I said her name again. "Felicia?"

Her eyes fluttered, then opened, and a pained exhale left her. Smiling at me, she whispered, "You do care."

Relief and irritation blasted me. "Not wanting to see you splattered all over the road doesn't equal caring."

Her smile only grew. "It doesn't equal hate either." I could hear sirens in the background, could tell that someone—probably the car parked on the other side of the street—had called the cops. We couldn't stay here, but I couldn't stop staring at her either. Her hand weakly came up to touch my helmet. "You feel something for me…" she whispered.

Grabbing her hand, I lowered it to the ground, away from me. "I do. I feel…regret." Her smile dropped, and the delight in her eyes faded. Something sharp in my chest told me I wasn't being entirely honest, but I pushed the feeling away. This wasn't the time or the place. "Now let's get you out of here before we both get fired."

Felicia gingerly picked up her bike. I could tell she was hurt worse than she was letting on. Her tight jeans were torn open at the knees, and I was sure the skin beneath them was a mangled mess. Since she wasn't wearing gloves, I was positive her hands were scratched to hell too. Luckily her bike was in relatively good shape, and started right away. Hopping back on my own bike, I motioned for her to follow me, then got us out of there as quickly as possible.

When it was clear that we weren't being chased by police or good, law-abiding Samaritans, I started looking for an open convenience store. Felicia needed to be bandaged up before the long journey home, or possibly taken to the hospital if her wounds were bad enough.

Spotting something to my right, I quickly pulled into the parking lot beside it. Felicia followed, and parked her bike right beside mine. Removing her helmet, she asked, "What are we doing here?"

Removing my own helmet, I indicated her ripped clothes. "Making sure you're really okay."

Her smile was warm, pleased, and inviting. She liked it when I showed that I cared about her. It made a confusing ripple of emotions go through me. Irritation and resistance to any sort of fondness for her, followed closely by memories of a time not all that long ago when I had been *extremely* fond of her. Fond enough to want to make her my wife.

"Thank you, Hayden," she murmured, her voice low and sultry. It spoke to the basest parts of me, and I hated that it did.

I wanted to respond to her by telling her that she could take a flying leap and it wouldn't bother me any, but I knew that wasn't the truth, so I remained silent. Seemed the safest course of action.

When we got inside the store, I had her stand still so I could examine her legs. Both knees had bloody road rashes that looked pretty nasty and probably stung like a bitch. While they'd bled quite a bit, I knew from experience that it was mostly superficial. We'd just have to clean and wrap them. There was a pretty deep gash in her palm, but it wasn't anything a little superglue wouldn't fix.

By Felicia's content smile, you'd think we were on a date or something. Seeing that grin annoyed me just as much as it brought back happier times between us. We'd been best friends before we'd turned lovers, and sometimes it was hard to shake that association. But the fact that she'd basically dragged our relationship over the concrete just as harshly as her knees had been dragged made it easier to push the past aside. I just wished she'd quit smiling.

I started walking down the aisles, looking for the first aid section, without even checking to see if she was following, and I only stopped when I found what I needed—bandages, gauze, wraps, peroxide, and glue. A racer's best friends.

As I picked up a bottle of hydrogen peroxide, I noticed Felicia discretely slipping a box of Band-Aids under her jacket. Her back was to the camera, but I glanced up at the front register anyway. The person behind the counter was engaged in a book, not paying any attention to us. "What are you doing?" I hissed at her.

She gave me a look that made it clear I had just said something strange and outlandish. "I don't have anything on me, Hayden. Just my driver's license, and that won't buy Band-Aids."

I gritted my teeth before telling her, "I'll cover it."

Felicia raised a defiant eyebrow; she hated it when I tried to pay for her things. It was such a familiar look, that my chest tightened and my heart surged. God, it had been forever since I'd seen that look…and in a sick way, I'd kind of missed it. "You'll do no such thing. And besides…we used to do this all the time, Hayden. Remember?"

I did, and those memories were dragging me under, taking me back to a time when Felicia had been my entire world. I'd been so sure about her, about us…

Shaking my head, I told her, "We were kids."

She immediately countered, "We still are."

No, we're not. "I walked away from this," I stated, my voice firm.

"From what?" she asked. "From having fun? From letting go and living a little? If that were true, you wouldn't be racing for Hookup." I hated what she was saying, but damn if there wasn't a small nugget of truth to it. I couldn't deny that a very small reason why I still raced for Hookup was the fact that it felt good.

Maybe seeing that she was getting to me, Felicia's voice grew animated. "You used to have fun, Hayden. *We* used to have fun. Don't you remember?" I started to look away from her pleading eyes, but she leaned in, and the intoxicating smell of jasmine brought me back to her. Face firm, she said, "You act like your life is carved in stone, unchangeable, but it's not, Hayden. You can change anything about yourself that you want. Anything."

I knew with certainty that she wasn't really talking about my life in general. No, she was referencing one *very* specific point, one she'd do anything to change. Felicia was basically telling me to choose her over Kenzie, to choose our past, our history, our shared connection. And there was a microscopic part of me that was tempted to go along with her desires. That was why when she handed me a bottle of superglue, I subtly slipped it into my jacket pocket instead of putting it back on the shelf.

Felicia gave me a crooked smile. "There's the guy I used to know."

Grabbing a few more things, I quietly told her, "Let's go."

She giggled as she darted for the door, but I couldn't share her merriment. A disorienting blend of disgust and excitement was coursing through me, and I couldn't decide if I was going to be sick, or if I was having a great time. All I knew was that everything I was doing right now was wrong. Really, really wrong. The second I was outside, I wanted to go back in and pay for all the crap we'd taken. It was too late though; there was no turning back.

We hurried to our bikes waiting for us in a dark corner of the lot. I tried not to think about all the ways I'd fucked up tonight as Felicia ducked between the bikes. My melancholy mood worsened as I wondered why she was kicking off her boots. When she started unbuttoning her jeans, I figured it out. "What are you doing?" I asked, knowing full well why she was undressing.

Felicia gave me an odd look, but didn't stop removing her jeans. "You wanted me to get cleaned up. Can't do much with super-tight denim wrapped around me."

I was assaulted by the sight of her long legs and barely-there underwear. Jesus Christ, if Kenzie knew...if she somehow came across us...I was screwed. Thoroughly, royally screwed. God, I was a horrible person. *I'm sorry, Kenzie.*

Felicia had her hand out as I stood there staring in shock and wallowing in shame. She cleared her throat and I finally realized what she wanted. As quickly as I could, I handed her the first aid stuff, then turned my back on her. Her deep throaty laugh met my ear. "I don't care if you look, Hayden. I like it when you look."

Heat rushed through my chest and up to my face, and I honestly couldn't tell if I was embarrassed for getting caught staring, or if I was enticed by her comment. I tried to bring the image of Kenzie in her underwear to my mind. It was surprisingly difficult to do…my mind was too full of the "now."

I heard Felicia hiss in a sharp breath, and turned my head to look at her. She was struggling with pouring the peroxide on her knees and wiping away the blood. Cursing under my breath, I shifted so I could help her. Grabbing the peroxide and gauze pad from her hands, I squatted down to get closer to her knees. Even though the dabbing and burning was obviously causing her discomfort, she flashed pained smiles at me whenever she could. Once she was as clean as I could get her, I gauzed and wrapped her knees. "Okay, you can put your pants on now," I murmured, avoiding looking at her lean, smooth legs.

"You sure?" she asked, her fingers threading through my hair.

Instantly, I stood all the way up, took a step back, and turned around. I hadn't been fast enough though. A tingle of excitement ran down my spine, which only made me feel worse. "Positive. Put on your pants so I can fix your hands."

She sighed, but I could hear her complying with my request. When she was decently dressed, I looked back at her. She had her palms out to me, almost in supplication. "I'm yours," she whispered. "Fix me."

I had to swallow a lump in my throat as her words struck a nerve. *No, you* were *mine, and I* had *thought I could fix you, keep you, make you happy enough to stay. But that hadn't been the case, and it will never be the case. You belong to no one but yourself. And I need more than that.*

I finished cleaning her up in silence. There was nothing more to say anyway.

CHAPTER 14

~Kenzie~

Time was moving so slowly, and yet, at the same time, it was speeding by faster than I could handle. It was already mid-July, and we were in Monterey, California for the fourth race of the season. The fourth race... There was only one left after this. One left, and I hadn't raced at all. I was missing everything. The hole inside me had grown so large, I didn't even recognize myself anymore. My dream was gone, my family was shattered beyond repair, and I was earning a living visually entertaining men. I sickened myself. I didn't even have Hayden to fall back on anymore. Not one hundred percent. He'd kept things from me, and the sting of that betrayal went deep.

Trust was such a funny thing. There were moments we were together when I would have flung myself into the abyss, trusting that Hayden would catch me. Then there were other times, darker times, when I doubted if he even wanted to be with me. It was a constant sword in my gut being pulled, pushed, prodded, and jostled; every direction I moved hurt, and there was no relief. Ever.

Obviously, today was one of the darker days.

"Hey, how are you doing, Kenzie?"

I looked over to see Myles and Nikki both giving me worried glances. Indicating the skimpy outfit I was wearing, I sarcastically said, "I'm great. Can't you tell?"

Myles's eyes drifted down my body. I could tell seeing me like that didn't please him though; he was scowling. "You should be out there riding, Kenzie. You should be right on my ass, chasing me to the final five. It should be you…not Hayden."

He still hadn't warmed to my boyfriend, and I didn't blame him. Besides the fact that Myles only briefly saw him at events, I was sure Nikki had told him everything about Felicia and Hayden's little texting habit. God, I hoped he wasn't still texting her. I'd considered stealing his phone and going through it on several occasions, but I hadn't stooped to that level yet.

"Hayden deserves it too, Myles. He's worked just as hard." He was currently sitting in third place, right behind Myles and Jimmy. Felicia was in fourth. Something I tried very hard not to think about.

Myles rolled his eyes and looked away, annoyance clear on his face. Instead of placing blame with my father, a man Myles deeply respected, Myles was laying one hundred percent of the blame on Hayden. I supposed it was easier that way for him. Being disappointed by someone you cared about left ugly scars across the soul.

"So," Nikki said, clearing her throat. "We're all going out tonight, right?" She looked at me when she said it. Myles was already in; he'd probably picked the place.

I shook my head. "Hayden won't be. He has a thing with Keith." I couldn't keep the sneer out of my voice. I was getting really sick of Keith stealing my boyfriend all the time. And parading him around at parties…it was a flimsy excuse, one that stretched my trust to its limits.

Nikki scoffed, like her trust had already snapped. "Right…well, guess it's the three musketeers then."

Over Nikki's shoulder, I saw Felicia walk by, a satisfied smile on her face. The three of us were sitting on a patch of grass in what was considered neutral territory, so Keith wouldn't bust Myles's ass. Felicia was holding two coffees, one in each hand. She was clearly walking back to the Benneti garage to get ready for the autograph session. Was one of those coffees for Hayden? Better not be.

Nikki saw my attention shift and looked over to see what I was looking at. She glanced back at me with a calculating expression on her face, then yelled, "Hey, Felicia! Come here!"

I almost reached out and smacked her. "What are you doing?" I hissed.

"Giving you peace of mind," she told me.

Right. As if that was possible anymore.

Felicia looked confused at first; Nikki didn't talk to her much, and I *never* talked to her. She glanced around like she was searching for an attacker, then she slowly sauntered our way. "What's up?" she asked, suspicion in her voice.

Nikki's smile was saccharin sweet. "We're all going out tonight, and we thought it would be great if you came along." I had to grab my hand and hold it in my lap to keep from socking her in the arm. What the fuck was Nikki doing?

Felicia's eyes widened in shock, then she smiled. "That's very sweet…but I can't. Keith is taking me to some party thing tonight. Sorry." She shrugged, then walked away. I felt like that hole in my chest had just tripled in size; next to nothing was holding me together now. She was going to Keith's thing too? What the fuck?

Eyes wide, I locked gazes with Nikki. She grimaced, and her face turned empathic. "Well, that backfired. I'm so sorry, Kenzie. I didn't know Keith took them both to these things."

Standing up, I brushed the grass off my ass. "I didn't either." Hayden had always sworn it was just him. When had that changed? And why the hell hadn't he told me?

When I found Hayden, he was just leaving a meeting with Keith and his crew chief. His green eyes sparkled with joy at seeing me. Then he noticed the look on my face. "Hey…you all right?"

"Funny thing," I snipped. "Nikki got a wild hair up her ass and invited Felicia to go out with us tonight."

Hayden's brows drew together. "Why the hell would Nikki invite Felicia? And where are you guys going? You know I've got that thing…"

"With Keith. Yeah, I know. That's the funny part…Felicia said the *exact* same thing. She's going with you," I hissed, my fingers digging into my palms. The only reason I'd been semi-okay with all of this, was because he'd been going alone with Keith. Now he was going to be with Keith *and* Felicia, and knowing Keith, he probably wouldn't be around much. It would be Hayden and Felicia…alone…all night.

Hayden closed his eyes and sighed. Annoyance and irritation morphed his face before it smoothed into resignation. Reopening his eyes, he told me, "It's the first time he's invited her. But it's just a work thing, Kenzie. It doesn't mean anything."

"Of course it doesn't," I said, my tone dripping with sarcasm. "The texts, the interviews, the onscreen kiss, and now the private parties—of course it all means nothing. What the hell was I thinking."

I spun on my heel and stormed off. I heard Hayden following me, calling my name, and I turned again with my hands out, stopping him. "Don't. Just leave me alone. I can't…I can't do this right now."

Hayden stopped where I'd asked him to, his shoulders sagging in defeat. A part of me knew he hated this just as much as I did, but I was too ticked off to care. As far as I could tell, Hayden was getting his cake and eating it too. He was still racing. He was on top of the world. He had me by his side, and his ex following closely on his heels. I had nothing, and he had the world in his pocket. It wasn't fair.

Not knowing where else to go, I returned to Nikki and Myles. They were both standing now, looking concerned. I hated people looking at me that way. I was fine. But as I stared at the question in their eyes, I began to reconsider whether I should go out with them tonight. Maybe I should hang back, stay close in case something happened with Hayden and Felicia at the party. Like I would know? Like I could do anything to stop it? Unless I wanted to spy on Hayden and follow him to the shindig, I couldn't do anything. And I wasn't about to resort to spying. Yet.

Maybe seeing my turmoil, Nikki quietly told me, "You're not backing out, are you? I think it would be good for you to come have fun with us. You'll only worry if you're alone." Stepping closer, she said, "You can't make him be faithful, Kenzie. He either will be or he won't be. And in a way, testing him like this might be a good thing.

If he's true to you, great, he's a keeper. And if he's *not*...then good riddance. He didn't deserve you anyway."

It sounded so simple put like that. So right...and yet, so hard too. Because *letting* Hayden go off on this thing with Felicia kind of felt like setting dry kindling on a pile of *almost* extinguished coals. Hayden was all I had left, and I didn't want to lose him. But Nikki had a point, and letting fear control me wasn't doing either of us any favors. And maybe she was right about testing the waters. Question was, with all the doubt hovering between us, I wasn't sure if we'd sink or swim. "Yeah, sure...I'll go out with you guys."

After the autograph session, I went straight to my hotel room and changed. Hayden and I were sharing a room, and it was really difficult to see his things spread everywhere. He was going out with Felicia tonight, and regardless of how he felt about it, she was going to be all over him. I hated it. All of it.

Grabbing my things, I left the room as quickly as I could. Maybe it was petty, but I wasn't coming back tonight. Let Hayden worry about *me* for a change. Nikki was already waiting for Myles in his room—she had a key—so I headed down the street to his hotel. Eager to get away from the track, I'd left "work" a little early. Okay, maybe I'd just been eager to get away from Hayden. I never thought I'd feel that way, but he'd been giving me puppy-dog eyes all day, and I just couldn't take it anymore.

Nikki let me in when I tapped on Myles's door; there was a look on her face that could only be described as disgust. "I think we need to have an intervention with Kelley," she said.

"What do you mean?" I asked. Then she let me inside, and I completely understood. We'd only just arrived here the night before, but Myles's hotel room was completely trashed, like he'd been here for weeks. "How does garbage follow him everywhere?"

Nikki laughed, then sighed. "I don't know, but if he ever wants a woman to stick around, he better fix this shit."

Nikki made us a drink from supplies she'd brought with her, while I tried to find a clean place to sit on the couch. Myles had upgraded his room to a deluxe suite, so it was decently sized with a jumbo TV and a private bedroom separate from the main sitting area. Even still, every inch of it was covered in clothes, energy drink cans and takeout containers. It was like he'd brought extra garbage with him.

He showed up just as Nikki was finishing our Cosmos. She threw a lime wedge at him the minute she saw him. "Kelley, you are such a slob!"

Unaffected by the surprise attack, Myles watched the lime wedge fall off his chest and land on the floor beside a discarded bag of chips. Grabbing a banana peel off the floor—the only evidence I could see that Myles had eaten something even partly nutritious lately—I said with a smirk, "Don't bother cleaning up for us or anything."

"Never do," he answered with a wink.

Nikki let out a loud groan. "You desperately need a woman in your life, Myles." Plugging her nose, she lifted a bag from the counter that was leaking a little.

Laughing, Myles told her, "Why do I need a woman, when I have the two of you?"

Giving him a blank stare, Nikki stated, "Sex, Myles. You need a woman—who isn't one of us—for sex."

Frowning, Myles nodded. "That's true. I've been in sort of a dry spell since moving up north. I just can't seem to find the right tactic for the San Fran crowd."

Looking around, Nikki told him, "Well, if your house looks even remotely like this hotel room—for the love of God—don't take your women there. You'll remain celibate for the rest of your life."

Sweet smile on his face, Myles flipped her off. Then he clapped his hands, truly excited. "Hurry and finish your drinks. I found the perfect place…" Nikki handed my drink to me as I was rolling my eyes at Myles. Of course he had.

The bar that Myles ended up taking us to later had a Bavarian theme to it. Jaunty accordion music was playing through the speakers, while the scent of bratwurst and sauerkraut wafted from the kitchen. Even the staff was in on the act. The boys were wearing lederhosen and feathered caps, while the girls had on super-short skirts and blonde pigtail wigs. It was year-round Oktoberfest.

How Myles kept finding places like this, I had no idea.

The three of us sat down at a table and ordered stout beers from a peppy waitress who spoke with a fake accent. While Myles and Nikki entertained themselves by counting all the goats they saw in the various paintings, I dwelled on the fact that my boyfriend was out with another woman. Kind of. I considered texting him, then changed my mind. What would I say? *How are you doing? Hope you and Felicia are having a great time? Don't sleep with her please.* No, I didn't want to say any of those things right now. I just wanted to pretend everything was fine for a few hours.

Myles snapped me out of my dark thoughts by asking a question that, in its own way, made me feel even worse. "So, Kenzie, how is your family doing? I mean…I know things are strained with your dad right now, but how are your sisters?"

A sour grunt escaped me. "Wouldn't know. All they did was bitch at me whenever I talked to them, so I just stopped talking to them."

Nikki's dark eyes widened in shock, then shifted to sympathy; I hadn't told her about that yet. I just hadn't been able to. "I'm sorry, Kenzie. That really…that really sucks."

Myles mumbled a similar sentiment, then silence enveloped the table. The waitress arrived with our beers a few minutes later. She said something in a foreign language that I assumed meant, "Drink up!" With pain and regret squeezing my chest, I immediately started sipping mine.

Myles had a mystified expression on his face when I looked back at him, like he didn't understand how things had gotten so bad between my family. It was a look I understood, since I often felt the same way. Setting down my beer with a forlorn sigh, I told them, "I'm the black sheep now, and everyone hates me."

"Because of Hayden." I was sure Myles had meant that as a question, but it sounded more like a statement.

Shaking my head, I told him, "Because I didn't let my dad dictate every single aspect of my life." After a moment of consideration, I nodded, "And because of Hayden."

"Is he worth it, Kenzie? Worth everything you've sacrificed? Worth everything you're…going through." Myles looked truly confused that I had traded in everything for Hayden. Sometimes it confused me too—especially now. Months ago, I would have told him it was absolutely worth it, but now…well, I just wasn't sure anymore.

Shaking that pain out of my head, I ignored his question and took another long swig of beer. Setting it down, I told him, "I'll race again, Myles." Somehow.

Myles studied me for a moment, then nodded. "Good. Because I really can't stand seeing you dressed up as a Benneti model. It's just…wrong…on every level."

"Amen to that," I said, holding up my glass. Nikki and Myles laughed as they clinked my glass, and I made a vow right then and there to get back on my bike by next year. I wasn't sure how, but I knew there had to be a way.

We all downed our beers, then ordered another. And another. Several hours later, we were in a cab, heading back to Myles's hotel room. Myles kept saying he was shocked to see me drunk. "You used to be so rigid. You wouldn't even drink two different forms of alcohol in one night. You said you couldn't afford to be off your game the next day, and now…"

"Now I don't give a shit," I tittered. Well, I did still give a shit, I just didn't have a "game" to be "off" of. Guess that was one positive thing about being a part-time employee in a job that required very little skill. I didn't have to spend my free time training. All I had to do was smile, look pretty, and be as friendly as possible to everyone I met. I was still working on that last one.

We all chipped in to pay the cab driver once we reached the hotel, then we stumbled inside and made our way back up to Myles's room. Myles immediately headed for the kitchen area to make more drinks, while Nikki turned on the TV. She found some music station and started dancing while Myles poured shots into disposable Dixie cups. I wasn't sure if I wanted to drink anymore, but I also didn't want to be called rigid again either.

Myles came over with a room service tray filled with enough tiny cups for a frat party, and I snorted when I saw it. "Jesus, Kelley, getting us drunk won't help your celibacy problem." Or help him race tomorrow. But Myles was one of those rare riders who rode better with a hangover. He truly was a freak of nature.

With a laugh, Myles shook his head. "This is all for me. I'm too lazy to pour shots all night, too classy to drink straight from the bottle." He winked after he said it, and Nikki rolled her eyes. Grabbing two cups, she downed them before he could even blink. I grabbed one too, while Myles protested that we were both cruel and selfish.

When the tray was littered with empty glasses, and the three of us could no longer stand, we collapsed onto the couch in a tangle of arms and legs. Myles broke free to grab the remote, then changed the station to some show about stupid stunts gone wrong. He snuggled into Nikki's side, and the two of them started laughing in unison as the show sucked them in.

The tug of excess alcohol was pulling me under, and before long I was yawning almost nonstop. Just as I was about to excuse myself to Myles's bedroom and leave the two of them on the couch, Myles suddenly grabbed Nikki's hand and pulled her to her feet. "Come be my spoon," he said, dragging her into his room. So much for that idea.

Nikki raised a weary hand in a small wave as she stumbled off with Myles. I could hear her giggling after the bedroom door shut, and I closed my eyes with a laugh. Wasn't the first time Nikki had been Myles's spoon. They were very cuddly friends, always had been and probably always would be. Whoever they ended up with would have to be very accepting of their relationship. Thank God Hayden and Felicia weren't like them, because I already knew I couldn't handle that. I couldn't even handle Hayden and his ex being on speaking terms. I supposed that situation was slightly different than two flirty best friends though.

I was too tired to grab the remote and turn off the TV, so I left it on and pulled a blanket from the back of the couch around myself. Just as I was drifting off, the TV started playing a movie that must have been on the kinky side. As sounds of huffing and puffing met my ear, I drifted off to sleep.

My inebriated slumber quickly morphed into a dream that felt so real, I immediately forgot I was dreaming. It was the middle of the day, and I was walking through my home, but everything inside it looked different. I didn't recognize the furniture, the decorations, the photos... nothing. It was like it was somebody else's house and it just happened to look exactly like mine.

I called out for Hayden to see if he was there. I could hear some sort of banging sound coming from the bedroom, so I headed that way. The sounds got louder the closer I inched, and they were mixed with heavy breathing and light moans. My heart started thudding in my chest as dread cemented my feet. "Hayden?" I whispered, hoping against all hope that he wasn't in the bedroom, and that those intimate sounds weren't coming from him.

The door was cracked when I stepped in front of it. I raised my hand to push on it, then stopped. There were two clear sets of erotic noises inside—one lower, like a man's, one higher, like a woman's. I suddenly knew that if I pushed open the door, I was going to see something I didn't want to see. *I can just walk away, pretend none of this is happening.* I was just about to do it too—just about to bury my head in the sand in a vain attempt to avoid the pain—when I heard the woman mutter, "Oh God…"

Rage pulsed through me, and I couldn't turn around anymore. I pounded on the door with my fist, shoving it open. The bed was right there in front of me, and the two people I absolutely didn't want to see together were there on top of it. Hayden and Felicia. They were completely naked, arms and legs wrapped around each other. Hayden was pushing his body into her while Felicia rocked her hips into his. Neither one stopped their movements, and their bodies thrust together over and over in an escalating rhythm that was clearly leading to something epic. Pure ecstasy was on both of their faces, and my stomach twisted and turned into a knot of disgust.

"Hayden…stop." Even though I was blazing with anger, my voice felt small and weak. Hayden heard me though. He opened his eyes and looked at me, but he didn't stop moving with Felicia, didn't stop having sex with her.

"Kenzie? I didn't think you'd be back until later." He groaned after he said it, then sped up his hips and closed his eyes again. I couldn't watch this, but I couldn't turn away either. I wanted to rip them apart, but I couldn't move. I could feel hot tears streaming down my cheeks. This couldn't be happening.

Hayden's jade eyes reopened, and he cringed in pleasure. "I'm glad you're here, there's something I need to—" His voice cut off as his mouth opened, and his face crumpled in euphoria. Felicia cried out beneath him, her dark silky hair fanned out around her head like a halo. The pair turned to face each other as they came, and I was finally able to move. I ran right to the bathroom, fell in front of the toilet, and began to throw up, but not before I heard Hayden whisper, "I love you, Felicia."

I woke up on the bathroom floor the next morning with the taste of vomit in my mouth. My heart was thundering in my chest as I tried to remember what was real and what wasn't. Was I home? Had I just walked in on Hayden and Felicia screwing? *Oh God, please no.*

My eyes fluttered closed and my cheek rested on the cool tile. As tears filled my eyes, memories slowly started returning. Myles. Nikki. The German bar. The tray of shots. Falling asleep on the couch to the sound of the damn erotic movie. A dream...it was a dream. Thank God.

But unfortunately, that dream had been too closely tied to reality. Shit. It could have happened. He could have had sex with her last night. It could all be over today.

Myles and Nikki stumbled out of the bedroom not too much later. I was still in the bathroom when Myles found me. I glanced up at him from the floor, anger in my eyes; his were blank, but his face looked kind of green. Well, if he needed the space, he was going to have to wait his turn. I wasn't going anywhere for a while. "I hate you, Kelley," I croaked.

He tried to smirk at me, but it came out more like a grimace. He wisely left the room.

It was at least an hour later before I felt well enough to leave the bathroom, and even then, I only truly left because I had to get to the track. Myles and Nikki were sitting on opposite ends of the couch, looking like they were on the verge of passing out. We'd all overdone it last night, but I was sure I was the one who had paid the biggest price; that nightmare was going to haunt me for hours. "Don't be late," I grunted as I gathered my things.

They both gave me some sort of response, but neither one moved. Today was going to suck. And what made it even worse was the fact that I had to go back to the hotel room to get my uniform. I'd really rather hold off on seeing Hayden for a few more hours. Maybe days. The image of him and Felicia together was just too strong. And it didn't help at all that he'd actually been with her last night. Hopefully not like my dream, but still...

I glanced at my phone on the cab ride over to my hotel, and saw that Hayden had texted and called at least a dozen times. At least I'd been on his mind. But for how much of the evening? Once I arrived at my hotel, I trudged to my room. I slipped my key card into the door as quietly as possible, but the unlocking sound still seemed loud to my ears. The door seemed extra heavy when I pushed it open too. I really just wanted to curl into bed and not move for several hours. Why was life so cruel?

Hayden was on me almost the instant I got through the door. "Where have you been? I was worried sick!" And he did look worried, like he hadn't slept at all. Was that because of me though, or because of *her*?

"Now you know how it feels," I muttered under my breath. I'd wondered where he was on more occasions than I wanted to count.

He heard my rumblings, and a storm of anger started brewing in his sea-green eyes. "That's not fair," he stated.

Hayden complaining about fairness instantly enflamed me. "None of this is fair! I'm a fucking model, and you're…living the high life."

His jaw tightened, causing a vein to poke out on his neck. "And it's all my fault, right?"

With a groan, I shuffled over to the dresser to grab my Benneti outfit. "I didn't say that, Hayden. Don't put words in my mouth."

Following me, he spat out, "But you were thinking it, right? I knew you'd eventually start resenting me. I never asked you to give up your dream for me."

That stopped me dead cold. "So you wanted me to break up with you? You wanted me to choose racing over you?"

"Now who is putting words in people's mouths? No, that's not what I want. I just…" he sighed, and some of the anger in his expression faded. "I'm trying…I wish I could…I wish I could explain, wish I could convince you…"

Hands on my hips, I turned to face him. "You could start by telling me what happened at the party with you and Felicia?" *Did you flirt with her? Dance with her? Go home with her?*

A spark of annoyance rekindled in his eyes. "Nothing happened. How many times do I have to tell you that I'm not interested in her? How many different ways can I say that you're the only girl for me? When will you believe me?"

And that was the crux of the matter, wasn't it? Because the truth was, so long as she was in the picture, I didn't think I'd ever one hundred percent believe him. Even if he was perfect. Even if he wasn't keeping things from me. My eyes began filling with tears as a desolate future of distrust filled my vision. "The painful truth is, Hayden...I'll never entirely believe you. I can't, not while she's in your life."

Hayden gaped at me, shocked. "Then where does that leave us, Kenzie?"

"I don't know." And it broke my heart not to.

Hayden and I were silent after that. There just wasn't anything else to say. I got dressed in my uniform, he got ready to go to the track. Then we went downstairs, hopped in his sporty rental car, and drove to the track, all in silence. The stillness was so thick between us, it was almost suffocating. But there was nothing that could be done about it, and that was the worst part. We were on paths neither one of us could change, and unfortunately, they were heading in opposite directions.

Hayden had a good day on the racetrack, finishing third while Myles finished second. Felicia snapped up fourth place, a fact that grated every nerve inside me. I hated that she was good at her job, I hated that she had a history with Hayden that wouldn't go away, I hated that she was here at all. Would Hayden and I be having all these trust issues if she were gone? Probably not. And that really made me wonder...were all successful relationships purely circumstantial? If everyone was tested like we were being tested, would every couple fail? Did love need optimal conditions to survive? That thought didn't make me feel good about anyone's chances.

CHAPTER 15

~Hayden~

Monterey was a disaster, on so many levels. My career was going amazing and I was racing better than I ever had before, but everything else was slipping. I couldn't keep doing this. I needed to stop street racing. The lies about parties with Keith…that now involved Felicia too…were getting out of control. It was time for my extracurricular activities to end. Problem was, they couldn't.

The more money I could approach Jordan with, the better; I probably had enough now to pay for about half the property in cash. He had to change his mind soon about selling. Financially, he couldn't hold out forever, and so far as Keith knew, we were the only bite Jordan was getting. Hopefully that didn't change in the next couple of months.

My bigger problem with trying to get out of street racing, though, was Hookup. He'd spill everything to Kenzie if I left. The only way to get myself out of this nightmare, was to get the track from Jordan, quit racing for Hookup, then tell Kenzie everything. It had to happen *that* way, in *that* order. Any other scenario ended in everything falling apart, I was sure.

That still left Felicia though. And unfortunately, I didn't have a carefully crafted schedule of events to guide me through that problem. I had no fucking clue what I was going to do about her. Except try to ignore her as much as possible. That was harder to do after my...fantasy. I was just too aware of her now. And Kenzie... God, I still couldn't look her in the eye sometimes.

Luckily the twisted fantasy hadn't happened again, but I was scared it might, and I was starting to feel reluctant around Kenzie. I'd managed to hide the reaction so far, so I didn't think Kenzie suspected the truth, but with everything else that was going on, not wanting to have sex with my girlfriend was the absolute worst thing that could happen to us. For the health of my relationship, I needed to get my shit together, and stop being afraid of another woman slipping into my love life. I needed closure. And that meant I needed to talk to Felicia. *Really* talk to her. Fuck.

Hearing a dog barking and a child laughing helped push away my dark thoughts. Buying Antonia that puppy was probably the only smart decision I'd made all year. The tiny Shih Tzu had acclimated to her new surroundings, and was no longer a quivering mess of fear. Antonia had named her Sundae, since she kind of looked like a hot fudge sundae. Sundae was currently licking Antonia's face with abandon, and she was giggling so hard, she could barely breathe.

When she started coughing and gagging, I worried that it was too much for her. I stood up to pull the dog off Antonia, but Izzy gestured for me to sit back down. "It's fine, she'll be okay." As I sank back down to the couch cushions, Antonia hacked a few more times, but then she was done. All smiles, she squeezed her puppy tight. Seeing that she was better made me relax.

Izzy smiled sweetly at her daughter, then cast a look at me. Rolling her eyes, she reluctantly said, "You might have been right about the dog. I think Antonia needed Sundae." I nodded at her correct assessment. Even if it did mean more work for Izzy, pets did wonders for the soul.

Sundae started sniffing around the carpet. "Need to go potty?" Antonia asked. She glanced at her mom, looking for permission.

Izzy nodded, and Antonia picked up the puppy and headed out back with her. After she left, Izzy turned her calculating eyes on me. "So…you're here during the day, when you're usually at the track. And you're here without Kenzie. I'm assuming that means you want to talk to me. What's up?"

I immediately shook my head. "Nothing is up. I wanted to see Antonia, and I just got back from an event a couple of days ago, so I don't really need to practice right now. It's cool."

"So why didn't you bring Kenzie then? I'm sure she'd love to see Antonia again, even if she did visit yesterday."

A sigh escaped me. *Because I need a break from the guilt I feel around her.* I couldn't say that, so I shrugged. "She…had plans. And just because we're together, doesn't mean we have to spend every second together, you know. We're still our own persons."

"Huh," she said, still examining me. "So, it has nothing to do with the fact that you've been secretly texting Felicia and going to all these parties with her?"

Heat instantly burst through my veins. "I'm not texting her or going to parties with her! She texts me, and I sometimes respond. And the parties are…coincidental." And being questioned about it was beginning to piss me off. Did no one trust me? And yes, I realized how that sounded, considering how often I lied to people.

Izzy's eyes widened at my outburst. "Wow, touchy subject."

Closing my eyes, I tried to regain my calm. It was surprisingly difficult. "I'm just…tired of arguing about it."

"Hayden…are you and Kenzie okay?"

I reopened my eyes to see Izzy giving me a look saturated with concern. "Yeah, of course," I told her. "We're fine." We would be fine, once all this was over.

She just kept staring at me, boring holes into me with her I-know-you're-lying eyes. I looked away from her, but didn't say anything else. I'd been telling the truth anyway. We were fine. Not great, not horrible…just…fine.

Seeing that I wasn't going to willingly spill anymore details, Izzy sighed and said, "All right, Hayden. But I hope you know what you're doing. For Kenzie's sake. And Felicia's."

I snapped my eyes to hers then. Did she think I was playing them both? I wasn't. I was being perfectly clear with Felicia; she just didn't want to listen. And with Kenzie, well, everything would be clear soon enough with her.

I was just about to tell Izzy to mind her own business, when Antonia walked into the room. She looked pained, and her face was paler than usual. Sundae followed close behind her, licking at her bare feet. "Mommy," she croaked, "I don't feel so good."

Izzy was instantly on her feet. "What's wrong, baby?"

My chest squeezed as Antonia put a hand on her belly. "My stomach hurts."

A look of relief passed over Izzy's face; seeing that calmed me down. "It must have been something you ate," she said to her daughter. "How about you go lie down, take a nap. Maybe you'll feel better when you wake up."

Antonia looked over at me, and I could tell she didn't want to be banished to her room while I was still here. Smiling, I told her, "How about a bedtime story?"

That immediately perked up her spirits. Always did. Girl loved to read. "Okay! I know just the book. I've been dying to finish it; I just *have* to know how it ends!"

I spent over an hour, sitting on the edge of her bed, reading her the last Harry Potter book. Antonia passed out when we had just 100 pages left to go. I considered waking her up so we could finish the book, but decided against it. She wasn't feeling good, and Izzy was right, she needed her rest. As I kissed the short hair on her head, I made a mental note to tell Izzy to not let her read any more of it when she woke up. Maybe that was cruel, but I saw a memory happening, and I wanted to be a part of it.

Izzy rolled her eyes when I told her, but she was smiling ear to ear. "You better come back soon then. I can't keep her away from that book for long."

"I'll come back tomorrow," I said, giving her a kiss on the cheek.

Izzy gave me a curious look. "With Kenzie?" she asked.

"Yeah…of course. Or maybe…during the day again. I could use some more time off." Fuck. I was *not* avoiding my life. I wasn't.

Izzy opened her mouth like she was going to—once again—tell me I was being an idiot, but then, wisely, she closed it. "Tell Kenzie I said hi," she said.

I nodded, but I wasn't really agreeing to her request. I couldn't tell Kenzie I'd ditched practice to come out here behind her back. She'd wonder why I hadn't invited her. Or maybe she'd understand that I wanted alone time with my family. Fuck, I didn't know how she'd react anymore. I really hated the uncertainty surrounding us.

After leaving Izzy's, I debated what I wanted to do. The street race was in San Diego tonight. I could go home, spend a few hours with Kenzie before bailing on her to go to the "party" with Keith…which would probably end in a fight since Felicia was now included in that lie. Or I could skip the drama entirely and just head to Hookup's now to kill time before the race. Making a quick decision, I pulled out my phone and texted Kenzie. *'Hey, Keith wants to head to L.A. early for the party. We're leaving right after practice. Sorry, babe. I'll make it up to you tomorrow night, okay?'*

I felt horrible as I pressed send. Now I was avoiding her all together. Great. But it was just a day. A day of peace, a day of not feeling guilty when I looked into her eyes, a day of not having to convince her that I was only in love with her, a day of not having to justify myself. Even if what I was doing warranted justification. God, I was so snarled in lies now, the way out was getting harder and harder to see.

It took Kenzie a while to get back to me, and when she did, it was brief. *'Okay.'* She hated these parties with Keith. Now, even more than before. Fucking Felicia. If she hadn't used *my* lie, Kenzie wouldn't be so furious about the whole thing. She'd just be moderately annoyed that I was gone all the time. Fuck, I hated that those were my options: furious or annoyed.

Starting my bike, I headed south to San Diego. Hookup had a place down there, not far from his childhood home, where we'd all spent the better part of our formative years. He said he hadn't moved away because he liked to keep it real. I think he just couldn't part with the community who loved and feared him. Hookup had made a name for himself here; he didn't want to have to start over, establishing himself somewhere else.

When I got there, cars and bikes littered the dry lawn. Hookup was rarely alone. He preferred to live like life was one perpetual party. Always going, going, going. It was almost like he feared what would happened if the party stopped.

I waved at the people I knew—most gamblers who bet on me at races. A lot of them I'd seen dozens of times over the years, and while they had no reason to not know who I was—who I *really* was—every single one of them called me by Hookup's lame-ass nickname. "Hey, Fun Killer! Good to see ya, man! Knock 'em dead tonight!" Right.

Opening the battered screen door, I strolled inside. Hookup was on his couch, a random girl draped over his lap. He lifted his hands into the air when he saw me. "Fun Killer! Ready for tonight?"

I nodded at him, then found somewhere relatively quiet to relax. I didn't want to be here. I didn't want to be doing this anymore. I just wanted Kenzie to be happy, and to not feel guilty every time I looked into her eyes. I wanted the lying to stop.

As I was contemplating how my life had turned to shit so quickly, a person stopped right in front of me, blocking my people-watching view. "Careful, you're starting to live up to your name, Fun Killer."

I glanced up to see Felicia standing there, holding a beer bottle out for me. "I'm not here to entertain people," I told her, grabbing the offered bottle. "I'm just here for the money."

Felicia debated something for a half-second, then sat on the small section of empty couch beside me. "For Kenzie," she stated. Not a question.

"Yep," I answered, taking a swig of beer. It was an IPA, extra hoppy, just how I liked it. But of course, Felicia would know that.

She studied me a moment, while I considered getting up. Ever since I'd started killing time before races with Hookup, she'd started hanging out with him too. Hookup said it was coincidence. I called bullshit. All it did was make me feel even worse about things with Kenzie. If she ever found out about all of this…well, I'd have one hell of a time talking my way out of trouble. I was betraying her on almost every level, just by being here, letting Felicia talk to me. I should go…

"Hayden…" Felicia said, her voice low, so no one around would hear.

I looked over to face her, and saw the nervousness in her eyes, if nowhere else. She was good at hiding her emotions, but not from me. I saw through her. Most of the time. "What?" I asked, surprised I was encouraging her to talk.

She licked her lips. "I was just… I…" Her eyes drifted to her untouched drink before returning to mine. "I hear

Kenzie's pretty ticked at you." I narrowed my eyes in question, and she filled in the blanks without me even having to ask. "Rodney. He said he saw the two of you fighting in the garage at Monterey. Was that...because of me?"

There was hope in her eyes now, like she thought I was switching sides or something. Unfortunately, I couldn't deny her question. That fight *had* been about her. Taking a quick swig of beer, I pointed my bottle at her. "You told Kenzie you were going to a party with Keith. You used *my* lie instead of coming up with your own."

It was a ridiculous argument, but it was the only one I had. Felicia pressed her lips together, annoyed. "It works for you, so I figured it would work for me too."

Rolling my eyes, I shook my head. "Yeah, except for the fact that Kenzie hates the two of us together."

Immediately after I said it, I knew I'd made a mistake. For one, Felicia didn't give a rat's ass if Kenzie was unhappy; it probably thrilled her to know Kenzie was miserable. But more importantly, I'd inadvertently shown Felicia a crack in our relationship. I'd been trying to hide that from her as much as possible; I wanted Kenzie and I to seem strong...even if we weren't. "Together?" she whispered.

"Not like that," I instantly snipped. "You and I are not together. Don't read anything into that."

She just smiled. Damn it.

Feeling like I'd cracked open yet another door, I quickly tried to close it. "Look, I know you and I have been thrust into the same circles lately, and I know we've had some...moments...but that doesn't mean—"

Interrupting, she quietly asked, "Moments?"

I wanted to smack myself over the head with my beer bottle for mentioning that. I hadn't meant to—it had just slipped out. I couldn't deny there had been a few times when I'd felt something around her though, like the past bubbling up, enclosing me with the warmth of its memories. But it was an illusion. Our history wasn't this peaceful, pleasant thing. There were sharp edges that cut deep, and dark valleys that blinded. We'd never been a perfect couple. There had been passion, explosions, fights, and temper tantrums. And she'd fled from every single one of them. Her slamming a door in my face was a common occurrence, because Felicia didn't compromise. She wanted things her way, all the time, and if she didn't get what she wanted, she took off…making me so distraught that I'd give her the moon when she returned. She'd wrapped me around her fingers for years that way, and I hadn't even realized I'd been manipulated by her. Not until Kenzie. She'd fought *with* me, worked *with* me, and had ultimately given up everything…for me. And this was how I was repaying her. Fuck.

"Why did you really come back, Felicia?" I asked in a low voice. Just by asking, I knew I was opening a can of worms that I would never be able to shut, and a part of me prayed she didn't answer.

Hope bloomed in her eyes as she spoke. "Isn't that obvious, Hayden. I came back for you. Because I still love you…and I hope some part of you still loves me too." Putting a hand on my arm, she quickly added, "I know I've been going about things the wrong way, and I'm sorry. Keith, he asked me to press hard, especially in public, and I was so desperate to fix things between us, I went along with it, even though I knew that wouldn't work on you."

Her smile turned sad and reflective. "You have to forge your own path, make your own decisions. When someone tells you not to do something, you go out and do it, just to show them that nobody owns you. We're a lot alike that way."

My mind was reeling over what she'd just confessed. Keith had asked her to pursue me? What the fuck? Why the hell was he dipping his fingers into my life? It wasn't right, no matter that I owed him everything.

Irritated, I snapped, "I don't fuck with people I care about, just to prove a point. But you...that's all you've ever done." Standing up, I walked out of the room.

I managed to avoid her for the next several hours, until it was time to gather at the race site. Hookup was giddy for the event, nearly bouncing off the walls as he hopped into his car with Grunts. I spotted Felicia heading to her motorcycle as I approached mine. She didn't look upset over the way our conversation had ended. Instead she looked determined, like she knew that if she didn't give up, I'd eventually come around. I didn't want to "come around", didn't want to understand why she'd left, didn't want to forgive her for tearing us apart. All I wanted from her was distance, I just didn't know how to get it; Felicia seemed to be everywhere I turned.

It didn't take us long to get to the location the organizers had picked for the race. Having grown up here, I knew the "course" inside and out. That gave me an advantage. Felicia too. Izzy, Hookup, Felicia, me...San Diego had been our stomping grounds, where we'd thought we were indestructible. And inseparable. Life was proving us wrong.

Hookup pulled up to the sidewalk sideways, and I tucked my bike next to his car. Felicia squeezed in the space right beside me. Keeping true to my commitment to keep my identity a secret, I left my helmet on. Felicia did the same this time. At least she was being smarter about her stupid decision to street race. I should really talk her out of it. Rekindling her friendship with Hookup wasn't worth risking her career. Of course, I knew Hookup wasn't the entire reason she was night racing. I wasn't a complete idiot.

I could feel Felicia staring at me, could sense that she wanted to restart our earlier conversation. I kept my back to her as much as possible. It didn't stop the heat I felt boring into me, but it did make it easier to ignore her.

The crowd up and down the street grew larger with every passing second, and an almost palpable energy vibrated in the air. The thrill of competition began to tingle up my spine, and a wave of missing Kenzie nearly knocked me over. She should be here beside me, cheering me on, encouraging me to help her make her dreams come true. But she wouldn't approve of any of this, so she wasn't here. And it killed me.

As I'd had to do several times recently, I forced thoughts of Kenzie to the back of my mind, and focused on the job at hand.

Hookup was waving Felicia and me over almost frantically. When we stepped up to him, he immediately started explaining the route. He'd explained it three times at his house already, so I tuned him out and shifted my attention to the competition. Three of the racers I could see were regulars to the circuit. So far, I hadn't lost to any of them, but assuming a win only assured a failure.

I started replaying past races with them in my head, and realized every single one of them had ended with a fluke accident that contributed to my victory. Shit. That meant they had all been close races, and Hookup had tipped the scales in my favor by messing with the other riders. That wouldn't be happening this time; I was on my own. But I was ready. I could do this.

Felicia was up first, so Hookup was sending her over to Grunts to have her helmet cam put on. Hookup shifted his attention to me once she was gone. He was smirking—never a good sign. "I totally saw that, by the way," he said.

"Saw what?" I said with a sigh.

"You and Felicia…getting snuggly on the couch." He wriggled his eyebrows, making a not-so-subtle innuendo.

It was pointless engaging him, but I couldn't help myself. "You saw nothing, because nothing happened." My phone vibrated from inside my jacket pocket, but I ignored it.

"Nothing," Hookup murmured. "Right. Just like Tammi and me were doing nothing for forty-five minutes in the garage earlier." He made a crude gesture with his tongue and his cheek, just in case I wasn't aware of what he was talking about.

My phone buzzed in my pocket again, but I ignored it again. There was an opportunity here to broach the waters with Hookup. "Hey, Hookup…you understand this is a temporary arrangement with me, right?"

His good humor instantly vanished. "What do you mean? You bailing on me?"

I instantly held up my hands. "No, but I can't do this forever. When I get enough money to help Kenzie…and the stars align and a crazy old man changes his mind about me…I'm out. I'm retiring. For good…no more comebacks."

Anger scrunched his face. "What the hell, Hayden? I've done everything you asked. Gave you most of the fucking cut, and kept my hands off the other riders. It's working. Why the fuck are you bailing?"

"Because this isn't my future, Hookup. Skulking in the dark, lying to everyone, hiding…being worried all the time. This isn't what I want for the rest of my life. Is it really what you want?"

A strange look passed across his face, a contemplative look, like he was actually considering his future for the first time, and he didn't seem too comfortable with the self-inspection. "Whatever, Hayden. You're just chickening out on me, like you always do. I can't say I'm surprised."

And I wasn't surprised that the conversation hadn't gone well. Hookup didn't like letting go once he had a good thing going. He'd targeted Kenzie last year in large part because she'd walked away. I really didn't want to justify my life to him anymore than I already had, and luckily, my phone buzzing for a third time gave me the perfect opportunity to move away from him.

Grabbing the phone, I slightly turned away from Hookup as I glanced at the screen. Seeing Izzy's name in bold letters made my blood turn ice cold. She never called me this late at night unless something was wrong. What could be wrong?

Ripping off my helmet, I hurried to answer the phone before voicemail kicked in. "Iz? What is it? What's wrong?"

Izzy's voice on the other end of line was so frantic, it made my heart pound in my chest. "Hayden..." Her voice hitched as a small sob escaped her. "It's Antonia. Something's wrong, something's really wrong...she's in so much pain..."

My grip tightened on the phone, and I began almost manically looking around myself, like somehow, I could spot Antonia in the crowd if I searched hard enough. "Are you at home? Where are you?"

"Children's Hospital," she choked out. "I just brought her in."

"I'll be there as fast as I can, Iz. It's gonna be okay." I didn't know if that was true, but I had to believe it was.

Disconnecting the phone, I shoved it back into my pocket. Turning around, I waved my hands over my head to get Felicia's attention. She noticed me immediately and popped her visor up. Her eyes were concerned, and I momentarily wondered what I looked like right now. If it was anything like how I felt, I probably looked wrecked.

Shooing Grunts off her, Felicia started heading my way. I turned back around to get Hookup's attention. He was starting to promote his racers, spouting untrue facts to the crowd like they were gospel. Stepping close, I tugged on his arm. "We have to go."

With a frown on his face, he yanked his arm free. "*You* have to go. Race. I have to stay here and make you seem even better than you are. That's how this works, Hayes. You know that."

Shaking my head, I patted the pocket holding my cell phone. "Izzy just called. Antonia's in the hospital."

Hookup's eyes widened for a second, but then he shrugged. "Kid's always in the hospital."

I wanted to throttle him, but I managed to control myself. "It's different this time, I can tell. Izzy's freaking out."

He still seemed unaffected. "She's always freaking out. Kid could have a cold and she'd start crying."

This time I did grab him. Just by the shoulders though. "There is something wrong with your niece. Your namesake! Get your ass in the car, and get to the fucking hospital. Now!"

Hookup seemed shocked by my outburst. Then his phone rang. I let him go and he reached down to unclip it from his belt. I knew who it was even before he answered it. "Iz? What's up?"

I couldn't hear Izzy's end of the line, but I knew what she was saying. "Ya, ya, okay...calm down. I'll be there soon." Frowning, he hung up and stared me down. Then he said over my shoulder, "Pack it up, Grunts. We're leaving."

The big man snorted some response, and Hookup's gaze shifted to him. "Don't argue with me, just pack it up." Grumbling, he closed his bet book. That was when Felicia's phone started ringing. Fuck...if Izzy was calling all of us in, it had to be bad. Really bad. *Please let her be okay. God, just...let her be okay.*

CHAPTER 16

~Hayden~

All of us sped to the hospital. We were in the city anyway, so it didn't take us long to get there. Iz was pacing the room, waiting for us. Her cheeks were wet, her eyes were red; she looked worn to the bone.

When she saw me, she ran my way and practically tackled me in a voracious hug. Knowing she needed to release some anxiety before she could tell us what was going on, I rubbed her back and murmured soothing words in her ears. All meaningless crap, since I had no idea what was going on.

After she calmed down, she pulled back to look at me. "How did you get here so fast?" she asked, sniffling. Then she finally noticed I wasn't alone. Her eyes bulged as she took in her brother, Felicia, and Grunts hovering behind me. "All of you…together…"

Her gaze snapped to mine, and fire sparked in her eyes. "Goddamn it, Hayden. Are you racing again?"

While I preferred seeing heat over devastation, I had questions of my own. Squatting down, I looked her in the eye. "Iz, what's going on? What's wrong with Antonia?"

That brought her back to the problem at hand, and her eyes started watering again. "She's in surgery… They said it was her appendix… She tried to warn me, but I just didn't think it was serious. I waited to bring her in. I waited too long…"

"Hey," I said, rubbing her arms. "It's okay. You couldn't have known what was going on with her. You didn't do anything wrong." She weakly nodded her head, but I could tell she still blamed herself. "How long will she be in surgery?"

"I don't know," she mumbled. "I just don't know…" She started crying again, and I held her tight.

A knot cinched my throat closed, and I turned to look at Felicia. She had a strange expression on her face, like she wanted to run and never stop running, but also like she was determined to stay no matter what. I wasn't sure what she'd end up doing; she'd fled for four years the last time something scary had happened with Antonia. That had been much worse than this though. This was just an appendix.

"It's okay, it's okay. They take out appendixes all the time. It's routine. It's totally routine."

That calmed her down again. I released her, and she headed over to Felicia. The pair shared a long hug before Izzy let her go to acknowledge Grunts, and then Hookup. She got teary again when she hugged her brother. "I can't believe you came, Tony. Thank you."

He rolled his eyes as he gave her a one-armed squeeze. "Well, of course I'm here. You were all crying and shit."

While I found his comment annoying, Izzy laughed and playfully socked him in the stomach. She always forgave him, no matter what he said.

We picked a spot to sit in the waiting room. God, I hated waiting rooms. There was always tension in the air; people waiting to be seen, or people waiting for good news. And since this was a children's hospital, it was even worse. Everywhere I turned I saw parents who were either concerned, or flat-out scared. It almost made me never want to have children—I didn't think I could handle that level of fear. Too late though. Antonia was mine, by choice if not blood.

My thoughts spun as I waited for the doctor to give us a report. I bounced my knees incessantly as I sat there, until Felicia put a comforting hand on my thigh. I froze, both because she was touching me, and because it helped ease the anxiety. She looked over at me, and I saw compassion in her eyes. She knew, she understood. Her hand turned over and opened, fingers spread in invitation. I knew I should decline the offer of support, but goddamn it, I needed it.

I clasped my hand with hers, and instantly wished I hadn't. Not because I hated it, not because it felt wrong… but because it felt so right. And that terrified me almost as much as not knowing what was going on with Antonia.

Memories swirled within me, threatening to drown me. Meeting Felicia for the first time. We'd both thought we knew everything, but we hadn't had a fucking clue. We'd faced every obstacle together though. Fought every bully side by side, helped each other deal with every failed foster placement, cheered each other on as we'd conquered racing the streets, swapped between friends and lovers so seamlessly, it had seemed normal that the two things were one and the same. She had been my world back then. And then she'd fucking left.

I tossed her hand aside, just as the emergency room doors slid open...and Kenzie walked in.

Her eyes were wide and frantic as she looked around for someone with information. She spotted me, and relief visibly filled her. Then she noticed who I was with, and her expression shattered, hardened. *Shit*. Leaping to my feet, I walked over to her.

Her wavy hair was secured in a haphazard ponytail; some of the pieces were still loose and free, like she'd missed them in her rush to get ready. Unlike us, Kenzie had probably been fast asleep when Izzy had called her. Damn it. It hadn't occurred to me that Izzy would call Kenzie too. But she was family now to Iz...and to me...it was only right that she was here.

"Babe," I said, wrapping my arms around her. The refreshing smell of lavender hit my nose as I squeezed her tight. Sometimes she put it on her pillow when she couldn't sleep. Was that because of me? God, I hoped not.

She was rigid in my arms, barely holding me back. "I thought you were in L.A. How did you beat me here?" she asked.

Relaxing my grip, I pulled back to look at her. Right. I'd told her I was at a party with Keith in L.A. Thanks to the "parties" we went to during ARRC events, she knew they typically went late. Really, really late. What could I say to her that would possibly explain how I'd magically appeared here before her? What could I tell her, except the truth?

"I...I um...well..." Words wouldn't form, and by the way Kenzie's brow was furrowing deeper and deeper, I knew I was digging my own grave with every stuttered syllable.

"Kenzie, thank God you're here. I'm freaking out!" Izzy engulfed Kenzie in a storm of hair and arms, and she was ripped from my grasp. I staggered back, then froze in place, trapped by the heat in Kenzie's glare. Fuck.

Kenzie forcibly pulled her attention from me so she could comfort her distraught friend. Izzy filled her in on the details while Kenzie discretely glanced around the room. Her eyes shifted from Felicia, to Hookup, to me, then back to Hookup. She had to be wondering why we were all calmly sitting around together. Last she knew, we all hated Hookup. Well, I did, at any rate. Did she believe that the power of mutual concern had momentarily rebuilt a burnt bridge? Or was she putting two and two together? Just how I'd gotten here so fast. How we'd all gotten here so fast...

And that was when Hookup decided to make my life living hell.

Stepping up to me, he loudly said, "Hey, Hayden...I don't want to seem cold here, but Antonia's gonna be fine. You said yourself, this shit's routine...so how about..." He leaned in and lowered his voice, but it still seemed like he was yelling. "Look, if we leave now, we can make the last heat. You can still win this thing, and I won't be out all my cash."

"Are you serious?" I hissed. Now was not the time or the place. Kenzie was close to us, but she seemed absorbed in what Izzy was saying. And what Izzy was saying was what we should all be thinking about. Tonight was about Antonia, not racing.

Hookup didn't look one bit abashed by his suggestion. "Yeah, I mean, we know where Antonia is, we know what's wrong with her now. It's cool, the docs will handle it, so let's go win some money!"

I was just about to tell him that none of this was cool, when Kenzie broke free from her conversation with Izzy. Stepping forward, eyes intense, she said, "Money? Does he mean race money? Are you...are you racing for him again?"

Her mouth popped open, and I could tell that, just like that, all the pieces had fallen into place for her with the force of an avalanche. "Oh my God, of course you're racing for him again. I'm such an idiot. There were never any parties. It was always about racing. You...and Hookup... and *her*..." Kenzie's gaze shifted to take in Felicia. Fire blazed in her eyes. When her gaze snapped back to mine, I could feel the heat on my face. "All this time you've been... You son of a bitch!"

Shit. It was over, I could feel it. Nothing was going to work now, no argument was going to be listened to, no reason would be seen. But I had to at least *try* to save this. "Kenzie, I can—"

She jabbed her finger into my chest while angry tears moistened her eyes. "Don't you dare try to explain this away. You said you would tell me the truth. *Always*."

I could feel a black hole opening in my chest where she was touching me, obliterating everything that was good about us. Fuck, I didn't want to lose her. "I did...and I planned to... I said I'd tell you the truth, Kenzie, and I meant it. I just...never said *when* I'd tell you." My argument made me want to sock myself in the nuts. *Really?*

Kenzie's expression turned ice cold. "That is fucked up, Hayden."

I know. "I'm sorry, I just...I didn't have a choice. You needed to race again. I was trying to get money to help you race. You belong on a bike." Hope surged through me at finally getting that off my chest. Surely she would calm down, once she understood my motivation.

But no, she didn't. She just turned even frostier. "Oh, so you lied for *me*? Is that your argument?"

"I..." I could feel her slipping through my fingers. I had no words to save us. It wasn't supposed to go down like this.

Kenzie lifted her chin, that smoldering defiance that had drawn me to her in the first place was back, full force. God, she was beautiful. "I never asked you to be my hero," she coldly stated. "All I asked from you was to be honest...and you couldn't deliver."

"Kenzie..." I murmured, reaching out for her. *Please don't go. Don't leave me too.*

She pulled away from me, and I knew right then, there was no going back. We were forever changed, altered by my repeated lies. Our relationship vanished in a puff of smoke...and it was all my fault. That black hole in my chest gnawed its way throughout my entire body, leaving only a void-filled shell in its place.

Spots of color brightened Kenzie's cheeks, and I could tell she was struggling with remaining calm and in control when she clearly wanted to attack me. "Don't touch me, don't talk to me, don't call me, don't come over. We're done."

Done. There it was...the word that would be etched on my tombstone. The word that would forever haunt my soul, until my body finally crumpled under the strain. "No, Kenzie, you can't... I did this for you!"

I surged forward, but hands grabbed me, holding me in place. Face expressionless, Kenzie turned from me, and started walking away. She was walking away from us. From *me*. And I couldn't let her go without a fight. I struggled with the person in front of me; I was so absorbed in my objective that I wasn't even sure who was blocking me until they spoke. "Hayden...I think you should go."

Looking down, I saw that it was tiny, distraught Izzy who was keeping me from my goal; she was so much stronger than she looked. What she'd just said made absolutely no sense though. "You think *I* should go? I'm family, Iz."

Sad smile on her face, Izzy shook her head. "I know. But so is Kenzie, and *you* wronged her, so *you* should be the one to go."

I stopped trying to get away from her, and just stared in disbelief. "Unbelievable. I did it for her, Izzy."

A slow exhale escaped Izzy as her eyes drifted to the floor. "I'm sure it started out that way," she murmured.

There was an accusation in her voice that sparked a fire in my cold body. "What's that supposed to mean?"

Izzy flashed a quick glance at Felicia, still sitting beside Grunts, a shocked expression on her face as she carefully watched everything that was happening. I returned my glare to Izzy. "This has nothing to do with *her*."

"I'm not the one you have to convince," she said with a raised eyebrow. Then she sighed again. "Just go, Hayden. It will make things easier if you're gone. I'll talk to

Kenzie, see if I can't smooth things over. And I'll call you the minute Antonia is out of surgery, okay?"

No, none of this was okay. But all of it was beyond my control. Maybe it always had been, and I'd just never realized it. "Fine, I'll go."

It took everything in me to walk out the door instead of storming over to Kenzie to continue our *disagreement*. She couldn't possible mean we were over-over. She'd change her mind once she'd had time to calm down. I was sure of it. But even still, I'd like to have some sort of assurance from her before I left.

The ER doors slid shut behind me, sealing in the sound, and for the first time in a long time, I felt utterly and completely alone. Everyone I cared about most in the world had just shut me out. Icy numbness ran through me as the desolation sank in. Antonia was sick, Kenzie was gone, and my family had just turned their backs on me. I was back at square one with nothing, and it was all my fucking fault.

Furious at life, furious at myself, I nearly shoved my bike over when I saw it. That fucking motorcycle had gotten me into more trouble than it was worth. But no, that wasn't entirely true. Motorcycles had saved me, given me purpose, meaning, hope… I needed hope again, but right now, I felt like I was being compacted into a ball, squeezed tighter and tighter. I couldn't breathe. *Everyone leaves…are you really surprised?*

Needing out of there, I slammed on my helmet, started my bike, and peeled out, leaving tire marks on the concrete. My chest pounded as I rode away from the hospital. Everything about this felt wrong. I shouldn't be leaving

Antonia, I shouldn't be leaving Kenzie. My whole world was back there, and I was running away from it.

I pressed my bike to its limits once I reached the freeway. What did I care if I got a speeding ticket now? If I got charged with reckless endangerment and Keith benched me, did it really matter anymore? Did anything? *She couldn't be gone.*

My entire body felt like it was vibrating when I got back to my apartment. I felt manic, like if I didn't do something, I was going to explode...I just had no clue what I was supposed to do. There was no one I could talk to, no one I could vent to, no one I could turn to. No one, no one, no one. Seemed to be a theme in my life, and I was sick and tired of it.

Pacing my living room, I debated walking over to Keith's. He hated Kenzie, and he probably wouldn't shed a tear over our breakup, but maybe talking to him would keep me from feeling like I was going to shatter into a thousand pieces. *This can't be happening.*

Maybe I could call Felicia. I hadn't done that yet, it had just felt too...wrong before. But now...if Kenzie and I were done—*God, please don't let us be over*—then what did I have to lose by reaching out to her. Pulling my phone out of my pocket, I stared at the dark screen for a solid ten minutes. Dark. No messages, no notifications. Nothing from Kenzie saying she was sorry, that she'd been rash and spoken hastily. Nothing to say we were still together. Just empty darkness. I wanted to fling my phone across the room, smash it into a million tiny pieces, then flush those pieces down the toilet. Anything to stop the device from silently screaming that I was on my own.

My grip tightened on the phone, my knuckles turning white. I cocked my arm back, prepared to launch it, when a timid knock sounded on my door. Kenzie? Was she reaching out to me already? *Yes, I'll take you back.*

Shoving my phone into my pocket, I ran the few steps to the door. Anxious for the apologies to begin, I yanked on the knob...and saw Felicia standing before me. For a second, my mangled heart thought the dark-haired beauty before me was my girlfriend. My ex-girlfriend now. But the subtle differences intruded on my fantasy, pounding the truth into me with the voracity of a hungry woodpecker. Heart sinking to the bottom of my shoes, I murmured, "Felicia? What are you doing here?"

"Can I come in?" she asked, ignoring my question.

I opened the door wide for her. Why the hell not? It didn't matter now, since Kenzie was... Since we were...

This had to be a dream, some fucked-up nightmare that I'd wake up from any minute. *Please let me wake up.*

Felicia sashayed into the room, and I closed the door behind her. Once she was inside, reality seemed heavier. More...real. "Why aren't you at the hospital?" I asked.

She worked her lip before answering me. "It was kind of...awkward after you left. Especially with Kenzie there ...killing me with her eyes." Hearing my girl's name on her lips was a dagger to the heart. Seeing the pain sweep over me, Felicia stepped closer. "But really, I just wanted to check on you. Are you okay?"

Her hand came up to touch my cheek, and I didn't have it in me to push her away. Was I okay? No. Absolutely not. "I'm fine," I muttered unconvincingly.

Her thumb caressed my cheek, reminding me of countless occasions where she'd been my rock—where my sanity had depended on her. "No, you're not, Haydey."

The tender word was too much, too jarring. Even if her touch did make a small amount of warmth return to my chest, we weren't those people anymore. Pretending nothing had changed wouldn't solve anything. "Don't call me that," I told her, pulling my head away from her touch.

She let me retreat unchallenged, but the disappointment in her eyes was obvious. Her lips firmed, and I could tell she was struggling with how she wanted to deal with me. I wasn't sure what I wanted…which meant she should probably leave.

"Hayden, I know you're hurting, but you don't have to shut me out. I'm here for you." Compassion swirled in the dark depths of her eyes, and I knew she meant that. But I also knew she was hoping for more. And I had nothing in me right now.

"You should go," I told her. Before she could respond, I turned and headed for my small kitchen area. Memories of Kenzie doting on me while my leg had healed bombarded me as I searched for a cure to my heartache. Whiskey. I was going to drown myself in about a gallon of it.

Instead of leaving, Felicia followed me. "You shouldn't be alone right now."

Finding a bottle, I set it on the counter and removed the cork. Flashing her a glance, I snarked, "And I should be with you? That's better?" I pulled a long draw off the bottle, and nearly sighed with relief when the numbing burn hit my throat.

Anger brightened Felicia's eyes. "Yes, being with me is better than drinking yourself into oblivion and drowning in your own vomit."

Grabbing the bottle from me, she hid it behind her back. Emptiness quickly turned to rage. I hadn't asked for a babysitter, and I didn't need one. "Give that back," I seethed, venom in my voice.

Unafraid, Felicia lifted her chin. "No. There are better ways to deal with this."

A sudden bubble of laughter erupted from my throat. Oh God, that was rich coming from her. "Yeah, you're right. I could just leave a note on the table and skip town. That's a much better plan."

Moisture filled her eyes, but her jaw hardened, so I didn't know if they were angry tears, or if I'd struck a nerve. "You can be such an asshole sometimes."

Returning to my cupboards, to search for another bottle, I retaliated with, "And you can be a bitch. Guess we were just too similar to last."

"That's not why we didn't last."

I spun around to stop her from talking. Stepping up to her, I snapped, "Don't. Just save it. Whatever excuse you've cooked up to explain away what you did, I don't want to hear it. I don't *ever* want to hear it."

Her jaw dropped as she stared at me. "You were never going to give me a chance, were you?"

Reaching behind her, I grabbed the bottle and yanked it away. Whiskey spilled over both of us, but I didn't care. "No, I wasn't."

While I took a long draw off the bottle, she calmly said, "I was pregnant."

The bottle slipped from my fingers, crashing to the floor in an explosion of alcohol and glass. I didn't even look at the mess. I couldn't. My mind was too wrapped up in what she'd just said to do…anything. "You were? What happened?"

My voice was a whisper, but she acted like I'd yelled at her again. "Doesn't matter. You don't want to hear it."

She started moving away, and I grabbed her arm. Pain and panic filled me, as I frantically searched her face. "What happened, Felicia? Stop messing around and tell me!"

Her face morphed into compassion once again. "I found out…right after Antonia was diagnosed. I was going to tell you, but…" Her eyes filled with definite tears. "Seeing what Izzy was going through, what everyone was going through…I just couldn't…I couldn't love something that much, and risk losing it. I wasn't strong enough for that kind of loss. So…"

Dread filled me. Dread and fear. Grabbing her other arm, I made her stay facing me. "What did you do?" I asked in a hushed voice.

She shook her head. "Nothing. It was a false positive. My period started the next month, and I was so relieved. And so…not relieved."

I couldn't believe what I was hearing. Why the hell didn't she talk to me? "If you weren't really…then why the hell did you leave?"

Reaching up, she grabbed one of my hands and held it in hers. "Because I realized that I was already risking it all …by loving you."

"I don't understand," I said, shaking my head.

Felicia nodded. "I know. It's just...everything I feared about loving and losing a baby, the thought of losing you was ten times—no, a hundred times worse. I knew that if something ever happened to you, if you...died...it would destroy me. I'd never recover. And I just couldn't ...I couldn't let you do that to me," she said, her voice trembling.

Pulling away from her, I stepped back. "You ruined... *everything*...because you loved me too much?" As odd as it sounded, I completely understood though. There had been nights when I'd woken up in a panic, terrified that I'd lost her. And then I *did* lose her, and all my nightmares had paled in comparison.

Crunching on the glass at our feet, she stepped forward and grabbed my hands; I was trapped against the counter now, with no hope of an easy escape. Mentally or physically. "I know it was stupid, Hayden, but I was a kid. I was scared. And you were...my entire world."

Shaking my head, I murmured, "You were gone for years, Felicia. *Years*. When we needed you most, when *I* needed you most, you just...left."

Tears dripping down her cheeks now, she dropped my hands and grabbed my face. "I know, and I'm so sorry. It took me so long to realize what a huge mistake I'd made. I thought I was saving us, Hayden. I thought it would hurt less if I left. I was so...so wrong...and I'm so sorry. Please ...forgive me."

Lifting, she placed a light kiss on my lips. It was like a gunshot went off in my head. Or fireworks—blinding, deafening. The remembered taste filled me as her mouth moved over mine—the softness, the sweetness...the fear. Even when we'd been together and happy, there had been an almost frantic fear between us, like at any minute everything would be swept away. It made the sex incredible, but it left an ache, a scar that never truly healed. And then my biggest fears had come true—and by facing my worst fears—I'd conquered them. Felicia, though, I don't think she'd ever faced her fears.

Breaking off contact, I gently pushed her back. "Stop."

Her wide eyes staring back at me were a mixture of desperation, fear and hope. "Hayden," she quietly said, her voice strained. "Please…"

She moved toward me again, but I held her back. "I get it, Felicia. I get why you left. I understand running from something you want, but you should have talked to me. If you'd just confessed your fears to me…told me you thought you were pregnant…we could have worked things out." With a sigh, I shook my head. "But you always had one foot out the door, ready to bolt at a moment's notice. This is going to sound harsh, but I think you leaving that last time was the best thing that could have happened to me."

Hurt instantly darkened her expression, and she pulled farther away from me. Wishing the truth didn't sting so hard, I told her, "You and I, we were never meant to be. I want more. I want permanent. I want a foundation I can trust. And that will never be you."

Fresh tears in her eyes, she looked away from me. "You're assuming I haven't changed." She returned her eyes to mine. "But I have. I'm still here, aren't I?"

With a sad smile, I nodded. "Yeah, but that's not going to change anything. I want Kenzie, and I won't ever give up on her."

Closing her mouth, she pressed her lips into a firm line. "Kenzie? She...she's done, Hayden. She doesn't want you anymore."

"I know," I said with a sigh. Collecting my thoughts, I paused for a moment. She searched me the entire time, like she was looking for a path back into my heart. "I loved you once, Felicia, I really did, and I will always cherish the memory of what we had. But we were kids, like you said, and we didn't really know what we wanted. Thank you for telling me why you left, and...I'm sorry I didn't let you tell me earlier. Because I get it. It stills pisses me off, but I understand."

More tears dropped down her cheeks as she stared at me. Her mouth opened and closed, but no words left her, so she merely nodded instead. The lingering attraction that had been popping up since her arrival faded to nothing as I locked gazes with her. Kenzie was all I saw when I looked into her eyes now. "I need to show you something," I told her.

She was naturally confused as she took my offered hand and I led her to the bedroom. When we stepped inside, her eyes darted to the bed. "I thought you...? Didn't you just say...?" She licked her lips, like she wasn't sure if she should keep objecting.

With a small chuckle, I released her hand. "That's not what I want to show you." Opening the closet, I rummaged through it until I found an old shoebox in the back. Pulling it out, I slowly turned around to face her. "This is what I wanted to show you." Opening the lid, I reached inside and pulled out the ring I'd been holding onto for way too many years now.

Shock passed over her features as she took the ring from my hand. Her eyes remoistened as she held it. "I was going to propose to you, but after Antonia got sick, I just couldn't ever seem to find the right time."

Eyes glued on the massive diamond, she gaped at me. "Why are you showing me this? Why do you still have it?"

Smiling at her reaction, I said, "I think I needed closure. A small part of me was holding onto the past—our past. But I can't keep holding on and move forward, so take it. Toss it, burn it, sell it…I don't care. I don't need it anymore."

With a sad smile on her lips, she held the ring close to her chest and said, "Hayden…Kenzie, she's…she's out of the picture. We can still… If you could just find it in your heart to forgive me, we could have our old life back."

"That's just it," I responded. "I don't want my old life back. And Kenzie will never be out of the picture. Not for me." My smile was unstoppable. "She has my soul, and I won't rest until I get her back."

Felicia's gaze grew wistful, and I knew it would take longer for the attraction to die from her side than it had from mine. She cringed again. "You really love her, don't you?" As I nodded, her eyes drifted to the ground. "I really thought you'd still be here when I came back. Even if you were taken, I thought you'd still come back to me." Lifting her eyes to mine, she shook her head. "It never occurred to me that you could fall in love with someone else. Not really. I always thought…you and me…" She swallowed a harsh lump in her throat, then shook her head again. "I'm sorry I left, more than ever now." She squeezed the ring in her fingers, and more tears dripped off her cheeks. "And I'm…I'm sorry I messed with your relationship." I could tell those words were really hard for her to say; I was a little shocked she'd said them. Her next words floored me though. "Keith has bigger plans to exploit us...but I'll...I'll respect your relationship with Kenzie. I'll tell him no."

Anger crawled up my spine, raising the hairs on my neck. "What plans?" I asked.

Felicia bit her lip, guilt all over her face. "Ever since he found out about our history, he wanted to play us up to the media. Make everyone think we were a couple. Get people talking about us, talking about his team. He's just about to seal an advertising deal for the two of us. Racy stuff...from what he's told me."

Felicia looked away from my glare like I'd burned her. "Thank you for telling me," I told her. "But you should go now."

She returned her heartbroken eyes to me, gave me a brief nod, then left me in my apartment, alone and seething. Fucking Keith. Pushing her to engage me, and now this? A racy ad? This whole "power couple" angle he was trying to manufacture was going to end right now. I was no one's puppet.

CHAPTER 17

~Kenzie~

I was so furious I could barely see straight. He did it for *me*? He lied, went behind my back with, with—*her*—for me? Bullshit. Hayden did it for *himself*, so he could play at being a hero. And I didn't ask for any of it. I had my own plans to fix my life, and none of them revolved around speeding down a city street at 100 miles per hour. The asshole could have been killed. Jesus, he could have been killed…

From the corner of my eye, I saw Felicia scoot out the hospital doors after Hayden. *Yeah, go. Go and be with him. We're done, he's all yours.* God…were we really done? Agony knocked on my shell of fury, but I pushed it away. I couldn't think about the aftermath of this fight, of what my words really meant for us; I was too pissed off.

Not able to stand still, I started pacing. Back and forth, back and forth, like a riled cat lashing its tail, telling the world it was angry without actually accomplishing anything. It wasn't satisfying enough. I wanted to act, wanted to do something…*anything*. The heat of inactivity was festering inside me, rank and putrid.

Izzy timidly approached me while I was maniacally bouncing between two support pillars. "Kenzie?" she asked, keeping pace with me. "How...are you?"

Her simple question sent a burst of rage up my spine, and I stopped to face her. "How am I? He lied to me for months! He was risking his life for months! He was going off with *her* for months!" I wasn't sure how long Felicia had actually been a part of that seedy world, but I didn't care. Once was too much. He should have told me.

Izzy raised her hands like she was fending off blows. "I know, and he's an asshole for doing it, but he had good intentions. That has to count for something, right?"

No. Right now he could take his good intentions and shove them. Good intentions didn't forgive bad behavior, no matter how you tried to spin it. And good intentions shouldn't have *ever* included his ex. Just how much had he reconnected with her anyway? Oh God...my nightmare was real. They'd rekindled their relationship right under my nose. I was such an idiot.

Shaking my head at her, I resumed pacing. "No, you know what counts, Izzy? Honesty. Honesty counts. Integrity counts. Faithfulness counts. Not being a lying asshole counts!"

"Okay, Kenzie...okay." Izzy sighed after her statement, and there was deep resignation in the weary sound. Hearing it opened a crack in my heart, and pain started to trickle in. How could he do this to me?

I tried to dam the cracks with hate, tried to rebuild the wall of indignation around me, but the grief was strong, and little by little, it was starting to pull me under. I didn't want to fall apart in front of Hookup; I could feel the amusement rolling off him in waves. But I didn't want to leave the hospital either. I'd come here for a reason, to support Izzy and Antonia, and drowning in my own pity wasn't doing a damn thing for either of them.

Guilt helped shove my feelings about Hayden into the farthest corner of my brain. It would haunt me later, but that was fine. This was infinitely more important. Inhaling a deep breath, I stopped pacing and faced Izzy. "Have you heard anything from the doctor yet?"

She grabbed her stomach as she shook her head. Putting my arm around her shoulder, I started leading her away. "Come on, let's go find someone who knows something."

Grunts stayed where he was, but surprisingly, Hookup followed us. He looked bored. Maybe he thought I was a walking time bomb, and any moment I'd explode into a dazzling display of out-of-control emotions. I honestly felt like I might, but for Izzy's sake, I was doing everything I could to keep it together.

Wandering the halls helped pass the time, and eventually Antonia's doctor found us. While he was updating us on her status, some sick, twisted part of me wished Hayden was still there, holding me, comforting me. What the doctor had to say wasn't good. Antonia's appendix had ruptured, and a bunch of that gooey crud inside it had seeped into her belly. The doctor had done all he could do, but the infection was slowly poisoning her. They were giving her medicine to help fight the onslaught, but ultimately, it was up to Antonia and her shot-to-hell immune system now.

She was out cold when we were finally able to visit her in her room. Even asleep, she looked awful with wan skin and darkly circled eyes. All the brightly covered walls, all the toys and stuffed animals, all the little friendly touches that the hospital used to make the kids feel at home here, somehow, it only emphasized just how sick she really was. She was a tiny, fragile doll—cracked, torn, and worn. It broke my already-broken heart.

Izzy climbed right into bed with her. Antonia stirred, but didn't open her eyes. I gave them their space, then glanced over at Hookup. He was standing by the door, like he was afraid to come any closer. His eyes were wide, like he couldn't process what he was seeing. Then he muttered something and kissed a pendant around his neck—a Catholic saint, from what I could tell. The ache in my chest squeezed so hard, I actually had the desire to comfort him—an emotion I never thought I'd feel. Instead of caving into the desire, I walked over to the other side of the bed and sat down. I smiled at Izzy cuddling with her daughter, then grabbed Antonia's hand and said my own prayer. *Please let her be okay...she's just a child.*

The night nurse eventually kicked Hookup and me out of the room; Izzy wasn't going anywhere, and the nurse knew that. We walked down the hallway together in silence, and I could tell when I glanced at Hookup that he was processing something big. He looked like a man who absolutely knew the world was flat being shown that it was round. I left him to his deep thoughts, since I had enough of my own.

Hookup sat down in the waiting room, clearly staying. I couldn't. I needed to be doing something. Walking outside, I headed for my bike. The sun was just starting to rise, and everything was turning a golden peach color. It was a beautiful sight, but it felt wrong, out of place. Nothing should be beautiful today.

Slamming on my helmet, I started my bike and headed home. Only I wasn't going home. Not yet. I had a few stops to make first. Antonia's random stroke of bad luck, Hayden's lies, my family, my job...life had pushed me around this year, and I was absolutely sick of it.

I was tired of being manipulated and left in the dark. I hadn't been acting like myself lately, and I was really starting to dislike the person I was becoming. I wasn't a doormat. I wasn't a victim. I was a champion...and it was time I started acting like one.

By the time I got to the practice track, it was early enough that people had started arriving. Since Keith hadn't found it necessary to give me a key, I headed around back, to Hayden's secret entrance. I opened it wide enough to fit my bike, walked it through, then sealed the hole shut behind me. After all this time, it still looked like a seamless part of the fence. Perfect. And yet another reminder that things weren't always what they seemed—like Hayden and me. I'd thought we were amazing together. I'd thought we would defy the odds and make it. I was wrong.

Hopping back on my bike, I rode around the complex to the parking lot. As I suspected, a few cars and trucks were there. I didn't see Keith's sports car though. The inner gate to the track was open, so I pointed my bike in that direction. Glancing to my right, I saw the empty Cox garages looming like a dark cloud—or a heavy burden—one I was ready to be free of. Free of the memories, free of the emotional ties, free of the past. Maybe it was the grief talking, but I was ready to release it all. And standing right in front of me was a golden opportunity to let it all go.

The practice track was empty, and the entrance was calling me like a forsaken lover. Since I didn't give a shit what anyone here thought anymore, I jumped on the chance and poured on the gas. My bike skidded out a little in the anticipation of intense speed, and by the time I passed the entrance and was on the actual track, I was already going fast. But not nearly fast enough. All of my training kicked into high gear as I hunched over the handlebars, and leaned low into the corners. My bike wasn't a performance bike like my Ducati, but it soared. It felt so good to be back on a track in daylight, that I started laughing, and happy tears clouded my vision. But they were bittersweet, because I knew this wouldn't last.

Like fate agreed, a man started stumbling onto the track, hobbling on a crutch with one hand while waving his other in the air like he was flagging down a taxi. Keith's face was bright red, and his mouth was moving like he was shouting something. Probably obscenities. I was in street clothes on a street bike; I clearly didn't belong on the track.

I had to slow my bike so I didn't hit him. I gave myself one extra lap—just enjoying it—then I stopped in front of Keith and removed my helmet. Now that I could hear them, his words struck me so hard I almost got whiplash. "What the fuck are you doing on my fucking track, Cox? And on that fucking piece of shit bike? You're lucky I haven't called the fucking cops yet. What the fuck were you thinking? And how the fuck did you get in here? Did one of those fuckers give you a key?"

Seeing him so riled up almost made me smile. "How I got in doesn't matter. All that matters...is that I quit. I'm done with Hayden's bullshit, and I'm done with yours." God, it felt good to say that. Although, it hurt too.

Keith's demeanor turned a complete one-eighty. "You and Hayden are done?" he asked, an eyebrow cocked under his aviator glasses. I didn't answer him, just gritted my teeth. He took my silence as affirmation.

With a sly grin, he said, "And here I thought today was going to be just another average day." A cruel laugh escaped his lips. "God, it's practically my birthday. You're gone from here, you're done with him, and Hayden can't blame me for any of it. It's a beautiful thing." His smile turned satisfied.

"Fuck you, Keith."

The smile quickly fell from his face. "Since you're no longer an employee, you're trespassing on private property. Now, get the fuck off my track," he finished with a snarl.

"Gladly," I murmured, putting my helmet back on.

I turned my bike toward the exit, and right before I punched it, I heard Keith yell, "And return the uniform to Nikki!" I paused to look over at him, and he added, "If you don't, I'll sue your ass for theft!" I was sure he would too. Asshole.

Since this seemed like a good day to confront everyone who'd been pissing me off lately, I headed to my father's house next. There were quite a few things I wished to say to my dear old dad. The house was dark when I got there. I was fairly certain my father was awake though; I highly doubted he'd given up his strict schedule just because he'd been forced into an early retirement.

Hopping off my bike, I strutted to his front door and started banging on the hard wood. It was an overly aggressive greeting, and I knew that, but I was too fired up to do anything else. Dad appeared a few moments later. His stern gaze and disapproving frown showed no signs of weariness; I knew he'd been awake. "Mackenzie, why are you trying to break down my door?"

"I thought you'd be interested to know that I just quit Benneti Motorsports." His eyes brightened at hearing me say that. He opened his mouth, but I didn't let him respond. "I also broke up with Hayden." A sharp knife slowly drew across my heart with that admission, but I didn't let the pain show on my face. Dad didn't get to see that.

His earlier happiness paled in comparison to the joy I saw now. "Mackenzie, that's—"

I lifted my hand to stop whatever encouraging words he'd been about to give me. "Neither of those two things changes anything between you and me. We're done too. Have been for a while, truth be told."

"I...that's not what I... Mackenzie, be reasonable." Dad was trying to make his face imposing again, but there was fear in his expression now, like he finally understood that he'd taken things entirely too far and there was no going back.

"I *am* being reasonable, Dad. You shut me out, because of a boy. You blocked off every avenue, closed every door. I wouldn't be surprised if you purposefully stoked Theresa and Daphne's anger toward me, all to make sure I was completely alone. If you could have corrupted Myles and Nikki, I'm sure you would have done that too." My hands clenched as I thought about that very real possibility. "Why go through such extremes? Because I didn't do what you wanted me to do? Is your pride that fragile?"

His eyes turned pleading. "I know you don't understand, but it was for *your* betterment. I was trying to help *you*."

Annoyance built up inside me like burrs under my skin; I was so tired of people doing horrible things for *my* benefit. "All you ended up doing, Dad, was ruining our relationship. And unlike what happened with you and Mom, no amount of counseling is going to save us. I'm done trying to understand you, and I can't forgive you for what you did." A warm numbness started blanketing me as my words sunk into my pores. It was sad that things were over, but it was the truth. A bridge had been burned, one that couldn't be repaired; there was no point mourning it now.

As I grew calm, Dad grew frantic. Stepping forward, he put his hands on my upper arms. "I'll get you a job, I'll make this right. I'm sorry if I took things too far, I was just trying to make you see—"

Brushing his hands off me, I firmly told him, "What I *saw*, was that Keith might have been right all along. You *can* be ruthless, relentless, and emotionless when you want something badly enough. That might have served you well as a racer, but they're not good attributes, Dad. And as far as getting me a job...don't bother. I'll refuse anything you send my way."

Shock turned Dad's face a pale white, and he looked about to interrupt. When he said my name, I steamrolled right over him. "No, I'm tired of being manipulated. I'm tired of reacting to things, instead of making them happen." With a sarcastic smile, I shook my head. "Congratulations, you successfully got me blacklisted from the sport—*your* sport. You single-handedly ended what could have been a family legacy, but I don't give a shit about that legacy anymore. If I can't race motorcycles, then fine, I'll just find a new sport to shine in. And I *will* be able to shine, because I won't have your shadow hovering over me anymore. I'll no longer be known as Jordan Cox's daughter first and a competitor second. I'll just be a competitor, same as everyone else, and that's more than enough for me." Hope bloomed inside my tormented heart, and, straightening my stance, I lifted my chin and stared him down; for once, I didn't feel like his inferior or subordinate. I felt...invincible.

Dad's eyes aged right in front of me as he struggled to maintain my gaze. "What are you going to do?" he asked, his voice subdued.

I couldn't contain my smile. Was this what true freedom felt like? "I don't know yet, but I'm excited to get started." Wanting to leave on that note, I spun on my heel and started walking toward my bike.

Dad's voice rose over the sound of gravel crunching under my boot. "Mackenzie, wait!" The tone of his voice halted my movement, freezing me in place. Swiveling my neck, I looked over my shoulder at him. Defeat on his face, he shook his head. "What I said about your mother was too much. It was cruel, and I'm...I'm sorry. Nothing you could ever do would have changed her feelings about you. She loved you, with all her heart, and she definitely wouldn't have approved of how I..." Hanging his head, he sighed, "I just... I wanted to push you in the right direction. I was desperate...but it was a horrible choice—possibly the worst one I've ever made." He looked up at me, tears in his eyes. "I truly am sorry, and I hope you'll change your mind and forgive me one day. I love you, Mackenzie."

Goddamn it, I shouldn't have stopped. I should have run to my bike and gotten out of there as quickly as possible. He didn't get to treat me like a pariah for months, then sweep it all under the rug with one phrase seeped in sentiment. And as angry as he'd made me...I wasn't used to hearing such tender words from him; it triggered something inside me. I wanted to run to him, toss my arms around his neck, and tell him I forgave him everything. But I had to be stronger than that. He'd been stone; I needed to be ice. Shifting my weight, I ignored his comment and resumed walking to my bike. My eyes stung with tears begging to drop. I didn't let them. He would *not* see me break down.

I put my helmet on as quickly as possible, and just in the nick of time too; a few tears escaped as I started my motorcycle. Not looking at Dad, because I wasn't sure what I would do if I saw his face, I backed up my bike, then turned up the driveway and left. As I pulled away from him, that jagged line of pain across my heart started to rip open. The tears started coming in torrents. Hayden was gone. My father was gone. My sisters...were as good as gone. My job was gone. Everything I'd once cherished had been set ablaze, and was now just ashes on the wind.

Myles's place was too far away—I could barely see through the tears as it was, there was no way I'd make it all the way to San Francisco—and I couldn't bother Izzy, not with everything she was going through right now, so I headed to the only person I could still count on. The only person I was positive still loved me. Nikki.

As I headed to her apartment, I hoped she was sticking to her usual routine of being late for everything. If she'd already left for work, I wasn't sure what I would do for hours until she got home. Probably cry on her front porch. Or pick her lock and cry on her couch.

The thought of breaking and entering Nikki's place made me think of Hayden, which restarted the vicious circle of despair. If only I could get the anger or numbness to come back. I'd do just about anything to keep from feeling the escalating grief. I'd lost it all…

Nikki's smart car was still parked in her appointed stall when I got there, and I said a quick thank you for her being a procrastinator. I rang her doorbell after I stepped up to her door; I didn't trust that I would be able to knock on her door without banging on it like I had at Dad's. It took Nikki a few minutes to answer, and I could hear her inside, muttering and cursing to herself. Probably for being late. Even though she was frequently behind schedule, it bothered her.

When the wood in front of me finally opened to reveal her face, she looked frazzled. But oddly, her eyes widened in surprise at seeing me, and she started closing the door. "Hey, Nik?" I said, putting my hand up to stop the door from closing all the way.

Throwing it back open, she gave me a half-hearted smile. "Sorry, Kenzie. I'm just…super late. What's up?"

Her eyes were darting everywhere but my face, and I instantly felt bad for adding to her stress. I needed her though. "I broke up with Hayden," I muttered. Her mouth dropped open, and she finally focused on me. "I also quit Benneti and told my dad I never wanted to see him again. It's been a busy morning…"

"Oh my God, come here." She instantly pulled me into a rib-crushing hug. "I'm so sorry. What happened?" she asked, pulling back to look at my face.

I was crying again, but I didn't care; I didn't think I'd ever stop. "Can we go inside?"

Nikki instantly cursed at herself, and stepped back, letting me in. "Yeah, yeah, of course." She no longer looked frazzled for time, but she looked…off. Eyes on my shoes, she pointed to the couch. "Have a seat." I schlepped that way and sat down. She bit her lip while standing nervously in front of me. "Want anything? Coffee? Whiskey?"

I cracked a smile, but shook my head. Nikki was still standing there, fidgeting with her hands. "You okay?" I asked her.

She instantly relaxed and sat on the couch. "Yeah… I'm great. So…what happened?"

She was holding her hands so tightly her knuckles were white. Since my own problems were swirling out of control, I ignored her oddness and spilled my story. "Hayden was street racing for his friend again. With Felicia this time instead of me…" Admitting the betrayal made my stomach fill with acid. I thought I might be sick. Holding my gut, I told her, "He even had the nerve to tell me he was doing it for me, to raise enough money so I could race again…somehow." I'd never let him fully explain how, but that didn't really matter. He'd lied. Repeatedly.

Nikki's faced morphed through a thousand emotions before settling on contemplation. "Do you think that's what he was really trying to do? Get you racing again? Because…that's kind of sweet."

My gaze hardened into daggers. "Lying to me all the fucking time isn't sweet, Nik. And I never asked him to get me racing again… I asked him to be honest. I asked him to be loyal. I'm pretty sure he failed at both."

Nikki's eyes shifted to the floor, and she started bouncing her toes up and down in an incessant pattern that was kind of driving me nuts. "Oh…so you guys are really over?"

Slamming my hand down on her knee, I bit out, "Yes, we're done. And Dad and I are done, and Keith and I are done. I don't have anyone…"

She immediately threw an arm around me. "You have me, Kenzie. Always."

Smiling, I laid my head on her shoulder and removed my hand from her knee. She immediately started bouncing again, but I tried to ignore it. "I thought Hayden and I were this great, epic couple. I'd thought we were going to be the happy version of Romeo and Juliet. We were so good together, but he still…"

Emotion closed my throat, and I had to swallow before I could speak. Nikki filled the silence. "Sometimes people change. Sometimes they do things they never thought they would, because it seemed like a good idea at the time, and they were really lonely, and maybe it had been a while, and maybe there was alcohol and stuff…"

I pulled back from under her arm to stare at her. "What?"

Eyes wide, she immediately shook her head. "Nothing. Just a bad analogy, or metaphor…or whatever."

Narrowing my eyes, I studied her. Chewing on her lip, her eyes darting everywhere, she was obviously nervous or anxious or something. And I didn't think it was because she was late for work. "What's going on with you?" I asked.

She tried smiling like she didn't have a care in the world. She failed miserably. "Nothing…I'm just worried about you. And Hayden. That totally sucks."

My annoyance at her avoidance actually helped curb the pain. Crossing my arms over my chest, I stared her down. "Tell me."

She leapt off the couch and started pacing. "There's nothing to tell except that I'm late for work, and Keith might kill me if I don't get there soon."

Guilt assaulted me, and I stood up with her. "Okay, I'm sorry. Do you mind if I crash here though? I don't want to go home." I really couldn't handle Hayden showing up on my doorstep.

Nikki's expression softened. "Of course, stay as long as you like."

She gave me a quick hug, and, after we broke apart, I said to her, "Hey, let's go up north this weekend and hang out with Myles. And maybe never come back." I laughed on the end of that to show I was joking, but Nikki looked absolutely horrified by my suggestion.

"No!" She quickly added in a softer voice, "I mean, Myles is training…he's busy."

I had never in my life seen Nikki turn down an opportunity to hang out with Myles. Those two were peas in a pod, nearly inseparable. The only thing that ever got Nikki down was the fact that Myles was so far away from her now. Her refusing to see him—*passionately* refusing to see him—was shocking. "Are you guys fighting?" I asked. That was unheard of too. Sure, they bickered, but it was all in good fun.

Nikki's expression was rigid as she stared at me; she looked marble she was so frozen. "Nope, we're good."

Obviously, they weren't. God, I was sick and tired of people hiding things from me. "I really can't deal with any more lies, Nikki. Tell me what happened. The truth."

She melted like she was made of butter. Sinking onto the couch, she put her elbows on her knees and her face into her hands; she no longer looked like she needed to be anywhere but where she was. "Oh God, Kenzie..." She peered up at me with a desolate expression on her face. "Myles and I...we kind of did the deed."

Not feeling any more enlightened, I sat down beside her and blankly asked, "What deed?"

Her face stiffened with annoyance. "*The* deed, Kenzie. We...slept together."

"You guys sleep together all the..." My sentence trailed off as I was hit over the head with understanding. "Oh my God...you had sex with Myles? But he's like your...brother."

Her face morphed into a disgusted expression that I was sure matched mine. Shaking her head, she said, "Ew, no, he's not my brother, he's more like...like my best friend. Which is why things are so weird now. We messed up, Kenzie. Big time. And I don't know what to do."

I couldn't believe what I was hearing. Myles and Nikki hooked up? It was like I was stuck in some alternate reality. Was this how Nikki had felt when I'd told her about Hayden and me? Probably. "Have you guys talked about this? How does he feel about it?"

She shook her head. "I don't know. We haven't spoken since Monterey."

"Monterey..." Again, understanding bashed me in the skull. "Holy shit! That wasn't the TV I was hearing that night in Myles's hotel room. That was you two...going at it..." I clutched my stomach, once more feeling sick.

Nikki looked equally horrified. "You heard us? Oh my God," she said, letting her head drop into her hands. "Now everything is weird."

Putting my hand on her back, I rubbed soothing circles into her skin. Looking up at me, she murmured, "Want to know the worst part?"

"Sure," I answered, not sure if I really wanted to know.

Straightening, she told me, "I can't stop thinking about it. It was the *best* sex I've ever had. Just thinking about his hands on me gets me horny." Her face shifted into a grimace. "But it's Myles, Kenzie. *Myles*! I can't get all hot and bothered about Myles!"

I had never wanted to be somewhere else more in all my life. While Myles was a best friend to her, he was a brother to me. And she was a sister. And the two of them "doing the deed" was *not* something I wanted to think about. "Well, I'm sure that will fade…just go have sex with someone else. But not Hayden."

I knew right after I said that, I shouldn't have. The thought of Nikki and Hayden together—of Hayden and *anyone* together—made bile rise in my throat. Nikki instantly understood the look of pain and disgust on my face. "God, Kenzie…I'm so sorry about you and Hayden. Want to watch sappy Lifetime movies all day with me?"

I could feel the tears building again, even as I nodded. "I thought you had to go, though. I thought Keith would kill you if you were too late?"

As a tear dropped down my cheek, Nikki gave me a sheepish smile. "No, I just didn't want to tell you about Myles. I'll call in sick…it'll be fine."

I lightly slugged her in the shoulder, then hugged her, then thanked her. Because I knew I'd never get through today without her.

CHAPTER 18

~Hayden~

I had trouble falling asleep after Felicia left my apartment. Not because of our conversation, or because I'd finally given her the engagement ring I'd been holding onto forever. No, I'd had trouble silencing my mind because I'd been brainstorming ways to get Kenzie back.

I'd finally closed the door on my confusing, unfinished feelings about Felicia. That part of my brain was blissfully silent, and I could now spend all my efforts focusing on Kenzie, like she deserved. But how in the world could I convince her that I didn't have feelings for my ex? I'd seriously messed up by lying for so long about the street racing, and Felicia being a part of that world only made things a hundred times worse. I really wasn't sure what I could do to fix it.

By the time I passed out from mental exhaustion, it was almost light out. When I finally woke up, it was almost noon. Goddamn it. Kenzie was slipping from me more and more with every passing second. Time was of the essence, and I couldn't afford to waste a single moment, not even with necessary sleep.

The first thing I did when I hopped out of bed was check my phone to see if Kenzie had called or texted. She hadn't, but there *were* missed phone calls from Keith and Izzy, and a couple of voicemails too. Hoping against all hope that the voicemails were somehow from Kenzie, I checked my messages.

The one from Izzy let me know that Antonia was out of surgery, but there were complications and she didn't know if Antonia was out of the woods yet. My chest squeezed so hard, I felt like I was having a heart attack. She had to be okay, she just had to be. Antonia was the closest thing I would probably ever have to a daughter, and I couldn't imagine losing her. I made a mental note to drive down there today and see her.

The second message was from Keith…not Kenzie. It was mainly a lot of incoherent yelling. Something about me having to answer for something, and I better get my ass to the track ASAP. The message was from two hours ago. Great. Knowing my ass would be grass if I waited any longer to leave—and I had a few things to say to Keith as well—I got dressed and made my way down to the track.

I was so late that everyone was there already. Everyone except Nikki. I didn't see her little car anywhere. Damn. I'd really been hoping to talk to her about Kenzie. If anyone could help direct me toward the right path, it would be her. I'd have to grab her as soon as she came in; hopefully I could talk to her before Kenzie did. Convincing Nikki to help me after she'd already been influenced by Kenzie's side of the story would make things so much more difficult.

Driving past Keith's sporty car, I drove my bike through the inner gate and headed for the garages. Almost everyone was outside for some reason—some practicing, some just walking around aimlessly. Rodney was standing where I usually parked my bike, leaning against the garage wall. When he saw me, he raised an eyebrow and said, "Hey, man, be on your toes if you're goin' in there. Keith's on a rampage, yelling at everybody."

I wanted to ask why, but something told me I should just go see Keith and ask him myself. And I might do my own yelling if what Felicia told me was true; Keith had no right to interfere in my personal life.

The garage was empty, so I stomped upstairs to look for Keith. I found him pacing the hallway in front of his office. He pointed his crutch at me when he saw me. "You! You're the reason she quit. What the hell did you do!"

Confusion trumped my anger. "Who quit? Kenzie? Was Kenzie here this morning? Did she look okay?" I asked, my voice a little frantic.

Resting his crutch back onto the ground, Keith scrunched his face in confusion. "Kenzie?" He instantly brushed aside my concern with his hand. "Yes, the little Cox bitch quit, but I don't give a shit about that. Felicia quit! *Felicia*! One of my best riders, and the other half of…" Looking flustered, he shook his head. "*She* mattered to the team, not your little gal-pal. And she quit, because of you!"

Surprise choked my response from me. When I could speak, I stuttered on the name. "Ken…Kenzie quit? This morning?"

Keith removed his glasses and gave me a hard stare. "And Felicia. You seem to be ignoring the most important part. What the hell did you do to your teammate!"

With a frustrated grunt, I ran my hands through my hair. Kenzie quit, then Felicia quit. I understood why Kenzie had given up her job, since she hated everything about it, but I didn't understand why Felicia had left—Keith was right when he said she was one of Benneti's top riders; she was the top female in the league right now. But then, of course, it wasn't all that surprising. Felicia bolting from a difficult situation was nothing new. Guess she hadn't changed after all.

Leaving was her decision, though, and if that was what she wanted, then that was fine. It wasn't my problem. Not anymore. "I didn't do anything to Felicia, okay? I just...told her she wasn't the one for me. Now what did Kenzie say when she quit?"

Keith's face skewed in anger. "You told her...? I had plans for the two of you, things that were going to cause a major buzz. Once that Cox girl was gone, the road was going to be wide open for you and Felicia. I was going to televise your fucking marriage for fuck's sake!"

Like the blazing sun eating away at the morning fog, the shock was wearing off and the anger was returning. "You had plans for us? And what about *our* plans? Yours and mine? You know, the plan for me to get the track from Jordan and give it to you...and in return you would give Kenzie a racing job. Do you remember that agreement? Or was it even an agreement? Was it ever really going to happen? Or were you going to screw me over? The way you screwed over Jordan by sleeping with his wife?"

Surprising the hell out of me, Keith lunged and tried to land a punch. He stumbled on his bad leg though, and I easily dodged the blow. Huffing, Keith spat out, "You ungrateful son of a bitch! I found you on the street! You live in my house, ride my equipment. You have no right to talk to me like that!"

Stepping up to him, I pressed my finger into his chest. "No, you don't have the right to butt into my life. You're my boss, not my father." I started to turn away, then stopped. "And you know what, you're not even that anymore. I quit."

Keith's jaw popped open and his sunglasses fell from his hands and clattered to the ground. "You can't…" His jaw snapped shut, and his expression hardened. "Get your shit, and get out of my house. But give me the key to your bike before you go. You're not welcome to ride it anymore." He uncurled his fingers slowly, like it was painful for him.

I debated telling him to piss off, I wasn't walking home, but he would just call the cops and have me arrested for theft. Digging into my jeans, I wrapped my fingers around the keys, dragged them from my pocket, and separated the bike key from the apartment key. Surely I could keep that one until after I'd cleaned out my shit. I handed the bike key to him without saying a word.

Hand still extended, Keith spit out, "Your key card to the track too. You're no longer welcome on the property."

Gritting my teeth, I took out my wallet, grabbed the key card and placed it in his open palm. Then I turned and left.

Fuck. In twenty-four hours I'd managed to lose my girlfriend, my apartment, my fucking job *and* my fucking bike. That had to be some kind of record. Stepping outside, I kicked a tire that was propped near the open garage door, making it fly toward the track. Fucking everything was going fucking wrong.

"Problem?" Rodney asked, still leaning where I'd left him.

"Yeah," I muttered. "Keith kicked me out of his house. And he took back his bike, so now I've got to walk home and gather all my shit before he tosses it." I couldn't believe I was telling *Rodney* all my problems, but I was still reeling. And pissed.

Rodney let out a low, long whistle. "I told you to watch out, man. Need a ride?"

I cocked an eyebrow at him, surprised. "You'd do that?" He'd been one of the biggest assholes to me last year. Sure, he'd mellowed some around me, but I wouldn't say we were friends or anything.

Shrugging, he said, "Beats hanging around here, waiting to get yelled at." He pushed himself away from the wall. "Keith's place, right?"

"Yeah, thanks."

We walked past my bike as we headed for the parking lot, and a forlorn sigh escaped me. I'd really loved that bike. And sure, I could buy another one with my earnings from street racing, but I was saving that money for Kenzie. At least now I had a genuine excuse to stop racing for Hookup. Couldn't race without a bike, and, unlike Keith, Hookup didn't provide equipment.

Fuck. I'd really done it. I'd quit…I wouldn't be racing anymore. Would anyone else hire me? Was my track record enough to compensate for all the negative gossip that had swirled around me last year? Would Keith spread rumors about me, making me un-hirable, like Jordan had done to Kenzie? Was my dream over too?

Shoving those worries to the back of my brain, I followed Rodney to his pickup truck. It was covered in dry dust, like he'd been squirreling around in the desert. Sounded like fun. A lot more fun than losing everything. As I opened the door and slipped inside the messy interior, a stray thought about Felicia floated through my mind. While I wasn't surprised she'd gone, I couldn't believe she was running again. Izzy needed her right now. Izzy needed *all* of us right now, and as much as I needed to get my shit together, I needed to be there for her more.

As Rodney started the vehicle, I looked over at him. "Hey, would you mind taking me somewhere else instead? In San Diego? I'll give you gas money," I quickly added.

Rodney shrugged again, like it didn't matter. "Sure. Where to?"

Gloom in my heart, I shifted my gaze to the windshield. "Children's Hospital…"

"Oh, you got a sick kid there?" he asked, concern in his voice.

I had to swallow the knot in my throat. What if Felicia *had* been pregnant? What if she'd still run away, and I'd never gotten to meet my child? Turning to look at Rodney, I told him, "Yeah, I do." Antonia was mine just as much as she was anyone else's.

"Fuck, sorry, man. I'll get you there quick."

True to his word, we were there in thirty-three minutes. I handed Rodney some twenties, thanked him, then opened the door to get out. He leaned over the seat to talk to me. "Are you gonna need a ride back? I could… hang out? Wait for you?"

His offer was surprising. Maybe he wasn't as much of a douche as I'd originally thought. "Nah, I'm good, man. I have family here."

He nodded. "All right, well…I hope everything works out."

Nodding, I shut the door. I did too.

As I walked down the halls, there was a dire mood in the air, lingering around every corner in sharp contradiction to the strategically painted, bright, cheery walls. Every inch of this place reeked with tension and sadness, and that feeling only amplified the closer I got to Antonia's room. When I pushed open the partially closed door, sunshine filled the vibrant room. It made the tiny sleeping child on the bed look even more pallid, like a dark cloud was hovering over her. Izzy was gone when I got there, and shocking the hell out of me, it was Hookup who had taken her place beside Antonia. He looked awful, like he hadn't slept at all.

He glanced my way when he heard me. "Hey, Hayden. Glad you're back, man. Izzy ran home to take a shower and grab some stuff, but she should be back soon."

"How's Antonia doing?" I asked, moving over to stand beside him.

With a defeated shrug, Hookup wiped a weary hand across his face. "Don't know. She's been sleeping a lot, off and on. She just seems completely out of it…" He let out a stuttered breath. "It's scaring the living fuck out of me, man. Even with all the shit she's been through, it never occurred to me that she might die. I mean, she's a kid…kids don't die." He examined my face like he was searching for confirmation.

I had to bite my tongue to keep from telling him just how untrue that thought was. All of us had the same chance in life. Nature didn't discriminate.

Hookup's gaze returned to Antonia's small form. "She can't die...she just can't. She won't, right?" he said, looking up at me again. The hope in his eyes was almost unbearable. It took every ounce of willpower I had not to avert my eyes; he was clearly on the edge, and needing something to hold on to.

"She's a strong girl. She'll fight this with everything she's got." I just hoped it was enough.

Hookup seemed bolstered by my comment, though, and he smiled before looking back at his niece. "Well, when she does kick this thing's ass, stuff's gonna change. She and Iz...I'm gonna take care of them...like I should have been doing all along." Glancing up at me, his expression turned somber. "You're a good man, Hayden, looking after Izzy and Antonia all these years."

I shook my head. "Taking care of her wasn't hard. It wasn't even a choice." *Love is a gift, not an obligation.* I'd heard that once, and it had always rung true for me. It wasn't a thought I could share with him comfortably, but I hoped he inferred it with my next comment. "She's family, Hookup, same as you."

He cracked a smile, and I thought maybe he finally did get it. Then he shook his head. "Don't call me Hookup, anymore. I'm done with that shit. Call me Tony." After he said it, his eyes once again drifted down to Antonia, his namesake.

"Okay, Tony," I murmured, hoping he meant it. The life he was currently living would only end one of two ways for him—dead or in prison. Iz and Antonia deserved better. And...so did he.

After a few minutes of silence, Hookup looked up at me. "You and Kenzie...you really done?"

A heavy sigh escaped me as I sat on the corner of the bed. "Until I can convince her otherwise, yeah."

"Fuck, man, I'm sorry." His expression turned curious. "Are you and Felicia...?" He raised an eyebrow as he let his question die.

"No," I said, firmly shaking my head. "We were over the day she left...nothing's changed there." He nodded, like he understood cutting ties.

Knowing I was going to need help for a while, and knowing I couldn't reach out to Izzy—not with everything she was going through—I decided to open up to Hookup—Tony. "Hey, I know this is bad timing, but, um...I quit my job, got kicked out of my apartment, and lost my bike... I know I'm an ass for even asking, but I need a place to stay."

I cringed as I finished my request, and felt like hiding in a very deep hole. Asking for help wasn't exactly easy for me. Hookup's eyes were huge as he stared at me. "Shit, man...I'm surprised you're sober right now."

A small laugh escaped me. "Yeah...me too."

Hookup nodded. "Of course you can crash at my place. Stay as long as you like. And if you need a car... here..." Reaching into his pocket, he fished out his car keys and handed them to me. "Izzy gave Grunts a ride home when she left, and I'm...I'm not going anywhere anytime soon. House key's on there too, so feel free to start moving shit in."

"Thanks, Tony. That means a lot to me." A small warm flicker of hope sparked inside my chest. At least one good thing had come out of all this shit. "I've got my phone on me, will you call if...if anything changes?"

Hookup nodded, and I added, "Give Izzy a hug for me when she gets back. I'm sure she needs one."

A wry smile cracked his lips as he nodded again. "Yeah…I will. Good luck moving your shit. I'd help, but…"

"No, you should be here. One of us should always be here…" Looking around, I noticed the Harry Potter book I'd been reading to Antonia on the nightstand. From where the bookmark was sticking out, I could see that she hadn't finished it yet. *She better be able to finish it.*

Feeling my throat swell and my eyes sting, I hurriedly turned and left. It was all too much, too heavy, too real. Everything was crashing down around me, walls caving at every turn. But there had to be an escape route from this mess. There was always at least one…you just had to find it before you were crushed. *Please, God, help me find it.*

Once I located Hookup's car in the parking lot, I headed home to start cleaning out my stuff. I probably shouldn't have burned that bridge with Keith right before the final race of the season, but he'd crossed a line, messed with my life. It was for the best that we were cutting ties. I hoped.

Thankfully, Keith was still at the track when I got back to my apartment. When I got inside, I started stuffing shit into garbage bags, since I didn't have any boxes. That was when I realized that a lot of my things were at Kenzie's. We hadn't officially moved in together—yet—but over the course of the year, small things had been left behind: clothes, toiletries, CDs, and other personal crap. There was a lot more of me at her place than there was of her over here at my place, that was for sure. The loss of evidence of her in my life struck hard as I cinched up the final bag of worthless junk. I should just leave it all behind, because what did any of it mean without her?

But maintaining some semblance of practicality, I trudged the bags down the stairs and shoved them into the backseat of Tony's car. I'd regret it if I let Keith keep anything; I'd even packed the toilet paper.

Climbing back into the car, filled to the brim with most of my worldly possessions, made a dull ache go through me. This couldn't be the way things ended. I couldn't just drive to Tony's and sit there useless and helpless, tail between my legs, licking my wounds until the storm broke. Not without at least trying to do something to change my fate. And there was only one thing I could think of left to try. It was a longshot, but it was better than doing nothing.

Instead of driving Hookup's peppy little car back to San Diego, I headed toward Jordan Cox's house, for one last-ditch effort to save my relationship. And maybe his own in the process.

My stomach clenched in anticipation as I drove up his driveway. With the adrenaline rushing through me, I felt like a race was about to start. Or a fight. Either way, I was geared up long before I knocked on Jordan's door.

Unclenching my fingers while I waited for him to answer was surprisingly more difficult than I thought it would be. It didn't help that Jordan flew to the door like he was expecting somebody. My hands were twisted in talon-like claws when the door suddenly opened.

Jordan filled the empty space so suddenly, I took a step back. "Mackenzie?" he said, eyes wide with hope. They dulled when they spotted me. Then they shifted to anger. "You. What do you want?"

Crossing my arms over my chest, I stared Jordan down. It took all my nerve; he was an imposing man. "You fucked up," I told him. "And you're about to lose your daughter because of it." His cheeks turned a flaming red, and his mouth opened in rebuttal. I didn't let him get the words out. Holding up a hand, I quickly stated, "I fucked up too. And I'm about to lose the woman of my dreams because of it."

Jordan's anger deflated. Surprisingly enough, I didn't see any joy in his eyes at the mention of Kenzie and I being on the outs. Maybe he'd finally realized that losing her in the process of trying to get rid of me hadn't been worth it. With a heavy sigh, I told him, "We both lost her. And there's only one way we're going to get her back."

A tenuous spark of hope lightened Jordan's weary face. "What way?" he tentatively asked.

"Can I come in?" I countered, indicating inside the house.

Jordan nodded, stepping back to let me through the door. As I crossed over the threshold, I was assaulted by memories of Kenzie. Inexplicably, her scent was all over the house, permeated into the walls from a lifetime of visiting and living here. Physical evidence of her was everywhere too; with each step I took, there seemed to be another picture or memento of her. Racing photos, family photos, trophies and medals. I wondered if Kenzie realized just how much of a shrine Jordan's house was; her photo trumped her sisters' photos two to one. Pride was thick in the air. If only Jordan had been able to express that feeling directly to Kenzie. She might not have felt so inferior around him, and neither one of us might be in the mess we were in.

Jordan led us to the living room, then sat down on a chair in front of a fireplace. He indicated a chair opposite him for me to sit, but I was too enthralled with a photo on the mantelpiece. It looked like Kenzie holding a baby, but I knew it wasn't. Walking over, I picked it up. "Is this your wife?" I asked, trying to be as respectful as possible. Regardless of what was between Jordan and me, he'd lost someone incredibly important to him, and I understood loss.

As Jordan stared at the picture in my hands, myriad emotions ran through his eyes. "Yes. With Mackenzie. Vivienne died when she was very young…Mackenzie never even got the chance to know her."

Nodding, I put the photo back. "I was a kid, too, when I lost my parents."

Jordan's gaze shifted to my face. "I'm sorry to hear that. I'm sorry for your loss." The words were clearly difficult for him to say.

I waved away his concern. "No, they didn't die or anything; they were just douches who never wanted a kid in the first place. State stepped in, took me away from them." Those words were hard for *me* to say, especially to him. I didn't talk much about my parents. There was just no point digging at that scar.

Uncomfortable, I sat down in the chair he'd indicated. "I just…I know what you think of me, and maybe I deserve your judgement…but my life sucked from the start. I did the best with what I had, and every day I strive to do a little better. In the end, I think that counts for something."

Jordan watched me with analyzing eyes, then he let out a soft sigh. "I suppose you're right." He cringed, like he hated admitting that.

Forcing myself to keep an even expression, I leaned forward and propped my elbows on my knees. "Kenzie means something to both of us, and we both dropped the ball while trying to make her life better. What *we* thought was better for her anyway." Maybe we should have just left all of it alone, and let Kenzie find her own path. That probably would have been a hell of a lot smarter.

Shaking my head, I focused on the now and tried not to worry about the past. "Kenzie quit working for Keith."

A small smile curved Jordan's lips. "Yes, she told me." He frowned. "And then she told me she never wanted to see me again."

Sounded very familiar. "Yeah, she told me the same thing. But I think…I think there's a way to change her mind. Or at least…a way to make things right." She might not ever forgive us, she might not ever take us back, but we could set her up with something great before we let her go.

Jordan raised an eyebrow. "I'm listening."

I held my breath, then let it out in a rush. "You let me help you with the track."

Jordan looked confused, then he frowned. "Are you asking me to sell it to you again? So you can give it to Keith? I already said no to that, and even after losing Mackenzie, I haven't changed my mind."

I shook my head. "No, I quit the team this morning. I'm done with Keith too. He's not…he's not a person I want to work for, and if that means I never race again…well, then I guess my career is over." And somehow, I would be okay with that, if it meant Kenzie was back on a bike.

Splaying my hands out to Jordan, I said, "Sign the track over to Kenzie. I'll use my cash to help with that…whatever you need. If the two of us work together, we can help her rebuild Cox Racing. We can give Kenzie the team, give her the track, give her the legacy she deserves. We can help her get her dream back, and, right now, that's all that matters." My dream could die, if it meant hers could live.

Jordan's gaze drifted to the carpet as he considered my offer. After a few agonizing seconds, he returned his gaze to mine. "All right. I'll help you."

CHAPTER 19

~Kenzie~

I ended up spending the night at Nikki's. Every time I thought about leaving, I found another reason to stay. Laughing over sappy movies with my best friend helped tame the pain, but it was there, waiting to attack when I woke up. My soul felt like I'd gone toe-to-toe with a heavyweight—everything hurt.

Nikki didn't want to miss two days in a row, so I faked as big of a smile as I could. "I'm fine; you should absolutely go to work."

She raised a suspicious eyebrow at me, but she nodded as she started getting ready. To go to work. To go see Hayden. To go see Felicia. Images of Felicia leaving the hospital, right after Hayden, slammed into my brain so hard my breath caught. Where had she gone? What had she done? What had Hayden done? Because there was no way in hell she hadn't taken advantage of that moment and tried to slip into his arms. And I doubted Hayden had pushed her away. Not after everything they'd gone through, everything they'd been doing lately. I wondered if he felt bad now, or if he felt like things were finally how they should be. Either way, he was an asshole; the sheets on my bed weren't even cold yet.

"Hey, if you see...? Could you not...?" My insubstantial questions trailed off as indecision and torment overwhelmed me. If Hayden *was* with Felicia now, did I want to know? Or did I want to stay blissfully ignorant? And if, by some miracle, he wasn't with her, and there was still some spark of hope for us...did I want to know that either? Which one was worse? I wasn't sure anymore.

Nikki's face softened as she studied my face. "I won't say anything about...anything...to anyone. Even you."

Grateful that she understood, I threw my arms around her in a quick hug. "Thank you, for everything." Pulling back, I looked her in the eye. "You should talk to Myles. I'm sure he's just as confused as you. Maybe you guys can figure it out together."

She rolled her eyes, but nodded again. "Yeah... God, that conversation is going to suck."

I laughed at her comment, then started grabbing my stuff. "Maybe you should have thought about that before you jumped his bones."

Annoyance on her face, she tossed a couch pillow at me. "Bitch."

I was laughing as I left her place, but the mirth didn't last long. The closer I got to my house, the more the past infiltrated my brain. Everything reminded me of Hayden, even stupid stuff that shouldn't have—the crack in the road that had been there for years, the crook in the tree in my neighbor's yard, the oil stain in my driveway. Everywhere I turned, I was assaulted again and again by the man who'd broken my heart. The grief was slowly crushing me.

My eyes were filled with tears when I opened my garage and pushed my bike inside. Seeing my dusty Ducatis in the corner made the tears roll down my cheeks. They reminded me of racing, they reminded me of Dad, they reminded me of Hayden. All I saw now was pain when I looked at them. I should sell them both, rid myself of the reminders. Just the thought of following through with that made me feel nauseous though. Telling my father I could start over in a new field was one thing, actually doing it was another. Racing was all I'd ever wanted…

Feeling wiped from head to toe, I stumbled into the house. Looking around the kitchen only made the emptiness inside me worse. We'd made love on that island…

Shifting my focus, I headed toward the living room. No reprieve there. We'd spent too many hours snuggled on the couch, watching random documentaries on the history of motorcycles. I knew my bedroom would hold the worst memories of all of them, so I stayed put in the living room. Maybe I'd go surfing. Maybe being on the water would wash away my pain. I doubted it. Nothing was going to help. But time.

Sighing in defeat, I laid down on my couch that still faintly smelled like Hayden, and let the grief out in wracking sobs that only ended when I ran out of tears.

* * *

I didn't move far from the couch for three days. Some small segment of my brain knew I would eventually have to pick myself up, dust off the hurt, and go make something of my life, whatever it was now. But every time I tried to move forward, I rewound to the past. Where had it all gone wrong? Felicia? Or earlier than that? If Cox Racing had survived, would my life be any different right now? Probably not. It had all started with my decision to trust Hayden, because, as it turned out, he wasn't trustworthy. I was a fool.

With that disturbing thought firmly stuck in my mind, I forced my stiff legs to rise off the couch. The ground around me was littered in soggy facial tissues. Whenever I thought I was done crying and no more tears could possibly form, another torrent brought me to my knees. I was starting to get a little sick of it.

My goal for today was to get out of my pity party funk and go see Antonia. She was still at the hospital, still not doing well. I'd talked to Izzy every night, but I hadn't made it out of my house to visit again, and I was angry and riddled with guilt over the fact that I wasn't there. Enough was enough. My first stop before I left the house, though, had to be the bathroom. I hadn't showered or changed my clothes in days—I was still avoiding my bedroom. Luckily, no one had dropped in to check on me. Nikki called frequently, but she was busy at the track and busy trying to work up the nerve to talk to Myles. Every time she talked to me, she apologized for not coming over. I always assured her I was fine, and it was fine, and I was getting by just fine. All complete shit, but she seemed to buy it. So, every day I was left alone, wallowing in grief. Until today.

The doorbell suddenly going off made me freeze in my tracks. My heart pounded as I waited for the telltale Christmas songs that would announce Hayden was waiting behind the dark wood. Please, God, no. If and when he came crawling back, wanting to talk about us, I wanted to look like a million bucks. I wanted to look like I was totally over him, had seamlessly moved on, like the breakup hadn't affected me at all. But if he saw me right now, he'd know that wasn't true. He'd see the devastation on my face, see the heartache in the tissues around me, sense the agony I just couldn't seem to shake.

I wanted to run, but I couldn't move. The doorbell rang again, but there wasn't a hidden melody in the sound, just the normal ring of someone trying to see if I was home. It wasn't him. Relief and pain hit me at the same time, and I could feel the tears resurfacing. God, I didn't want anyone to see me like this. If I ignored them, surely whoever it was would go away.

"Kenzie? You home? I know you're mad, but please open the door..."

The familiarity of the woman's voice made a pang go through me, and I had to put a hand on my chest to massage the ache. Theresa? I hadn't heard from her in so long. Because every time we'd talked, she'd berated me for hurting Dad. She hadn't once listened to my side of the story, and that really pissed me off. Anger hurt a hell of lot less than despair, so I greedily embraced it.

Filling myself to the brim with rage, I nearly pulled the door off its hinges, I yanked it open so hard. Theresa and Daphne were both standing there, forlorn expressions on their faces. Theresa's eyes watered as she examined me. "Oh, Kenzie..."

The sympathy in her voice was more than I could handle. "What the hell are you doing here?" I snapped, my gaze going past Theresa to include Daphne as well.

Daphne bit her lip, looking uncomfortable. Theresa sighed. "We messed up, Kenzie. We let Dad convince us that you were the one being cruel, saying mean things, shutting him out. He made it sound like he was innocent, like he was the one wronged, and we bought it—hook, line and sinker."

My mouth hung open in shock. I was the one saying horrible things? Far from it. Dad had gotten his digs in whenever he'd had the chance, and I'd held back more often than not. Dad was the cruel one, not me. Seeing my expression, Theresa shook her head. "After you...cut ties with him, he finally admitted he'd been lying, about everything. We're so sorry we believed him. We're so sorry we didn't give you a chance."

Damn straight they'd messed up. "You both acted like I was a horrible person. You took Dad's side on *everything*, you left me with no family at all...and why? Because Dad didn't like my boyfriend? That's fucked up." They both cringed at my words, like I'd physically struck them. "I thought we were all closer than that. I thought we were family, unbreakable. I didn't think family did shit like that to each other. Obviously, I thought wrong."

I started closing the door, but Theresa put her hand up, stopping it from closing. "Kenzie, please. We're sorry. We know we screwed up, we should have believed you, but you know how convincing Dad can be, and you *have* been doing things that are so unlike you. What were we supposed to think?"

My anger cooled somewhat, I was well aware of how manipulative Dad could be, but they hadn't given me a chance to properly explain my side of the situation. "If the tables were turned, I would hear you guys out, no matter what Dad said you did."

Theresa let out a shaky exhale. "Dad said Hayden was corrupting you—changing you. He told us about the street racing, Kenzie. Was that true?" Biting my lip, I nodded. Yes, unfortunately, that part was very true. Theresa shook her head. "He told us about the gambling, the lying, and the way you just gave up your dream for Hayden, the way you crushed Dad…it was all so surreal. Dad said Hayden was dangerous, and you were choosing him over your family. He said we had to be hard as steel to get you back. And we believed him." A tear fell to her cheek, and my heart broke at seeing it. "We were hurt, and scared, and angry, Kenzie. We thought we were losing you."

Everything inside me wanted to run to my sister, wrap my arms around her in a fierce hug, and tell her I forgave her. But she'd hurt me so much; my insides were radiating with pain so badly, I felt like I might have to be admitted to the hospital soon. My throat was tight with emotion, but I managed to croak out a response. "Oh…" The word felt insufficient, but it was all I could say.

Daphne stepped forward, so she was even with Theresa. Her pale blue eyes examined me from head to foot, much like Theresa had when I'd first opened the door. "Are you okay, Kenzie? You look…awful."

I had to laugh at that, and a trace amount of pain left me. "I feel awful. I thought I'd had it all…but I lost everything that mattered."

"Maybe not," Daphne said with a small smile on her face. Mischief blazed in her eyes, and her happiness was unmistakable.

"What do you mean?" I asked her.

Theresa was the one who answered. "Look, we know we're not your favorite people right now, and we know you're not going to forgive us for what we did anytime soon, but...we'd really like to show you something. Will you come with us?"

Suspicion and irritation ripped up my spine. "Where?"

Theresa's smile was small and sad. "Just trust us, okay?"

Trust. I wasn't sure if I believed in that word anymore, but there was nothing left, so what did I have to lose? "Fine. But can I shower first?"

They both gave me wide, satisfied smiles. "Of course," Daphne beamed. "We'll just come in and wait for you to finish."

I opened the door wider to let them in, and it felt odd to have them there, like they were strangers, not beloved family. A part of me wanted that feeling to go away, another part of me wanted to hold it close, stoke the fire of separation. They had done this to us after all.

But I wouldn't be that petty. I would put aside my pride and hear them out. Only I could heal us now, and I didn't want to let my demons get in the way of the possibility of getting my family back. Part of them anyway. I didn't have the same desire to reconnect with my father. He'd gone too far.

I languished in the shower, letting the hot water soothe my internal aches and pains. I had no idea what they wanted to show me, or how it could possibly fix things between us, but just having them around was already slowly mending something inside, and for the first time in days, hope began to bloom.

They both jumped off the couch when I reentered the living room. I could feel the stress coming off them in waves, and I knew they felt badly about what they'd done.

Did Dad? Or was he just upset that things hadn't worked out liked he'd wanted? "All right, I'm ready." *Let's get this over with.*

We climbed into Daphne's gargantuan SUV, and I again asked them where we were going. They only smiled as they turned to look at me in the back seat. "You'll see," Daphne chirped.

It only took a handful of miles for me to figure out where we were headed. The track. Which was the last place I wanted to go. My healing heart was much too fragile for that level of stress. "If we're going where I think we're going, you can turn this thing around right now. I'm not going back there."

Theresa's eyes met mine in the rearview mirror. "You said you would hear us out, Kenzie. You said you would trust us, so just…keep an open mind."

Technically, I'd only said *fine*. I wasn't sure that meager word covered everything she'd just said, but unless I was going to jump out of a moving vehicle, I was at their mercy. "Whatever," I muttered, turning to gaze at the familiar landscape racing past the window.

Long before I was ready, Daphne pulled her SUV down the road that led to my personal hell. When we got to the outer gate, she slipped in a key card, something I thought was odd since all the Cox Racing issued key cards had been collected. I was too annoyed to ask her about it, but my curiosity was piqued. Why were we here?

She drove through the parking lot to the inner gate, then drove through that and headed toward the old Cox garages. I purposely kept my gaze from the Benneti side of the track, but my entire body burned with the knowledge that Hayden was nearby.

As we got closer to the Cox buildings, I noticed something odd. The garage door was open. My first thought was that the Bennetis had broken in and trashed the place—a very real possibility since Keith was even more pissed at my family than he'd been before—but then I noticed Dad's truck parked in the empty garage. Oh, hell no.

"Stop the car and let me out, Daphne," I snapped.

She sighed as she kept her slow pace toward our father. "No, Kenzie. This is going to happen, just accept it."

Anger roiled in my belly as I shifted my glare to Theresa. "I said I'd listen to you guys. I never said anything about listening to Dad."

Theresa turned in her seat to look at me. "You're going to want to hear what he has to say. Trust me."

I was sick of hearing that word, sick of people keeping me in the dark, sick of a lot of things. But I was also tired of being alone. "This better be good, Theresa."

With a smirk, she turned back to face the front. Under her breath, I heard her mutter, "Oh, it is..."

Rage and hurt were battling within me as she stopped the car in front of the open garages. For a moment, I considered staying in the SUV like a pouting child, but I wasn't a kid anymore, and I could face my father. And besides, unlike every other confrontation I'd had with him, I wasn't the one begging for something. The ball was in his court now.

Shoving open my door, I slammed it shut behind me. Daphne gave me dagger eyes for a second before fixing her face into a forced smile. I almost apologized for being rough with her vehicle, but Dad stepped out of the open garage door before I could. And he wasn't alone.

My heart seized in my chest as Hayden walked out of my family's garage…with my father. It was such an improbable scenario that, for a second, I was positive I was hallucinating. Then Hayden smiled at me, and the ache of loss broke open the tender seal holding my mangled heart together. His dirty blond hair was shaggier than before, distressed, like he was constantly running his hand through it. A thicker than usual layer of stubble blanketed his jaw line, and his jade eyes were worn, like he was holding on by a thread. The smile on his full lips was small, sad, and there was tension in the way he was standing; it was almost like he was holding himself back.

I opened my mouth to speak, but no sound would come out of me. My father shifted his weight between his feet, for the first time ever looking very unsure of himself. Hayden's eyes wouldn't leave mine, and I felt frozen in place, waiting for something to happen.

Finally, when the tension couldn't possibly get any thicker, Theresa sighed and said, "Dad? You wanted to tell Kenzie something?"

Her tone of voice was encouraging, a mom urging her child to do the right thing. Dad frowned at her, then cleared his throat. "Yes, I…uh…" Inhaling a breath, I watched as he focused and centered himself. When he spoke again, his voice was firmer, and he unflinchingly held my gaze. "I was wrong trying to control you, trying to determine your future, and…I'm sorry. It won't happen again."

My eyes widened in surprise, but I remained silent. What did any of this have to do with Hayden? Why was he here? Like he knew I was wondering about him, Hayden stepped forward. "I'm sorry, too, for the lies...for going behind your back...for being fucking stupid."

Dad glared at him for swearing, but surprisingly didn't chide him for it. "Hayden and I, we've...come to terms," Dad said, indicating Hayden beside him. "We know we can't change what we've done, but we want to make it right."

His words loosened my tongue. "Make it right? What could either of you do that could possibly make up for screwing me over and over..." *Love me, no matter what... that's what you could do, Dad.* Shaking aside that heartbreaking thought, I focused on their answer.

Dad and Hayden exchanged looks, and Hayden nodded. Looking back at me, Dad said, "I transferred the track into your name. It's yours, all of it. Sell it, keep it...do whatever you will with it."

Shock struck me so hard, my knees almost buckled. Mine? How was that even possible? "You can't...you owed money on it? A lot of money. You can't just transfer a loan to someone else like that."

Dad looked over at Hayden, and Hayden smiled. "You can once the loan is paid off. You own this free and clear, Kenzie."

Understanding nearly knocked me over. "You...you used your winnings to pay the loan off...so you could give it to me? That was your plan?"

He shrugged. "More or less."

My amazed eyes shifted to my father. "And you're okay with this? With a Benneti buying you out?"

Dad gave me an oddly calm one-sided smile. "He's not a Benneti anymore, and he's not taking control of the track. You are."

My eyes snapped to Hayden's. Not a Benneti? Why hadn't Nikki told me? Oh right...I'd asked her not to. "You quit? With one race left in the season? Are you crazy?"

Hayden's eyes studied my face for a second. "Maybe..." he said, his voice wistful. "I quit right after you did. Racing isn't what I want."

By the heat in his voice when he said that, I knew that what he *wanted* was me. He should have realized that earlier, before he started lying and cavorting with his ex. Pain pounded my chest as I stared at him. Had she claimed any of that perfection since we'd ended things? Yes, I was sure she had. I forcefully returned my eyes to Dad's; it hurt less to look at *him*.

"This doesn't instantly fix us, you know." I meant that for Hayden, too; I just couldn't look at him while saying it.

Dad nodded. "I know. But it was the right thing to do. The track was meant for you. Maybe that's the real reason why I couldn't sell it."

Pain and confusion bombarded me as I tried to wrap my mind around this new possibility. I could revive Cox Racing. I could *be* Cox Racing. "I don't know how to run a team, how to run a business..."

"I could help you," Dad quietly offered. My face must have hardened, because he instantly raised his hands. "I could offer advice and suggestions, but you would be the boss. All decisions would be yours."

Theresa put a hand on my shoulder. "Daphne and I will help out too. Whatever you need, Kenzie."

I still couldn't believe any of this was happening. "What about equipment, bikes, staff? It's so much money." There was so much that went into running a team that I had no clue about, but I knew all of it was expensive. That was what had gone wrong with Dad. He simply hadn't been able to afford it.

Hayden cleared his throat. "I can help you with that, Kenzie. We can do this."

We? There was no we. Not anymore. But...if I was actually going to do this, going to reform my dream from the ashes of its death, then I would need his help. I couldn't agree to it though, so I only stared at him blankly.

Dad broke the silence. Stepping forward, hands out in supplication, he said, "Please, Kenzie. Let us try to fix what we broke. Let us help you."

Hearing him say my shortened nickname was stunning; he'd never once called me Kenzie. My answer stumbled off my lips before I could stop it. "Okay, let's do this."

Daphne squealed and clapped her hands. Theresa was beaming. Dad looked relieved, and Hayden...his expression was unreadable. My head was spinning with plans as I stared at Hayden. I'd have to steal Nikki from Benneti. Hopefully I could get Myles from Stellar Racing. I would ride, of course, and I already owned my bikes, so that would save some money. There was so much to do, so much to plan...but, if this worked, I could race again.

"What are you thinking about?" Hayden asked me, tilting his head to the side.

His question snapped me back to the present, and thoughts of being on the track again fell from my mind. I didn't want to talk to him—I wasn't ready—but I didn't really have a choice if he was going to be the money behind this operation, something I still wasn't sure how I felt about. I didn't want anything from him, but I needed him.

"Just absorbing this. I never thought I'd ride for Cox Racing again…"

Hayden smiled at hearing the wonder in my voice. His grin reminded me that I shouldn't be opening my heart to him. He'd only smash it into a million pieces. "Look, I appreciate all you've done—all you and my father have done—but it doesn't change anything. We're still not okay."

The smile fell from his face, and the grief in his eyes was almost too much to take. "I know, Kenzie. That's not why I did this." Pursing his lips, he amended his statement. "Well, it's not the *only* reason I did this."

He gave me a sad, wistful smile that twisted my heart so badly, I had to look away. That was when I realized that my father and sisters had disappeared into the garage, giving the two of us space. Seeing my father do anything even remotely supportive of my relationship with Hayden made me reconsider if I was truly awake. I had to still be on my couch, in some state of severe delirium that would probably get me committed when someone finally checked up on me. My life no longer made any sense at all.

"Kenzie," Hayden whispered, stepping toward me. "I know I screwed up. I know I should have told you what I was doing, but I swear I didn't do anything with—"

I interrupted his attempt at an apology with a raised hand. "You swear? You promise? You give me your word? That's where all our problems started, Hayden. I. Can't. Trust. You." Biting my lip, I quietly added, "I can't work with you either. I just…can't. It would kill me. It *does* kill me…" Unshed tears clouded my eyes, hazing the beauty of his tortured face, and I prayed they didn't fall. Not being able to see him clearly made things a tiny bit easier.

I expected an outburst from him, maybe a demand that I give him a racing spot since he was paying for everything. And he deserved a spot on the team, just on the merit of his talent. But I couldn't come into work every day and see him. That was more than I could bear.

His fuzzy shape took another step toward me, and his voice was quiet when he spoke. "I know, Kenzie, and it's okay. I never expected you to... I'll find someone else to hire me. Don't worry, I'll be fine. I'm just glad I could do this for you. Making you happy was all I ever wanted. I just... I wish I'd been better at it."

Just as I was wishing that he'd been better at it too, I felt him lean down and place a soft kiss on my lips. The tears broke free as the feeling of his mouth on mine reduced me to a pile of emotional goo. How would I ever recover from him?

He pulled away after a short eternity, his breath quicker. "Goodbye, Kenzie," he whispered in my ear. Then he kissed my cheek, and walked away.

CHAPTER 20

~Kenzie~

The first thing I did to commemorate the re-opening of Cox Racing was remove the *For Sale* sign in front of the garages. From what Nikki told me that night, Keith was in a rampage when he heard about the deal I'd made with Hayden and my father. He'd thrown things across the garage, then started clutching his chest like he was having a heart attack. Convinced he was about to die, he'd had one of his guys take him to the hospital. He wasn't in cardiac arrest, though, just angry and bitter; he really needed to deal with his feelings better. The doctor had prescribed yoga and a calming hobby like painting or gardening. Somehow, I didn't see Keith doing any of those things.

The next thing I did was overnight a new sign and have the old Benneti-only one removed. Keith had again blown up at his staff, but then he'd grabbed some golf clubs and sulked off the track. Guess he was actually trying to follow his doctor's orders.

My life was now a blur of activity. With only a month and a half to get everything up and running, and to get my body back into peak performance before the last race in

New Jersey, I felt wholly unprepared. But I didn't care. I was racing again.

As I soon discovered, there was a plus side to being mind-numbingly busy. The rush of plans and preparations helped temporarily patch the hole in my heart that Hayden's absence had created. But, busy as I was, I wasn't entirely fooling myself, and I knew the grief would catch up to me as soon as I rested. My solution was to never be at rest, and since my dream was back on track and I had too much to do anyway, it was pretty easy to avoid the thoughts that caused me pain.

"So, Dad, did you contact John?"

John Taylor was Dad's old crew chief. He'd been pretty upset with Dad for closing the business like he had, and they hadn't spoken much since they'd parted ways. I needed him though. He'd been Dad's mechanic back in the day, and he had a tremendous amount of experience. His help would be invaluable—assuming he would talk to us.

Dad frowned. Not a good sign. "He answered, then hung up when he realized it was me. I called back and left a message, but it might be better if you talk to him."

Of course. I should have realized that from the beginning. Dad burned bridges wherever he went, or so it seemed. Things were slowly getting better between us—there was just too much pain there for any sort of instant forgiveness—but I couldn't wait around for John to forgive Dad. I needed him by my side *now*. "Great. Guess I'll add that to the to-do list."

Dad started to apologize, but I held my hand up to stop him. We were in a falling-apart, nearly-empty building. I had no crew, no riders but me, and little to no equipment. My plate was overflowing, and I didn't have the energy for a meaningful conversation with Dad. My fragile heart couldn't take it right now—I needed more time. "It's fine. While I'm taking care of that, will you find out what I need to do to get signed up for the race?"

I could see the debate in his eyes before he spoke, and, when he did, his words were tempered with patience. He was trying at least. "This is up to you, of course, but have you considered holding off until next season? You won't accomplish anything with one race, Mackenzie. Why rush this?"

I'd been expecting that question from him, so I wasn't too surprised. "I've missed an entire year of racing, Dad. I won't miss another second." If my only accomplishment this race was being in it, that was enough for me.

Dad opened his mouth, then shut it and remained quiet. His willpower impressed me, and a small smile cracked my lips. I don't think he'd ever bit his tongue with me. Dad grinned in response to my smile, then shook his head in amusement. Baby steps.

Just as I was turning from Dad to head up to the office above the garage, Nikki crashed through the door and slammed it shut behind her, a completely unnecessary act since the garage doors were rolled up and wide open. "Nikki? What are you doing? Is everything okay?"

Nikki had her back flush to the door, like she was holding it closed against gale-force winds. "Yeah…no… I'm not sure."

Stepping toward her, I asked in a rush, "What happened?"

Closing her eyes, she let out a big exhale. "I told Keith I quit. He freaked out on me, which I expected, but then he started chanting like a he was a monk or something." When she reopened her eyes, they were wide with concern. "I'm not entirely sure what that means, but my guess is he's about to bust down the doors and drag me back over there."

I smiled over her assessment of Keith's mental state. "You quit?" Her confession touched me. I hadn't had time to ask her about joining the team yet. And, to be honest, I'd been a little nervous to bring it up. Just because Cox Racing was back, didn't mean it was stable and unbreakable. She had a good, secure job now—even if it was for Keith. Asking her to give it up was just hard.

Nikki smiled, like she completely understood my reaction. "Yeah...I can't be a Benneti if Cox Racing is alive again. And besides, you're going to need me for Jersey," she said, lightly flicking my arm.

Feeling like everything was falling into place, I pulled her away from the door and encased her in a warm hug. Then I pulled her over to my dusty Ducatis. "I don't have tools or equipment yet, but do your best."

Raising an eyebrow, she gave me a very droll expression. "And what exactly do you expect me to do without any tools?"

It was a valid question, and one I didn't have an answer for. "You're a genius. You'll figure something out."

Nikki rolled her eyes while a wave of uncertainty went through me. Hayden had paid for the building, gotten Cox Racing out of debt so it could be revived, but he didn't have an endless supply of cash. I'd had enough to buy the basics needed to race—tires, gas, small parts, basic screwdrivers and wrenches, but it wasn't enough. Not by a long shot. I'd worry about it later though. I had to, because there was too much to do now.

The very next afternoon, a solution arrived on my doorstep, and it wasn't one I'd been expecting. "Hookup? What the hell are you doing here?" And how did he get in? Damn, I really needed to patch the hole in the fence.

Looking uncomfortable, Hookup shifted his feet. "I'm going by Tony now. I left that shit behind." The look on my face must have been disbelief. Raising his hands, he said, "I swear, I'm done, Kenzie. There's more important things in life than money…"

I couldn't believe what I was hearing, but he hadn't really answered my question. "I agree with you, but what does that have to do with me?"

Hookup looked around my mostly empty garage. "Hayden told me you were hurting for equipment. Write me a list of what you need, and I'll get it for you."

Indignation was the first emotion that hit me. No, that wasn't true. Hurt came first. Hearing Hayden's name ripped open a raw seam in my heart. The surge of pain was nearly incapacitating, so I focused on anger instead. It helped contain the flood. "I can't have stolen stuff, Hookup. This is a legitimate business, and it has to have fully paid-for merchandise. Receipts and everything."

Hookup gave me a look that was laced with strained patience. "It's Tony. And I *was* talking about legally purchased material. I told you…I gave that shit up."

It was hard to believe. How could he have changed so much in such a short amount of time. But if he *was* serious… "Why would you help me?"

Frowning, and looking uncomfortable, he scratched his head. "Hayden's been living with me, you know." He paused, waiting for me to acknowledge that fact, but I couldn't. I was too stunned to respond. Of course Keith wouldn't let Hayden remain living with him after quitting the team, but...Hayden had picked Hookup as a replacement? I thought for sure he'd bunk with Felicia.

Hookup shrugged when I didn't speak. "Anyway, I told him the other night that I wanted to start living better—like he was—and he gave me ideas on how I could do that. I wronged you, so I feel like...like I owe you."

He'd tried to sabotage my bike, something that could have killed me. Yeah, I supposed he did owe me. He owed a lot of people. A part of me couldn't forgive that fact, but another part of me wanted to give him a second chance. If he really had changed his ways, I didn't want to send him backpedaling to his old life by rejecting him. Antonia and Izzy needed him to be a better man.

"Okay, let me make you a list."

Three days later, the once-empty Cox Racing garages were full of everything I might possibly need. Even the upstairs gym was full of training equipment. I couldn't believe Hookup had actually pulled through. And Hayden. His influence in all of this was all-too apparent. It made the fact that I hadn't seen him in almost a week that much harder. But it had to be this way. It couldn't get easier if it wasn't difficult first. Somehow that thought wasn't as comforting as it should have been.

My life was a storm of preparations, but whenever I wasn't at the Cox garages, desperately trying to get everything ready in time, I was at the hospital, trying to keep Izzy's spirits up. Antonia was still there, still fighting. It seemed like every morning the doctors were hopeful that her numbers would be on the rise soon, then that evening they were surprised and disappointed when nothing had changed. It was beyond frightening now.

Visiting Izzy made me uneasy. I couldn't stop myself from scanning every nook and cranny when I entered the hospital, like I was afraid Hayden was going to jump out at me at any moment. I'd managed to avoid running into him so far, but I wasn't trusting my luck to always be with me, and I wasn't sure what I would do if I saw him again—when I saw him again. Thank him for giving me my old life back? Beg him to be a part of it? Curse him for hurting me, for lying, for gambling, for risking his life…for cheating on me?

Just thinking about that conversation tied me in knots. That was why I hadn't responded to any of his texts, hadn't picked up the phone when he'd called, hadn't listened to his voicemails. I just couldn't handle it right now, and I prayed every day that he kept giving me space and didn't just show up on my doorstep, begging me to talk to him. There was no point talking. I couldn't trust him, so we were done.

When I peeked into Antonia's room, only Izzy was sitting beside the bed, holding her daughter's hand. A quick sigh of relief escaped me, but it was instantly squelched by the sight of the small, sick child flooded in the orange glow of the fading daylight.

Antonia was awake, and frowning at her mom. She looked annoyed, and I took that as a good sign. Irritation had to be better than exhaustion. "I want to go home, Mom. Please? I haven't seen Sundae in forever."

Izzy sighed, like she'd heard this a million times already. "I know you want to, honey, but the doctors need to make sure you're okay first, and you're still not—" Izzy spotted me walking into the room, and her objection trailed off in a wide smile. "Hey, you. How's the business going? Tony told me he sent your new equipment over."

Walking around to the other side of Antonia's bed, I shook my head at Izzy. "I still can't believe he did that. I keep thinking I'm going to wake up, and everything's going to be gone." Again.

Izzy's warm smile shifted to her daughter. "He's changed...he's finally changed." She slicked back Antonia's short, newly grown hair, and I knew what she was thinking. Tony had finally grown up because Antonia had been on the brink. Could still be on the brink. Her frail body had been through so much already. But no, she'd make it through this. She had to.

Sitting down, I placed my hand on Antonia's arm. "Hey, kiddo. You done being in here yet?"

Antonia groaned and rolled her eyes, just like any normal kid. "Yes, but Mom won't let me leave."

With a small laugh, I told her, "You just keep trying. Eventually, you'll wear her down."

Pursing her lips at me, Izzy mumbled, "Thanks." But then she smiled, and I knew she was actually looking forward to every single complaint that came out of Antonia's mouth.

A small knock on the doorframe met my ear, and I looked up before I could stop myself. Standing there, leaning against the frame, holding a bouquet of flowers, was Hayden. Seeing him again punched a hole straight through my chest, ruining any amount of healing I'd managed so far. His dirty-blond hair was scruffed to perfection, but his jaw was layered with a thick amount of stubble now, like he'd completely given up on shaving. The fading sunlight caught his eyes, making the green gems gleam as they locked onto mine. I saw such a mixture of pain, happiness, and hope in his gaze, that I felt my chest compress and my lungs seize. All my internal systems froze at the sight of him, and I was suddenly dizzy, lightheaded, and a little delirious, like I hadn't eaten in days. *Why today? Why now? I'm not ready.*

His smile suspiciously casual, Hayden stepped into the room. "How are all my favorite girls doing tonight?" he asked.

I wanted to scoff at his remark, but hearing him say it hurt so badly, I couldn't. Turning to Antonia, I leaned down and kissed her forehead. "I gotta go, but I'll come back tomorrow and check on you, okay?"

She frowned, either unhappy that I was leaving, or that she might be here another day, but then she nodded. "Okay, Aunt Kenzie."

Her term of endearment warmed me, but not enough to make me stay. I couldn't. Shifting my gaze Izzy's way, I told her a quick goodbye, then prepared to storm from the room. Hayden, of course, wasn't about to let me slip away that easily. "Kenzie, wait."

I didn't. I slipped away from his extended hand, and darted out the door. I could hear his boots as he immediately followed me. "Wait, please." Bitterness surged through me at hearing his words. Wait? Why should I wait when he couldn't be honest? That was all I'd asked for—honesty. I quickened my pace, but it wasn't enough. His firm hand closed over my arm, pulling me back to him. *No.*

I spun to face him, and the sudden, unexpected movement crashed our bodies together so his rock-hard chest was firmly pressed against me. I instantly took a step back, but not before the memory of our bodies tangled together rushed through my mind. Sadly, I really missed him, and now that he was right in front of me, mere inches away, the grief was too much. While just a few moments before, every organ inside me had felt like solid ice, now everything was raging like a river released from a dam, flooding the world in agony.

Yanking my arm away, I spat, "Don't touch me."

He instantly raised his hands. "I'm sorry, I just didn't want you to leave like that. We can still…talk, Kenzie. You don't have to run from me."

His eyes were laced with pain and sadness, but it was the lingering hope I saw deep within them that killed me. There was no hope for us, and the sooner he realized that, the better. "We can't be friends, Hayden. We never could be friends. We were rivals, then competitors, then lovers…" My mind spun with images of his hands, his lips, his mouth. "We were never friends…"

His jaw tightened, and I could tell he was struggling with what to say to me. "I don't want to end this. I love you…" He started to reach out for me, then stopped himself. "Please, Kenzie. I gave you time, I gave you space, but I need you. Can we just…talk about this?"

I could feel my eyes watering, my throat tightening. I was barely holding on, and a "talk" right now wouldn't go well. "There's nothing to talk about, Hayden. We're over."

His mouth popped open, before closing and firming. "I don't want to be over."

My heart was pounding in my ribcage, but I lifted my jaw in defiance. "Then you shouldn't have lied to me."

His eyes grew fiery. "I did it for you. To get you the track back. To give you Cox Racing, which I did."

Knowing that his motives were pure only made everything harder. "Was meeting up with Felicia behind my back for me too?" I asked, my voice cold.

Hayden sighed, the anger fading from him. "I never planned for that part. I never wanted that part."

Crossing my arms over my chest, I made myself ask, "And when she followed you home the night we broke up…did you want that?"

I was purely guessing about her following him home, but by the way his eyes widened, I knew I'd hit the nail on the head. "Nothing happened," he whispered.

The thudding in my chest hurt so hard, I almost wanted to flag down a nurse and tell her I was having a heart attack. She really had gone over there. I'd known it…but knowing something in your gut and hearing a confession were two entirely different things. She'd gone over there. And *nothing* had happened. That part, I couldn't believe. "Nothing?" I whispered, my voice hot.

Hayden's eyes drifted to the ground, just for a second, but the guilt on his face was enough to confirm my suspicions. *Something* had happened. God, I was going to be sick. "Kenzie, it's not what you—"

I interrupted him with quick, clipped words. I didn't want to hear about his romantic reunion with his ex. "Thank you for the track, Hayden. For giving me back my dream. I really can't ever repay you for that. But you and I…we will *never* be together again so, please, stop trying. Stop calling, stop texting, stop asking about me, stop everything."

I backed away with my hands raised, and then, when I was positive he wouldn't follow me, I turned and fled. As I was leaving, I heard him softly say, "I'll never stop, Kenzie."

When I got outside, I hunched over my knees, drawing deep breaths like I'd just run a marathon. My chest burned, my stomach roiled. He'd done something with her. He'd touched her, kissed her, caressed her...had told her he loved her, made love to her—something. I felt the bile rise in my throat, and had to swallow several times to stop my stomach from emptying. Was this really happening?

Needing to clear my head, my heart, and my soul, I climbed on my bike, started it, and tore out of there. Away. I needed away. Hours passed as I lost myself to the curve of the road. The sun sank beneath the waves of the ocean, leaving the Earth dark and dreary. I pressed my bike faster and faster, my speed dangerous on this winding road, but at the moment, I didn't care. Concentrating on the asphalt stopped my mind from thinking about anything else; it was cathartic.

I didn't slow down until I saw something that shocked me—the Golden Gate Bridge. Somehow, in my torment, I'd driven all the way to San Francisco...and Myles.

A small smile brightened my mood as I pulled into a rest area so I could call him. He answered almost immediately. "Hey...Kenzie. What's up?"

There was an oddness to his voice that I instantly recognized. He probably wondered if I knew about him sleeping with Nikki, and if I was about to berate him for it. While that wasn't a bad idea, it wasn't why I'd called. "Hey, Myles. I'm in town...can I come over?"

"You're in San Francisco? Why?"

"It's a long story. Where's your house?" He rattled off an address followed by directions, and I told him I'd see him in a few. When I put my phone away and replaced my helmet, I hoped I could keep the numbness at bay for just a little while longer. It would be so much easier to find Myles's place if I wasn't searching for it through a haze of tears.

Even with his directions, it took me a while to find where his duplex was hidden. When I knocked on the door and he let me inside, I was shocked by what I saw, or what I didn't see—the place was spotless. "Myles…do you have a housekeeper?"

Myles laughed, then nervously ran a hand through his dark hair. "No, I just remembered what you—and Nikki—said about my messy tendencies. I'm trying to do better." He looked sheepish a second, then added, "I've been cleaning since you called."

A small laugh escaped me, but the look on Myles's face grew more concerned at seeing it. "What's wrong? You look like you're about to have a meltdown."

"I think I am," I said, collapsing on his couch with a sigh. His face was a mask of confusion as he sat beside me, so I tried to explain it as best I could—without breaking into sobs. "Well, you know Hayden and I broke up…" Just saying it made my insides feel like I'd swallowed razorblades. Would it ever not hurt?

Myles looked shocked at my admission. "You did? When?"

Ignoring his question, I said, "And you know Hayden and my father worked together to get me Cox Racing back, right?"

He again looked startled. "What? That's...odd...but amazing. Congratulations, Kenzie."

Seeing that he clearly didn't know anything, I sighed and said, "You still haven't spoken to Nikki, have you?"

His delight instantly shifted to guilt. "Not since Monterey. Things are kind of—well, we kind of..."

"I know," I said, interrupting his sad attempt at an explanation. "You guys had sex and now things are weird." I understood the feeling, since Hayden and I had started out in a similar way. We just hadn't been friends first. Or ever.

Myles's dark eyes nearly bugged out of their sockets. "She told you? And you didn't say anything?"

Frowning at the almost insulted tone to his voice, I said, "I haven't had time." And that was something they really needed to work out for themselves. Shaking my head, I told him, "But I need you guys to figure it out, because I really need both of you right now."

My voice turned soft, distant, and Myles could easily see the hurt I was dealing with. "Okay, Kenzie. I'll talk to her. What do you need from us?"

Smiling at his answer, I told him, "I want to race in the final race of the year...in New Jersey. Nikki has already agreed to be my mechanic. She actually quit Keith's and came over to my side without me even having to ask her. She's pretty amazing."

A small smile lifted Myles's lips after I said that. "Yeah, I know." Clearing his throat, he shifted uncomfortably. "If you're asking me to race Jersey with you, I don't think I can. Luke's a dick, but I'm under contract. And...I could win this thing, Kenzie. I'm so close."

I knew all of that, and I never would have asked him to switch it up like that with only one race left. "No, no, stay with Stellar for Jersey…but come race with me next year?"

Suddenly scared, I bit my lip. If Myles won the championship with Luke, he might not want to leave Stellar. Racers could be very superstitious, after all, and clearly, he had a good thing going on over there, even if he did hate almost everyone.

Myles was quiet for a long time as he studied me. He was trying to think of a way to let me down easy, that was the only explanation for his delay. Well, he didn't need to do that. I was a big girl. And besides, I'd dealt with a lot of disappointments this year. What was one more?

"It's okay, Myles. I get it. You're happy."

Myles started laughing. "Happy? I hate 99% of those fuckers. I'm yours, Kenzie. Next season, I'm a Cox Racer again. And I'm betting anything, I can get Kevin and Eli to come with me too. We'll have most of the band back together."

His answer overjoyed me. I flung my arms around his neck, then pulled back and smacked him in the arm. "Why did you wait so long to answer me?"

He laughed again as he rubbed his arm. "I was just building the anticipation. Maybe I took it a little too far."

"A little," I scoffed.

Myles smiled, but then it faded. "I'm sorry about you and Hayden. Okay, I never really liked him, so I'm not *all* that sorry to see him gone…but I know you did, and I'm sorry you're hurting."

His words made tears instantly cloud my vision. God, how I wanted to stop feeling like I could cry at the drop of a hat. "Thank you," I mumbled.

Myles pulled me in for a hug, and just the friendly feeling of comfort lifted my spirits. Wanting to shift the subject in any way I could, I pulled back and told him, "By the way, Nikki said it was the best sex she's ever had. Like, can't-stop-thinking-about-it good." That made me nauseous for a completely different reason, but it did alter the mood in the room.

Leaning back further, Myles gave me a cocky grin. "Really? She said that?"

The giddy, boyish smile on his face made me roll my eyes. "You're an idiot. You both are."

A strange expression passed over his face. "I know…" he murmured, his voice haunted. I expected him to say something mocking or teasing, but he didn't. He just sat there, his expression thoughtful and serious. And a little sad.

CHAPTER 21

~Kenzie~

A little over a month later, Dad, Nikki, and I were in New Jersey, getting ready for the last race of the year—my first and only race of the year. I couldn't wait to be back on my bike, chasing a victory, but it had been forever since I'd truly competed, and nerves and excitement rampaged inside me. Strangely enough, the emotions were a welcome change; they helped block out all how lonely the last several weeks had been for me.

If it hadn't been for this race, for spending every spare moment preparing myself mentally and physically for it, I would have been a blubbering mess, barely leaving my couch. Hayden and Dad's gift had given me hope and vigor, just when I'd needed it most, a fact that filled me with even more conflicting emotions; it was odd and unnatural to simultaneously feel gratitude *and* anger. Hopefully one day I'd only feel one emotion at a time.

With only three of us on the newly revised Cox Racing Team, it felt strangely hollow and empty in our large garage bay at the event track. I kept looking around the mainly vacant space, waiting to see things that I normally saw before a race: Ralph about to throw up, Eli cracking lude jokes, Kevin blushing and apologizing, Myles laughing at it all. Next year.

"Hey, Nik, Dad and I have to go to a mandatory meeting before the autograph session. Are you good here with the bikes?" Nikki was obsessively cleaning and organizing her tools; she did that sometimes before a race. It was so good to see her in Cox blue and white again; I never wanted to see Benneti colors on my best friend again.

Nikki nodded absentmindedly and answered without looking up at me. "Yeah, yeah...it's all good...all good." She started mumbling something else, but I couldn't understand her. She'd been acting really weird the last couple of days. She must be going through a bad bout of nerves too. This weekend would be the first time since Monterey that she'd seen Myles.

I'd made her call him several weeks ago. She'd just kept putting it off and putting it off, and, without my interference, they'd probably still be giving each other the silent treatment. That forced call had been awkward and silent at the beginning, but by the end they'd been laughing and chatting just like old times. And so long as they didn't wind up in a bed together again, physically interacting shouldn't be any different than their frequent phone conversations.

"Hey, you and Myles are going to be fine. You know that, right?" I said, placing my hand on her shoulder.

When she finally looked up at me, there were tears in her eyes. "Think so?"

Surprised by the emotion I saw on her face, I wrapped my arms around her in a quick hug. "I know so."

Dad cleared his throat behind me, but didn't say anything. That was his not-so-subtle reminder that we had somewhere to be and this sappy stuff could wait. I'd never in a million years thought my dad could hold his tongue about anything, but so far in our business arrangement, he'd only offered advice when he'd felt it was needed, then he'd step back and let me handle the information in whatever way I saw fit. It was a bizarre new reality I'd been thrust into, but I had to admit I loved it.

Letting Nikki go, I looked back at Dad and gave him a stiff nod to let him know that I understood his message. Just as we were moving toward the door, someone walked through it who surprised me: Dad's ex-pit crew chief, John Taylor.

His presence stopped me dead in my tracks. My dad hadn't had any luck convincing him to join us. Me neither. "John, what are you…? Are you here to…help us?" I didn't want to get my hopes up, but I could feel the anticipation rising.

John crossed his arms over his chest and cast a slow glance around the quiet garage. It took a solid minute for his eyes to finally rest on me. "You gonna see this through to the end?" he asked, his voice gruff.

Resolution firmed my spirit. I would never see Cox Racing die again. "The very end."

A faint smile graced his lips, and he gave me a small nod of approval. "Then I'll help you in whatever capacity I can."

Relief coursed through me in a wave. *Thank God.* "Good," I said, keeping most of my glee contained so I appeared somewhat professional. "We were just about to head to a meeting. Join us?"

John nodded, and fell into step behind Dad. I flashed a quick glance back at Nikki, and a wide grin burst out of me. We were one person closer to where we used to be.

While it was the same old meeting I'd been to several times before, it felt different this time. I wasn't just a rider, I was an owner. This was my business now, not just my job, and that put a different spin on things. I felt more secure, more confident, and more at peace with my world. This was where I was meant to be. Even Keith glaring at me with murder in his eyes all meeting long couldn't diminish my fire. My dream was alive again, and I was back where I belonged.

During the meeting, my eyes scanned the crowd of owners and riders. Whenever I caught myself doing it, I immediately forced my gaze back to the speaker. I was searching for Hayden, and that was something I didn't want to do. He wasn't here anyway. He'd quit. He was done. His dream was over. And as angry as I was at him, the fact that he'd given up this world killed me. Hayden belonged on a bike just as much as I did. Maybe Keith would take him back next year? But even as I thought it, I knew it wouldn't matter if Keith wanted him. Hayden had cut ties with his boss, so he must have finally gotten sick of the man's meddling. Hayden had given up everything Keith had offered him—stability, a home, a bike, a future. If Hayden had walked away, he must have had good reason, and that reason would probably keep Hayden away for good. So, unless someone else was willing to take a chance on the former street racer, Hayden's days of racing were over.

And knowing I could give Hayden the chance he needed only made me feel even more conflicted. I couldn't work with him though. I just couldn't.

After the meeting, I headed to the autograph session while Dad and John headed back to the garage. Since I'd been out most of the year, I wasn't sure if I'd have any fans today, but I was pleasantly surprised to see a line already waiting for me when I got to my assigned spot. Most of them were wearing T-shirts proudly displaying my racing number—22—and several were holding presents and cards; one young girl even had flowers. Tears pricked my eyes as I went to sit down. They'd missed me.

I was an emotional mess for the first few people in line. I could barely say thank you without my voice warbling. When the girl with the flowers finally made it to the front, I had to wipe away the tears. It was the best welcome I could have asked for, and I again thanked fate that I could be here today. It might not matter in the rankings if I raced or not, but to my soul, it meant everything.

About thirty minutes into endlessly signing my name across multiple 8x10 glossies of my face, another familiar, unexpected person stepped in front of me. "Antonia?" Her dark-brown eyes and dark-brown hair—that was now long enough to put into two tiny ponytails—was as unmistakable as her effervescent smile. "What are you doing here?"

Immediately standing up, I gave her a hug, and that was when I noticed who she'd come here with. Hayden. My heart instantly started racing as I drank him in. He was dressed in street clothes, jeans and a T-shirt, and had a baseball cap pulled low over his dirty-blond hair. His eyes were hidden behind dark sunglasses, but there was a small, sad smile on his lips. My chest ached at the sight of him, and every nerve was instantly pulsing with pinpricks of pain, like I'd just jumped into an icy lake. I hadn't seen him since that night at the hospital, when I'd told him to never contact me again. He hadn't...and while that was what I'd wanted, what I'd needed, it kind of broke my heart.

I was still stretched over the table, holding Antonia tight, eyes locked on Hayden. Antonia giggled and squirmed to get free, and I instantly remembered that I was holding her. I tried to ignore Hayden and focus on her, but that was impossible; it was like trying to ignore a spotlight being directed at my face, blinding me.

Letting her go, I pulled back and peered down at her sweet face. "What are you doing here?" I asked again. My skin felt on fire as the intensity of Hayden's gaze burned me.

Her joyous smile reminded me of the day she was finally released from the hospital, the day she'd finally fought off the infection that had crippled her for so long. She was one tough cookie, there was no denying that. With a playful shrug, she told me, "I wanted to see you race."

I unintentionally looked up at Hayden for confirmation. His smile grew just a bit wider, although he didn't look any happier. "She hasn't stopped talking about coming here to watch your comeback race, so Tony and I talked Izzy into letting us take her."

My eyes instantly narrowed in suspicion. "Hookup is here?" If he did something, hurt a rider to win money, well...I wouldn't keep my mouth shut this time.

Hayden shook his head, like he knew exactly what I was thinking. "He's just here to watch. We all are..."

His voice was so sad, my throat constricted. A part of me wanted to run over to him, wrap my arms around him, tell him I was stupid, I was sorry, and I wanted him back more than anything. But I couldn't trust him, and what future did we have without trust? It was better this way, for both of us. I just wished doing the right thing didn't hurt so much.

Blinking away tears, I looked down at Antonia. "How would you like to sit and sign autographs with me?"

Antonia's face turned sympathetic, like she understood just how much pain was coursing through me. Then her face sparkled with excitement as my words sank in. "Can I? Really?"

She looked back at Hayden, and he smiled and nodded. "Sure thing, Bookworm. I'll come back for you later." With a squeal, Antonia dashed around to my side of the table and sat down in the empty chair next to me. Hayden grinned at her, then shifted his gaze back to me. His smile slipped as he said, "Thank you, Kenzie."

Again, emotion locked my throat, and all I could do in response was nod. Hayden didn't leave after thanking me. He just kept staring, and even though I couldn't see his eyes, I knew he was trying to come up with something to say to get me to change my mind about us. Whatever he came up with would be painful and heartbreaking, and I just couldn't handle that right now. Even though it felt like I was stabbing myself in the chest, I looked around him and motioned for the next person in line to come forward.

The guy patiently waiting glanced at Hayden, unsure if he should move around him or not, but then he stepped past, pushing Hayden into the background. A flutter of relief trickled through me at the small piece of distance the stranger had put between us. I tried to stay focused on the fan, but even still, I was acutely aware of Hayden. He watched me for a solid thirty seconds longer, before finally turning and leaving. I blatantly stared at his retreating form, until dryness burned my eyes. It had to be this way.

Once the weight of Hayden's presence was gone, I could focus on the fans and Antonia. Her utter joy at being a part of the festivities lifted my spirits, and, for a microsecond, I actually forgot that Hayden was going to be in the stands...watching me race.

When the allotted autograph time was over, Antonia was alive with energy. Clapping her hands, she proclaimed, "I want to be a rider when I grow up! I want to inspire people like you do! And go really, really fast!"

A laugh escaped me as I put a hand on her shoulder. "Your mom is going to love that. She worries about you enough as it is."

She pursed her lips in annoyance. "You, Uncle Hayden, and Aunt Felicia do it, so how dangerous can it be?"

Her comment made a stab of pain go through my gut. Felicia. Would I ever hear that name without wanting to throw up? Oddly enough, I hadn't thought of her once since coming here. I hadn't seen her either. I flicked a quick glance at the Benneti section, but all their riders had already cleared out. Had she qualified below me...or above me? I didn't think I could handle her being above me. But it would be fine if she had; she wouldn't be above me for long.

Just as I was thinking of some way to answer Antonia's question without either scaring or encouraging her, someone came to collect her. It wasn't Hayden though. No, it was Hookup who stepped up to the table. For some reason, I felt protective of Antonia with Hookup right there in front of me. That was stupid, though, since she was his niece and he was there for her. I resisted the urge to hold her back as she surged toward him. "Uncle Tony! I'm going to be a motorcycle racer, just like Aunt Kenzie."

Hookup laughed as he put an arm over her shoulder. "Kid, don't give your mom another reason to kill me."

His comment made me want to smile, but I resisted the reaction. "Hayden said you were just here to watch. That true?"

If he gave me any inclination that wasn't the case, I'd contact the officials immediately. And if they didn't believe me, I'd find another way to cancel the race, even if that meant giving up my only chance to compete this year. I'd rather miss the opportunity than risk anyone getting hurt.

Hookup sighed as he met eyes with me. "Yes, I'm just here to watch, like all the other spectators. I gave that shit up, Kenzie. I don't bet. On anything. I can't…"

His eyes turned sad and remorseful, like he finally understood that there were instincts he couldn't control, compulsions that managed his life for him. But a part of him still wanted to let them lead the way. He had to resist the desire, just like I had to resist my desire for Hayden. We were both struggling to get away from disastrous cravings, and we both knew it. It was hard to believe I actually had something in common with Hookup now. When did that happen?

Feeling more at ease with Hookup being here, I inadvertently asked, "Where's Hayden?" I instantly regretted asking, as the question brought him to the forefront of my mind again.

Hookup looked uncomfortable, and seeing that expression on him made me nervous. Was Hayden with Felicia? Had he found her? Did it matter? "He, uh...he's sitting in the stands. Said he...needed some time alone. I think it's hard for him to be here...you know?" He scratched his head and looked around, like he was searching for an escape route. Obviously, he didn't like serious conversations.

Sympathy flooded me. I knew what it felt like to be at the track but not able to race. It was hell. But I'd had Hayden to get me through it. Hayden...didn't have anyone. No one who understood what he was going through, at any rate.

Eyes on the ground, I quietly asked Hookup, "Do you know which way he went?"

When I peeked up at him, he pointed over to the top corner of the stands. "That way."

I thanked him, then slowly began making my way to Hayden. Every step I took toward him was slow, deliberate, and painful. My heart shouted at me to turn around and leave him alone, that what I was doing would hurt too much to handle. But my head told me he was in pain, and I couldn't let him suffer alone. He'd done too many good things for me; I couldn't completely abandon him.

It didn't take me long to spot him. He was sitting by himself, in the highest section of the stands, the vast empty track before him. He'd removed his hat and glasses, and was leaning over his knees with his head in his hands. A picture of defeat, if I ever saw one.

He didn't notice me approaching until I was walking down his row of bleachers. Then he did a double take, like he was sure he was hallucinating. "Kenzie?" he asked, when I was right beside him. "What are you…?"

Wondering if I was doing the right thing, I sat down beside him. "Hey," I quietly said, my heart pounding in my chest. "Hookup said you were up here, said you were…having a hard time."

Hayden's eyes drifted to the course. "I just…it didn't hit me that it was over until I saw the track. My career's over, we're over. Everything's…over."

His voice was so sad and quiet, my heart just couldn't take it. I put my hand on his leg, and instantly wished I hadn't. A familiar warmth traveled up my arm, all the way to my aching soul. It had been so long since I'd touched him. His eyes immediately snapped to the point of contact, then slowly lifted to mine. The depth of feeling I saw in his gaze made my breath quicken. "Not everything is over," I whispered.

He tilted his head as he straightened. Somehow, the movement brought him closer to me. "It's not?" he asked, equally quiet.

I bit my lip, and his eyes wandered to my mouth. "No…" His nearness was intoxicating, the scent of sand and sun strong, and I wanted nothing more than to close the distance between us. But I couldn't. Inhaling a calming breath, I told him what I'd come out here to tell him. "You can still race."

Hayden retreated a little, and a moment of disappointment flashed through his eyes. Shaking his head, he said, "No one's going to hire me, Kenzie. Keith told everyone I was a street-racing lowlife. He even started a rumor that I stole from him, and that's why he fired me. I'm un-hirable. No one will take a chance on me."

"I will." The words were out of my mouth before I could stop them. Shit. But as Hayden's eyes widened, and the shock wore off, the words rang true. Regardless of what had transpired between us, Hayden was a natural born racer. He deserved the chance to be on a bike, and...I...I needed high-quality riders. From a purely professional standpoint, I needed him. "Ride for me next year," I stated, my voice confident.

Joy and relief instantly brightened Hayden's expression, and his hand immediately shot out to cup my cheek. He brought our foreheads together in one smooth, intimate movement that left me reeling. He was so close, he smelled so good, felt so good...all I had to do was let go and let him back in, and we could have everything again.

"Oh, Kenzie, thank God. Thank you, I was so worried you'd never forgive me, never let me back in. Things will be different, you'll see. I'll never lie to you again, I promise."

His head began to shift, his lips drawing closer and closer. His words sparked a painful memory, words I wished I could forget. *You said you would tell me the truth. I did...I just never said when I'd tell you.* His version of telling the truth, and my version of telling the truth were too different to be compatible. As much as I wanted him, we wouldn't work.

With every bit of willpower I possessed, I pushed him away. "Stop..."

His expression was confused as he pulled back to look at me. "What's wrong? Don't you want this?"

Sadly, I did. But it was something I couldn't let myself have. "No. You and I are still broken up. That's not what I was offering you. I just want you to ride for my team. That's all. Can you do that? Work with me but not be with me?" God...could *I* do that?

Hayden studied me for several long seconds, and, as I watched, some of the light faded from his eyes. "Yeah...if it has to be that way, and if it means I get to ride, then... yeah, I can work with you without...being with you."

My chest cracked in two, and I wondered if either of us could actually do this. Like he was thinking the exact same thing, he grabbed my hand. "Kenzie, I swear, if you give me another chance, I can fix this. I can fix *us*, I just need you to—"

I instantly stood up. "When we get back to California, come by the garage. John will get you set up."

With that, I turned and walked away. I sped away from him so fast, I might as well have been racing, and I didn't stop until I reached the Cox Racing garage. After slipping inside, I pressed my back to the wall, closed my eyes, and took a moment to just breathe in the silence. What the hell did I just do? I'd spent all this time trying to keep away from Hayden, and now I'd just invited him into my personal sanctuary. But he would be good for the team, and that was what mattered—the team.

As I was recovering from the heart-wrenching moment with Hayden, I heard laughter in the room, disturbing the momentary calm. Opening my eyes, I looked over to the source of the noise. Surprise flooded me as I spotted both of my sisters standing next to Nikki, John, and my dad. What were they doing here? This race was turning out more people than I ever thought it would.

"Daphne? Theresa?" I said, stepping toward them. "What are you guys doing here?" I felt like I'd asked that question about twenty times today.

My two tall, blonde sisters immediately turned my way at hearing my voice. Daphne gave me a sheepish wave while Theresa put a hand to her heart. "God, Kenzie, it's so good to see you dressed like that again. As much as this life scares the hell out of me...it suits you."

She stepped forward to wrap her arms around me, but I was still so shocked to see them, all I could do was repeat my question. "What are you doing in New Jersey?"

Daphne giggled. "We're here to see you, of course. It's your first race since...well, it's been a while."

Theresa's expression fell. "And we haven't been very supportive lately. We both felt we owed it to you to be here."

She looked over at Daphne, and her smile faded. "Yeah, not being here wasn't an option. You were there every step of the way for my wedding last year, and I know I was kind of...intense..." Theresa started laughing, making me smile. Daphne smacked her in the arm. "Anyway, I know I was a handful, but you put up with me anyway. I should have done the same instead of listening to..." Her voice trailed off as she flicked a glance at Dad. He frowned, but didn't say anything. Once again, Dad was keeping silent.

My sisters had already apologized, and I'd already forgiven them, but having them come all the way out here, just to see me do what I loved...it meant the absolute world to me. Holding in the tears was a struggle, but I was managing just fine until I happened to notice Nikki behind Dad; she was crying like a baby. And she hardly ever cried.

Fanning my face, in some vain attempt to curb the tears, I snipped at my best friend, "Stop it, Nikki."

She was smiling as she cried now. "I'm trying."

Doing my best to ignore her, I grabbed my sisters and pulled them in for a hug. "Thank you, guys. I really appreciate you being here."

I took things as easily as I could after that; I needed a break from emotions for a while. I did have a race to compete in after all. But once I felt emotionally stable, I started filling with eager excitement. Just when I was at my limits, vibrating with energy, rearing to get to work, it was go time.

My heart pounded in my chest as I waited in my grid box. I wanted to soar. Discretely, I looked around for Felicia, my rival in this race. Oddly enough, I didn't see her anywhere. She didn't make the qualifiers? With how well she'd been doing this year, I found that hard to believe. Which meant…she wasn't racing. Was that of her own accord? Or Keith's?

Pushing that mystery from my mind, I focused my attention on the task at hand. I had a lot of eyes watching me, but I felt freer than I ever had before. I wasn't racing to prove something to my peers, I wasn't racing to impress my father, and I wasn't racing to save the team from financial ruin. No, I was just racing for the sheer joy of racing. Anything could happen today, and it would be fine, because all that mattered was the fact that I was here.

The bank of red lights before me shifted to a glorious shade of go-get-'em green, and releasing the dam of pent-up energy, I surged forward. I shot past three people without even trying, then I dialed in on the person in front of me. One at a time. That was how races were won.

My bike flew over the concrete, creating the illusion that the ground was liquid, malleable, like I could reach down and scoop it into my hands. Leaning low into the corners, I recalled every scrap of training I'd ever been given, and kept my form as close to perfect as I could get it. I raised the bike and adjusted my position at the last possible moment, enhancing my speed, and as I watched in amazement, more competitors trailed behind me.

Even though every corner of my brain was focused on the task at hand, I couldn't contain my smile, couldn't stop saying to myself—*I can't believe this is happening.* It was everything I'd been missing over the last several months. And yet, it wasn't quite as perfect as it could have been. Something…or some*one*…was missing.

There was no number 43 to chase, no smug nod of his helmet, no cocky smack of his ass. But while he wasn't down in the trenches with me, I knew he was still here, cheering me on in the stands, goading me to do better than he would have, and that phantom drive kept me going through the mental and physical exhaustion.

My body felt numb from the strain of holding my muscles so tight for so long, but I was too close to relax now; the final lap had been flagged…and I was in third place. It would be a monumental personal victory if I could end the race in this position, but the competitive side of me wanted to go for more. Just *one* more spot, to give me my highest finish ever. That would make my comeback so much sweeter.

Myles was in the lead position, I could just make out his colors and number from where I was. The person in front of me was my old teammate and rival, Jimmy Holden. He'd left Cox Racing when we'd needed him most, so flying around him now would be icing on top of an already amazing cake. He was well within my reach, less than a foot away from my front tire. All I needed was the perfect opportunity to scoot around him, and he'd be mine. The finish line was coming up fast, sparking a bit of reckless impatience inside me, but I squashed it immediately. I wasn't going to make another careless mistake that could cost me a handful of places. I was going to practice utmost control, and wait for the right moment.

It only took a few more seconds to show itself. A gap, just large enough for me to squeeze by. With a satisfied smile on my face, I punched it through the hole he'd left me…and shot across the finish line in second place. *Holy shit. I did it, I actually did it!*

As euphoria flooded through me, I thrust my fist into the air in celebration. Maybe it was my imagination, but it sounded like everyone in the stands burst into applause, cheers, and whistles—all for me. Myles had his hand up, too, celebrating his own victory. Glancing back, and seeing I was behind him, he slowed his bike until we were level. Grabbing the throttle with his left hand, he held his right out for me. I eagerly grabbed it, grateful for the friendship and support, and we rode our way to the winner's area hand-in-hand. God, it felt so good to be back.

CHAPTER 22

~Kenzie~

The next forty-five minutes were a blur of emotion and activity. Myles, Jimmy, and I gave our interviews. The press asked Jimmy how it felt to have second place ripped out from under him at the last moment, and they asked me how it felt to make such a triumphant return. It was glorious, and, for once, I didn't mind answering their questions. I even had a few insightful, heart-felt answers for them, since having my dream yanked away had given me a lot of time to think about things.

"Mackenzie, would you mind explaining for us just what happened earlier this season? You weren't able to get on a team, and with your record and background, that seems unfathomable to me."

I smiled at the female reporter before me. The look on her face was pure disbelief, like she really didn't get it. I instantly liked her. Knowing that I no longer had to hide anything from anyone, I told her the truth. "My father disapproved of a fellow racer I was dating at the time. He made sure no team would take me, to try to get me to change my mind about my boyfriend."

The reporter's eyes widened in shock. There had been speculation and rumor surrounding my departure, but no confirmed facts. "Your father, Jordan Cox, had you blacklisted…because of a boy?"

As I nodded, I felt my cheeks heating in residual anger. It was going to take a long time to get over that betrayal. "Essentially, yes."

She still seemed baffled, and I was sure the remainder of our conversation would be about this topic. "But when you reopened Cox Racing, you hired him as a consultant, correct?"

Again, I nodded. "Yes. His poor parenting skills don't have anything to do with his knowledge about racing. But, trust me, it has been well-established that he has no say on my personal life anymore."

She smiled, like she was happy to hear that. Yeah, I'd give this reporter an exclusive anytime. "And the boy? Are you still together? Can you tell us which lucky rider sparked the War of the Coxes?"

With a sigh, my smile finally left me. "Actually, we're not. He betrayed my trust too. Guess that's a theme in my life."

The reporter's smile shifted into sympathy. "I'm sorry to hear that, but at least your career is back on track. You're doing better than ever, and I can't wait to see what happens next season. Congratulations, Mackenzie."

She reached out for my hand, and I gladly shook hers. "Thank you. It's great to be back."

It was better than great to be back, but I was a little worried that if I started gushing about racing, I might never stop. And I might cry, and I didn't want to break down on camera.

After the interviews were done, points were officially tallied, and the winner of the championship was declared. It didn't surprise me at all who had clenched it. "The winner of this year's ARRC Championship is...Myles Kelley!"

Myles was standing next to me when his name was announced. He thrust both of his fists into the air, his grin a mile wide. Nikki was on the other side of me, sobbing. As Myles climbed the steps to the winner's podium, I looked over at her with concern and confusion on my face. Nikki wasn't a crier, but today alone she'd already had a couple of breakdowns. Myles's victory was great news, but it wasn't all that shocking; he'd been the points leader for a while now.

"You okay?" I asked, my voice nearly drowned out in the crowd of cheering spectators.

She nodded, then shook her head, then nodded again. "Yes, no, not really." She started crying again, but not in a happy way this time.

Really concerned now, I pulled her to the edge of the boisterous crowd. "What's going on?" I asked. "Ever since you and Myles..." I couldn't even say what they'd done without cringing. "Ever since you guys...you know... you've been a basketcase. I thought you two patched things up? I thought the weirdness was gone?" Or at least at a manageable level. Nikki crying at the drop of a hat didn't seem very manageable to me.

Sniffing, Nikki wiped her nose on her dirty sleeve. "We did. We talked it out, and totally fixed us. Then my body had to go and betray me."

If she was saying she was still sexually attracted to Myles, I didn't think I could get through the conversation. "What...do you mean?"

With large, red, watery eyes, Nikki sullenly said, "I'm pregnant."

Nothing short of Nikki quitting would have shocked me more. My eyes dropped to her stomach, then her face, then back to her stomach. "You're...what?" I started putting my hand on her belly, looking for some sort of physical confirmation, but Nikki smacked my fingers away. Returning my eyes to hers, I asked, "Is it Myles's?"

Nikki frowned at me. "He's the only one I've been with, so yeah, it's his."

"Does he know?" I asked, glancing up at the stage. Myles was shaking up a bottle of champagne, getting ready to spray it over the crowd. He sure seemed clueless.

When I looked back at Nikki, she confirmed my suspicion. "No, he doesn't know. And I don't want him to know. I don't want any of this." She raised her head and firmed her jaw, like she could will away the situation and replace it with one of her own choosing. I completely understood the desire to do that, but I also understood just how impossible it was. You couldn't wish away reality.

I wrapped my arms around her in an all-encompassing hug. Twisting us so I could look up at Myles showering the crowd with alcohol, I told her, "It will be okay, Nik. I promise."

She started blubbering again in my arms, and I silently prayed that it really would be all right.

Myles started heading our way, so I pushed back from Nikki and hurriedly helped her clean her face. She still looked a little weepy, with tearstained cheeks and puffy eyes, but Myles was riding high right now, so I doubted he'd notice. He ran right up to Nikki and scooped her into a playful hug. She started laughing as he swung her around, and I couldn't help but think that even if they only ever remained friends, the two of them would make great parents.

I was just about to give Myles my own congratulatory hug when I felt a tiny tap on my arm. Turning around, I saw Antonia standing there with Hookup and Hayden. Hayden was beaming as he stared at me, and the love on his face was almost unbearable. He shouldn't look at me that way anymore. Surprisingly enough, Hookup was shooting big, happy grins at me too. Had he bet on me or something? No, he'd seemed convincing when he'd said he'd given all that up. Maybe he was just…happy for me. Wow, that was a foreign concept. Getting used to this new reality would take some time.

Antonia had a wide-eyed, dreamy expression on her face as she looked up at me. "That was amazing, Aunt Kenzie! The way you weaved around people…" She paused to mimic racing with her hands. "It was like they weren't moving at all!"

I was sure it wasn't quite that dramatic, but I appreciated her enthusiasm.

"Yeah, not bad, Kenzinator. I always knew you had mad skills." Hookup nodded his head in approval, still smiling like he'd just won big.

After thanking them both, I tried to return my attention to Myles; I just didn't have it in me to handle another heart to heart with Hayden. He didn't let me ignore him though. Cupping my elbow, he quietly said, "I knew you could do it, Kenzie. No doubt in my mind." The feel of him touching me, the look in his eyes…it made it very hard to forget the fact that we were over. God, how the hell was I going to work with him next year?

To put some sort of distance between us, I asked him a question I never thought I would. "Why didn't Felicia race today? Is she even here?" Maybe I should have lifted Nikki's promise to be silent about all things Hayden and Felicia; I had no doubt Nikki knew what was going on. Although her plate was a little full right now...

A bit of Hayden's smile fell as he absorbed my question. I wasn't sure what that meant. Was he missing his lover? God, I hated the thought of the two of them together. "She…quit," he told me, his voice subdued. "Same day as me."

"She quit the team? Why the hell would she do that?" She was Keith's golden child, his secret weapon, his media darling. Why the hell would she walk away from all that? Immediately after I thought of the question, the answer struck me like a hammer. "She quit because of you."

Hayden flinched, then shrugged. "I don't know if she…" With a sigh, he shook his head. "Yeah…I think she quit because of me."

Of course she did. She'd follow Hayden to the ends of the Earth, and if he jumped off the Benneti cliff, then she'd plummet to the ground right along with him. Well, if she thought I'd hire her, too, she was sorely mistaken.

Instantly outraged by their tight-knit bond, I spun on my booted heel, and left. I felt bad walking away from Antonia, but I couldn't handle another second in Hayden's presence. He shouted my name, asking me to stay, but I ignored him. Now if only I could do that every day for the rest of my life. Goddamn it.

My father and my sisters took me out to celebrate that night, and I was grateful for the distraction. It was a little odd to be with that circle of people again, but I knew I was going to have to try if any of us were going to move forward. And I really didn't want to be stuck in the past, so I sucked it up and got through it. And by the third round of drinks, I was actually beginning to enjoy myself.

But when the festivities ended, and I was once again alone in my hotel room, my thoughts turned to Hayden. Hayden, the charming, seductive rogue. And Felicia, his childhood sweetheart. Reunited again, after all this time. It was so damn sweet, almost like a fairytale romance. But I was the girl in the middle. The obstacle that had to be removed. The two of them getting their happily ever after, ruined my chances for one. And as bitter as I was about that, something else was bothering me even more.

Felicia was giving up an obvious, God-given talent, and a legitimate, legal way to exploit that talent…for a man. A fact I was all-too familiar with. Regardless of how much I disliked her, I hated seeing something special like that go to waste. And realizing that gave me a sudden, new-found appreciation for what my family must have felt when I quit racing. If nothing else, I could appreciate the sentiment behind their horrible actions.

Staring at the hotel room ceiling, I debated how to get Felicia and her career out of my head. Thinking about Hayden's new fling was about the last thing I wanted to do. I'd rather call up Nikki and have her describe in detail everything she'd done with Myles in Monterey. God, I couldn't believe she was pregnant.

Just when I was about to text Nikki and ask her when she was going to tell Myles, my phone chirped with a message. Grabbing it out of my bag, I glanced at the screen, then frowned. It was from Major Asshat…Hayden. I didn't want to hear what he had to say—especially since I'd asked him not to text me anymore—but curiosity compelled me, and I unlocked my phone so I could read what he'd sent.

'I'm sorry if I upset you today, that wasn't my intention. I'm so proud of you, Kenzie. I hope you are enjoying the moment. You earned it.'

The simplicity of his message touched me, and I could clearly see him, hunched over his phone, hand running through his hair, anxious expression on his face as he waited for me to respond. If he was exploring his old relationship with Felicia, why was he still trying to engage me? It made no sense. *You can't have it both ways, Hayden.* Even still, I texted back. *'Thank you.'*

His reply was almost instant. *'Can I come over? Just to talk?'*

There was nothing to talk about. I shouldn't haven't encouraged him into thinking there was. We were over. Turning off my phone, I tucked it into my bag, crawled into bed, and hoped that sleep came quickly.

Maybe it was delirium. Maybe it was because I'd tossed and turned all night long, but an idea implanted itself into my brain, and no matter what I did, I couldn't shake it. So, the next day, when my plane touched down in California, there was only one course of action left for me, and I couldn't believe what I was about to do.

Turning on my phone, I called Izzy. "Kenzie! Hey, congratulations! I watched the race on TV. You were amazing!"

"Thanks, Izzy," I said, walking to my truck. "Hey...I have a huge favor to ask, and it's going to sound strange, but I'm really hoping you'll help me."

She was quiet for a moment, then she softly said, "Okay, what is it?"

Inhaling deeply, I held my breath for a few seconds before releasing it. "I need Felicia's address. Do you know where she lives?"

I could hear her trepidation coming through the phone. "Kenzie, I don't think... Whatever you're planning, it's not a good idea."

A soft, humorless laugh escaped me. "I can guarantee you, it's not what you think. I just need to talk to her. Please, Izzy."

Izzy let out a long sigh. "Okay, but don't make me regret this, Kenzie." She rattled off the address so fast, it was like she was trying to get it all out before she changed her mind. Once she was done, she said, "Don't do anything stupid, okay? Hayden is amazing, sure, but he's not worth going to jail for."

Getting arrested was about the last thing I planned on happening today, but I supposed stranger things had occurred recently. Thanking Izzy—and ignoring her comment about incarceration—I hung up the phone and hurried to my waiting vehicle. Best get this over with before I changed my mind.

The drive from the airport to Felicia's house was far too long, and I had too much time to think. I talked myself out of my plan every other minute, but then I talked myself right back into it. I'd never feel completely at peace if I didn't speak my mind. About a few different things. When I finally got to the address Izzy had given me, I was shocked at how similar Felicia's house was to mine. Did she plan that on purpose? So Hayden's transition from me to her would be as seamless as possible?

Annoyance bubbled up inside me, but I pushed it back; she couldn't possibly have known what my house looked like when she'd rented this. It was pure, stupid coincidence. Shutting off my truck, I mustered all my confidence before stepping outside. *Don't show fear* was my mantra as I strutted to her front door. Along with, *Just breathe*.

I rapped on the door a few times, then waited. Doubt crept back in as I stared at the white wood separating me from the person Hayden was sleeping with. Don't hit her, don't start something. Say your piece and leave.

The door cracked open, and Felicia's face filled the void. For the first time that I'd ever seen, she looked awful. Her hair was a tangled mess, her eyes were red and bloodshot, and she was wearing I-don't-give-a-fuck sweats. What the hell?

She seemed to be thinking the same thing as she stared at me. "Kenzie? What are you doing here?"

Coming back to the task at hand, I indicated her house. "Can I come inside?"

She blinked in surprise, then stepped back and opened the door wider. "I guess so."

With a calming breath, I stepped into her home; it even smelled like mine. Felicia shut the door behind me, then, like she'd just realized what she must look like, she began smoothing her hair. "Why are you here?" she asked again.

"I just..." Her red, irritated eyes were a dead giveaway that she'd been crying. Were her and Hayden already done? Did that matter? I couldn't take him back. I wouldn't.

Annoyed at that thought, I changed what I'd been going to say. "Are you okay?"

Felicia flashed me a small grin. "Are you really concerned about me?"

No. *Then why was I here?*

Before I could answer her complicated question, she shook her head. "I'm fine. This weekend was just difficult for me." She sat down on the edge of her couch, and grabbed a tissue from a box nearby. "I never imagined just how much I'd miss racing. I never even thought I cared, until it was gone..." She dropped her head back and groaned. "Jesus, isn't that the story of my life." Readjusting her head to look at me, she lifted a questioning eyebrow. "Have you ever felt like you're your own worst enemy?"

A scoff escaped me. "All the time." Clearing my throat, I decided to get to the heart of why I was here. "Did you quit because of Hayden? Because he quit too?"

Felicia looked surprised at that. "Hayden quit?"

Her answer was extremely confusing. How could she not know Hayden had quit? "Yeah...he said he quit the same day you did. I just assumed you quit because of him."

She gave me a half-smile. "I suppose I did. I quit that morning, before he got in. I just couldn't be around him anymore."

Now I was extremely confused. "You couldn't be around Hayden? But...aren't you guys...?" *Screwing like rabbits*? He'd hinted that something had happened between them. He had all but confessed to me that they were lovers.

Felicia sighed and dabbed at her eyes. "It's no secret that I want him. Hell, I came back for him. But...the truth is, I lost him ages ago. I was holding onto a dream, and that dream is over. It's time for me to wake up."

This wasn't how I was expecting this conversation to go. I thought she'd admit they were in love, and then I'd chew her out for how they got together. But what if they'd never gotten together? "Did you...have sex with him...the night he and I broke up?" My throat closed as I waited for her answer. *God, please say no.*

Felicia stared me down, her dark eyes intense. Then she shook her head. "No. He wouldn't..." She bit her lip, her face pained, then she sighed. "He was loyal to you, even when he didn't have a reason to be."

As my mind spun at hearing confirmation that my worst fears were totally unfounded, Felicia walked over to her purse. With a resigned expression on her face, she rummaged through her bag until she found something; I watched in stunned silence when she pulled out a gigantic diamond ring. "I think maybe this rightfully belongs to you," she said, handing the ring to me.

"What is this?" I finally whispered, fingering the sparkling gem on top of the silver band.

Felicia's voice was subdued when she spoke. "Once upon a time, Hayden was going to marry me with this ring, but he never got the chance to propose. I left before he could." She looked up at me and sadness transformed her face. "He gave it to me recently...as closure. Said he and I would never work, because his heart belongs to you now, and it always would." Smiling through the tears in her eyes, she said, "I was his first love, but you...I think you're his last."

The world started hazing, and I had to sit down on the couch before I fell. "I just assumed... He made it seem like the two of you..." They didn't sleep together? He was...faithful? Shaking my head, I told her, "Even if you two didn't do anything, he lies so much, how can I ever...?"

I couldn't even form complete sentences, but Felicia seemed to understand what I was saying. "I've known Hayden a long time. He's always been fearless, a little reckless, and utterly devoted to those he loves. It was that insane commitment that ended up pushing me away. It was too much, too intense, and I was too young, too scared of what would happen to me if I lost him...so stupidly enough, I let him go. And it was the biggest mistake of my life." As a tear dropped down her cheek, she held my gaze. "Don't make my mistake, Kenzie."

Stunned, I blurted out, "And don't make mine."

Now Felicia was the one who was confused. With a half-smile, I explained. "I gave up everything I loved for a boy. I gave up my dream." Swallowing a painful lump in my throat, I tried to control the swirling emotions within me. My voice was passionate when I could speak again. "Don't stop racing because of Hayden. If being on a bike is where you're meant to be, then don't let him stop you from doing that. Get your ass on a bike."

A small smile cracked her lips. "I'm surprised to hear that, coming from you. If I do what you say, then we'll be competitors again."

"I welcome competition." *So long as it has nothing to do with my boyfriend.* But...since Hayden and I weren't together anymore, that was no longer an issue.

Felicia's expression turned thoughtful, and I knew she was considering my comment...just as I was considering hers. My eyes drifted back down to the ring in my fingers. Hayden had held onto this for so long, maybe as a reminder of his pain, a reminder to never love that fully again. Or maybe it was hope that had made him cling to the piece. Hope that Felicia would return, and they could resume what they'd had when she did. But then, when she *had* returned, and they'd been free to be together—no guilt, no worries—he'd rejected her, and let go of that last physical tie between them. He'd let go of his past, because of me. Because he loved me too much to be with someone else. Because he wanted to be with me. Only me.

My heart began surging in my chest as that realization washed over me. Everything had been for me—the good, the bad—all of it. I had his heart, wholly and truly, and he would never let me go. Not without a fight. And now that he knew, now that he fully understood just how deeply I detested him lying to me, I had a feeling that would never come between us again. He'd be honest to a fault now, which might cause very different problems, but I welcomed *that* challenge.

I felt dizzy, and I knew I was breathing harder than I should be. *He loves me. Just me.* "I should go," I whispered to Felicia.

She nodded, like she understood. As I stood on shaky legs, I handed her back the ring. "I think you should keep this," I told her. "Keep it as a reminder, to not run away from the things that scare you." That might be something else that we had in common; I'd fled from Hayden just as surely as she had.

With a sigh, Felicia wrapped her fingers around it. "Maybe I'll give it to Keith. Get him to take it as payment for rehiring me."

That made a genuine laugh escape me. "I don't think you'll have any problems getting Keith to take you back." He'd put her on the team just to spite me. Although...I didn't really feel jealous or spiteful of her anymore. As a rider, she was fine. She was an equal I could test myself against. As a person, though, well, I still wasn't sure about that.

I turned around to leave, then stopped myself. I'd come here for a reason. I couldn't do that without saying *all* of it. Twisting back to her, I said, "If I *do* take Hayden back..." and that was a very large *if*... "then the two of you can't be—"

She cut me off with a raise of her hand. "I already deleted his number, Kenzie. I'm well aware that the two of us can't be friends. Not anymore."

Relief coursed through me at hearing that. Maybe I wouldn't have to fight her every step of the way. I still wasn't sure if I was going to take Hayden back, but it was nice to know she wouldn't be interfering if I did. And that begged the question...was I going to?

CHAPTER 23

~Hayden~

I couldn't sleep. I'd been tossing and turning for the last several hours, my every thought centered on what I'd be doing in the morning. I was going to be racing...for Kenzie. She'd be my boss, and I'd be her faithful employee. And that was all we'd be, since she still couldn't forgive me.

I really thought she'd cool down if I gave her space, but no...something was still sparking her anger, reigniting it over and over again. I'd hurt her so deeply, and that really fucking killed me. All I could see in the darkness of my room, was the look in her eyes when she'd realized I'd been lying to her. I didn't think I'd ever get that haunting grief out of my mind.

Since sleep was eluding me, I tossed off the covers and hopped out of bed. I needed something to shut off my mind. Grabbing a blanket, I shuffled out the door and wandered to the living room. I could watch some mindless TV while I waited for exhaustion to overtake me.

Hookup's house was surprisingly empty. Even though it was the middle of the night, there were usually people here, crashed on the couch or playing a late-night game of poker. But ever since Hookup had announced that he was giving up the life he'd known for so long, things around here had quieted down. The party was finally over, and while typically I was grateful for that, tonight I kind of wanted the distraction.

Sitting on his couch, I turned on the TV and started looking for something halfway decent to watch. I ended up finding replays of the race from this past weekend. Watching the bikes fly around the course was bittersweet; I'd known I would miss it, but I hadn't realized how much until I was there—watching, and not participating. It was torture. Slow, agonizing torture. But Kenzie...she'd nailed it. Everything she'd done out there had been spot-on perfect. I'd never been prouder of her. And had never felt so distant, like I was on the outside, looking in. Watching her triumph, and not being able to celebrate the victory with her, that had been worse than not racing. She was all I wanted, and she was completely out of reach.

"Oh good, you're up."

I turned my head to see Hookup shuffling out of the kitchen, a tall glass of milk in his hand. God, he really had changed. Not that long ago, he would have been walking out with a six-pack under his arm. "Yeah...couldn't sleep."

Hookup nodded, like he understood insomnia. Sitting beside me, he drank a bit of his milk, then set it on the coffee table. "So, uh, I was going to wait until morning, but now seems as good a time as any."

Curious, I asked, "Good of time for what?"

Hookup skewed his face in reluctance, like he didn't want to tell me what he had to say. "I've been thinking a lot, and I've decided...I'm gonna sell this place. I'm thinking it will go pretty fast, too, so you should probably start looking for somewhere else to stay."

My jaw nearly hit the floor. "You're...? Are you serious? You love this place." Hookup was the king of this particular jungle, and I was floored that he wanted to leave his kingdom behind.

Hookup rubbed his jaw. "Yeah...I did love it...once. But I want to be closer to Izzy and Antonia. I was actually thinking of buying a place for all of us. Something close to the hospital, but outside of the city. Something with a big backyard for Antonia. Something nice...she deserves nice. They both do."

I just kept staring at him, stunned. It was like he'd been abducted and replaced by...by a caring, thoughtful creature who put other's needs first. Hookup wanted to live in the suburbs? Willingly? I still couldn't get over it.

Hookup looked around his place, and I knew he was seeing more than the cracks in the walls. "And besides," he said, "I'm kind of over...all this. It's time to move on, you know?"

I did know. I'd wanted to move on from this a long time ago, and I'd tried—several times—to do just that. Smiling at him, I nodded. "I think that's great, Tony. Antonia will love having you around."

Hookup grinned, then his face turned more serious. "She wants you around too. Maybe you could find a place near us?"

"Maybe. I'm gonna be pretty busy though. Kenzie hired me as a rider for Cox Racing."

Hookup's face nearly split in two he was smiling so wide. "Dude, she did? That's great!"

"Yeah," I said with a smile. "I was going to tell you on the way back from Jersey, but it, uh, didn't feel real at the time. Still doesn't actually. That's why I'm not sleeping. Just trying to wrap my head around...my life."

Hookup playfully socked me in the arm. "I thought for sure you two were splitsville for good. I'm glad she finally got over it. And it's not like much happened with you and Felicia anyway. A little reunion sex is to be expected, but it's not like you were bangin' her every night." His expression grew contemplative. "Or were you?"

A long, weary sigh escaped me. "For the millionth time, I wasn't sleeping with Felicia. Not once since she's been back. No sex. At all. Period."

Hookup looked disappointed as he shook his head. "Yeah, all right. I don't get it, but all right..." He smiled and slugged me in the arm. "Either way, I'm glad your woman got over it and took you back."

I sighed again, but sadly this time. "She didn't. I'm racing for her...but that's it. She still doesn't want... She wants to stay broken up." And I had no idea how I was going to be around her all the time, but not be with her. Just thinking about it made a sharp pain slice through my chest. The real torture was only just beginning.

Hookup was silent a moment. Then he grabbed his milk and took another swig. At that moment, I really wished he did have a six-pack. Or a fifth of whiskey. "Sucks, man...sorry," he finally said.

"Yeah," I murmured, my eyes refocusing on the race highlights currently showing Kenzie's flawless form. "I'm sorry too." For so many things.

Hookup went back to bed after finishing his glass of milk. I stayed on the couch, watching numerous different sports recaps until I finally, thankfully drifted off to sleep. When I woke up, nerves were eating holes through my body. Shit. It was time to see her. To see her and act like absolutely nothing was off between us, like me being her employee—and only her employee—was completely normal. Yep. Just another day at work.

Hookup's place was pretty far from the racetrack, and I still didn't have a vehicle, so I borrowed Hookup's car and started making my way back to Oceanside. I needed to get my life together. With Hookup selling his place and moving somewhere with Izzy, I'd need to find my own place soon. My own place, and my own vehicle; it was time for me to truly stand on my own two feet, with no one helping me up. It was something I should have done a long time ago, then maybe I wouldn't have felt so indebted to Keith.

When I finally got to the turnoff for the practice track, I stopped Hookup's car so I could take in the fresh new sign along the road. *Cox Racing / Benneti Motorsports Practice Track*. God, it was so good to see Cox Racing back up there; the sign had looked incomplete without it.

A few moments later, when I reached the outer gate, I realized that there was a small problem. I no longer had a key. I'd have to ride around back and break in, but I really didn't want to do that. If I was going to truly leave that world behind me, then I needed to start doing things by the book. That meant taking out a loan when I needed money. It also meant not breaking and entering.

Pulling my phone out of my jacket pocket, I debated if I should call Kenzie and ask her to let me in, or call Nikki. Nikki would certainly be the easier way to go, but taking the easy road hadn't gotten me very far lately.

Chewing on my lip, I scrolled down to Kenzie's number. That was when I noticed a motorcycle stopping at my window.

Looking over, I saw a woman sitting there, staring in my direction, a dark helmet covering her face. Kenzie? I instantly glanced down at the bike. No, not Kenzie. Felicia. I hadn't talked to her since I'd given her the engagement ring. After Keith had said she'd quit, I kind of thought she'd taken off again. Even though Izzy had said she was still around, it was shocking to see that was true. What was she doing here at the track though? I would think this would be the last place she'd want to be.

I rolled down my window while she popped open her visor. "Going inside?" she asked, tilting her head toward the gate.

Curiosity killed me as I nodded. "Yeah. Can you let me in?"

She nodded, then pulled forward to the gate. Inserting her key card, she punched in the code and the gate instantly began to open. She still had access? Obviously she hadn't turned hers in once she'd quit. I kind of wished I hadn't turned mine in either.

The gate rolled open, and she punched it, so I had time to follow her through before it started closing. Once she was on the other side, she stopped and waited for me. "What are you doing here?" she said.

With a short laugh, I told her, "I was just about to ask you the same thing."

She smiled, then sucked her lip into her mouth, a nervous habit. "I'm about to storm into Keith's office and demand that he takes me back. Or beg him to take me back, whichever one I need to do."

For the second time today, I was stunned. "You're going to race for him again. I thought you were done?"

She gave me a small smile. "I thought I was too, but then someone convinced me that I shouldn't give up on my dream."

Her lips curved up into a strange, knowing smile that truly baffled me. I had no idea what secret message she was trying to convey, but then I started thinking about her words. Someone had convinced her to not give up on her dream—her racing dream. "Kenzie?" I blurted out. "You talked to Kenzie?"

Felicia laughed at my reaction. "Yeah, I was shocked too. She came by my house, told me I shouldn't throw away my dream for a boy. I still can't believe she *wants* me to race."

Pain and guilt lashed across my soul. Don't give up your dream for a boy? *See, Kenzie...I knew you'd resent me.* Shaking my head, I told Felicia, "I think she just doesn't want to see another person have to walk away from something they love to do." Hope rising inside my chest, I hesitantly added, "Did she...did she mention me?"

Felicia frowned, and I felt a bit of despair creep in. "Yeah, you...came up."

"And...?" *Did she say if she'd ever forgive me?*

With a sad smile on her face, Felicia said, "I told her she didn't have to worry about you and me anymore. That ship has sailed."

I was surprised to not only hear her say that, but to hear her confess she'd told Kenzie that. I wanted to thank her, but it felt inappropriate, so I stayed quiet on the subject. Not sure what to say, I mumbled, "You didn't run?

When Keith said you'd quit, I thought for sure you'd bail again."

Her smile widened, but didn't grow any warmer. "I told you I changed..."

For her sake, I hoped she had. "Good luck in there with Keith. You won't need it, but good luck all the same."

Her smile finally turned bright. "Thanks."

I turned my gaze to the parking lot, and was nearly assaulted by the sight of Kenzie's truck. She was here... this was happening.

"Hey, Hayden..."

Turning back, I saw Felicia still sitting there on her bike, studying me. When she had my attention, she said, "Good luck with Kenzie."

"Thanks," I mumbled, not feeling my chances were anywhere near as positive as hers were with Keith.

Felicia's eyes searched mine, and her voice grew soft. "Don't let her go, Hayden. If you really want to be with her, then keep fighting for her."

Her advice made me smile. "I plan to." No, if there was one thing in this world that I would gladly spend every moment of the rest of my life doing, it was winning Kenzie back. Nothing else mattered.

Felicia nodded, then twisted like she was going to leave. "Hey, Felicia," I said, stopping her. She turned back to me, and I held my breath. What I was about to say wasn't easy, but I knew I needed to say it. I knew from experience how awful it felt to not have someone's forgiveness, and I couldn't keep punishing her for a mistake she made over four years ago. "I forgive you for leaving, and for not telling me what you were going through. I forgive you for all of it."

Her eyes lit up with a combination of hope and joy. "Really?"

An overwhelming sense of relief came over me as I nodded. "Yeah...really." What I'd forgotten was that it felt just as good to forgive as it did to be forgiven. I'd been hanging onto that pain for far too long.

Felicia grinned, looking more pleased than I'd seen in a while. "Thank you," she whispered, then she turned toward the track and sped off, to go chase her dream with Keith Benneti. I wished her luck. Hopefully it wouldn't bite her in the ass like it had me.

It physically hurt to park next to Kenzie's truck. Being that close made a flood of memories go through me. The fights, the passion, the sex...the love. There was so much about her that I missed, so much about her that I knew I couldn't live without. Back when I'd been with Felicia, I'd thought I'd had that intense level of love, of companionship, but I'd only scratched the surface. I just hadn't realized it until I'd met Kenzie. And now it might be too late to fix it.

Shaking off my melancholy, I shut off the car and stepped outside. Walking up to the track was a new experience for me; I usually rode my street bike right up to the garage. Or I used to ride Keith's street bike to the garage, I guess I should say. Getting my own motorcycle was high on my list of priorities. Just under getting back with Kenzie and finding a place to live.

My eyes drifted to the left side of the track when I entered the main complex. The way things ended with Keith still left a bitter taste in my mouth. So did the way he'd tampered with my personal life. Wanting me to race better was one thing, wanting me to date better was another.

Without wasting another second reminiscing over my career with Keith, I turned to my new home with Cox Racing. The garage doors were rolled open, and, even from where I was standing, I could hear Kenzie's voice. The sound of her laughter was painful music to my ears; it was a sound I'd give anything to be able to produce from her again.

Hands in my pockets, I forced myself to calmly continue walking over to the Cox garages. *I can do this.* A rider was leaving the track right as I walked past the entrance. I glanced over to see who it was, then stopped when I saw Rodney popping open his visor.

He smiled at me, then nodded over to where I'd been headed. "Starting your new gig today?"

A humorless laugh escaped me. "Keith knows about that already?" I asked, not really all that surprised.

Rodney's face turned incredulous. "You know how small this world is. He's pissed, by the way. Thinks you betrayed him by going over to the enemy."

Right, I betrayed *him*. "You agree with him?"

He considered me for long moment before answering. "Nah. You tried to work things out with Keith, but from what I could tell, he was being an insufferable dick. I would have quit too."

His comment made me happy, but I had to wonder...things between us were actually improving, would that end now that we were no longer teammates? "Do you think the Cox/Benneti ban will be back in effect? Now that Cox Racing has reopened?" If so, he shouldn't be on the track right now, since it was technically Cox time. And we shouldn't be talking; during the old ban, that was a fireable offense.

Rodney sighed, like he wasn't sure if the ban should be in place or not. "I don't know. Since it's Kenzie's team now, and not Jordan's, maybe Keith won't be so strict about the whole thing. I mean, I understand not getting too friendly with the competition..." He frowned as his thought faded, then he shook his head. "Nah, fuck that. No harm in hanging out as far as I can tell." Tilting his head, a sympathetic look touched his face. "How's your kid, man? Get out of the hospital okay?"

Touched that he was asking, that he seemed to want some sort of friendship, I nodded and grinned. "Yeah, she's home and doing much better. Thanks."

Rodney grinned too. "Good, glad to hear it. Guess I better go report to Keith. Even though the season's over, he's acting like the first race of the year is about to start."

He rolled his eyes, and I laughed at the gesture. "Yeah, well, I think he might be in a good mood when you get back. He just rehired Felicia." I wasn't sure if he had—I supposed he could have turned her down out of spite—but odds were good she was a Benneti again.

Rodney's eyes widened in shock. "Really? Damn, that is good news. That girl is so fucking hot." Clearing his throat, he quickly added, "And talented, too...of course."

Of course. Well, if he wanted to make a play for her, he was welcome to it. Maybe if Felicia was dating someone else, Kenzie might finally realize that I wasn't interested in her, and she'd take me back.

I waved a quick goodbye to Rodney, and turned back to the garages. Each step closer was a mixture of excitement and trepidation. Would today be the day we worked everything out? I hoped so. When I got close enough to the doors, I could see Kenzie standing there, talking to Nikki. Nikki looked like she was trying not to be sick, and Kenzie's face was scrunched in concern for her friend. God, I loved that look on her. I loved every look on her—even pissed.

Suddenly, she twisted around and looked right at me. Our eyes locked, and my breath caught in my throat. Jesus—the wildness in her wavy hair, the fullness of her kissable lips, the intelligence in her eyes...Rodney had it all wrong. Felicia wasn't the hot one. Kenzie was. I stumbled on my step, caught off guard by the intensity in her gaze. Kenzie turned away with a heavy exhale, like she'd been trapped by my stare. Then she said something to Nikki...and walked away. The disappointment nearly crushed me where I stood. She wasn't even going to talk to me? We'd never be able to work together this way. Something had to give.

My face felt rigid as I walked into the garage. Nikki still looked green, but she waved when she saw me. "Hey, Hayden. Kenzie had to...well, she said..." With a heavy exhale, she gave up trying to make up excuses for her friend. "She just needs more time."

Heaviness settled over me. More time. I'd already given her weeks. If she couldn't even—shit. There really was no hope for us. "Thanks," I told Nikki, my voice subdued. Shoving aside my own problems, I quietly asked her, "You okay? You look like you're about to throw up. Bad breakfast burrito or something?"

She immediately slapped a hand over her mouth. Her eyes hardened into daggers, like she was blaming *me* for her stomach, then she bolted from the room, heading for the locker room. Damn. Was it something I said?

Someone behind me felt the same way. "What the hell did you say to her, man?"

Looking behind me, I saw Myles walking into the garage. He was holding a duffel bag in one hand, his racing helmet in the other. He was moving in today, same as me. Only I didn't have anything yet. Keith had provided everything for me, so I was showing up empty-handed; not a good feeling. "Hey, Myles. I didn't say anything to her. I think she ate something bad."

Hopefully that was all it was. I couldn't handle someone else I cared about being truly sick. And I *did* care about Nikki. She'd been a great mechanic, and, even though she'd always kind of been in the middle of Kenzie and me, she'd been a good friend too. Hopefully I could return the favor one day.

"Congratulations on winning the championship. That was an amazing race," I said, trying to change the subject, since Myles seemed unconvinced.

From the look he was giving me, it was clear he was trying to find some sort of hidden meaning in my praise. *Search all you want, I'm being sincere.* Finally, his lips curved into a barely-there smile. "Thanks." Glancing over at the locker room, he said, "I better go check on Nikki."

I nodded, but then put a hand up to stop him from moving. "I know I've said this before, but I really am sorry about what happened to you last year." I hesitated a second, debating, and then I added, "I didn't directly have anything to do with the accident, but...a friend of mine did. I didn't know until it was too late, and then...I didn't do enough to stop him. I felt stuck. I felt responsible. I felt obligated to stay silent for him. I felt...like shit. And I'm sorry. I'm sorry you got caught up in what he was doing, I'm sorry I didn't do more. I hope one day you can forgive me, because I really respect you."

Holding my breath, I extended my hand to him. I'd never quite so bluntly admitted that much to him, and I hope he took it as closure, instead of ammunition that he could take to the officials. His dark eyes scrutinized me for seemingly countless minutes before finally setting his helmet on a table and grabbing my hand. "I'm assuming this...friend...is no longer a problem?" he asked.

Smiling, I shook my head. No, somehow Hookup had finally grown up. "He won't touch another bike again. And, if for some reason he ever does, I'll turn him in myself."

Myles cracked a genuine smile as he let go of my hand. "Welcome to the team, Hayden. This should be an interesting year."

I couldn't disagree with that.

After Myles disappeared, I looked around the garage for Kenzie. She was nowhere in sight, so I had to assume she was upstairs in her new office.

As I trudged my way up the stairs, I looked around at the small changes Kenzie had already made to the garage—there was new paint on the walls, new windows in the garage doors, new signs on the walls. Where everything had looked rundown and forgotten before, it was bright and alive with new energy now. Kenzie's energy. She'd even revitalized the Cox Racing logo, freshening it up for a younger feel. When I reached the upstairs, I noticed her handiwork there too. It was like the entire building had heaved a grateful sigh of relief that she had come and saved it; I understood the feeling.

Kenzie's office door was closed, her name proudly displayed in large chrome letters, along with the title—*owner*—underneath it. Seeing her position made me smile as I rapped on the door with my knuckle. *Silence.* I tried again, a little harder this time. When there still was no answer, I rolled my eyes and said, "Come on, Kenzie. I work for you now…you can't ignore an employee."

The door instantly opened. "Technically you haven't filled out the paperwork yet, so you're not actually an employee."

I frowned as I considered that. "Did you change your mind about hiring me?" *Please say no.*

Kenzie sighed, then walked over to stand behind her desk, like she needed the heavy piece of furniture between us. "No. I still need a rider of your caliber on my team." I raised my eyebrow, testing her, and she sighed. "I need you, okay?"

Her words singed me with an unexpected jolt of pain, and I cringed. *I need you.* God, how I wanted that to be true. Like she understood my reaction, she quickly added, "On the team. I need you on the team."

Forcing a smile, I nodded. "Good. This is where I want to be." *You're where I want to be.*

Kenzie's mouth popped open like she'd heard my mental addition. Licking her lips, she grabbed some papers off her desk and began nervously rifling through them. "I've got some stuff for you to fill out—standard employment paperwork. Do you have your driver's license with you? I'll need to make a copy…"

Stepping over to her, I put my hand over hers, stopping her incessant shuffling. "You're nervous. Do I make you nervous?" I'd made her several things since I'd met her, but nervous had never seemed to be one of them.

Fire instantly sprang into her eyes. *There's my girl.* "No, you don't. I just have a lot to do right now, and I told you to meet with John, not me. If you can't listen to simple instructions, then—"

A laugh burst out of me before I could stop it. She was mad at me for not following directions? For wanting to see her? Bullshit. She was mad because she wanted me here. And she didn't *want* to want me. It was our age-old problem, resurfacing its ugly head. "Nikki said you needed time. Is that true? Are you thinking about...?" Firmly pressing my lips together, I stopped myself from asking her about us.

Kenzie pulled away from where I was touching her. Sighing, she put down the papers. "Felicia told me that you guys didn't sleep together. She told me you were faithful, even when you didn't have to be. She said I shouldn't give up on you..."

Hope squeezed my heart so hard I thought it might burst. Was she giving us a chance? I moved around to her side of the desk, but she put her hand up, stopping me. "Even if you didn't sleep with her, even if you never did anything inappropriate with her...you still lied to me. How can I ever trust you, Hayden? How can we possibly work?"

Panic surged inside me; I knew I had one shot at fixing this. *One.* That was it. "I'm thickheaded, I know that, but I've learned, Kenzie. This lesson has sunk in."

She rolled her eyes, but I grabbed her arms, holding her gaze. "Being without you all this time…it's been hell. And if you're offering me a way out of hell, then there's no way I'd ever risk going back. If you set me free from this prison, I'll do everything in my power to stay free, to stay true, to stay with you. You have every piece of my heart, and I can't imagine any reason on this Earth why I'd ever lie to you again. I don't think I even could. You're my best friend, you're my family, and nothing feels real if you're not there with me. I can't function without you. I don't want to. I don't want to go another day without you by my side."

I couldn't think of more to say except begging her over and over to forgive me, and I didn't think that would sway her. My heart was pounding as I stared into her eyes. *Please say something before I explode.* She didn't though. She just kept looking at me, analyzing me, trying to determine if she could trust me. I couldn't take the silence, I couldn't take the scrutiny. I needed action.

"Fuck it," I murmured, then I leaned forward and found her lips. Hot fire surged through me as we connected. God, I'd missed this.

I expected Kenzie to get pissed and shove me away, expected her to end this immediately. But she didn't. She did the opposite. She attacked me. Her arms wrapped around my body, her fingers dug into my scalp, and she let out a groan that sent shockwaves of pleasure to my cock. Fuck, yes.

Our kiss intensified, and I had to steady my feet to keep from falling over. As I engulfed her in my arms, a part of me wondered what this meant. Had she forgiven me? Taken me back? Were we fine? Because I really needed us to be fine.

When her tongue stroked mine, all coherent thought escaped me, and pure, animal instinct took over. Leaning down, I cleared off her desk with one swoosh of my arm. Paper, pens, and a Cox Racing mug that I hoped was empty went crashing to the ground. Kenzie groaned again as I backed her into the desk. She dropped her head back, and I instantly trailed kisses along her neck, lower and lower, to the top of her chest.

Her shirt had half-a-dozen buttons keeping it modest. I didn't want modesty at the moment, and popped open the buttons. When I could see a black-lacy bra peeking at me, I swept aside her shirt and kissed a gloriously rigid nipple through the fabric.

Kenzie exhaled a shuddering breath, then finally pushed me away. She scooted back until she was sitting on her bare desk, then held up both hands, warding me off. "Wait...wait," she panted. "This isn't what I wanted."

My body was hard, ready, and now it was starting to ache. Stopping wasn't something *I* wanted to be doing. "What did you want then?" I said through clenched teeth.

"I wanted time. I wanted to take things slowly." She gave me a soft smile on the end, like she understood she was killing me.

But her words eased the ache, and a smile stretched over my lips. "Take things slowly? As in...together?"

She laughed, and her hand fell to my chest. "Yes... together." Her expression grew more serious. "I don't trust you right now, and that's a serious problem. But...I think I *could* trust you, and because of that slim possibility, I'm willing...to try again."

With a relieved exhale, I pulled her to her feet, and hugged her with every ounce of love I possessed. "Oh, God, thank you. Thank you. I didn't know how the hell I was going to work with you and not go crazy."

She giggled, and my heart soared at hearing it. "Yeah, I hadn't figured that one out either." Pulling back, she stared into my eyes. "But I'm serious about the going slow part. I want to know my heart is safe before I give it to you again."

I cupped her cheek, and she closed her eyes, savoring the contact. "I'm fine with going slow, Kenzie. I'm fine with anything, so long as it's with you."

Lowering my lips to hers, I gave her a soft, chaste kiss. *My forever is with you.* I didn't think that sentence sounded slow and easy, so I kept it myself, but my heart sang with the truth of it. She *was* it for me, and so long as she was open to giving me a chance, I wouldn't stop until she knew the truth of that too.

CHAPTER 24

~Epilogue. Kenzie~

Things at the track were going—really well. It was a few weeks after New Jersey, and while it was typically a slow time of year for racers, *both* teams were bustling with activity. It thrilled me to see so much life in the Cox garages, and, even though I had a lot to do and a lot to learn, I cherished every day I got to walk into my father's—no, *my*—building.

I wasn't sure why Keith had his team practicing so often, but I had to believe it was mainly because he didn't want to feel like we were showing him up or something. We'd already had a handful of arguments. The first disagreement was about the sign. In keeping with tradition, I'd placed Cox Racing before Benneti Motorsports on every sign around the track. Keith was furious. Said I'd had no right to design the signs without his input. He had a point, but I'd put up with so much shit from him that I didn't care. Cox Racing had always been first on the sign, and I wasn't about to change that.

The next major argument we'd had was about practice times. Keith had wanted to reinstate the noon switch-over time. I'd flat-out told him no. So long as my guys didn't interfere with the other riders, I didn't see any reason why our teams couldn't mingle, both on and off the track. Assigning times to keep our teams apart only created animosity and filled the air with tension. Not exactly an environment conducive to excellence. There was no reason our two teams couldn't get along, and I knew from experience that a little healthy competition could drive a rider like nothing else. It was in everyone's best interest to keep the track open and friendly. Keith didn't see it that way, but I wasn't budging on the issue. He could complain as much as he wanted.

"Ready to go home for the day, sweetheart?"

I looked up from my desk to see Hayden leaning against the doorframe of my office, smiling at me with an expression that was full of both amusement and love. He hadn't called me a pet name in a while, and I knew he'd been dying to. I crooked a smile at him as I set my pen down. "In a bit."

My smile turned into a frown as I wondered if his question had been some sort of subtle invitation. We'd agreed to take things slow, and so far, we'd been taking things *really* slowly. Hayden hadn't even come over to my house yet. We met up when we went out, or we went out in groups. Maybe I was taking "slow" a little too literally, but…to be completely honest, I was nervous. I didn't want to jump right in with both feet only to have my heart stomped on again. I was dipping my toes in the water, and praying they didn't get bitten off.

But Hayden never once complained about the sloth-like pace of our relationship. He just kept telling me: *Whatever you need, I'm not going anywhere.* And considering the fact that Keith had rehired Felicia, and she was a stone's throw away from Hayden all the time, I found his patience very comforting. He wanted this. He wanted me.

Hayden smiled, like he understood the change of my facial expression. "Let me know when you're ready, and I'll walk you to your truck."

He turned and left, and all I could do was grin like an idiot at the place where he'd been standing. He was so sweet, so warm and loving. It made it very difficult to resist him, and I wasn't sure how much longer I could keep going slow and steady. Hayden just had a way of making me want to go fast.

Refocusing on my job, I forced my eyes to return to my desk. I hadn't realized before just how much paperwork my father's job had entailed, and I now understood why he used to stay so late every night. But if I was going to do this job long-term, I needed to find balance. And that meant I needed to let this go until tomorrow, clock out, and go home. After letting Hayden walk me to my truck, of course.

Standing up, I began organizing my desk so coming in here tomorrow wouldn't drive me bat-shit crazy. My dad walked in just as I was finishing up the last to-do pile. Glancing up at him, I frowned. "Dad? I thought you went home hours ago."

A small smile cracked his lips. "I'm used to being the last one out. I guess it's hard to break that habit."

Setting down my stack, I walked over to him with a smile on my face. "Well, you don't need to do that anymore. Go home, get some rest."

He nodded, then his smile faded. "The girls and I... well...we'd like you to come over for dinner this weekend. You and...Hayden."

A grimace swept across his face, but it was gone so quickly, I almost could have imagined that I'd seen it. "You want to share a meal...with my boyfriend?" Just having dinner with me would have been a big step, but Hayden being there too—they really were trying.

From the look on Dad's face, I could tell he wasn't happy about what he was about to say, but then the annoyance shifted into a genuine grin. "It's possible that I might have...misjudged him, and if you took him back, then there must be something in him worth keeping. I'll just have to look harder."

From his tone of voice, it was clear he thought that was an impossible mission. I was touched though. "Thanks, Dad. I'll talk to Hayden. We'll see you this weekend."

Dad's smile widened, and he started to turn around. Stopping himself, he asked, "Do you need any help with that?" He pointed at the pile of work waiting for me on my desk. I knew if I said yes, he'd stay here all night until everything was finished. But I didn't want him sacrificing his life anymore for the business, or doing my job for me. I'd never learn the ins and outs if I wasn't at the helm.

"Nope, I'm good. Thank you."

Dad gave the desk a forlorn glance, like I'd taken something away from him, but then he nodded. I followed him out the door, then locked it tight behind me. Hayden was waiting for me in the garage. He was standing next to Myles and Nikki, apparently keeping them company while Nikki put her tools away for the night. Myles had a strange, resigned expression on his face while he listened to Hayden talking about something. While he hadn't exactly warmed up to Hayden, he was a little more willing to be around him now. Slightly.

I said goodnight to Dad, then headed over to my friends and boyfriend. Nikki shot me a guilty look when she noticed me approaching. That glance made me swear under my breath. She was supposed to tell Myles about being pregnant today, but obviously, that hadn't happened. Damn it. If I left this up to Nikki, she wouldn't tell him until after the baby was born.

Myles turned and grinned at me, so I quickly fixed my face. "Hey, Kenzie. We were thinking about going out for drinks. Want to come?"

I shifted my eyes to Nikki. "Drinks? Really?"

Her face turned sheepish. She'd successfully hidden the fact that she wasn't drinking from Myles for a while now—ordering her own non-alcoholic drinks at the bar, or secretly flagging down the waitress and changing her order—but she wouldn't be able to keep that crap up forever. She needed to tell him.

Myles clearly didn't understand what my comment really meant. He rolled his eyes. "Come on, Kenzie. I know you're back in full-on training mode, but I'm living testament that having fun on occasion won't kill you, or ruin your racing. I'm number one, baby. Remember?"

Nikki snorted. "Number one… You're never going to let us forget that, are you?"

Grinning, Myles shook his head. "Nope. I'm having it monogrammed on all my clothes. Especially my underwear."

Nikki groaned and tossed a rag at him. Hayden laughed at the pair, then languidly turned his eyes to me. "What do you say, 22? Want to unwind for a little while?"

I could see the hope in his eyes, and I knew he wanted me to say yes. It was what I wanted, too, so, biting my lip, I nodded. "Yeah…sounds good."

Myles started talking about where he planned on taking us. Inching closer to Nikki, I leaned over and said, "You know, tonight would be as good a time as any to tell him."

Nikki's brows drew together in clear warning that I should butt out, then she said to Myles, "Hey, Kelley, we should see if Ralph, Kevin, and Eli want to come too."

All the old Cox members had gleefully returned after the end of the season, and, while having them along sounded like great fun, I knew Nikki had only invited them so she had an excuse not to talk to Myles. *Well played, Ramirez. Well played.*

Myles's eyes lit up, and he pulled out his phone. I shook my head at Nikki, while she grinned in triumph. *Procrastinator.*

Hayden held my hand as we walked, and a feeling of contentment mixed with excitement surged through me. It was almost like how I'd felt during the New Jersey race—like everything was right in the world. He kissed my fingers in goodbye when we got to my truck, and my skin sizzled where his lips had touched me. Hot damn. Saying no to this boy was going to take all my willpower. But when we finally did cave, it was going to be so worth the wait.

Twenty minutes later, we all arrived at Oysters. It was a quaint little seafood bar and grill down by the pier that we frequented. In fact, Nikki and Myles used to come here so often during the off-season, that the manager, Glenn, had named a drink after each of them. I had stopped in on occasion too, but back then, I'd been far more regimented. Or uptight, as Myles used to say.

Our group was treated like long-gone soldiers returning from the war, with lots of hellos, hugs, and congratulations—apparently it had been a while since our last visit. By the time we were ushered to a back table big enough for all of us, the waitresses already had drinks in hand—either a fruity pink drink garnished with gummy bears, affectionately called the Nik-o-Rita, or a swirling blue and green drink that was known simply as The Myles.

"For my best customers," Glenn said. Then he gave Myles the evil eye. "Who promise to come in more frequently, now that the season is over."

Myles grinned at seeing his drink, and assured Glenn that he'd be in a lot. Nikki's eyes went wide with fear. Her tan face paled, and she remained absolutely silent. She couldn't hide not drinking when the drink was already waiting for her. When she recovered from her shock, she slid the drink over the table to me. "Here you go, Kenzie. Figure you could use this after a day like today. You seemed to be drowning in paperwork up there."

Knowing she was taking the easy way out, once again, I slid the drink back to her. "I'm good with one. And besides, it's named after you…you have to drink it."

My smile was almost as large as my face, and so was Nikki's scowl. I could practically feel her burning me with her brain. While most of the table was enjoying their drinks and not paying any attention to Nikki, Myles had looked over and happened to notice her annoyed expression. "Oh my God," he said. "Don't tell me you don't like Nik-o-Ritas anymore. Do you know how hard I had to fight to get Glenn to name it that? It's not even a margarita."

I could see the fury building on Nikki's face, but just underneath it was panic and pleading. She'd do *anything* to be able to get out of having this conversation. I knew I could throw her a life preserver and easily get her out of this predicament, but, for her own good, I wasn't going to.

Throwing on a casual smile, Nikki turned to look at Myles. "No, I just want water tonight. Still love the Nik-o-Ritas...they're the best."

Myles raised an eyebrow at her. "Water? You don't even drink water when you're thirsty."

"Thanks," she muttered. "You're making me sound like a lush."

Myles shrugged. "Just pointing out facts. So, what's up with you? Still sick or something?"

Nikki instantly latched on to the escape route Myles had just offered. She grabbed her stomach for emphasis. "Yeah...it's acting up again."

I wanted to fling my gummy bear stick at her, but I made myself stay silent. She had to tell him herself. Myles groaned at her comment. "Why did you want to come out tonight if you weren't feeling good? We could have gone out tomorrow instead."

Nikki bit her lip as she thought of something to say. "I was feeling fine earlier...it just kind of hit me."

Disappointment clear on his face, Myles said, "Do you want to go home?" He looked so sad, it was pretty obvious he wanted to hang out with her; I hoped Nikki didn't crush him by saying she was done for the night.

Nikki stared at him for a few long seconds before finally nodding. "Yeah...I do...sorry."

"Oh my God, Nikki, just tell him." I slapped my hand over my mouth, but it was too late. I'd said too much. Far too much. Hayden next to me had been idly listening to all the conversations around the table, but he was fully invested in this one now. So was Myles.

Seated across from me, Myles shifted his gaze from me, to Nikki beside him. "Tell me what?"

I closed my eyes, then flinched when I felt a slimy stick of candy hit my cheek. She gummy-beared me? Seriously? My eyes flared open, but the intensity in my gaze was no match for hers. "You had *one* job," she sneered.

"And you're being ridiculous," I snapped. "He's going to find out sooner or later, just tell him and get it over with."

Nikki's dark eyes flashed to Myles, and filled with tears. Now Myles looked concerned. Hayden too. He was looking at me, searching for a clue. I hadn't told him anything about what was happening with Nikki.

"What's going on, Nikki?" Myles asked.

The seriousness in his voice silenced the table, and all eyes fell on Nikki. She swallowed a few times, and I thought she might actually be sick now. "I…um…I'm… I'm kind of…"

"You're kind of what?" Myles asked, panic beginning to blossom in his voice. "Jesus…are you really sick? Like…sick-sick?"

Now Myles looked scared. Nikki instantly began shaking her head. "No, no, I'm just pregnant. It's okay."

Then her eyes widened, like she couldn't believe she'd just said that. Myles's face morphed into a shocked expression that matched hers. "You're…?" His gaze drifted to her stomach, then back to her face. "You're pregnant? Wow...I'm...wow...congratulations."

By the way he said it, I could tell he wasn't getting it. "Myles," I whispered. "It's your baby."

Myles lifted his lip in an incredulous half-smile, like he thought I was pulling his leg. "Right, it's..." His expression blanked, and he snapped his eyes to Nikki. "It's mine?"

Cringing, Nikki nodded. "Yeah...it's yours."

Myles shot to his feet like he'd just been electrocuted. "You're pregnant? I'm pregnant? We're pregnant?" He ran his hands through his hair, distress all over his face. "How the fuck did that happen?"

Every silent set of eyes at the table shifted to look at him. Myles's cheeks bloomed bright red. "I mean, I know *how* it happened...but how did it happen? Weren't you...on something?" he said to Nikki, sitting back down.

Nikki's eyes narrowed, and she cast a quick glance at her audience before answering. "I wasn't in a relationship at the time, and I hadn't been planning on having sex with my best friend, so, no, I wasn't on anything." Myles opened his mouth, and Nikki shoved her finger into his chest. "And don't even try playing the blame game. You didn't use anything either." Sighing, she stopped stabbing him. "The fact is, we both fucked up, but that really doesn't matter anymore. This is happening, and we have to deal with it. And I honestly don't know how I'm going to deal with it." A tear fell down her cheek. "My landlord just upped my rent, and I'm barely getting by as it is. I don't know what I'm going to do when the baby arrives..."

Myles swallowed three times before answering. "I'll help. Obviously. You're not alone, Nik."

Nikki gave him a small smile. "I know you will, Myles. I didn't mean to make it sound like I was on my own...I'm just freaking out."

"Understandable," he muttered. "I'm kind of freaking out too."

Nikki extended her hand to him, and he grabbed it; they both looked so lost. I wished my little one-bedroom house had more room, so she could move in with me, but I doubted she wanted to live on my couch. Myles moving in with her wasn't really an option either. Eli, Kevin, and Myles had all moved into a swanky house after coming back from San Francisco. It was a total bachelor pad, and way out of their price range individually. He was kind of stuck there for a while, at least until the lease was up.

Myles's face was scrunched in an almost comical way as he desperately tried to come up with a solution. Looking down the table at an uncomfortable Eli, Ralph, and Kevin, he said, "You could move in with me?"

Nikki gave him an appreciative, but dismissive smile; clearly, she'd considered that option already. "While moving into the Party Palace would be a lot of fun, it's not a good place to raise a baby." Her gaze shifted to Eli and Kevin. "And I would never ask you guys to make it baby friendly." Turning back to Myles, she added, "And besides, it's only a three-bedroom house. We'd have to shack up...and that would be weird."

A frown graced Myles's lips. "I'm having a baby with my best friend. All of this is weird."

With a humorless laugh, Nikki nodded. "True."

Hayden cleared his throat. "I just found out this morning that I'm going to need a place to stay soon. *I* could move in with you? I've got a steady job now, and I'm great with kids," he said with a charming, megawatt smile.

Nikki was grinning, but I was surprised. "Hookup sold his place already? That was fast." Hayden had told me just a few weeks ago about Hookup's plan to become a responsible human being, and find a home in a nice neighborhood for Izzy, Antonia, and himself. I was still shocked.

Looking over at me, Hayden nodded. "Yeah…I have three weeks to move."

I felt like he'd just poured ice water down my back. "Oh…wow…" Hayden and I had talked about what he would do when Hookup sold his place, but we hadn't come to any real conclusions. I thought we'd have more time to figure it out. Months maybe.

Hayden's expression turned earnest as he studied me. "I meant what I said the last time we talked about this, Kenzie. I don't want to stress you out or make you feel like we *have* to move in together. We're taking things slow, and I like that we are. I don't want to change things, and I don't want to pressure you. He looked over at Nikki. "Which is why I think the two of us living together would be the best solution for everyone. What do you say, Nikki?"

Nikki looked both excited and unsure. "I could really use the help, but…" Her eyes drifted to mine. "Are you okay with us living together?"

A part of me wanted to say no, but it was a small part, easily ignored. Smiling wide, I nodded. "I think it's a great solution. But I do have to warn you…he's a bit of a slob."

Nikki scoffed and rolled her eyes. "He's got to be cleaner than Myles."

Myles playfully scowled at her comment, then grinned. "Well, good...that solves that. You and Hayden will live together." There was an oddity to his tone that I couldn't quite place. Annoyance, resignation...jealousy? He probably wanted to be the one providing for his child. Well, he'd get plenty of chances to do that.

My feelings on the matter were...complicated. I was grateful Nikki was getting the help she needed, and I also feeling a bit guilty that I wasn't the one helping her. I was happy Hayden would be closer to me—his commute right now sucked—but I wasn't thrilled that he'd be living with another woman, even if she was my best friend. It also felt strange that Hayden wasn't going to be staying with me. We might be taking things slow...but it hadn't always been that way. We'd been on track to move in together. That course had been forcefully derailed, but the lingering feeling of us moving backwards instead of forward was still there, bubbling just under the surface.

Pushing all that aside, I settled on contentment as Hayden and I relaxed with our friends and colleagues. I was racing again. I was with Hayden again. My two best friends were finally on the same page, and all was right with the world.

Hayden grinned at me, and I could see the same peace I felt reflected on his face. Leaning down, he whispered in my ear, "I'm dying for us to be far enough along in this new relationship for me to be able to tell you that I love you. Because I do. You're my heart, my soul, my everything."

My insides felt like they were splitting apart with happiness. A playful laugh escaped me as I did my best to contain the glee. "Well, maybe one day you'll get to tell me that. And then I'll get to tell you that I love you too. With all my heart."

"I can't wait until that day," he murmured, his face softening.

He leaned in to kiss me, and I playfully pulled back. "Personally, I can't wait until we can have sex again."

Hayden blinked in surprise, then let out a pained groan. "God…you and me both, babe."

I couldn't help but laugh at his reaction. He brought his lips to mine while I was still giggling, and my laughter subsided as I reveled in the sweet, sultry contact. I didn't know what the future held for us, but I knew we could face it together. So long as we remained truthful. Keeping things hidden only gave those things power. Bringing them into the light was the best way to diffuse them before they exploded. Honesty was our secret weapon, and it was going to work this time. I hoped.

* * * The End * * *

ABOUT THE AUTHOR

S.C. Stephens is a #1 *New York Times* bestselling author who spends her every free moment creating stories that are packed with emotion and heavy on romance. In addition to writing, she enjoys spending lazy afternoons in the sun reading, listening to music, watching movies, and spending time with her friends and family. She and her two children reside in the Pacific Northwest.

You can learn more at:

AuthorSCStephens.com
Twitter @SC_Stephens_
Facebook.com/SCStephensAuthor

Printed in Great Britain
by Amazon